La Florida

Books in the Thomas Night Crime Novel Series

La Florida

A Thomas Night Crime Novel

Book I

Paul Casper Scherer

Soul Attitude Press

Book I

The author relied on *Florida's First People, 12,000 Years of Human History*, by Robin C. Brown, Pineapple Press, (pp. 8 and 9), 1994 as a source for general information about and the identity of pre-European cultures and native tribes who inhabited that area of the present USA that is called Florida. Pre-Columbian natives developed unique and complex cultures which were not accurately portrayed by these natives in any writing and therefore the author relied on the opinion of archeologists to describe pre-Columbian culture.

The author also relied on various letters and writings by European participants in the exploration of the New World contained in that collection of documents, writings, paintings, maps and drawings titled *Settlement of Florida*, compiled by Charles E. Bennett, 1968, University of Florida Press.

Published by Soul Attitude Press
Pinellas Park, FL
www.soulattitudepress.com
0 3 1 4 2 3

ISBN: 978-1-946338-48-8

Printed in the United States of America

There is a Rhythm to Life:

Start; Stop; Start Again.

Table of Contents

Preface

This novel, titled "La Florida", together with a series of four subsequent novels, tells the story of the civilization of the southeast United States, Florida, from 15,000 BC to 9-11-2001 AD.

Important first questions the novel answers are, how, when, and who inhabited Florida?

Scholars and scientists have concluded that Paleo-Indians were the first human inhabitants of Florida. Ancestors of these Paleo-Indians were discovered to be the occupants of the peninsula named "La Florida" by the Conquistador Ponce de Leon. He landed and was confronted by these people near Daytona Beach in 1513. For his trouble, Ponce de Leon was summarily driven from the shore and back to his ship in a hail of darts tipped with sharp rock points fired by the Native Americans using a throwing stick called an "atlatl".

Paleo-Indians were an ancient people; they were great wanderers, and the first big game hunters. They traveled with herds of megafauna (giant, now extinct animals), relying on these animals for food, clothing and shelter. Their travels have been traced to Central China. Some 47,000 years ago, they encountered an impassable natural barrier, the Bering Sea. They could not travel north or east any further.

The Paleo Indians and their prey, the megafauna, were trapped living in Siberia. A change in climate over time allowed the land and ice bridge known as "Beringia" to be formed between Asia and Alaska during a period of sustained cold weather. Science tells us there was such an ice age 20,000 years ago. (See map 2b) The extreme cold froze the sea and when the bridge appeared, at least some of the animals headed east into Alaska and some of the Paleo-Indians followed. We know this because scientific evidence (linguistic factors, distribution of blood types and DNA) links Native Americans in the Western Hemisphere to eastern Siberians in Asia.

Beringia probably formed and melted then re-formed on more than one occasion with the Paleo-Indian and megafauna traveling back and forth. As a result there were Paleo-Indians in Asia and in Alaska who settled into respective sides of the land bridge. Then, the climate warmed and changed again. Beringia again became part of the Bering Sea. The animals could no longer cross. There is evidence the Paleo-Indians might have been able to move back and forth with boats made of hides and wood braces, but they could not transport large, live animals such as Mastodons and Giant Sloths. Once the animals were locked out of Asia, the animals began to migrate again.

The Paleo-Indians in Alaska continued to chase the animals and the trail shows they moved in two groups. The first moved east into Alaska and then south along the west coast of the Western Hemisphere from British Columbia to South America. Scientific evidence shows they moved as far south as Patagonia.(See map 1, p. 12)

There is evidence that a second symbiotic pairing of man and beast settled for a time in central Alaska, but their course was impeded by a thick glacier. Then an ice free corridor developed. This corridor in the glacier allowed a line of travel across Canada and into the Great Plains and then to the Mississippi Valley and from there the Paleo-Indians could access the hunting grounds of La Florida. (see Map 1, p. 12)

By traveling over these two routes, Paleo-Indians were able to migrate across the entire Western Hemisphere. Proof of this accomplishment is found from evidence of the manufacture, use and trading of weapons, scrapers and blades which were distributed randomly across the Hemisphere and unearthed by modern day archeologists.

We also know that the hunting culture of the Paleo-Indians depended on a particular projectile name: the Clovis point, for the weapons they used. We know that those spear heads and arrow and dart points, together with blades, cutting tools and awl points have been scientifically dated to 10,000 to 13,500 years ago. We also know Clovis points were in use by the Paleo-Indians when Ponce De Leon landed somewhere north of Daytona Beach and south of Ponta Vedras on the east coast of Florida in 1513. The conquistadores engaged the Indians in battle and saw their weapons. Ultimately Ponce lost his life to a wound from a Clovis point dart hurled on a throwing stick wielded by a Native American during another voyage to Florida in 1521.

It is intriguing that when the Paleo-Indian war party and the Ponce and his men fought on the beach they knew nothing about the other's culture. Each side in the battle was repulsed by the appearance of the other and their natural reaction was to destroy each other.

These were alien peoples: short, squat European explorer/conquerors dressed in steel with explosive smoking weapons, some riding war horses; versus tall, athletic, tattooed, nude warriors slinging darts and spears tipped with razor sharp flint rocks that could pierce the body of an enemy, in one side and out the other.

They were like Martians meeting Earthmen. But, how could they not have had some knowledge of the other? DNA tells us that all of mankind came out of east-central Africa. Man moved through Europe and into Asia and then men crossed Beringia into North America then south throughout the Western Hemisphere.

And, if there was a line of travel and trade it is logical that there would have been a line of communication along this route of migration. There must have been some long term disruption of communication or trade that resulted in the divisions of the civilizations of the world to be lost to one another.

Man focuses on his ancestry. Civilizations kept sacred the names and sequence of their leaders who were revered as gods. Could history have been so profoundly disrupted that the Mayans of the Western Hemisphere would not know the Egyptians? These were great kingdoms with intricate cultures, covering large geographic areas that lasted thousands of years and which established trade routes that bridged cultures and allowed the proselytization of religion. Yet these divisions of man, the European and New World Native Americans, were unaware of each other.

We have to accept this as true, hard as it is to believe. And accepting as fact that these societies never knew or were aware of each other, we begin to understand the distrust these opponents felt for each other and build the history of the New World which began in La Florida in 1513 AD.

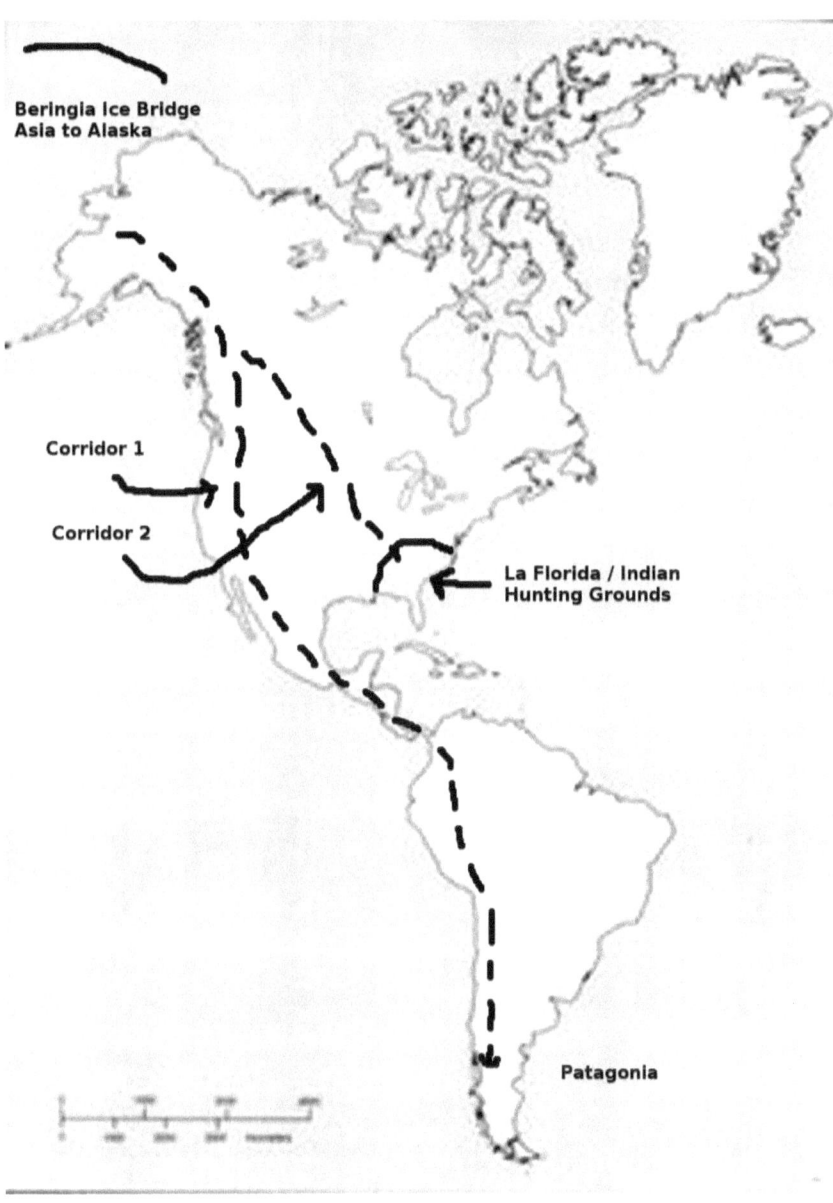

Map 1: Western Hemisphere

Part I

History of La Florida

Chapter 1

Early Florida and its Pre-Columbian Inhabitants

Paleo-Indians emigrated to and permanently and continuously inhabited the lands that are now identified as the state of Florida between 12,000 to 15,000 years ago. Recent archeological finds suggest that even thousands of years prior to that time man regularly visited Florida to hunt for large game and they carried the meat back home to the Mississippi River Basin.

Humans living in Florida faced danger of attack from large animals including alligators and crocodiles, giant sloths, short-nosed bears and saber-tooth cats. If the humans could survive, Florida was a source of nutritional riches. They could hunt deer, peccary, Mammoths and mastodons. Fish and turtles and frogs were abundant. They harvested huge mounds of shellfish. Turkey and fowl were found in great flocks. Eventually Indians settled the land and planted corn, beans and squash and harvested wild persimmons and grapes and other fruits, nuts, acorns and berries.

These Natives formed tribes and not only survived, they flourished to fully populate the Florida peninsula to the east from Mobile Bay to the Atlantic Ocean near Jacksonville and then south to Biscayne Bay and the Florida Keys. Archaeological evidence proves that Indian tribes completely settled the peninsular of Florida before the year 1492 (See Map 3, p. 297). The Native American population was estimated at in excess of 200,000 inhabitants.

The Indians of Florida lived in towns. They established separate political systems or tribes. The tribes defended their land with deadly weapons tipped with rock points. Flint and Chert rocks were also manufactured into cutting blades, hatchets and spearheads. Some arrows were propelled by bows. Special arrows and darts were hurled through the air with great accuracy and great speed using a throwing stick called an *atlatl*. This weapon system allowed the arrow to fly with such force as to pierce the body of an enemy, through and through. The atlatl was unique to Native Americans.

The tribes' lands became well established in Florida. Each tribe had a central city and outlying villages to secure their borders. The Natives primarily used rivers and bays to distinguish the boundaries of their territory. The Apalachee, the Yustega, and the Utina lived in the Northwest. The Saturiwa and the Freshwater were in the north and east between the shores of the St. Johns River and the Atlantic Ocean. The Acuera tribe lived between Daytona and Cape Canaveral. The Potano and the Ocale were located in the center of the peninsular. The Tocobaga were in the Tampa Bay area and the Calusa were on the west coast from Sarasota Bay to the Ten Thousand Islands. The east coast from the Banana River basin south to Miami was inhabited by the Ais, the Jeaga, and the Tequesta. (See Map 3 for the location of the tribes)

The tribes' political systems were diverse. Some tribes were led by single strong men or by birthright or there was government by committee. The tribes established laws and policy for their members and declared war and made treaties with their neighbors. All of the tribes had religious beliefs primarily honoring the sun and the moon. Burial rituals were part of their religion. Until the 1400s their burial practices universally prohibited cremation.

Chapter 2
Culture of the Indian Nations

The Native American tribes created works of art in the form of unique wood sculptures and pottery, and they wove fabric and rope and carved articles such as pipe bowls from stone. They engaged in trade and traveled across the Gulf of Mexico to Central America and they visited the islands of the Atlantic Ocean and the cayes of the Caribbean Sea. Evidence of trade among the tribes of Paleo-Indians was found from the fact that Florida's tribes were found in possession of precious jewels and metals, including pearls, gold, silver and jade, which were not mined in Florida. The natives also collected pearls from oysters and mussels and they strung the pearls and shells to create necklaces and bracelets.

The natives traveled overland by foot, some tribes carried their leaders in chairs during ceremonies. They did not ride animals, and were unaware of horses, cattle, or swine until the Europeans arrived.

Some tribes established cities surrounded by protective walls made of poles and earth. Within the walls they constructed mounds of earth upon which they built houses for their leaders and altars for their religious ceremonies. Other tribes assembled middens or mounds which consisted of their refuse, primarily shells and animal bones. Some tribes also buried their dead in these mounds. One tribe (the Acuera), located near present day Titusville, interred the remains of their members in peat bogs or ponds which preserved the bodies underwater in the low oxygen environment. Some tribes employed special members to handle the dead and they had char houses where the bones of the bodies were sorted, collected and cared for. The bodies of the dead from some tribes were placed in wooden boxes.

Each of these tribes protected their territory through war and battle, but they also employed diplomacy and treaty to maintain their political units.

Unfortunately, the Florida Indians did not leave a written language to explain their beliefs or their history. We have to rely on the European explorers, settlers and Catholic priests to describe the life of the natives and their activities. In 1614 a Catholic priest created a dictionary of one tribe's words.

The Catholic Church converted the Florida Indians and built missions and churches and employed priests to teach them to read and write language and music. Bishop Gabriel Calderon described the natives and their dress when he wrote his pope after visiting the towns created under the Catholic mission system where the Indians lived after they were converted to Catholicism.

The French artist, Jacque le Moyne, who accompanied the explorers Rene de Laudonniere and Jean Ribault to northeast Florida in 1562, produced many engravings of the Indians. These drawings show how the natives lived, fought, traveled, conducted councils, treated their captured enemies, and how members of the tribe treated those who were ill and dying, and how the chiefs conducted war.

Chapter 3
European Presence in Florida

When Europeans landed on the native lands compromising Florida there was conflict. Ponce de Leon explored the east coast of Florida in 1513. He and his men disembarked their ships and encountered aboriginal people who drove Ponce from the land. He returned in 1521, this time to the west coast of Florida. Yet again, Ponce de Leon fought with the native Americans (the Calusa tribe). In the attempt to conquer the natives he was gravely wounded by a dart during battle and he died of the wound after he returned to Havana, Cuba.

Despite the Native American's military prowess in the art of warfare and the technology the Indians developed with their special arrows and darts propelled by bows and atlatls, the natives were decimated in battle after battle by the Europeans. The Conquistadors' implements and weapons made of steel (body armor, swords, crossbows and lances) and the use of explosive powder in canon and harquebus, and their war horses and war dogs provided a superior force and the invaders defeated the Indian armies, although the Indians had much greater numbers in their force.

Some of the Native Americans attempted to make friends with the Europeans and they invited them into their homes and offered them the favors of their women. As a result of these contacts, these natives contracted the foreigner's viral diseases (small pox, chicken pox, measles and influenza). However, the efforts of the Indians to resist or placate the Europeans failed. As a result of

battle and sickness, and the efforts of the Catholic Church to pac-
ify the Indians, none of the tribes of indigenous Florida Indians
had survived by the end of the 1700's.

Other Indian tribes from the southeast lived in the Mississippi
Basin outside the territory of the Florida Indian tribes. These
Indians were members of the Creek Confederacy collectively
called the Mississippian Indians. With the decline of the native
Florida Indian tribes, the Creeks relocated to Florida from what is
now Mississippi, Alabama, and Georgia.

The Mississippian Indians were fierce warriors. They fought
beside the Europeans and were used by the whites to fight the
Florida Indians. Later, the Mississippians became proxies and
mercenaries for various European nations. They fought the
Spanish in West Florida and later they fought for the French
against the British, and later still the Americans employed them
to fight the Spanish.

In return for fighting as mercenaries, the Mississippian Indian
tribes attacked the Florida tribes; they enslaved the Indians they
captured and later they imitated the whites by taking African
slaves. The Mississippian Indians took land formerly occupied by
the Florida Indians (the Apalachee and Yustega) and they settled
on former Florida Indian farms in the north of the territory.

For a period of 50 years (1750 to 1802) the Mississippian Indians
lived like the Europeans, farming using slaves until their lands
were desired by the Europeans. The Mississippi Indians who had
migrated to Florida were known as the Seminoles, or "lost men"
or "run-aways". The Seminoles were then driven from their farms
in the north of Florida to the center of Florida south of Tampa Bay
as the whites proliferated in North Florida from Pensacola to
Panama City, to Tallahassee, and to Gainesville and St. Augustine,
and to Jacksonville.

In an attempt to protect the land they took from their Florida
Indian brothers, the Mississippian Indians who were now called
the Seminoles participated in three wars, called "The Seminole

Wars" in the early 1800's. The last war was concluded when these Indians were relocated to the Midwest United States to the Arkansas Territory by treaty with the US Army. If they refused to be resettled, the Mississippians were driven farther south to live in exile in the Everglades.

From the earliest time there was war over the possession of land between the Florida Indians and the Mississippians and the Europeans. Since they discovered humans living in Florida, the Europeans fought with and murdered the indigenous peoples of the land until the Europeans had eliminated, cleansed, colonized, converted and assimilated the members and the political units of the natives (the tribes) had been disenfranchised.

Chapter 4
War Between Europeans

The separate European nations also fought with each other over possession of La Florida carrying the hatreds of the nations of Europe to the New World. The Europeans were attempting to control the lands of the southeast which were known as the Indian Hunting Grounds (see map 1), and the seas and sea lanes that allowed the treasure from the gold and silver mines in Peru and Mexico to be transported to the coffers of the king of Spain. These sea lanes passed near Florida and were infested with warships of pirates and privateers of the French, Dutch and English who were hunting the wealth of the New World carried in Spanish ships.

Ponce de León claimed all of the lands of "La Florida" for the King of Spain in 1515, but he was killed in 1521 before he could establish a permanent settlement in Florida. Cartographers delineated "La Florida" to be all the land north and east of the Rio Grande to and including the Carolinas. The size of Ponce de Leon's discovery, which was further delineated by the explorations by Panfilo de Narvaez in 1528 and Hernando De Soto 1539-1542, was found to include all the lands of present-day Florida and Georgia, the Carolinas, Mississippi, Alabama, and Louisiana. Spain considered these lands as being their possessions, but they did not establish a presence in Florida. Instead, they used Cuba and the port in Havana as the bridgehead for forays into these new lands. (See Map 4)

Spain's claim to La Florida was not contested until 1562 when the French landed below a bluff on a large river (now called the St.

Johns) at what is now Jacksonville, Florida. The French explorers called the river, The River of May. The French, led by Jean Ribault and Rene de Laudonniere, did not stay at the site, but erected a stone column there claiming the site for France. Later, these explorers sailed north and erected a second column to designate the land between the columns as French soil. They also founded a colony in what is now Paris Island, South Carolina. The settlement built at that site was called Charles Fort. But the settlers at Charles Fort suffered from hunger, Indian attacks, and mutiny. The settlement failed and the settlers returned to Europe.

By 1564, Laudonniere and Ribault had obtained new backers and they sailed back to Florida with hundreds of soldiers to establish a colony for Protestants (the Huguenots). They chose a site at the mouth of the River of May which they named Fort Caroline. This settlement remained viable. After a year, Ribault returned to France and enlisted an additional 800 new settlers and five ships and he arrived back at Fort Caroline in August 1565 with these reinforcements.

The Spanish (Catholic) king became aware of the French (Protestant) fort on lands Ponce de León had claimed for Spain. The king appointed Don Pedro Mendez, a military leader who was based in Cuba, to establish a colony in Florida and rout the French Protestants from Fort Caroline. Spanish warships and crew landed at the site of St. Augustine from Cuba in September 1565.

The French learned the Spanish had landed and the French were determined to drive the Spanish from Florida. After leaving a contingent of guards to protect the women and children at Fort Caroline, Ribault set sail to destroy the Spanish. There was a skirmish at sea between the French and the Spanish that was interrupted by a violent storm that dispersed the French fleet.

The Spanish were able to land their ships at St. Augustine during the storm. Don Pedro Mendez gathered his soldiers and ordered them to march from St. Augustine, which was south of the French fort, through the remnants of the storm to Fort Caroline some 30 miles away. The Spanish made a surprise attack, and 200 Frenchmen and 50 other women and children at Fort Caroline surrendered. The French men were told that they would be executed if they did not renounce their Protestant beliefs. The men refused and they were slaughtered. The women and children were taken to St. Augustine. That settlement became the earliest continuous settlement in what became the United States of America.

Jean Ribault and more hundreds of his men had escaped from their ships that were sunk by the hurricane near what is now Daytona Beach. They tried to march north to return to Fort Caroline but were impeded by the swamps and a large inlet north of the Tomoka River Basin. They were captured in two groups (over a hundred men in each group) by the Spanish troops who were searching for them. These Frenchmen faced the same fate as their brothers at Fort Caroline. They were killed if they did not accept Catholicism. It was reported that all the men in both groups of men were slain after they refused to deny their beliefs. Ribault was beheaded and his head was quartered and displayed at the corners of Fort Caroline which the Spanish occupied and renamed San Mateo. The location of the slaughter of Ribault and his men was called Matanzas Inlet. The word "Matanzas" means massacre.

This military action between the French and the Spanish was said to be the first international conflict in the New World between European armies.

The French did not suffer the loss of Fort Caroline and the massacre of its citizens and soldiers without retribution. In 1568, the French attacked the Spanish fort at San Mateo and captured all of the Spanish soldiers at the fort. The French then murdered all the Spanish soldiers in retaliation for the deaths of Jean Ribault and his men.

Chapter 5

Three Hundred Years of World War (1550-1843 AD)

For a period of 300 years, there were wars between the Europeans over the New World. The conflict was continuous, and even involved the Colonial Patriots in America in their wars with England in 1776 and 1812. The intent of the parties was to establish a balance of power by act of war. Europeans sought a final solution or treaty among the nations in Europe that would be forced on the parties by war. By the 1800s the international conflagration among the Europeans stretched upon the lands of the earth from the American Colonies and the St. Lawrence River basin and down the Mississippi and the Louisiana Territory, East and West Florida and south to the West Indies, the Mediterranean and Africa. In addition to the battles on land, naval battles were fought throughout the world.

During those 300 years, the Spanish in La Florida held a shrinking territory. The English squeezed the borders of the land from their settlements in the Carolinas and Georgia. The French pushed down the Mississippi River to New Orleans. The Creek Confederation allied with the English. They fought with the Governor and the South Carolina militia. The Creek Indians, led by Governor James Moore, invaded and razed St. Augustine and later they attacked the Spanish mission system and destroyed it and killed, captured or enslaved the 20,000 Florida Indians who had disbanded their tribes, converted to the Catholic faith and were living peacefully in the Spanish enclaves.

Chapter 6
Treaties

Meanwhile, during that 300 year period there were treaties that attempted to normalize the physical positions of the parties which were established by the battles fought in these various wars. The effect of those treaties on the New World changed the government in Florida. The Spanish controlled Florida from 1565 until 1763. Then The Treaty of Paris required the Spanish and their citizens to abandon Florida. War was brewing in the Thirteen Colonies but Florida was loyal to the British after the Spanish ceded Florida as a result of the treaty.

During the Revolutionary War, West Florida and East Florida and their ports were protected by the British navy. The British army occupied the two major cities, Pensacola and St. Augustine. Because of the strength of the British military in Florida during the war the territory experienced a period of peace and the population of the territory ballooned. The new residents primarily lived in the vicinity of the major cities. The newcomers to Florida were mainly British loyalists from the Carolinas and Georgia who escaped the American rebels who drove them from their homes. The British loyalists established farms in Florida that provided the British troops with crops and timber for ships and naval stores and barrel staves to aid their fight against the American rebels and their allies: the French, the Spanish, and the Dutch.

After the Revolutionary War (which was resolved by treaty in 1783 after Spain captured Pensacola in 1781) Spain retook possession of Florida from England. As a result, 16,000 British loyalists escaped from the re-ceded Spanish Territory to the

Bahamas, Canada, England and the land west of the Mississippi, or they assimilated deep into the Florida Frontier.

This was a period of great transition in the Florida Territory. To understand, after the War of Independence there were numerous wars in the South. The War of 1812 resulted in the burning of the US Capitol and war in Louisiana. The Creek Confederacy erupted in a civil war called the Red Stick War in 1813 and 1814. The Creek Civil War involved battles in what is now Georgia, Alabama and West Florida. The Spanish and the British backed the Red Stick Creeks who fought the Americans because the Americans looked to expand into Creek lands in what is now Alabama.

Initially there were skirmishes between the Spanish and the Georgia and Tennessee militias in the Creek lands north of Florida. Then, Americans, led by Andrew Jackson, brought a large force into the Creek lands and down the Apalachicola River into Florida. This action was not sanctioned by the US government. The conflict allowed the white American farmers to raid the towns of the remnants of Florida's Indians (Apalachicolas, Tallahassees, Alabamans, Lower Creeks and Seminoles). The whites used this war to settle scores. They stole Indian slaves and confiscated Indian farms. The action into Florida in 1818 was the first of the three Seminole Wars.

Chapter 7
Seminole Wars

The Seminoles are an amalgamation of Indians of the Creek Nation. Two Creek tribes under Chiefs Secoffee and Micca Hadjo had relocated their people in 1750 to the lands of the Miccosukee Indians who lived in Alachua (Gainesville) Florida. Beginning in 1813, the Seminoles fought with Spain against the Americans because the Seminoles anticipated the expansion of America into Florida which threatened their farms.

In the Red Stick War the Creek Nation suffered the loss of much of their land in Georgia and Alabama in 1814. Then the Spanish withdrew from the conflict in 1819 and agreed to cede East and West Florida to the United States of America. The Seminoles were left to defend Florida from the Americans in three wars.

Americans led by Andrew Jackson won the first war and took command of Florida in 1821. There then came a period marked by battles and negotiations between the Indians and the US Army, interrupted by massacres of innocents by both sides. The US government attempted to obtain the agreement of the Seminoles to voluntarily move from Florida to the West (known as the Removal Policy). There were numerous treaties but no sustainable peace resulted and almost continuous conflict occurred. The Seminoles refused to give up their land claims in Florida.

The Indians under Chief Osceola were able to hold their own in battles at the beginning of the second Seminole war. Hundreds of US Army soldiers were killed in battle and many more died of disease. The white Floridians and their slaves, who had appropriated Indian land during the first Seminole War, were driven from the Indian farms in the Florida frontier by the Seminoles in the second Seminole War. The large plantations in northwest Florida were burned. The fighting dragged on. Some Indians were captured. The US Army won battles through an act of treachery. Indians who were invited into the army's camp under a white flag of truce were taken prisoner. These Indians were forcibly moved to the West.

The second war morphed into a third war which was fought in the swamps of south Florida with the US Army chasing Indian families down the East Coast and then into and through the Everglades.

Ultimately, the Seminole Wars were concluded in 1843. The reason the conflict ended was through attrition. Essentially, the US Army said they could find few of the enemy. The Seminole Indians the army found were relocated by force to Arkansas.

Thereafter the land from Daytona north to St. Augustine was safe from the Indians for resettlement by white families. This novel begins with a fictitious family, the relatives of Bea O'Brien who migrated from Savannah, Georgia to Holly Hill, Florida. (See Map 6)

Part II

The O'Brien and the Barnes Families

Chapter 8
The O'Brien Family

In 1847, Bea O'Brien's ancestors settled on land south of St. Augustine in the Territory of Florida that became known as the O'Brien Homestead, or simply, the Homestead. The O'Brien family members were indentured workers from the isles of Guernsey in the English Channel who had fulfilled their obligation to their masters in return for their passage across the Atlantic Ocean by working in a dairy in Savannah, Georgia. The family had arrived in America in the early 1800s as a result of the efforts of Governor James Oglethorpe who needed immigrants to populate the Territory of Georgia. The O'Brien's worked hard and saved every penny they earned and with their savings they purchased 800 acres comprising the Homestead in what became known as Holly Hill, Florida. The sale transaction was handled by a lawyer representing the estate of the original settlers who had died trying to wrest the Homestead from a band of warring Creek Indians. The settlers lost the fight and their lives.

After the second Seminole War was concluded in North Florida, the Homestead together with thousands of acres that had been plantations and other major farms had been abandoned due to the Indian Wars. Plantation houses and farm buildings had been destroyed by the Indians and were never rebuilt. The Homestead had been part of a larger plantation called the Bulow Plantation which had over 2,000 acres of land planted in cotton and indigo. The Homestead was primarily woodlands heavily timbered with long leaf pine. The property also had a dairy which was the O'Brien Family's trade. They intended to produce cheese and fresh milk.

The O'Brien's, with their animals, three cows and one steer of the Milking Devon breed, and chickens and two horses pulling a wagon, walked south from Savannah on Old King's Road. The pathway was an old Indian trail along the Atlantic coast that had been improved by the British. The road ran from North of Savanah to New Smyrna Beach, South of Mosquito Inlet in Daytona Beach. The family left Savanah in the fall and headed South past the port at Brunswick, Georgia and crossed the cattle ford on the St. Johns River in Jacksonville then rested in St. Augustine.

The family spent three days in St. Augustine and purchased supplies. The city was still inhabited by refugees, mostly Minorca's, who feared a continuation of the Indian wars. The last landmark before Holly Hill were the ruins of Bulow Plantation. They could see how grand the farm had been and they made mental notes of items they could salvage for use at the Homestead. The 150 mile trip took three weeks, but the clan of five suffered no losses or illness and arrived with all their animals and the wagon with their goods. (See Map 6)

When the Homestead land was sold and the money passed hands, the O'Brien's were told there had been a dwelling on their property. This information was only partly true. The Indian war party left only that part of the cabin standing that had failed to burn when the previous owners came under attack and were killed. There was a large hole in the roof. The damage was covered with a tarp and the O'Brien's were dry that first night. There was a stream of good potable water within 50 feet of the cabin.

A stream flowed north to the Tomoka River and provided good drainage for the land. There was a small milking barn and a corral made of sticks and branches. The livestock settled in and there was good forage for feed. The cabin, barn, and the animal enclosure were all tucked under three massive live oak trees that were centuries old. The trees provided cover in the rain and from the wind, and shade in the heat of the day from the sun.

After 1847 there was a passable peace. There were renegade Indians who still harassed settlers but the main bodies of the Seminoles were driven south of Fort Dade in Tampa and so the O'Brien's were able to build up their herd of cows for the dairy. They also trapped and domesticated wild pigs and bred them and raised swine, resold their piglets and butchered the animals and prepared the pork with salt and smoked hams, butts and shoulders. They let the long leaf pine grow naturally, but did clear a wet area of the land and grew rice and sugar cane.

The O'Brien men also worked as drovers. The cattle industry in central Florida employed men on horseback who collected wild cattle that were living on the prairie grasslands in the center of the territory near Kissimmee. The unbranded steers were the remnants of herds of cattle introduced by the Spanish. These animals escaped and ran wild and grew fat and healthy on the prairie grasses on thousands of acres of land north of Lake Okeechobee. Each year the O'Brien men and other workers known as Cracker Cowboys built a herd of thousands of animals chasing them out of the brush. The cattle were then driven overland to Georgia and sent to the northeast by railroad to provide protein for the Eastern European immigrants who worked in factories in Pennsylvania, New Jersey, and New York.

The O'Brien women cared for their children and bred the milking cows and swine and oversaw the 800 acres until their men came home from the cattle drives. The men were paid in gold with US Dollars by investors in New York City who traded the wild animals on the commodity exchange.

By the 1860's America was in the Civil War. The cattle herded by the Cracker Cowboys now fed the Confederate soldiers and the South. The South would have starved after the supply of meat from the West was cut when the Confederacy lost the city of Vicksburg. Florida's range cattle prolonged the war.

The O'Brien's contributed one family member to the fight. Joshua O'Brien was killed near Tallahassee defending the State capital. The rest of the clan, luckily too young or too old or female remained at home in Holly Hill during the Civil War where they married and increased their numbers.

After the Civil War, there was the Reconstruction, depressions, bank failures and upheaval. Some family members were restless and went to the Wild West and resettled or were killed in the Indian wars in the Dakota Territory. Then came the Spanish-American War and the O'Brien's herded cattle to Tampa and the animals were shipped to Cuba by Lykes Shipping Lines. The family rebuilt the cabin twice and finally decided to build a more permanent structure and they reconstructed the farmhouse on the Homestead with coquina rock and used many of their pine trees.

World War I brought more business for cattle ownders but after the war there came the Spanish Flu epidemic and the O'Brien's were decimated again, losing 20% of their clan.

After the flu epidemic, the Homestead and the families living in the environs nearby languished through the Great Depression.

Chapter 9
The Barnes Family

One of the closest neighboring families across the Halifax River from the O'Brien's Homestead was the Barnes' Family. They owned a plantation and citrus grove. The Barnes Family moved to the Ormond area in 1920 because the Mother, Ann, suffered from tuberculosis. The son, Frank Barnes was away at Georgia Military Academy during his mother's illness. He was 16 when he returned home to live after his mother had passed.

The Barnes family purchased a portion of the Bulow Plantation outlands known as Plantation #7. Bulow had been parceled into tracts. The Barnes' land consisted of an "Old House" and cooking vats and chimneys and over 100 acres of a citrus orchard planted between the Halifax River and the Atlantic Ocean. The grove was less susceptible to a freeze because it was planted near the water.

Frank's father Francis Aloysius Barnes (who was known as: The Senator) had purchased the property on the bank of the Halifax River from a family that became old and went bust and was now anonymous.

The Senator moved his wife from Atlanta on doctor's advice. She came with her family's expensive furniture and library to the Old House on the plantation. The Senator trimmed back and re-planted the citrus groves and purchased what was left of the rendering plant and chimneys at the Bulow Plantation and rebuilt the plant so it boiled cane syrup into molasses. The Senator had his workers mix the low-grade molasses with grain for animal feed. The feed was his first commercial product. He peddled the feed himself and the O'Brien's became a steady customer. Because he acted as a salesman the Senator came to know almost everyone in the county who had a cow or chicken, which was everyone.

The Senator was an entrepreneur. He did not let grass grow under his feet. He built a dock into the Halifax River which was part of the Intercostal Waterway. The waterway was used by the rich to travel by water from the Northeast to Miami. When a yacht came by, the Senator rowed out into the river to greet the wealthy, interstate sailors. He was a talker. He sold his citrus fruit and then sold jars of his jelly and jam cooked in the kitchen of the Old House on the plantation. His guava jam was prized.

After a few seasons, the rich boaters were familiar with his business and they docked at his place; toured his grove; had a meal; purchased his preserves and fresh fruit, and laughed at his jokes. They surely admired his boy, Frank, and talked up his products, especially the guava jelly, to their friends and relatives up north. The Senator found a market in department stores in New York and Boston and Philadelphia for the guava jelly, the marmalades, and jams.

The Senator had great affection for his family and for people in general. He wanted to help everyone and move everyone along to success. He was elected to the Florida legislature and represented the folks in Volusia and Flagler Counties and helped hold the state together during the 1920s and 30s.

His son, Frank Barnes, knew Bea O'Brien for her whole life. They attended the same grade school for six years until Frank was sent to the military school when Frank's mother's illness became worse. The O'Brien Homestead was across the river and south a few miles from Plantation #7. Bea and Frank had played in the river and fished and dipped for shrimp and gone clamming as they were growing up. They were best friends. (See Map 7)

The O'Brien family had a rough turn of events. Bea lost her mother and father to an undiagnosed illness. It was not unusual for citizens to succumb to disease. It just happened. Bea was only

14 and after her parents died she lived at the Homestead with a cousin, his wife, and their four children. The cousin was her legal guardian. Locals had been lining up to see who could steal the Homestead with the dairy and the planted pine forest and the swine herd from Bea. Though she was female and only 14 years old, Bea successfully convinced the judge to resist all offers and proposals to sell the land to the consternation of her cousin. Bea was stubborn. The Homestead was her land.

Frank had been at the academy while his father dealt with the death of his mother.   After he returned from military school in the second year of high school he saw Bea at a dance in Ormond at the end of the school year. It was only one night, but she became pregnant.

Though they were young, they were to marry. Bea insisted. The Senator spoke to the judge. Bea's cousin wanted to return to Georgia. The Senator would move Bea into the Old House at Plantation #7, and she and Frank would marry and Bea would have their child. The judge agreed. This was what Bea had wanted. She would name the child after her parents--either James or Jennifer. The Senator would oversee the dairy farm and the tree lot until Frank and Bea were of legal age and then he would release the property to Bea. Everyone acknowledged the Homestead was her property.

***

THEREAFTER, fifteen (15) years elapsed and the story continues...

(The form of the work is collage/novel. The Editor.)

Chapter 10
Broken Conversations (Collage)

"Is this woman so stupid? Or am I just so smart?" said Miss Petunia. The pig was so proud. She had a natural set to her lips that seemed to be a permanent smile. When she walked, she pranced and kept her head tilting upward and her eyes darted about. She licked her chops as she led her piglets out of the pen.

"I can open the gate raising the latch using my snout and I can sneak through the high grass along the lot line and head next door to the flowers and the sweet roots." Miss Petunia loved the potatoes and the turnips and the parsnips and the carrots in the neighbor's garden. Sometimes a ripe tomato was left on the vine. But it was rare though, now that the summer was over.

"No more hot—hot. Now it will be cool—cool," said Miss Petunia to her piglets.

"I have to sneak over to the garden and I have to keep my mouth shut. If I drool and slobber and suck the juice in my mouth I will grunt and she will hear me. Quiet, quiet, I must be quiet. I need to root in the dirt now and suck the roots and munch the blooms on the flowers."

**

"Bob, Bob, come help, that fat sow is in the garden again." Bob's mom got the broom. It was a big tool with a thick staff. She whacked the sow on the rear. Mom poked the pig in the ears and the brow above the eyes. Bob was small but he grabbed Petunia's tail and lifted up and the pig squealed in pain and protest. Bob tried to rip the tail from the butt of the animal to teach it a lesson. Stay out of the family vegetable garden.

Bea Barnes came then, huffing across the road to retrieve her larcenous wandering pig.

"Ohooo, pig. You come here to me. How did you get out of the pen? SoooHee. Come back pig. Come back Miss Petunia," hollered Bea who, at 30 years old, was best described as dowdy-short, over-weight and prematurely gray. Unattractive on her best day.

Miss Petunia knew the feast was over. The humans had been quick this time. She just got a root or two and they were on to her. Her little piglets were following across the dirt road. They had caused the alarm to be sounded by the humans. The piglets had squealed as they followed their mother out of the wallow in the pen and across the road. They followed her everywhere. Miss Petunia was a smart pig. They were all smart, particularly when food was involved.

Bob's mom, Mary Johnston, worked with Bea Barnes to return the large, fat sow to the pen on Bea's property with her sty mates. Miss Petunia lived with an old de-tusked razor-backed boar that had fathered generations of hams and jowls and butts and bellies.

Mary Johnston didn't say anything to Bea about the damage to her garden. Bea said what she always said. As soon as the next pig was slaughtered and the animal was parceled up she would share the meat with Mary and her family to compensate her. Bea could afford to give the meat away. Bea was a land owner. They owned 800 acres of land with the pigs, a dairy farm and planted pine timber. Bea Barnes operated the pig farm and her husband, Frank, managed the dairy. Bea turned the meat into cash. She sold the animals on the hoof by the pound. Mostly, the money went to the doctor for the care of her boy Jimmy. Jimmy had never walked or talked. But he smiled and seemed to have great joy with any attention he was given. He particularly enjoyed Bob. He cooed and blew bubbles at the side of his mouth when Bob came up beside him and peeked over his bed and said: "Boo."

Jimmy looked at Bob intently. No telling what he was seeing. But he loved Bob. You could see it in Jimmy's face.

Mrs. Barnes devoted her life to her son. She washed his bed clothes every day. Jimmy was laid on the softest lamb's wool. Bea

Barnes turned her son from side to side every two hours, day and night. It was to prevent bed sores. She washed the walls, floor and ceiling of his room with pine-sol to kill any possible infection. Before you were allowed in Jimmy's room you had to clean your hands and fingernails with soap and a brush.

Bob had seen Jimmy when he was nude while he was being washed. There wasn't much to him. He was very thin. But everyone who lived on Flomish Road was thin. No one had enough to eat except for Miss Petunia, the selfish pig, and the Barnes family.

Mary Johnston never got mad at Mrs. Barnes for the actions of her pig. Mary laughed and bent her body back at her waist with her hands on her hips in a great guffaw. She gave the pig one more whack and sent her on her way with the piglets scampering at her heels back home to the wallow and the pen. The other pigs waited for her at the open gate. They never left their sty. Even the old toothless boar stayed put. Somewhere deep in his memory there must have been a stirring of what it meant to be free and to roam the woods rooting in the sweet grass and gathering live oak acorns with his snout. But the boar had been taken when he was young and his mom was killed. He stood shivering at her side when the man with the blade gutted his mom and her offal fell at his feet. He was traumatized by the sight of what became of his mother. Then he was put in a flour sack. He smelled the sweet, whole wheat dust inside the burlap. The powder coated his hair. He didn't grunt from that moment in his life. A mute pig. He grew up and did his business breeding the sows. He never missed a lick.

There was no reason for any of the pigs in the pen to leave. They had everything they wanted. Miss Petunia was indulged her occasional romp which satisfied her and supplemented her routine of finding something sweet tasting in the swill they were fed. Miss Petunia may have caused trouble but she produced the most desirable offspring in the county. They became fat pigs and sold easily at auction to eager bidders.

There was an old farmhouse on the acreage called the Homestead. The farmhouse was built of coquina shell rock and long leaf pine timber. It was built to accommodate the entire O'Brien clan.

But their numbers had dwindled. The prodigy of the O'Brien's now only consisted of Bea and Jimmy. The farmhouse was spacious, with large rooms and high ceilings. However it was vacant though it was fully furnished. Some nights Bea and Jimmy and Frank stayed there. Bea had inherited the acreage with the planted pine timber, the old farmhouse, the dairy, and the cows and the pigs from her parents. The Homestead was in Holly Hill, Florida, a small town just north of Daytona Beach and south of Ormond Beach, a mile west of the Halifax River.

Bea was married to Frank now for over fifteen years. Frank owned no property. Frank's father, Senator Francis Aloysius Barnes owned land know as: Plantation #7. The property was located on the Halifax River in North Ormond Beach, Florida (north of Holly Hill and on the opposite side of the Halifax).

The Senator had also purchased a large swath of land in the south west corner of Volusia County. It was over 40,000 acres of mostly cut-over swamp. The Senator was trying to decide what to do with the big property. He had not gotten any farther with his plans than to construct a simple saw mill that cut pine logs into 2X4s. This was rough cut lumber. It was not dressed, planed and kiln dried. The boards were used to make forms but there was little call for the wood. There was little opportunity now. Florida was economically depressed.

The Halifax River was part of the Intracoastal Waterway and in the winter, the rich would motor by the plantation in their yachts. The rich would tie up at the plantation and buy jams and jellies that Bea produced at the farmhouse and sample the citrus fruit. The Senator made a little money and they survived.

Bea and Frank and Jimmy had lived at Plantation #7 on the river in the Old House with the Senator since their marriage. The house was a large, two-story house with a screened porch that wrapped around the entire building. The porch was like heaven even in the worst of the summer. The breeze rolled up over the river and wafted into the screened area. It was almost cool.

Before dawn every day Bea and Frank loaded Jimmy in a cradle, special-built into the front seat of their 1932 Ford truck and drove from the plantation over the Granada Bridge then south on US 1 to Flomish Avenue to the Homestead. If Frank had no school, Bea dropped Frank at the dairy and Bea went to the farmhouse to produce jams and preserves.

There was a big kitchen containing large prep tables and a wood cooking stove. She lifted Jimmy from the cradle in the Ford truck and carried him into the farmhouse and put Jimmy in a seat on the floor of the kitchen so he could watch her work. Bea was talkative speaking happily to her son. She answered for her son and to encourage the repartee, she played the radio and listened to the music and the news. Jimmy blew bubbles and followed the sight of his mother with his eyes as she moved across the floor to complete her daily tasks.

Through the Senator's efforts, Plantation #7 had become a tourist attraction and Bea made jams and jellies in the kitchen at the farmhouse of the Homestead to sell at the plantation's store. This land comprising Plantation #7, north of Ormond had been part of the old Bulow plantation. The Bulow Family had grown sugar cane and indigo on 2,000 acres of prime land when it was first in operation in the early 1800's. There was a cane mill and there were old rusted iron cooling vats that were still in place. The warehouse containing the mill and vats had been destroyed by a fire set by the Indians that had burned so hot that the brick chimneys had crumbled and fallen to ruins. Over the years the locals had salvaged what they could of the Bulow's property. When Bea drew water in the kitchen at the farmhouse at the Homestead, the pump she used in the process had once belonged to Bulow.

There was also a citrus grove at Plantation #7. The grove was planted in the 1890s. Most of the tourist activity occurred when the fruit was in season in the fall and winter when it was cold up North. The daily routine for Mrs. Barnes was to take Jimmy to the farmhouse at the Homestead and cook and prepare the jams and jellies during the day and then pick up Frank at the dairy and return to the Old House on the river at night together with the jars of product she had cooked and bottled during the day.

***

Once the pigs were secured, Mary and Bea had a chance to talk. They went in the farmhouse so Mrs. Barnes could listen for Jimmy, who was now in bed. Jimmy really made little or no sound but Mrs. Barnes would know if he stirred, she was so sensitive to his movements.

Both women enjoyed this time.

Dowdy Bea had not finished school and she had the constant care of her child for 15 years. She was worn down. Bea saw Mary as a woman of refinement. She was beautiful but gaunt. Mary was struggling too. She had the care of two children and an infant. She was pregnant too or she thought she was probably.

Mary and her husband were ready to move on from the little house on Flomish Avenue with the vegetable garden. Mary's father, called Pa, had a home on an acre in Daytona Beach. The Johnson's found a house near Pa's little farm. Mary could plant a garden on Pa's acre of land. Her father was trained as a logger. He had operated the circular saw at the saw mill in Deland until he went blind with cataracts. The mill had paid Pa next to nothing. Mary's father was 75 years old.

Mary's husband, Big Al, was around sometimes but he only came home when he was not working. He was pretty much on his own because he was always working. His kids had no real memory of Big Al.

"What are you going to do if you have another child?" asked Bea.

Mary had confided to Bea that she thought she was pregnant again. "I am worried," said Mary.

Bea was secure. The Homestead made money. It was free and clear of debt. The farmhouse was a big house made of coquina rock. It was solid.

Almost weekly, if Bea, Frank, and Jimmy stayed overnight in the farmhouse, Bob was allowed to stay with them. When he stayed over, Bob helped with Jimmy. He could hear the boy when he stirred and he would sneak into the big bedroom past Mr. Barnes and he would rouse Bea and she would go in with Bob to care for the boy.

Jimmy needed to be changed regularly. When he was nude, Bob could see he wasn't a baby. He was about the size of a two-year-old except he was a skeleton, flesh and bones. Bob was four years old, almost five. They said Jimmy was 15. He was not supposed to live, expected to die at birth. They said the nurse at the hospital walked Jimmy slowly down the hall from the delivery room to the nursery to give nature a chance, to give Jimmy a chance to decide to die. But he was willed to survive by Bea who saw him and loved him and coaxed him to breathe and suckle and exist in his simple world. What kept him alive was Bea's love.

"I don't know what I will do without Bob when you move to town," Bea admitted. "He has been a real honest help with Jimmy. He's the only one who accepts him."

Bob had other thoughts and desires regarding Bea and Frank Barnes. The Barnes' fed him well when Bob stayed over. The three Johnson kids were scrawny and wiry. Bob got most of his calories from Bea and her family. When Bob was not helping Bea with Jimmy at the farm house he went down the road to the dairy voluntarily and helped the men move the cows in and out of the chutes leading to the milking parlor. "You have to slap their boney hips to get them going."

Mary encouraged Bob to help the Barnes operations. She had Bob spend as much time as he could with Bea and Frank because Bob always came home with milk or cheese or cream. Sometimes Bob carried home meat from a dairy cow or a pig that was culled and slaughtered. Mary and the kids survived from the food donations from the Barnes' family larder. Mary's family was starving and the Barnes' had food to give away. Bea saw Mary's struggle and she saw an advantage.

She wanted Mary to give Bob to her.

"I want to adopt him." Bea told her husband. "It's already like Bob is our own child ... Frank, you could take him hunting and fishing. He would grow up to run the dairy. You cannot run the dairy and run all over doing all the things your dad wants you to do. Think about it," Bea said as she cuddled Jimmy in her arms. "Jimmy's not going to be with me very long. I can't live without a child. I need Bob."

***

Mary loved the woods and that's why they had bought out in the country near the Homestead. They had a little cash when they came from New York. Big Al got a job salvaging timbers and heart of pine floors and siding from the barracks the U.S. Army had used for the training bases near the airport west of Daytona Beach. They shipped the salvaged wood out to the Northeast and it was sold in a market hungry for building materials to house the soldiers and their new families since WWII.

The Senator had built the sawmill that had produced the rough cut pine lumber that had built the barracks that housed the soldiers while they were being trained to fight WW II. Now the barracks were being deconstructed for salvage. All the soldiers wanted to wipe the slate clean-to forget the war. They wanted a wife and kids and their own home. So there was a market for all the used lumber Big Al could salvage and that the Senator could produce in the saw mill. There was business and there was money. There just wasn't much profit.

***

"I have to move the kids into town," Mary told Bea. "Bob has to start school. If he stays out here he will have no school. He will make nothing of himself."

Mary had finished high school in New York State. She passed the Regent's exam. She had gone on to business school. Mary knew the value of an education. When the war started she worked at army bases as a secretary for the officers. She was very competent, always got her work done on time. She was beautiful-striking, a brunette, tall, high cheeks, German features. The men on base were always on the lookout for a pretty skirt and she ran a gauntlet from her apartment in town to the office at the base where she worked. That's where she met Big Al. How could a Master Sergeant win the heart of a woman wooed unsuccessfully by Generals? He had to be a liar.

***

"Jimmy and me need help, Mary, and if you are pregnant again you will need to see a doctor. You almost lost your last child,

Jenny, trying to live out here in the country. It's too rough and rugged. You need to be in town for the sake of your children. You know I helped you save the baby. Jenny was small. I gave you food. Jenny would have died without that food. Why don't you give me Bob?" begged Bea. "You have three and a fourth child on the way. I would give you $2,500."

Twenty-five Hundred Dollars.

Mary had been saving now for three years since Bob was born so he would have a home in the city where they would be near school and friends and a church. The family lived in a small two room house Big Al built on a small lot on Flomish Avenue near the Homestead. The family was always threatened with foreclosure and always behind in their payments. In three years Mary had only managed to set aside $428.23. But if she was pregnant again the doctor would take $250.00. To save, she would have the baby at home this time. They still owed the hospital for birthing Jenny. The County government would pay the hospital bill but Mary refused to let the County pay the bill. Mary paid the hospital $10 a month when she could pay it. They were charging interest now and she kept going backwards but she insisted she would pay the bill. She was always awake at night worried about money matters. The lack of money kept her worried and thin. She really was tempted by the $2,500.

***

"I couldn't sell my son. That would be out of the question. How could I?" said Mary as she mulled over the thought. "He could agree to stay with you and work for you maybe."

Bea could see that Mary was wavering. She had watched as the family stressed. Big Al worked a lot of hours but there was no money to be earned in Florida. The state had never emerged from the Depression. The only money that came to the State was during the boom portion of the real estate cycles (boom and bust).

Finally during the war the hotels along the beaches were filled. The hotels housed soldiers injured in the fighting and soldiers training for battle. But the money stayed on the coast with the rich hotel owners. The money did not trickle down.

The Florida coast had resorts along the beaches. Then there was a strip of homes across the river for the middle class and the professionals. They were paid good money to service the rich. Then further west (inland) were the workers' homes. Then came the railroad tracks and just beyond the tracks was colored town and then it was the forest.

Northwest Florida contained millions of acres of pine trees. The forest was thick with green needles. A fire would have been catastrophic. The air was tainted with the scent of pine sap. It was overbearing in the heat of the day. It made you dizzy.

The trees were planted by the DuPont's or the Dodges' or the Carnegie's. Someone fantastically rich who wanted to smooth out their investments with agricultural real estate. Plant the trees and let them grow. The trees grew five percent every year. The gross domestic product did not grow that fast on average. No one understood the value of trees except the very rich. They did not participate in the boom and bust cycle. The rich grew trees and earned a steady five percent.

***

"You would not be selling Bob if he worked for us," Bea reasoned over Mary's compromise. "He would stay with us and you could move to the city. I will buy your little house here in the country from the bank. You would owe no money and you would have enough for a down payment for a house in Daytona near Pa and the church and the school. You know we love Bob. We would take good care of him. He would have a full time father, someone who could show him how to be a man."

Mary was not worried so much about Bob being a man. Mary died a little every time she served a meal to her children that had not been subsidized by the Barnes' kindness. If the Barnes' had not donated protein for the meal, Mary was left to cook mostly pasta, egg noodles with tomato sauce from a can. The older kids would bloat up on a meal of starch and sugar but be starving a short time after. To ward off their hunger, Mary would always save something for later. Vegetables cut up and lightly salted, grown in the garden—potatoes and yams with a little butter. The vegetables would get the kids to sleep. She still nursed the baby but to do that she had to have calories and if she ate as much as she should the children would be hungry. Mary became confused when she was hungry. The milk she produced deprived her body and her mind of the nutrients she needed to function. She knew that. She knew she was losing her beauty. Her husband used to beat her, claiming she was running around. He didn't beat her anymore; both of them were being ground down.

***

"Bob should go to school. You know how smart Bob is. There is a school in Ormond that is very good," said Bea.

"Do you think you could send him to school there if Bob stayed with you?" asked Mary.

Bea would want to be proud of Bob if he was her boy and she would give him everything. She was only sad he would not actually be her blood. She was jealous of Mary being able to give birth to beautiful babies. Mary Johnson was like Miss Petunia. It was unfair to compare Mary to a pig but that is what Bea thought when she was upset with her own lot in life. Mary's children were a picture, especially the daughter, Jenny. Mary's kids could grace a box of children's cereal. Of all the children, Jenny was the most handsome. But she was scared of men. The young boy, Little Al was healthy but a little scrawny. Bea knew they needed food. A good Christian would help and that's what she was doing, helping her fellow human being who had less and was in need.

***

"I know you want that house by the church and the school," said Bea. "If you bought the new house I would make sure Albert and Jenny had food and milk. You could just tell me what you needed and I would help.

"If Bob could stay with me," said Bea, "Bob would go to school. I would send him to school in Ormond if you wish."

Mary began to cry.

"This is the best I can do for them," said Mary. "I will give you my boy, Bob."

THEREAFTER, one year later, the story continues.

Chapter 11
One Year Out

Bob was almost six years old now. It had been a confusing year. He had moved in with Bea and Frank at the house on Plantation #7. His natural mother, who he now called "Mary", had moved to Daytona Beach with his brother and sister. He saw Mary when they came to the dairy on weekends. He played with his brother, Little Al, and the baby Jenny. The baby was a little over two years old. She was always given affection by everyone. She was a beautiful child.

Mary, Little Al, and Jenny would visit the Homestead regularly to retrieve the food Bea had promised for the Johnsons for so long as Bob remained with her.

Little Al loved the farm. Bob took Little Al with him to the milking parlor to watch the operation. There were milking machines at work; there was noise and the smell of cows. The dairy was a modern operation. The raw milk was removed from the cow's teats by suction machines and pushed through clear plastic tubes to a stainless steel vat. You could see the froth of the liquid as it gushed through the tubing. There were 12 milking stations and there was one worker at every two stations. The men stood in trenches to the side of and below the cows and attached the machine to the teats. There was a large water hose that was used to spray the ground to rinse away the milk that fell to the concrete floor. The slurry of water and waste milk went into a stainless steel drain and pipe, and then went to a collection pond that drained into the stream that ran through the Homestead and eventually drained into the Tomoka River.

Bob showed Little Al each part of the process. One of the workers would normally joke with the young boys squirting them in the mouth with liquid directly from a teat. The boys loved the warm rich milk.

Mary visited the dairy to pick up food. The Johnsons had moved to Daytona but they were still barely making it and still depended on food from Bea and Frank.

***

"Why am I here?" Bob asked Mary. Mary told Bob it was better for everyone that he was with Bea and Frank. She told Bob how proud she was that he had a job. He was working helping Jimmy. She always asked if Bob was being fed and if he was still planning for grade school. She brought him picture books and did not leave the dairy without teaching Bob a new word from the picture books. Bob always thanked Mary for the time she spent with him. He always complimented her on the way the children, Little Al, and Jenny looked. They were always clean and their hands and faces were scrubbed. The visit ended with an ice cream from the dairy store. Bob packed the cones. He gave the children extra- a little more.

Every visit Mary would sit with Bob by themselves and talk about his days and nights. Was he getting enough sleep? It was his job to wake up Bea Barnes if Jimmy stirred or was in distress. Regardless of whether Jimmy stirred, Bob had to turn him every two hours at night to prevent bed sores from forming on Jimmy's body. Jimmy could not reposition himself. At first Bob needed an alarm to wake up. He told Mary he never slept deeply except in the daytime. It was then when he got a nap. Then when he napped he dreamed. Mary would hug Bob mightily when they left in Big Al's old black Studebaker. Bob rarely saw Big Al. He was a long distance trucker now. He worked for the saw mill carrying bundles of 2x4 inch boards up North where they were used as building studs in new tract houses being built for the new families up North.

***

There were always changes. On the last visit, Bob learned Mary and Big Al. and the two kids were now living with Pa in the house with the one-acre lot on Seagrove Street. Mary had lost the house she bought with the $2,500.00 she got from Bea. Mary only had the new house for a short time. Bob had only visited the new house one time when Mary was sick and Mrs. Barnes brought food to the new house.

Now they were in the house on Seagrove—Pa's house. The house was painted gray inside and out. Mary and Little Al and Jenny all slept in the same room. Pa had a room to himself. He wore old blue jean dungaree overalls and a white T-shirt. He chewed tobacco. Wads of it. He had cataracts and couldn't see well enough to work as a sawyer anymore. He had a one half-acre plot in his yard planted with vegetables and he worked at that grubbing through the dirt on his hands and knees feeling for the vegetable plants versus the weeds. He was blind but his hands and fingers could feel the difference.

The government provided Pa an old age pension of $20.00 a month. Between that cash and the food supplement from the Barnes and the wages Big Al doled out when he came home when he was off the road for a week or two, Mary was able to make do. Not having to pay the mortgage payment on the house they purchased and then lost allowed her to balance her budget so long as there was no more expense or an emergency.

Mary had over extended with the purchase of the new house. She had forgotten all the added expense of a home. There wasn't just the down payment. There were taxes and insurance and maintenance if something broke. The house looked fine when they first moved in but there was the leaky roof and rotten wood and an old furnace. The money was spent. The money was gone. And the bank foreclosed. This gave Big Al more to complain about. He and Mary hardly talked to each other. Both of them were relieved that his job on the road kept them apart.

Mary had hoped that she would have her fourth child, but she miscarried. Thereafter she was cold to Big Al.

For his part, Big Al had not been faithful to Mary particularly since he was on the road. There were too many temptations. There was the boredom of the highway and it was hard to turn down a trick.

Mary knew he was not faithful and they argued when they were together. Pa would get into it and tell Big Al to leave his house. Big Al would go to the bar and drink his fair share making the Busch Brothers secure in their mansion in St. Louis, Mo.

Big Al would not even come home most times when he was in town and not on the road hauling timber. He would lay up with a lady and not be around for months. Mary would hear from him through Bea. If Big Al ran out of money he would go to the dairy and see Bea. Bea did not want him around. She found that he would leave if she gave him a little money, so that's what she did. She didn't want him around Bob. There was always some evil that would come out of Big Al's mouth. The words were mixed with the odor of peptic gas and bile that hurt to the quick.

"Who's your father?" Big Al would ask Bob.

Bob was told to walk away from his old man by Bea and Mary and Pa. Bob followed the advice mostly, but it was hard to walk away. Big Al was his father.

***

When Mary and Big Al and Bob and Little Al and Jenny lived in the little house next to the farmhouse on the Homestead Bob liked to sit on the porch of the little house his father had built. After, Mary and Little Al and Jenny moved to Daytona Beach and if Bob missed them, he would sneak over to the little house. He would go inside and sit on the little front porch. Mary left Bob's small rocker there. If he was lonely he would go to the house his father had built with scraps of wood and sit in the chair and rock and rock.

Bea had discovered his hidey hole and she left it to him for his privacy. She knew there was a load on his mind and he had to have a release. After Mary moved to Daytona, Bea purchased the little house from the bank for a couple hundred dollars as she had promised. After discovering Bob on the little porch rocking she decided to keep the house so that Bob had his place to think. Bea would watch him. He would talk to himself like a mute. He mouthed long sentences with emotion but no sound. He would laugh silently and he would cry though Bea saw he had difficulty crying without making a sound. Sometimes he would wail, spreading his mouth but emitting no noise. Bea would join in, tearing up and sobbing silently.

By buying the little house Bea had tried to do something about Bob's melancholy. She felt he had to express himself and he had an outlet on the porch of the little house. She talked to Frank and though he did not understand the problem, he would help his wife. They had a successful relationship and Frank knew how much Bob helped Jimmy and he would do what he could for Bob. They took one evening a week and Frank spent that time with Bob.

Bob loved sports. Daytona Beach had a colored college (BCC/Bethune-Cookman College) and there was an opportunity to see college football and basketball games at the school. There were great rivalries between Bethune-Cookman and Grambling and Howard and other colored college teams. Frank took Bob to the games. They sat with the colored folks. There were only a few whites that attended the games. Most of the whites at the games were men who had played ball and who recognized the superior talent they saw in the colored players.

Of all sports, Bob liked baseball the best. In the summer the Islanders played minor league baseball in Daytona Beach. Most of the players were white but some were brown and black from Central America and from the Caribbean. Bob made a friend named Tony at the ball game and Mr. Barnes let Bob sit with Tony. Sometimes they would carry Tony to the game with them. The boys practiced their swing and pretended to catch and throw the ball and when Christmas arrived there was a glove, ball and bat for Bob and Tony from Santa.

When Bob had time to play and wander he explored the 800 acre Homestead. In the south west corner of the property he found an outcropping of lime rock near a rivulet of clear water that drained into a pond. The pond ran to the stream that eventually ran to the Tomoka River.

The lime rock had been worked by man and chips of Chert points had been manufactured from the hard rock and created into arrow heads and spear heads. Bob collected examples of the work from the site and took them to Bea. Bea showed Frank and Frank had Bob take him to the site. Frank surmised the site was a factory where Indians had manufactured points for weapons and for trade. There was evidence of trade. Frank and Bob dug around with a pick and shovel and discovered caches of shells that had holes drilled in them so they could be attached to a thread made from the fiber of a Century plant to make a necklace. Bob and Frank made a collection of the items and put them in a display case in the dairy to show to visitors and customers.

***

Bob settled in with the Barnes family. He took good care of his "little brother". It was odd because as Bob grew Jimmy stayed the same. Bob was now double the size of Jimmy. Bob was able to wake up without an alarm every two hours to move his brother. He checked to see if he needed to be changed and if he did, Bob woke Bea. Bob would wake up three times a night. He adjusted to the schedule and was able to fall back to sleep quickly. Bob would nap in the afternoon. It became a routine that was only varied when Jimmy got sick.

Jimmy was susceptible to congestion and if a cold took hold he developed sniffles and a cough. He was normally better in a couple of days. There were times though when he needed to be looked after at the hospital. He needed oxygen and a course of antibiotics. Penicillin was probably the thing that allowed Jimmy to continue to survive. He should have been dead long ago. There were medical studies in journals in which his case was reported. The doctors believed penicillin was the miracle drug for Jimmy.

During the summer after Bob first came to live with the Barnes', Jimmy was hospitalized twice. Jimmy was lucky because the personnel at the hospital in Daytona were very skilled. They had cared for the most difficult pulmonary cases from the war. Some of the doctors upon discharge from the Army remained in the area. They had Jimmy as a patient. They kept informed on the latest treatment for lung infections. Jimmy was most susceptible to lung infections and the infections were susceptible to penicillin.

Bob visited his little brother each time he was in the hospital. Jimmy recognized Bob and smiled and greeted him with bubbles.

On Jimmy's second hospitalization, Frank had taken Bob to the cafeteria for dinner. A surprise—Little Al and Jenny were in the dining room. Jenny was with Big Al sitting on his lap and Little Al was staring at his soft drink twirling the ice in the glass with his straw.

Jenny saw Bob and squealed. Bob went to her and touched her arm and she jumped up in his arms. Little Al was less involved with his brother. Big Al shook hands with Mr. Barnes. They talked about business. The saw mill was being closed for maintenance and the workers would be idle. He hadn't made a trip with a load of timber for a couple of weeks. The men went outside.

Big Al quietly told Mr. Barnes that Mary was in the psychiatric ward. He had come home and she had not taken care of the kids. A neighbor had the children. Mary was alone in the house in bed. She had been there for days.

Mr. Barnes told Big Al that he would have Bea drop by the hospital to see if she could help.

Big Al said it wasn't necessary; that Mary was "strong as a horse" and she would be out soon.

"Where is Pa, Mary's Dad?" asked Frank.

"He's with his daughter up North. He has prostate cancer. He was complaining he hurt so much that Mary called her sister. The sister took him home. They are going to have to sell Pa's house," said Big Al. "We'll have to leave and go back North. The kids don't know it yet."

Mr. Barnes just nodded and the men went back to the kids.

Later in the car, Bob told Frank Barnes that Mary was in the hospital. Bob related what Little Al told him, that Mary was yelling at the children and Little Al had gone to the neighbors. Pa was gone. The police came and took Mary away. The police located Big Al at a bar and he came home with the police to Pa's house. Little Al said Big Al had been with them since then.

Bob asked Frank what was going to happen to his brother and his sister. Frank said they would talk to Bea once they got home.

"We can't let anything happen to Albert and Jenny."

Frank Barnes had come to respect Bob for his honesty and hard work. Even though he was a child he had never missed a night watching Jimmy. He had never feigned sickness though Mr. Barnes knew it had to be hard for a six year old to wake up from a sound sleep to care for their handicapped son. Bob was a person of his word, even if it hurt if he told the truth.

***

Bob insisted that he and Bea visit Mary at the hospital. "It is very important that we see Mary."

Bea agreed. They went the next day. Bea told Bob to stay close and listen. "I'm going to speak to the nurse."

They learned that Mary was being treated with a new drug, Phenothiazine. She had gained weight after a week in the hospital. She was not at risk of death but she was very ill. When he heard this from the nurse Bob was distressed and confused and he began to whimper. Bea held him close and they walked over to Mary. She recognized her son and gave him a stick of gum. Bob took the gift but did not unwrap the gum but put it in his pocket. It was a memento of sorts.

"How are you Mary?" asked Bea.

"I feel fine, fine," she fawned over Bob. "You look good Bob, when did I see you last?"

Bob did not reply. He could tell Mary was different than the last time when Little Al and Jenny visited the dairy. That was the last time Bob saw Mary. Mary looked thin to Bob then. Now Mary was heavier, thicker and when he touched her arm and felt her muscle, it was quivering. "Are you cold, Mary?"

"No, I am fine, fine." She was trembling.

Bob didn't remember much of the conversation with Mary. Bob just listened, in a day dream. Bea and Mary talked about the children and Pa and Big Al. Mary knew Pa was up North with her sister but she didn't know where Big Al was. She didn't know where the kids were living. She thought they were in the house by the church and school. She forgot that the home had been lost to the bank for non-payment of the mortgage.

Bea felt the conversation was strange. Mary was ambivalent about everything she had once cared for.

Bob was impressed by the fact that the ward where they were visiting in was more like a living room than a hospital. There were no beds in the room. There were clusters of couches and chairs for patients and visitors to sit at. There were people speaking in little groups of two or three people-visiting like you would at home. There were no nurses or doctors that he could see except for the lady who greeted them at the door and answered Bea's questions. There was a large picture window that looked out over a yard of grass and a large live oak tree. The window made you feel you were inside a house, not a hospital. The yard was enclosed with a tall fence. There was no gate in the fence. How do you get in or out, thought Bob.

What Bob remembered most was that when they left after Mary hugged him that the nurse used a key to unlock the door and after they went out the door, Bob could hear the latch close with the bolt in the lock snapping shut.

***

Bob and Bea said nothing as they drove in the truck from the hospital in Daytona back to the farm house at the Homestead in Holly Hill. Frank Barnes had cared for Jimmy while they were gone. Bob went over to Jimmy and talked to him. Jimmy had become his friend and Bob imagined Jimmy always had something positive to say. Bob was never condescending to Jimmy and always eager to listen to his brother but Jimmy could only converse by blowing bubbles and smiling.

That night the four members of the family, Bea, Frank, Bob and Jimmy, stayed at the farm house. They would have some privacy there. The old man, Senator Barnes was back from Tallahassee staying at the Plantation on the river. The Senator was cranky. He drank rye whiskey. He was big and strong and disruptive. The Senator wanted to be the center of all conversations and he wanted to give advice and his advice would be the final word.

The question of what Bea and Frank Barnes would do for Bob's brother and sister was a personal, marital matter. The Senator would not have a say.

Frank asked his wife her opinion of Mary. Bea felt Mary was fragile and unable to care for her children or herself.

"What is your opinion of Big Al?" asked Bea.

"He's not a strong man. The reason Mary is so beat down is that he hasn't helped. He will leave first chance he gets. We're lucky he's still with the kids now."

The pair decided that they would try to take custody of the children if the court would allow it. Frank would contact his friend Tom Night for his advice and they would take it slowly one step at a time. Frank believed that Big Al had burnt his bridges so far as custody was concerned.

Bea shared that at the hospital Mary had asked Bea for help. Mary told Bea the doctors wanted her with someone who could take care of her. The doctor had told Mary someone also needed to help with her boy and the little girl. Mary recognized her husband could not be relied upon. Bea was impressed that Mary was thinking clearly on that score. But everyone recognized that she needed care and she would not be able to care for her children. She would be a danger to her children. They would not be able to defend themselves if she suffered a setback and had a schizophrenic episode like she had before she was hospitalized. Luckily, Little Al had asked a neighbor for help.

***

After she was hospitalized, Mary's doctors had prescribed a compound first prepared in the late 1800s called Phenothiazine to counter her psychosis. It was interesting that a variant of the compound was introduced by DuPont Chemical Company as an insecticide in 1935. The compound could be a poison or a cure. Mary's body chemistry accepted the medical compound and she could think more clearly when she took the drug. The question was whether she would take the medication once she stabilized. If she failed to take her medicine she would be unable to take care of herself, let alone care for the children.

Mary's doctor was insistent that Mary no longer have custody of the two young children if she did not have assistance. Big Al complicated the matter. He wanted nothing more to do with Mary. Mary's sister said she would take her in and care for her and make sure she took her medicine but she could not take the children.

Big Al refused to return to Pa's home if Mary returned, he told his lady friend he intended to divorce Mary and turn the two youngest children to the care of the State. Since Big Al would not stay home if Mary was there, Mary's doctor would only agree to allow Mary to return to the young children if Bob was back with his mother. If Bob was back in the family circle he could help his mother care for his brother and sister and sound the alarm if Mary failed to take her medication or suffered a setback. The doctor was fearful that Little Al, who was only four, might not recognize his mother was becoming more ill or had failed to take her medication. However, the doctor felt Bob was mature enough to care for his mother.

Frank and Bea did not want to lose Bob. He was family now. They decided Bob had to stay with them. To keep Bob they would take Little Al and Jenny too. It was important for Jimmy to keep Bob in the fold. But that fact was their secret.

Chapter 12

How Everyone Became Rich the First Time / Tom Night

Thomas Night was a lawyer. Tom and Frank Barnes met in college. Tom was on a fast track program to obtain a law degree at Stetson College of Law. He could finish his undergraduate degree in two years and then enter the law school and complete the requirements of his law degree in three more years. The program saved him two years of study.

In the 1930s it was not necessary for a prospective lawyer to obtain a law degree but you had to pass the Florida Bar Exam to obtain a license to practice law before the courts. In order to sit for the exam you were required to have a degree from an accredited law school or you had to be employed as a clerk for a licensed attorney who would teach you the law. The supervising attorney would decide when you attained minimum competency to practice the law and at that time he recommended you were eligible to take the Bar Exam. The Florida Bar also investigated your background to approve your good character. If you were colored or a woman the Florida Bar performed a very thorough investigation and the proctor who graded the colored had a very sharp pencil.

In any event, Tom went to Stetson, which was an accredited law school. Graduates from Stetson had a 100% passing rate on the Bar Exam for as many years as anyone could remember. The year Tom took the Bar Exam; Stetson students maintained the schools 100% passing rate yet again.

Frank Barnes was an agricultural sciences student at Stetson. This was a logical area of study. His family owned citrus groves and the jam factory at the Plantation, and his wife owned a dairy, a pig farm and a large stand of timber, so Frank wanted to bring the latest agricultural knowledge to the family interests and expand the operations. Frank helped out when the baby came, but the baby was ill from the start and did not thrive, did not walk or talk or grow. Frank had to work in the dairy. Bea devoted herself totally to the baby. She did not graduate.

The Senator insisted Frank go to college. Frank tried to satisfy all needs. He would work and attend school. The Senator suggested Stetson University because it was the closest university to the farm in Holly Hill. Frank could take the back way to Canal Road and then US 92 and be at the campus in an hour. He would milk the cows at 5:00 am then leave the care of the animals to the workers.

He would arrive in Deland early and study in the library and take his classes and then study in the library again in the afternoon and he was home by 7:00 p.m. Most afternoons Frank and Tom were in the library together studying. While he was in school Bea would check in at the dairy in the afternoons and collect receipts and pay the bills. Otherwise, if Frank was not in school Frank worked at the dairy all day.

***

The Thirties were unimaginably tough economic times for the nation. Florida's economy was always racked by boom and bust cycles, but it was not prepared for the downturn. The state was hard hit by the Great Depression. In spite of the fact that there was a depression, Tom Night's parents held their jobs as teachers in St. Petersburg, Florida. They were lucky.

Then, the family caught a new strain of the flu. The illness was isolated to a pocket on the west coast of the state. Tom was the only family member who survived. Penicillin would have saved his family. It had been discovered but it was not yet an accepted treatment regimen. Tom was born and had grown up in St. Petersburg on Florida's west coast near Tampa. He was a junior in St. Petersburg High School when the family became sick.

After he was orphaned, Tom had two aunts who took him to live with them in Deland, Florida near the East Coast. Tom's aunts taught Humanities at Stetson University. One of the few perks for the teachers at the university was free tuition at the school for children of the faculty. The school encouraged Tom's aunts to apply for the scholarship for Tom even though he was not their natural child. During the Depression there were few students enrolled in college and there was room for Tom in classes at the school. The Firestone family had established an endowment for children of the faculty for tuition. Therefore, the money for tuition was available, so long as no one objected if the benefit of free tuition was given to the orphaned nephew of the two professors. It was to everyone's advantage for Tom to go to university. There was no objection.

Tom had residual physical problems from his bout with the flu. He had weak lungs and he was susceptible to colds. Once he was in college, Tom developed a terrible addiction to nicotine and he smoked up a storm in spite of his lung affliction. Tom's doctors did not advise against smoking however. They looked at smoking as purgative. Tobacco was an expectorant that kept Tom's lungs clear. Most doctors smoked. They participated in advertisements for cigarettes touting a brand's mild flavor and so on. It seemed most doctors began to smoke when they were confronted with the odor of death while studying a cadaver. Whether it was the smell of the body or the phenolic disinfectant, the doctors all seemed to use tobacco in one form or another. The smoke or the chaw or the snuff got into the farthest recesses of the medical student's nasal cavities and masked the smell of the corpse.

***

Tom Night and Frank Barnes were both lucky. They had the ability to attend school during the Depression. Tom had the scholarship and the financial help of his Aunts and a small inheritance from his parents and insurance benefits from his parents work as teachers and a small residual from the parent's pension.

Frank's mother was deceased. His father was a State Senator and even during the depression, politicians knew where the roads were going to be built and which company was going to receive a contract to provide a service or a purchase order for a State expenditure. If the politician had some cash and he had inside information provided through his position then he could invest on the inside trade and make money. There was nothing illegal with a politician making money on inside information gained through his elected office.

The Senator had an eye for a good deal. He saw the value of ownership of Plantation #7 and the prime grove land that sat on 130 acres between the Halifax River and the Atlantic Ocean on the north side of Ormond Beach. The plantation's jams and jellies were sold throughout the Northeast United States. Even in the Depression he saw that the jellies were favorites at holiday meals and most families would purchase the sweet exotic taste of the guava, fig or oranges grown at the grove behind Plantation #7. The Senator realized that in order to keep his market share after 1929 he had to reduce the size of his glass jars and reduce the price. By having the ability to cut back and having a persistent market for the product the Senator was able to sustain his business and he kept his employees. And there was still enough cash money left over to send Frank to college.

***

The Senator's shrewdest move was the purchase of a 40,000 acre contiguous block of swamp land. The property was located between Deland and Daytona Beach. He was able to purchase the land at a tax sale for a little less than $5 per acre. The Senator had driven past the land every time he drove to Deland, the County Seat of Volusia County. There was a "for sale" sign that was erected in 1929. No one had any money but by 1939 the signage had deteriorated and had about lost all its paint, except for a phone number in Daytona (CL2-2448). After driving past the sign for ten years, the Senator made a call to the number on the sign. The phone was out of service. The Senator figured it was time to move on the property.

While in Deland, Senator Barnes visited the Property Appraiser and found an assistant who had some knowledge of the property. The land was titled in the name of a Delaware Corporation. The taxes had not been paid for five years and the Volusia County Tax Collector had not even received a bid for the tax certificates on the land. The County hoped to eventually recoup the amount owed for the taxes plus statutory interest. Times were very bad. So bad that if the County took property by judicial sale for all the land in the County for which the taxes were unpaid, the County would own almost all the property in the County. That would include the property belonging to all the County officials and even the tax collector himself. Times were so bad that no property owner could pay their taxes.

So if there was a way the County could sell these 40,000 acres they would accommodate a purchaser. At least that is what the assistant tax assessor told Senator Barnes.

The Senator consulted with Frank about the purchase. The Senator told Frank it was time for his education to pay for itself. Frank felt that the property, though wet, was not swamp. Frank enlisted Tom. Frank and Tom rented a plane and a pilot from the airport that was located just north of the parcel.

By flying over the land at a constant altitude and photographing the land they were able to acquire an aerial survey. The photographs showed the property contained the headwaters of the Tomoka River. The property drained to the northeast and emptied into the main branch of the Tomoka.

By studying the photographs Frank was able to determine which of the stream beds on the acreage would drain the most surface water into the river. Frank felt that if the natural drainage system was cleaned and unclogged the land would drain and dry. Even though the timber on the land had grown slowly due to the wet conditions much of the timber was mature and merchantable and was ready to be harvested. But the land had to be drained so that the loggers could reach the trees.

The original owners had purchased the land to sell for residential development but they failed to attract buyers because the property was considered swamp. They had also failed to successfully harvest any of the timber except the trees growing on the side of the highway because of the wet conditions.

Senator Barnes felt he could pay for the land with the timber if he could cut the trees. The market for timber was coming back. There was war in Europe and all commodities, including pine and cypress timber would be needed by the country once the United States was in the war. The US Government had the ability to print dollars so the government would be the market to purchase the timber. Senator Barnes was up all night considering the possibility of the value of the land if he owned it. They could be rich. He enlisted every person he knew who owed him a favor to help him.

When the Senator was with Tom and Frank he pounded on his hand and gestured like he was giving a stump speech: "And I want you boys to investigate the possibility of building a saw mill. We are going to be in a war. We can cut our timber and all the timber south to Mims in Brevard County to supply the troops. We can put the mill on our property. The bank will loan us the acquisition and development money if the Army will give me a contract. I know the US Army will build barracks buildings here. This is Florida. You can train 365 days a year. Up North they will need to be in-doors due to the weather. And the military can fly here all year long. They will build airports here, or enlarge the airports that are already here. I know they will need one right here on our prop-erty. The Army will drain our property for nothing."

The Senator kept talking as he got in his car and drove off to the next meeting and the next problem he needed to solve. Frank was left to sort out the plausible from the fantasy. Frank was dogged. He stuck with it and he leaned on Tom to help him think through the problems his father left him. Once they started the project it exploded in a positive direction. The Senator's idea was sound. Frank and Tom were mostly chasing dollars to pay for everything. But the banks were willing to lend if they could show how the loan would be repaid. The government was always willing to give a purchase order and that promise to pay for the timber, so long as the Senator produced the mill and the timber, was proof the Barnes family could repay the loan.

America's involvement in the war began. The Senator got loans for the purchase of the land. They built the saw mill. Everything was leveraged except Bea's farmhouse and the Homestead in Holly Hill. Now, the banks sought out Senator Barnes with the intent to make him a loan. He was golden. The government had bought all his timber, and part of his land for a huge training base near De-land. The saw mill cut timber 24/7 and the Senator's transporta-tion company, Commercial Carriers Corporation (CCC) delivered the processed boards throughout the South for military construc-tion projects.

When the war was over and timber was no longer needed to build barracks for the troops, CCC shipped the processed wood to New Jersey to be used to build tract homes.

***

Over time, Frank and the Senator bought more land and built more mills over time. But the family was always on the edge of bankruptcy. Senator Barnes was always purchasing something. He diversified his investments; the bigger the better. He bought a trophy commercial office building on Peachtree Street in Atlanta. He secretly bought 600,000 acres in British Honduras. He and some partners bought and sold timberland throughout the Southeast. At one point they owned over a million acres. All of the land was purchased with a signature. No cash changed hands.

But after Tom graduated from law school he spent most of his time in the air flying one or two days a week to closings for the purchase of timberland or to court because someone had sued one of the Senator's corporations for non-payment of a debt. Plantation #7 was the headquarters for all the operations. Tom couldn't stand the pressure at the Plantation and so he moved back to St. Petersburg so he could avoid the Senator. If he had stayed in Volusia County, Sen. Barnes would have been at his office all the time, pounding his fist on Tom's desk. Besides, if Tom kept his distance he maintained some credibility in his dealings on behalf of all the Senator's businesses that were over time consolidated into Corporate Carriers Corporation (CCC). CCC seemed to owe money to every bank in the country.

The Senator became crafty the deeper he got in debt. He cross collateralized his holdings so that all the banks and lending institutions had an interest in his property. To get repaid, the banks would have to fight with each other or they had to cooperate. Tom found that there was no one more vicious than a banker trying to be repaid. The Senator's loan strategy was sound. The bankers were all suing one another trying to establish priority over the collateral.

Tom countered avarice and greed with honesty. Tom's approach was to tell the creditors that they would all be paid if they would just be patient and not upset the latest deal that was cooking. The creditors came to trust what Tom said because new deals were struck and Tom and Frank were able to dole out funds from sales to the creditors to at least get the banks partially paid.

Finally, in 1948, a deal was struck with a large corporation that owned a number of paper mills in the Southeast. Everyone would be paid. It was the Senator's idea and Frank's tenacity that made it work.

This was the Senator's idea: CCC, the Senators most liquid company had been purchasing timber leases in close proximity to the paper mills of a company called Worldwide Paper Company (WPC) and CCC was supplying the WPC mills with pulpwood from the land leased by CCC. Pulpwood is a tree too small to cut into a board. Pulpwood is mashed and cooked to make white paper, brown paper, craft paper, card board and corrugated board. CCC owned saw mills in the area of the WPC paper mills. When CCC clear cut the land it had some timber it cut into board and the rest of the trees that were thin were sold to WPC to be digested into fiber for paper.

Worldwide Paper came to realize that the cost of their pulp wood had increased. The reason was that CCC owned and controlled WPC's resource stream. When WPC's buyers attempted to purchase timber leases on the open market they discovered that CCC owned all the timber leases in close proximity to their paper mills. And if WPC went farther away from WPC's mills to purchase timber they had to use CCC's trucks to haul the timber and CCC's transport fees were very expensive.

What Worldwide Paper realized was that they were being squeezed on price for the resource they needed to manufacture their paper and corrugated board. As a result Worldwide was beginning to lose market share because they had to raise their prices to pay for the increased price for the pulp wood resources that CCC owned and delivered to WPC's mills.

Worldwide finally realized what had happened. The President of WPC knew they were had. He disliked the Senator but regularly spoke with Frank and opened negotiations with Frank to purchase the CCC's operations that fed timber resources to WPC's paper mills. CCC would still own the mills and timberlands that were not near WPC's plants. The one property Frank wanted to retain and replant was the original 40,000 acre parcel near Deland.

Sen. Barnes tried to take over the negotiations as soon as he heard about the possible deal. Tom and Frank told the Senator that they would quit if he intervened in the discussions. Sen. Barnes agreed to leave the preliminary negotiations of the sale to them. It was agreed that Senator Barnes would help with the final decision on price once the preliminary discussions were completed.

Tom was able to keep the other creditors at bay. These creditors did not have any lien or encumbrance filed against the CCC properties that Worldwide was interested in purchasing. So these creditors knew they could be left hanging and they would be paid nothing unless they became more reasonable. Tom was able to work out a compromise of the amount of the debt owed to each creditor. These unsecured creditors entered into a forbearance agreement so that the sales agreement with WPC could be completed without the creditors interfering with the purchase of the CCC land by Worldwide Paper. Once CCC was paid by Worldwide all the other creditors would be paid.

Sen. Barnes was tasked with finding permanent financing so that there wasn't a constant fight to find enough cash to make purchases of land and businesses and to operate the new purchases. Frank and Tom refused to continue working for CCC if they had to continue operating hand to mouth and starving and near financial collapse all the time.

The Senator said he knew just who they needed for permanent financing. He claimed he knew of a financial institution that had plenty of money and experts to help CCC with decisions involving purchases of land and mills for ongoing operations. The financial institution was involved in loans to agricultural and industrial businesses. The company was looking for entrepreneurs who would put together a business plan based on an idea that would satisfy a need. The institution, Farm and Timber Financial (FTF), would look at the proposal and make the loan, and stick with the owner over time, and provide additional financing if needed to fulfill the borrower's dream.

Tom and Frank hated the idea. It was just more bankers selling loans. Tom and Frank concluded that FTF was just inflating the Senator's ego and they would sell him a high-priced loan with the Senator's company paying all the accounting and legal fees.

Frank and his father were at loggerheads. The Senator said he would agree to the sale of land and timber to Worldwide Paper, but only if he got the deal with FTF. The Senator had Frank over a barrel. Frank gave in and agreed FTF would be CCC's banker after the deal with WPC was completed. Frank also had a mild heart attack.

Ultimately, the deal was for CCC to spin off the mills and land and leases that WPC wanted to a new corporation named CCC/WPC and then CCC would receive shares in WPC plus sufficient cash for CCC to pay all of the other creditors who Tom had been holding off.

As a result of the transaction Senator Barnes became the largest individual shareholder in Worldwide Paper Company owning 450,000 shares in the publicly traded corporation and a $2,000,000 certificate of deposit. The net proceeds of the sale were tax free. The WPC stock Senator Barnes received contained a restriction that prevented the sale of the shares for a period of five years. The Senator retained his interest in Plantation #7 and CCC paid off all outstanding debt on the assets it did not sell to WPC.

Frank's share was 50,000 shares of Worldwide. He received $500,000 cash. He also received 30% of all other land holdings owned by CCC but which had not been purchased by WPC. Many of these land holdings had been purchased as side deals by the Senator when he would make a purchase or sale of CCC lands. As a result Frank owned a 30% interest in over one hundred cut-outs and parcels that could be used for gas stations or small residential development, or commercial properties. The Senator owned the other 70% of these land holdings. All of the debt had been paid on these properties. The land was free and clear. Included in this land was the 40,000 acres near Deland.

Tom was paid his legal bill. CCC owed him $150,000. Tom paid cash to buy an office building in downtown St. Petersburg for his law practice and he had money in the bank.

Part III

The Johnson Family - Post World War II

Chapter 13
Big Al and Frank

Albert Johnson Sr. felt he was owed something for all the care he had given his three kids during their lives. He was aware Mary had been given $2,500 by Bea to obtain Mary's permission that Bob spend nights helping Bea with Jimmy. Big Al had gotten no more from the $2,500 transaction than what he could steal from Mary's pocketbook. In his opinion purchasing the house in Daytona Beach near to the church and school was a waste. It turned out he was right when the bank foreclosed and the house was lost.

Big Al had big ideas. He knew how to make money. But to make money you needed to have money and he never had any money. When Mary was locked in the psychiatric ward he had his chance to put some money in his pocket. Mary wouldn't be able to spend the money foolishly on a house. In fact, now that she had been declared incompetent she couldn't legally enter into a contract.

Big Al knew Bea wanted all his kids and to get them she and Frank would need his permission or prove he was unfit. The Barnes' attorney, Tom Night had written him a letter and inside the letter there was a form called "Consent to Adoption" that Tom asked him to sign before a notary and two witnesses. Al refused.

***

Frank and Big Al had known each other for two years. Al had bought the lot on Flomish Avenue from Frank and Bea. Big Al had built a small house on the lot. He intended to resell the little house for a profit. Mary wanted to live in the country. While he built the little house, Al had been working at the abandoned US Army base salvaging building materials from the barracks buildings. Everything in the small house he built for Mary and the kids was from the Army. They joked that the construction materials came from the lowest bidder. But to Al's mind there was nothing wrong with the wood and windows and doors and tubs and toilets just because they were used. When he sold the goods he argued to potential buyers that the supplies were just now broken in, and hardly used. He was honest and he made a living. But it seemed that as soon as the government got cranked up to fight the war, the war was over. Big Al was out of the army and he was working in Daytona.

After the war came the market for housing. The war effort was scrapped and the consumer economy ignited. There had been 15 years of little or no manufacturing; no new washing machines and cars and houses owing to the Depression and the War. And what was manufactured was for the war and not the consumer. First came the Lend Lease Program and then the actual fighting. Afterward, there was pent up demand for consumer goods. It took a while but after the war, Al's next job was driving a truck for CCC delivering finished lumber to the northeast to build new homes. Al's job came as a result of the consumer economy.

But now, Big Al was sick and tired of long distance hauling. He needed a new start and he would get that, he promised himself. The plan to get what he wanted, money, required him to keep the kids close since Mary was sick and living with her sister in upstate New York.

Big Al exercised his right of care, custody and control over Bob, Little Al and Jenny. He moved back to the small house on Flomish near the Barnes' farm house with the three kids. He would not let Bob spend time with Bea or spend the night helping with Jimmy.

Big Al would only let the children stay with Frank and Bea when he was on the road driving the lumber truck for CCC.

Frank explained the problem he was having with Big Al and the children to Tom Night. Frank was honest explaining how it came to be that Bob lived with them and took care of Jimmy. How Bea paid Mary $2,500 and that Bea gave Mary food for the children. How Bea had bought the little house on Flomish from the bank. Now, after Mary lost the house in Daytona and was unable to care for the children, Big Al had moved back into the little house on Flomish with the children.

Bea complained to Tom Night that she wanted to sue Al to get back the $2,500 because Bob wasn't staying over and helping with Jimmy. Tom advised Bea and Frank, they should not sue Al because Al had valid defenses to such a claim. Bob was a minor. He was too young to work. The contract with a minor was illegal and unenforceable. Further, Bea gave money to Mary, not to Big Al. And besides, Big Al would argue that Mary and Bea couldn't enter into an agreement to sell Bob to Bea. Al would argue it was slavery.

Bea became upset and Frank explained that they should follow Tom's advice. Finally, Bea agreed they would let Tom handle the matter legally.

Bea worried if she could still give the children food. She didn't know how Big Al would take care of Jenny. She needed special care. A grown man shouldn't take care of a little girl. It wasn't right, she thought.

Tom said Bea could be a good neighbor and if that meant that when Al was on the road she could care for the children and let them stay over at the farmhouse and Bob could help with Jimmy at night. There would be nothing wrong with it. Al had an obligation to care for the children now that Mary was with her sister up North. Al was using Bob as a babysitter when he worked. Mary wasn't expected to come back to Florida and was worse off mentally now than when she was with the children. So Al had no one to care for the children except Bob or Bea if she volunteered.

Other than the advice to be neighborly, Tom gave Frank and Bea no other advice. Time was on their side, said Tom.

The Barnes were very wealthy now after the sale to WPC and they could afford to care for Bob, Little Al and Jenny. Tom asked, and he was assured by Bea and Frank that the only reason they wanted Al and Mary's children was that they had grown to love them and they wanted them to be part of their family. Bea was satisfied with Tom's advice as time went on because the three children were with her and Jimmy most of the time. Al was always on the road so the kids were at the farm house. He didn't make enough money to support the kids and himself. When he came home there were always problems he had to face. The latest was that the Constable for the Justice of the Peace (JP) had visited the small house and left a card wanting Al to stop by the JP's office in Daytona.

Al knew not to ignore the law. When he showed up at the JP's office, the JP said there were complaints that Big Al was not at home with his kids at night.

"I wonder who made that complaint?" asked Al.

"It's confidential," said the JP. "You have a duty to protect your kids."

"That's true, and I do."

"Is Bob in school?" asked the JP. "School started last week and no one's seen Bob."

"He had a cold. I will get him in there next week if he is better."

"We are concerned for the kids," said the JP.

"Understood."

When Al asked if he was under arrest, the JP offered that he wasn't under arrest "at this time".

Al knew he needed to tread lightly. He took time off from work and registered Bob for school. He stayed with the kids. The JP visited the small house two days in a row and that was enough to make Al phone long distance to Tom's office in St. Petersburg to see when Tom would be over in the area next.

"I need to talk to you," said Al.

***

Tom did not have an office in Volusia County. He didn't want to meet Al at the Plantation or the Homestead so they met in a conference room in the courthouse. Tom brought his secretary, Marla, to take notes. She was a notary and she would file court papers with the clerk if that was needed. Tom intended to file a Petition for Adoption and if Al did not voluntarily accept service and the jurisdiction of the court for the termination of parental rights and an adoption of the children, he intended to have a process server serve the petition.

There was little small talk.

Tom asked if Al still had the consent form.

Al said he did.

Had he read the form?

Yes, he had.

Did he understand the form?

Yes, he did.

Tom explained that Frank and Bea intended to press forward with the adoption of the three children.

"I understand it would be illegal to pay me for the children?" said Al. "I spoke to a lawyer."

"Do you want to have a lawyer present for this meeting?" asked Tom.

"No. I was looking for some advice and got what I needed and I don't want to pay for or hire a lawyer."

"If you consent to the adoption, I intend that you see a lawyer of your choice if you desire. We will pay the reasonable value of your expenses in the adoption, including the cost of a lawyer, but we are not going to pay you for the children. You will need to decide that this is the best thing you can do for your kids and that will be the only reason you sign the consent form. There will be no other reason. Otherwise we will go forward with the proceeding alleging that you are unfit to have custody of the children, and that the children are in danger, and we will let a judge decide the issue."

"What about Mary?"

Tom had been in contact with Mary through her sister. "We have her consent to the adoption and the statement of her doctors here and up North. The doctors believe a change of custody to Frank and Bea is in the best interests of the children."

"Can I visit the children after the adoption?"

"That would be agreeable for now so long as there was sufficient notice of a visit. But you would have no right to visit if Frank and Bea object later."

"Would I be able to speak to Bea, you know, call her from time to time to see how the kids are doing?" asked Al.

"No problem, as long as Frank and Bea consent," said Tom.

Al took out the papers he had received in the mail from Tom's office and he scanned them again. "I went over these papers with the attorney I consulted," said Al. "He explained that if I sign the papers a judge can sever my parental rights of my children. Are those the correct words?"

"Yes, your rights to the children would end."

"The attorney said that even though I sign the papers the court will have to find that an adoption would be in the best interests of my kids. So this is not the end of the process, just because I sign the consent."

"That is correct," said Tom. "In fact you will be given notice of the hearing on the Petition for Adoption and you can appear and object at that time. But your signed consent to the adoption would be put in evidence and the judge would give it greater weight."

Al rubbed his jaw. "Ok, I have considered the matter. This is the best for them and for me and for Mary."

"It's your decision," said Tom. "You can see another lawyer first if you want."

"No, that's all right. You said you would reimburse me for the money I spent on the attorney I talked to?"

"Yes. Do you have the bill?"

"Yes."

Al gave Tom the invoice in the amount of $25.00. The invoice was marked paid. Tom took a trust check from his file and made it out payable to Mr. Albert Johnson in the amount of $25.00 for reimbursement of legal fees and expenses. Big Al took the check, shook hands with Tom and left the conference room.

***

"This seems too simple a way to give up your children." Marla teared up.

Tom advised Marla that she needed to control her emotions.

Marla apologized and said it wouldn't happen again.

Chapter 14
The New Routine

Following the adoption, the new and enlarged Barnes family fell into a routine. Everyone except the Senator moved out of the big house on the plantation and lived at the Homestead on the 800 acres. Bob was enrolled in Catholic school in Daytona. Frank was spending most of his time at the timber farm and sawmill that was located half way between Daytona Beach and Deland on US 92. Bea was overseeing the dairy at the Homestead.

Frank drove past the grade school on his way to the office for the saw mill and so it was convenient for Frank to drive Bob to school. Frank took Little Al with him to work. He was his shadow. They were inseparable. Jenny stayed at home with Bea and Jimmy.

Bob's school was run by nuns, the Dominican Sisters. The school taught grades one through eight. All eight grades were in one large room. There were only four nuns, one nun for two grades. The room was noisy but the children were respectful and paid attention to their lessons and progressed.

Bob was taking first and second grade at the same time so he could catch up. He had missed most of the first grade because of the situation with his mother in the hospital. The teacher doubled up his workload and he was expected to complete the first two years in one. Bea helped him at home with his numbers and alphabet and simple math. They used flash cards as a teaching aid. Bob liked the cards because it was like a game. All the children participated and they all began to learn. Jimmy was even included. Frank and Bea found a chair that hung from the ceiling by a rope. They could sit him in the small chair and prop him up with pillows and he was positioned in the room with the other children. He was about as tall as three-year-old Jenny when he was seated and they were all together playing games. Jimmy followed the other kids with his eyes.

Bea and Frank knew that Jimmy probably could not comprehend what was happening except he was interacting with other human beings and that made him happy. Jimmy did understand joy and he was able to receive joy and give joy to the other children.

Jenny came to be Jimmy's best friend. She would talk to him. She was sometimes very serious, speaking low and slow and she was convinced he understood her. Bea came to believe also but Frank couldn't believe it. No matter how much he wished he could have a regular conversation with his son he couldn't believe the gurgles and grunts that Jenny could elicit from his son was a form of communication.

***

Frank was happy with his buddy, Little Al. The pair dressed the same. If Frank had a red shirt, jeans and boots, that's what Bea laid out for Al. Frank had a place for Al at the office so Al could play and color and nap while he went in the mill. But other than keeping Al out of the mill and away from the equipment the two were together. Al went to meetings with bankers and lawyers and salesmen. He listened carefully and would ask his dad questions afterward. Frank was amazed that he understood the crux of the conversations. You need money. You want a new saw. He got it. Sometimes, Frank would ask Al what he should do in a particular case with a problem if Frank was stumped. Al would just shrug. Frank would laugh and Al would join in in a deep voice imitating Frank.

***

Bea had bought the small house that Big Al built from the bank after it foreclosed on the property. Bea transferred the lot and the house to Big Al so he had a place to go that was close by if he wanted to visit his children. But he never stayed in the small house. He would call and talk to Bea to find out how the kids were. The calls became less frequent as time went by. Mary never called. Big Al said he visited Mary. They were still married but they never lived together again. Mary was still on medication and it caused her to gain weight. Mary was with her sister. Pa died. Mary didn't mention the children much, Big Al reported in one of his phone calls.

***

The tree farm near Deland was originally 40,000 acres. Frank hung a map on his wall and identified the names of the owners of the agricultural and timber tracts that were contiguous (abutting) to the Barnes' land. He wrote letters asking the owners if they had an interest in selling the "dirt". He would let them sell the timber on the property to the Barnes' sawmill and he would buy the land. Frank had in mind to cut all the timber on the outlying parcels and then replant as he cut. He wanted to use best forest practices that he learned at Stetson and follow the advice of the state foresters.

Frank had begun to survey the original 40,000 acres to determine which parts of the land were worth replanting after the timber was clear cut. The idea was to leave the swamp alone and let the timber in the swamp regrow naturally. The hardwoods would reseed and grow quickly and the hardwood timber that was cut would be used for pulp, plywood and furniture. The mature cypress trees would be cut from a pond or head and the small trees in the pond would continue to grow to maturity. Cypress was for boards, siding, fencing, etc.

Pine would grow best if it was replanted in a plantation. The best practice to replant pine land that was wet, was to clear cut the trees from the land and then chop the stumps and burn it and then plow it and then form the ground into beds-similar to the way a farmer prepares a field on which he intends to plant corn. After the land was clear cut, chopped and burned, plowed and bedded, the farmer plants 850 seedlings per acre in the top of the beds. The end result was a field of seedlings that were planted on

top of a mound of earth so the seedlings would not be in the water. And by chopping, burning the land and plowing the land before bedding it, the farmer killed any competition and the pine
seedling could feed on all of the nutrients in the mound and from
the soil in about a four foot circumference around the seedling.

If the land was dry and hilly, the pine could be planted without
bedding the soil. All of the pine land owned by CCC was wet and
needed to be bedded and Frank bought large CAT bulldozers and
John Deere tractors to do the work. Almost all of the land that
surrounded the Barnes' tree farm was similar to Frank's, so once
he cut and replanted his land, he purchased his neighbor's land if
they would sell and he moved on to remold their property using
the same farming regime.

Few foresters were critical of Frank's methods. Because he did
not fill the swamp and the cypress ponds and let the hardwood
and cypress regenerate naturally on their own, the land overall
was not a monoculture that consisted of only pine tree plantation
but instead the pine land was interspersed with river, stream,
ponds, cypress and hardwood together with the commercial pine
plantation. From the air you could see that Frank had made little
change to the natural lay of the land except he had bedded the
pine plantation so that the pine trees had the best chance to grow
in wet low lands. If the land was not bedded the trees would
drown or be stunted.

Little Al loved to run in the furrows between the newly planted
seedlings. If he saw a tree that was planted in loose soil he would
form a fist and pack the dirt around the roots of the seedling by
punching around the little tree. He also enjoyed visiting the farm
that grew seedlings. The farm tried to improve the trees by collecting seed from superior trees and culling seeds that were from
inferior trees. Over the years the seedlings became faster growing,
producing more fiber than trees planted in years past. Little Al
told Frank he thought he would like to grow trees too.

Within five years of beginning the program of buying just the dirt and replanting seedlings according to best forest practices, the Barnes' Tree Farm consisted of 72,000 acres. The profit generated by the sawmill was used to purchase the dirt and the cash flow of the mill paid all other expenses.

***

Bea still managed the dairy. The 800 acre wood lot was clear cut. The acreage was mostly used for pasture for the cows. She continued to modernize the operation and improved the milking parlor. She was so proud of the operation that the dairy had a tour every Saturday for anyone who dropped by. During weekdays of the school year students came by with their classmates for tours of the facility and a free ice cream cone. Bea wanted the youngsters to understand that milk came from an animal and not from a bottle. She wanted the children to know what a cow smelled like.

The dairy, the farmhouse, and the wood lot were owned by Bea individually. She wanted to keep ownership in the asset in her own name and not in CCC's.

Every day when Little Al and Bob were out of the house, Jenny and Jimmy went with Bea to the dairy and they gathered the receipts from the day before. Bea had meetings and spoke to the employees discussing their concerns. She reviewed the accounts with Frank. He was proud of her. Her gross margins were better than his at the saw mill. But Bea didn't have the Senator to deal with, thought Frank.

The Senator was like a vacuum. He grabbed up every dollar that he could find. Frank actually had to hide money in savings accounts so there were sufficient funds to pay payroll and the cost of maintenance. Otherwise Senator Barnes would buy something else. It was like he was trying to spend himself out of his wealth and back into debt. Frank had been able to prevent the Senator from leveraging the stock in CCC, which still owned the out parcels and cut outs and the Barnes Tree Farm.

The banker, FTF, convinced the Senator to have CCC borrow money to construct commercial and residential structures on the out parcels and cut outs. Once these properties were built out they were sold or leased. The cash flow from the completed projects paid construction and operating loans to the Senator's "friends" at Farm and Timber Financial (FTF). Between interest and expense charges from FTF, CCC's construction projects were broke. They never made even a gross profit.

In order to obtain additional credit the Senator was convinced by the bankers at FTF to assign the interest payments from the two million dollar CD to guarantee the payments owed to FTF, even though there was no default in the principal or interest balance owed to FTF. FTF felt "insecure", or so they said, and the loan documents allowed them to acquire additional collateral from the Senator if they felt they might not be paid. The interest payments from the CD satisfied FTF for about a year and then FTF wanted not only the interest from the CD but they wanted the CD itself.

Frank had anticipated that FTF would try to get their hands on the CD as additional collateral for their loans. To block FTF, Frank made his father assign 30% of the CD to Frank in return for Frank advancing funds from the operating accounts of the sawmill to pay loan debt to FTF. Then when FTF demanded the CD itself, Frank refused to agree to allow the transfer of the CD because he had the prior lien to 30% of the CD. FTF would have to pay him $600,000.00 to obtain priority in the CD. FTF refused to pay him.

Then FTF tried to get the Senator to transfer his 70% interest in the CD to FTF. The Senator realized they bank would have all their assets if he did not object. When the Senator refused to assign the 70% interest in the CD as additional collateral, FTF sued Frank for interference with their advantageous relationship with the Senator.

Frank hated lawyers but sometimes they were necessary. Frank knew he had to talk to Tom. Tom had been left in the dark. When Frank finally called, Tom thought it concerned the kids and the adoption. Then he was told it was a business matter and that Frank had been sued.

When Tom asked Frank what the defense was to the suit, Frank explained that the best he could figure, FTF was paid in full and there was no money due on the loans. The bank was anticipating a breach. What Frank and his Dad and CCC needed was help to refinance and get off the billing cycle the bank was charging in fees and interest and penalties. What they also needed was an accounting from FTF for all transactions from day one.

Tom had not acted as counsel for Frank or his father or CCC since the transaction with Worldwide Paper had made them rich. After hearing Frank's story Tom said the way things were going they would be going from rags to riches and back to rags.

Tom meant it as a joke but Frank wasn't laughing.

Tom asked who was representing Frank and the Senator and CCC in their dealings with FTF. Frank said the bank provided them with one of their attorneys.

"FTF hired our attorneys and CCC paid the attorney," said Frank.

"Where are CCC's legal files?"

"I do not know. We seemed to have a different attorney every time we had a new loan or new business."

"Was it the same law firm?" asked Tom.

"Yes. The law firm has its office in FTF's office building."

"Well, you need to call and arrange to pick up your file."

"Ok."

"Do you have any of the billing or paperwork from FTF?"

"If we do it's at the plantation offices. That's where the Senator works."

"See what you can do. I need the paperwork to defend the suit," said Tom and he added, "When were you served with the lawsuit?"

"Two weeks ago."

"Have someone drive the paperwork to me today. You only have 20 days from the day you were served with the complaint to file an answer, so we need to get on this right away."

"Ok."

Part IV

*Industry, Agriculture
and the Law in Florida*

Chapter 15
Discovery

"Thomas C. Night, Esquire" was the name on the business card that Tom handed to the receptionist who sat at a raised dais and looked down on clients who entered the reception room of Duffy and Phillips, Attorneys at Law.

The receptionist fingered the card as she looked at Tom sizing him up.

Tom wondered if her stare was meant to crack his "old boy" veneer. Tom was sure the beautiful woman seated before him had broken many hearts. She was an impeccable woman out of "Gone with the Wind", tough as nails with black hair and green eyes. Tom wondered why the firm placed an object as cold as this woman at the front desk, unless to communicate that they were distant and better than you.

Tom ignored the woman and took a seat. There was a Wall Street Journal on the coffee table and he sat down and read. His appointment was at 9:00 am and he was a little early.

The first thing Tom had asked Frank to do when Frank hired him was to pick up the Barnes' files from the firm of Duffy and Phillips. The law firm refused his request for the file.

The law firm claimed all the files pertaining to CCC and the Barnes' family belonged to FTF. At that point Tom became involved and he requested his client's files but the law firm replied that all the files in their possession belonged to FTF. None of the files in Duffy and Phillip's possession belonged to CCC or the Barnes family.

FTF admitted that CCC and the Barnes had been paying the legal bills for the work contained in the files to Duffy and Phillips for the last five years since CCC had entered into the agreement with FTF to provide a line of credit for the operations and development of the out parcels and cut outs owned by CCC. Tom believed that if his client paid for the legal work, the files belonged to the Barnes' family.

The reason Tom was there in Atlanta was that the Florida Supreme Court had agreed with Tom's argument. Tom had a final court order authorizing Tom to retrieve his client's files. He had an appointment with Samuel Smith, Esq., the managing partner of Duffy and Phillips. The named partners were long ago deceased. The firm had practiced law from its offices in the FTF Building on Peachtree Street in Atlanta, Georgia for over 100 years, since before the Civil War.

Mr. Smith was prompt. He personally came to greet Tom and they walked together through one floor of the firms' offices that were housed on three floors of the tall building in Twenty-Five Thousand (25,000) square feet of what was known as the "FTF Building".

Quite impressive.

Tom practiced out of a small office building he owned in downtown St. Petersburg, Florida. The walk through the offices was for show and to intimidate Tom. But Tom was not to be intimidated, he was here in Atlanta because the Circuit Court Judge assigned to the lawsuit entitled FTF vs. Frank Barnes, *et al*, had granted Tom's motion to compel FTF to have their attorney, Duffy and Phillips, produce all of the documents in the law firms' possession for work performed by Duffy and Phillips on the FTF/Barnes account. The court ruled that if Frank Barnes or the Senator or CCC paid Duffy and Phillips' billings they were allowed to see the notes, records and other work product for the legal work that had been produced. Tom couldn't be intimidated. He had won. FTF had appealed the court's order twice. The second appeal was over. FTF lost twice on appeal.

FTF had been billing the Barnes' and CCC not only for the work Duffy and Phillips had done for the Barnes and CCC, but also for the work Duffy and Phillips performed for FTF. This practice was illegal if Frank had not agreed to the arrangement. There was no evidence that this practice was authorized by Frank or CCC.

FTF, by objecting to Tom's discovery motions, was hiding FTF's unauthorized billing practices. But the delaying tactics were at an end.

Based on the court's ruling, Tom would be able to read all of the work product and confidential communications between FTF and Duffy and Phillips. This part of the court's ruling was most troubling to FTF. Not only was FTF concerned about its billing practices, FTF was concerned because scattered among the thousands of pages of documents and letters in the files was advice Duffy and Phillips' lawyers had provided to FTF that stated the method FTF used to charge penalty interest was illegal and constituted usury.

If the loan charges were usurious, the debt could not be enforced. The entire debt Frank and CCC owed to FTC could be uncollectable. Tom had never reviewed the documents so he was unaware the letter and legal briefs on the subject of usury existed. But if Tom was persistent he would discover that fact at some point as he waded through all the documents that he now confronted stacked in over a hundred boxes on the floor of a large conference room.

Mr. Smith opened the door to the room. The law firm hoped Tom would see the hundreds of thousands of pages to be reviewed and give up. He asked Tom how much time he would need to review the files. Tom said he wasn't sure but he had taken a room in the Hilton and he had an open reservation. Tom said he wanted to work from 9:00 a.m. to 5:00 p.m. daily until he finished the review.

Mr. Smith invited Tom to dinner. Tom accepted the invitation. Tom offered that he could meet at the Hilton at 6:30 that evening. Smith said he was fine with that.

"Well," said Tom, "We are making progress. The dinner arrangements are the first thing we have been able to agree to."

Smith laughed. "Well maybe we can come to some agreement at dinner tonight. We'll see what you find today."

***

The law suit between FTF and CCC had been going on now for years. The case had bogged down in the discovery phase. Tom was trying to obtain CCC's files and FTF resisted claiming the files belonged to FTF not CCC. The judge decided that since CCC paid for the legal work then CCC owned the work product that CCC paid for. The court's ruling was appealed to the district court and then to the Florida Supreme Court. CCC was winning.

But time was not on Tom's side. His clients had cut back mightily on all expenditures and had sold most of the projects they had built and the raw commercial land that was slated to be developed. The two million dollar CD was tied up in litigation and FTF was still collecting the interest from the CD that had been assigned to it to pay the interest that FTF claimed was owed on prior loans. Frank was able to stay afloat on the cash flow from the saw mill but he was no longer buying any land for the Barnes' Tree Farm or planting any seedlings. Plantation #7 still produced a profit on the sale of jams and jellies but it was a meager profit. Bea was not sharing the profits from the dairy.

The one good thing that occurred from the litigation was that the Senator was not able to buy anything on credit and he could not leverage any property because all the property had been sold, or was already collateral for an existing loan.

Since Senator Barnes was unable to make additional purchases, he spent his time at the plantation greeting customers who came to visit the factory where the preserves were manufactured, bottled, boxed and shipped. Senator Barnes held court telling tales of the early days in the Florida legislature. He was first elected as a member of the House of Representatives and then he went to the Senate for a total of 20 years. He retired from office without being forced to resign or being indicted. Thus, he was an august member of the body. He just hoped he could get back to the position where he could wheel and deal in property as he had in the recent past.

Frank didn't intend to let that happen.

***

As Tom reviewed the documents in the conference room of Duffy and Phillips he began at the beginning when the business relationship with the Senator and FTF began. He began with the billings.

Evidence in the billing showed the Senator had been wined and dined, plied with liquor and women. FTF charged the Senator's account for the privilege of being solicited as a client. Tom recognized one name in the billings. One lady the Senator was provided as a date had the same name as the receptionist for Duffy and Phillips. No wonder the black haired, green eyed beauty was so cold, thought Tom, she probably knows her name is mentioned in the billing. Tom wondered if she had actually been paid to have sex with the Senator or if CCC just paid the $100 billing for dinner. In either event, CCC should not have been charged for the social activity. The billing agreement did not list courtesan services as a billable item. Nor did Duffy and Phillips have the right under the agreement to bill for electricity or gas or water and sewage for their office. Duffy and Phillips billed for everything whether there was a contractual right to bill for the expense or not.

Tom loved what he was seeing.

Later in the afternoon, Tom came upon the smoking gun—the letter with the brief signed by S. Smith, Esq., that laid out the problem with the usurious penalty interest charges. The letter stated that FTF could not charge penalty interest on top of penalty interest. The result of the double interest charge was that FTF was charging more than 25% per annum on loans collateralized with real property. The charges were akin to loan sharking according to Florida's usury law as interpreted by Mr. Smith. Smith backed up his legal conclusions with case law in his memo. Some of the cases were as recent as five years ago and they were written by the Florida Supreme Court. There was no question FTF was violating the usury laws.

At 5:00 p.m. Tom closed the file he was reviewing and asked for copies of the letter and legal brief that had been written by Mr.

Smith regarding penalty interest. Once he had his copies he went to the Hilton and showered and changed into slacks, a sport coat, and tie for dinner.

***

Samuel Smith stood when Tom came to the table. Smith was early. Tom was on time.

Smith began discussing the case as soon as Tom sat down.

Tom took a long, slow drink of water.

Smith began expounding the strength of FTF's case—that the agreements were clear, that all charges were as per the agreements, and that the Senator, old fool that he was, would be stuck with what he signed.

Smith ordered a steak with mushrooms and onions, mashed potatoes with rich brown gravy, and Lima beans.

Tom ignored Smith as the FTF lawyer prattled on. Instead he considered the Lima bean and thought about what his dad had said about Lima beans. Tom's dad grew up on a farm. When his dad was growing up, Tom's grandfather always grew a thirty acre patch of Lima beans because they were the richest crop if you got them to market. They were more work because they had to be shelled by hand. When the crop came in, Tom's grandfather would not let the family eat any of the Lima beans because they were the cash crop for the farm. The Lima beans were too rich for the poor.

Tom's grandfather would say, "We can't afford to eat the Lima beans."

If the harvest of Lima beans wasn't abundant enough, they could lose the farm. Their livelihood depended on the success of growing Lima beans. But Tom's dad said it wasn't worth all the work if you couldn't partake of the Lima beans. So he took just the smallest of the beans in one of the pods and put it secretly in his mouth. He chewed. It tasted awful. How could this be, he thought? So he took another and it had the same slimy skin and dry hull and no taste. Bland as a bug, it was. He took one more Lima bean and assured himself that that's all there was. It was nothing special. But it was gold.

Tom asked the waiter for a bowl of Lima beans.

"Anything else, sir?"

"Maybe some butter and salt and pepper."

"You can have more than that," said Smith motioning to the large menu. "The dinner is my treat."

"I don't think I will want what you are offering. I will just have the Lima beans."

"Well what do you really want?"

'I want honesty and you don't know what that is." Tom raised his head and looked in Smith's eyes and said, "I intend to put you out of business."

"Are you crazy?" said Smith.

"Is that a question?" asked Tom.

"What do you and your clients really want?"

"I want your license and I want your client out of business," said Tom.

"We are not going to do that," said Smith, who was now red in the face but was controlling himself and not yet yelling.

"No, I didn't expect that would happen." Tom looked at Smith. Tom's face softened. Tom laid the copy of the letter and legal brief on the table that had been written by Mr. Smith to the president of FTF. The letter admitted FTF had committed numerous violations of the law as far as the loans that were made to CCC.

Mr. Smith glanced at the paperwork, and after he paged through the document he pushed it back toward Tom. Smith said, "We will waive all interest, penalty and cost in return for your client repaying the money we actually loaned your clients."

Tom knew CCC could not refinance the loan. FTF had ruined their credit. Therefore, Tom's counter offer was, "CCC will agree to pay back only the principal due on the loans, less a credit for all payments CCC has made to FTF to date. In addition, FTF will pay back the interest FTF collected on the $2 million CD."

"Yes," said Smith. "I have authority to agree to do that. My client will agree to that."

Tom looked sheepishly at Mr. Smith.

"I suppose you also want us to fund the loan," said Smith.

"Yes, that would be necessary." said Tom. "The problem is that this lawsuit has ruined my client's credit. CCC has no ability to repay the principal balance of the original loan in full at this time."

"Are you saying FTF will have to loan CCC the money needed to settle the case?"

"Correct. We would accept your proposal of settlement if you loan us the money to repay the principal owed to FTF," said Tom.

"And the money would have to be loaned to your client at a reasonable rate?" asked Smith.

"Correct."

"I need a minute to make a call." said Smith.

"Take your time." Tom mashed the Lima beans in the butter.

***

"We can loan you the money," said Smith. "But we have to rewrite the loan. It will be a write down and the original loan will remain on FTF's books. The original loan will be satisfied when your client successfully repays the new loan. Also, your clients will be required to sign a confidentiality agreement so they can't reveal the terms of the settlement."

"Sounds like you need to bury this new loan in your books."

"Yes we do. Deep, very deep," thought Smith. He was smiling.

Tom understood that what FTF's officers were doing was hiding the settlement from the shareholders and directors. If FTF's shareholders and directors knew how this loan had been handled and the losses realized by FTF, the corporate officers and Smith's law firm, Duffy and Phillips, would be fired.

***

"These Lima beans are awful," said Tom smiling. "They are bland and slimy."

"Yeah, that's how they taste," said Smith.

"I don't know why people would want to eat them."

"I guess you have to develop a taste for them," said Smith.

Chapter 16
Dinner at the Homestead

To celebrate the reversal of their loss of fortune, Frank and Bea invited Tom and Marla James to the farmhouse for dinner. Marla had been Tom's secretary since he opened his office in St. Petersburg in 1947. She was young, intelligent and beautiful—tall, blond and slender. They had been dating for about a year. They both knew a romantic relationship between a lawyer and secretary was tentative. She had worked for Tom for almost five years. No telling if their relationship would lead to anything serious—they still had separate living quarters. But they were very close. Marla shared in Tom's victories and losses emotionally, and that may have been part of the basis of their mutual desire. Certainly the win over Florida Timber Fund (FTF) was spectacular and Marla felt, rightly so, that she had earned a place at the table in Bea's farm house at the Homestead for the victory dinner for her hard work on the case.

***

The O'Brien Homestead had been in Bea's family for over 100 years. The farmhouse on the Homestead had survived fire, hurricanes, and floods. The Timucua Indians had hunted the homestead lands and later the Seminole Indian people felt they had as much right to the use of the land as the whites and the Indians fought the whites for possession of the land. As a result, the Seminoles had to be driven from the land.

There was no member of the Timucua tribe still living by 1900, but the tribe still had a presence in Florida via the names of local landmarks such as rivers and parks. The Tomoka River, which flowed north of the property, was named after the great Timucua

Chief, Tomoka. The Timucua and the Alachua had ruled the Northeast of Florida. The Spanish settled in St. Augustine on Timucua land. Over the next 200 years the Timucua were removed from their cities to missions by the Spanish. The French, then the British and then the Americans used Indian allies, the Creeks and the Seminoles, to drive the Spanish and the Timucua out.

The last 12,000 Timucua Indians were captured by James Moore, the Governor of South Carolina and they were enslaved by the Americans and removed from Florida to Carolina and they were worked on Southern Plantations.

The Seminoles, an amalgamation of Creek tribes, settled on Timucua lands near Gainesville. These Indians together with the Miccosukee tribe imitated the Europeans and became farmers and land owners and had cattle and African slaves. It was only a matter of time until the whites became jealous of the land held by the Seminoles. The whites began to move against the Seminoles in the early 1800s and the first Seminole War began in late 1817. The Indians counterattacked and raided into Georgia. The citizen militias of Tennessee and Georgia fought in Florida along with the US Army which attacked the Indians in Florida and drove the Seminoles off their farms. The whites took the Indian lands. The Seminoles became roving bands of marauders. They drove the whites off the farms. America acquired Florida from the Spanish in 1843. By this time most of the Seminoles had been removed from Florida to Arkansas. The 100 or so Seminoles who were left in Florida were driven into the Everglades. Thereafter the land in the northeast was safe for resettlement by the whites.

After the Seminole Wars, ownership of the land south of St. Augustine, in what became St. Johns, Flagler, and Volusia Counties, was sold and re-sold. Large plantations like the Bulow Plantation in Flagler County were divided and sold. The plantation was burned and the Bulow family abandoned the large farming operation.

Bea's ancestors, the O'Brien family had arrived in Georgia in the early 1800s as a result of the efforts of James Oglethorpe and his followers. They settled the Savannah, the Territory of Georgia, in order to complete their indenture. The family worked off their debt for the cost of ship passage on a dairy farm producing milk and cheese.

Once they paid their debt the family purchased the Homestead and migrated to Florida. They followed an old Indian trail that was improved by the Europeans called King's Road. The O'Brien's walked beside their wagon from Savannah, passed the port of Brunswick, and then passed St. Augustine and resettled on an 800 acre section of wild land east of the St. Johns River and south of Bulow Creek, and south and west of the Tomoka and the Halifax River. (See map 8)

The O'Brien's built a trail through their property to the east to meet other wagon trails that connected to King's Road. The O'Brien's hunted their land and the surrounding lands. They grew cane which they processed into raw sugar as a cash crop.

Because they owned land, the family felt they had a stake in Florida when the Civil War broke out. They sent their boys to fight for the Confederacy. In 1865 the one son, Joshua, was killed in the Battle of Natural Bridge near the port of St. Marks, Florida. The Union landed its Army at St. Marks and intended to march north and take Tallahassee, the state capital. But a group of students, irregular troops, and elderly southern citizens from the city beat back the Federal soldiers and saved Florida's capital from being sacked. Tallahassee was the only rebel capital that was not taken by the North during the war.

The Spanish imported cattle, horses and swine to the state. Florida's Central prairies north of Lake Okeechobee became populated by cattle which roamed wild and free on the grasslands through the center of the State. Florida's value to the South in the Civil War was beef. After the South lost the west in the battle of Vicksburg in 1863, Florida beef cattle became the primary source of protein that sustained the Confederacy.

Following the war the reunited nation still needed beef and Florida still had cattle that roamed through the center of the State. Cowboys called "Crackers" rounded up huge herds of animals and drove the cattle north to the rail head in Lake City, and they were sent to market throughout the country. The O'Brien men joined in the cattle drives and their women remained on the farm. The women raised prime beef cattle to eat and cows for milk. The O'Brien's built a sawmill and the men cut timber, mostly long leaf pine, that was manufactured into masts for sailing ships. The resin or sap from the trees also produced naval stores (resin) for caulking the seams of ships. Transportation of the timber was primarily by ship or rafts. The O'Brien farm was about two miles by wagon to the pier in Ormond on the Halifax River. From the river they had a cheap economic connection to the country and the world. The wagon trail to the river that connected the O'Brien's to international commerce was named Flomish Road.

The O'Brien farm was about a half mile from Flomish Road. Later a short line railroad was built south from Jacksonville to Ormond. Short line railroads coursed north through the woods to St. Augustine and Jacksonville, and then another short line railroad ran west to Lake City.

Another railroad, the Yulee Line, ran to Cedar Key on the Gulf of Mexico from Fernandina on the east coast. From Cedar Key, the businesses of the state sent their goods for trade to the ports along the Gulf of Mexico—Pensacola, Mobile, New Orleans, and Galveston. The interior lands south of Tampa were wild Indian lands that were the home of the Seminoles, who refused to surrender to the US Army.

The O'Brien's lost two rustic cabins to fires. Finally, they decided to build a home of local rock and long leaf pine from their mill. The stone was quarried from the coquina rock naturally formed in the Atlantic Ocean near Flagler Beach. Small periwinkle shells coalesced and formed a soft stone called coquina. An outcrop of coquina was found at the edge of the Atlantic Ocean 20 miles north of a fishing village near Ormond. The O'Brien's used a barge to haul the rock to Mosquito Inlet near Daytona and from there brought the cargo up the Halifax River to the pier at Ormond. The rock was then hauled by oxen to the home site. The stone had to lie on the site to harden or cure for three years before it could be used as a building material. The farm house at the Homestead was completed in 1880.

In the late 1880s, Henry Flagler, a director of Standard Oil, consolidated many of the short line railroads in the northeast of Florida. Eventually, the Florida East Coast Railroad extended along the east coast of Florida from Jacksonville to Key West. The train line was built by Flagler to connect his real estate developments and resorts along the East Coast. Florida had become a tourist haven for invalids during the winter.

In 1887 a developer named John Anderson built a bridge across the Halifax River from Ormond on the West side of the river to Ormond Beach on the East side of the river. He built a large hotel (the "Ormond Hotel") in 1888 in Ormond Beach to bring the Yankee tourist to the Atlantic Ocean. Henry Flagler then bought out Mr. Anderson and increased the size of the hotel to 600 rooms.

The beach on the Atlantic side of the barrier island that stretched from the inlet near New Smyrna Beach to Ormond Beach consisted of pure white sand packed so hard that you could drive a car on it. Sir Malcom Campbell attempted to set the world land speed record on the beach in his car the Bluebird in 1935. Ormond was west of the barrier island. The railroad developer (Flagler) built a station in Ormond and improved the bridge to the hotel for his guests.

John D. Rockefeller, Flagler's partner in Standard Oil, built his winter home, the Casements, across the street from the Ormond Hotel and their friends (Henry Ford, et al) built homes along the river on John Anderson Drive.

The O'Brien farm was south and west of Ormond. Flagler's train passed within a half mile of the farmhouse and the O'Brien's could hear the train whistle warning traffic on Flomish Road that the train was about to pass on its North/South route.

US Highway 1 was built through Volusia County in the early 1900s. It was cobbled together by connecting existing north/south roads. The highway ran parallel to the railroad tracks. The Halifax

River ran parallel to the railroad and across the river the large barrier island that ran from Sebastian Inlet south of St. Augustine to the Mosquito Inlet south of Daytona Beach was built up with small resorts, hotels, golf courses and tourist attractions.

The building activity and the rich tourists and their service workers needed the basics along with the exotic. The O'Brien's had produced prime beef cattle and cows for milk since the family had arrived in 1847. They upgraded their operation in the early 1900s and concentrated on producing milk and cream products. They used a breed of cows called the "Milking Devon." Soon they were making deliveries of their products to the Ormond Hotel, which was claimed to be the largest wooden structure in the South. Once the hotel endorsed their products, which were superior to all the dairy products in the state, the O'Brien's began to enlarge their market to the Casements and the homes along John Anderson Drive and to the restaurants and small hotels along the beachfront, and then they supplied their milk, cream and butter to the railroad which connected to the Northeast.

Most every business in the area, directly or indirectly, depended on the trade produced by the railroad and the Ormond Hotel and tourists.

Frank's people, the Barnes' family, came later after US 1 had been completed and John Anderson Drive extended north to the Tomoka and Halifax River basins. The Barnes' land, located on 130 acres between the Atlantic Ocean and the Halifax River, grew the citrus and fruits for the tourists. The jams and jellies were so prized that they were taken home by the visitors and later sold in the northeast in large department stores in the biggest cities under the logo or trade name: "Plantation #7".

Then came WW I, then there was a land boom and bust and the Great Depression. The colony surrounding the hotel and the families servicing the hotel survived. The local business thrived during the downturn. The rich still wintered in Ormond during the Depression from 1929 to 1939. The names of the rich changed, but America still produced wealthy patrons for the Ormond Hotel and its colony of businesses. The towns the locals inhabited on the mainland along the railroad and US 1 (Flagler, Bunnel, Holly Hill, Ormond, Daytona, South Daytona, and Orange City) were incorporated and there were schools and courts and prisons erected.

The Spanish Flu pandemic struck Florida in 1918 after WW I like a horrible afterthought, killing 100,000 people. Bea's family was decimated by the flu and Bea's parents were the only O'Brien's left after the scourge. They lost their two children to the flu in 1919. Bea was born in 1920. Her parents died of a fever when she was ten. She married Frank in 1935 when she was 15. Jimmy was born in 1936. It became apparent that Jimmy would survive his birth but he would need constant care.

Frank and Tom entered college, became friends, and later business associates with the Senator developing the 40,000 acres called "The Wetland," which the Senator purchased near Deland. While Frank and Tom completed college and developed the Wetland, and the Senator completed his duties as a legislator and managed Plantation #7, Bea took care of Jimmy and the operations at the diary and the pig farm at the Homestead.

***

When America entered World War II, both Frank and Tom attempted to enlist. The Senator would have none of that. If Tom and Frank were in the Army they could not develop the Wetland. In the Senator's mind if the boys developed the Wetlands they would contribute as much to the war effort as if they were shooting a rifle.

The Senator did not have to intervene on Tom's behalf with Selective Service. Although Tom was intelligent, handsome, and looked healthy—he was six foot tall and muscular—Tom couldn't pass the Army physical due to damage to his lungs caused by pneumonia. Tom, as a child, had suffered from the same pulmonary infection that killed his entire immediate family (his mother, father and twin brother).

After the Senator explained to the Selective Service the value Frank contributed to the war effort building the air base in Deland, the Agency voted that Frank had reason to remain at home.

They also took into consideration Jimmy's medical condition and Frank was exempted from active service.

The fact that the Senator influenced the Selective Service System on his behalf made Frank very angry. The Senator salved Frank's conscience by having Frank appointed as a Commodities Commissioner for the War Department. The Senator was also a Commissioner and had been since the First World War. He had taken many trips to Honduras, Belize, San Salvador, and Mexico in order to identify timberlands and mines that could produce vital resources that the USA would require to prosecute a war. The Commission office was located in Atlanta. Frank was at the office of the commission several days a month. He wore a brown shirt with red epaulets to show he was involved in the war effort.

The resources needed in WW ll were heavily dependent on biological produce such as rubber, copra (palm oil) and resins from trees. Frank's education involved horticulture and biology. Frank realized that his education could help the Allies win the war. Frank and his father helped locate lands that would produce naval stores for the shipping industry and resins to make gunpowder and palm oil to grease the machines of war. Frank realized that by obtaining contracts to the resources from the countries in Central America, the US would supply our troops and deny access of these necessities to the enemy. The Senator argued Frank's work as a Commodities Commissioner was as vital and as important work as carrying a weapon. So when asked what he did in the war, Frank was proud to explain his participation in the victory.

Chapter 17
Coquina

Neither Tom nor Marla had visited the Barnes' farmhouse before the invitation for the dinner to celebrate the victory against FTF.

Tom had heard that the footings, basement, and first floor walls of the 4,000 square foot, two-story building, were constructed of coquina rock. The material, consisting of small shells welded together by wave action over the centuries, was mined from a quarry in Flagler Beach over 70 years ago. The Spanish were the first to use the material in construction to build their fort to protect their major port in St. Augustine. The fort, the Castillo de San Marcos, was built of the coquina quarried from the shore of the Atlantic Ocean. The fort covered 20 acres and was over 400 years old.

The O'Brien family brought the rock by barge from Flagler Beach south in the Atlantic Ocean to the inlet south of Daytona, then north up the Halifax River to the port at Ormond. The rock was then transported by oxen and wagons to the home site.

Coquina is an unusual and rare material. After it was quarried it was soft and easy to cut. But while it was in its soft state it could not be used in construction, as it would crumble. After it was cut it had to be cured by laying in the elements and it would harden into a strong solid material over time.

Tom became fascinated with the masonry work at the front door of the Homestead and he coursed the seams of the masonry work with his fingers while he and Marla waited at the door to the porch. The seams were as tight as the stonework ascribed to the Incan people that he read about.

When Frank and Little Al came to the door of the farmhouse, Tom had numerous questions about the construction. Tom had been to the fort, the Castillo de San Marcos, when he visited St. Augustine, but he was unaware that the huge structure with walls 20 foot thick in places was built of a local material. In fact, the building stone is found in quantity only in Florida and Australia and England. The Spanish found the coquina to be perfect for a fort in the age of the cannon because a cannon ball fired at a coquina wall would sink into the relatively soft material and not explode the wall the way other rock walls would shatter if they were hit by an iron projectile.

Marla had become accustomed to Tom's peculiarities. He would become stuck on a subject and he couldn't get away from it. He kept tracing the seams of the coquina rock with his fingers. Finally, Marla took Tom by the arm and pulled him into the house where the rest of the family was waiting.

Bob was a teenager. He had almost finished high school. He was a good football player, and the coach at Stetson University in Deland was eager that he join the team if he went to Stetson. Tom's Aunts were retired now, but he and Frank still knew professors at the school and they encouraged Bob to enroll at their University.

Little Al was 10 years old and still shadowed Frank. Bea still dressed them in similar clothes, but they no longer looked like a full size and the miniature of the same person. Little Al had become a businessman, learning from Frank. He wanted to do everything his adoptive father did and Frank had no objection so long as Al did better and tried harder than he.

Jenny was a beauty even at eight years of age. She looked like her mother, Mary. Bea could see the resemblance and was happy Jenny had captured her natural mother, Mary Johnson's, good looks. Bea considered herself plain looking.

Bob and Jenny still helped Bea with Jimmy. Bob still had duty at night, and during the daytime Jenny played with the man that Jimmy had become. Bea knew she and Jimmy would not be able to rely on Bob and Jenny for many more years, but they were happy with what time she had to help. Frank insisted that when Bob went to college, Bob would live at school and establish his independence.

Frank, like Bea, knew it would probably kill Jimmy when Jenny left the house. The pair had a special relationship. Jenny had been able to communicate with her oldest brother because when they first began to interact they were the same age mentally. In fact Jenny was more mature. Jimmy was stuck in first gear. Jenny was able to push him along but got no further than to get affirmative and negative responses from him for simple questions. (Tired? Hungry? Thirsty?)

But what their children were able to do with Jimmy amazed Bea and Frank, and they were grateful. They could now do more than simply hold their child. They could communicate. Frank, in particular enjoyed the simple conversations he and his son could have through Jenny.

Jenny took Tom and Marla in to see her brother. He was asleep, but woke as Tom clumsily hit the bed post.

Awake?

Nod.

Hungry?

Shake.

Wet?

Shake.

Tired?

Nod.

Jenny stroked Jimmy's head and his eyes closed.

Tom could see Jimmy's face. He had wispy long eyelashes and a few strands of facial hair. He was covered in sweet smelling bed clothes.

Jenny rolled his miniature body to the side and propped pillows to his back and front and he slept as they left the room.

***

At the table Bob proposed a toast, to Tom and Frank, for unleashing them from the "pangs of litigation" as he put it. Bob was allowed a glass of beer. Jenny and Al had grape juice.

After the dinner of prime rib, Frank and Tom went to the porch. Tom was drinking rye whiskey. Frank had a beer. Marla finished the dishes and went to the porch. The children stayed in the living room. They played a board game and were quiet. Tom went for another drink. Marla just stared at him. Her gray eyes were glaring.

"It's a celebration," said Tom, directing his comment to Marla.

The adults sat on the porch in swing seats and they made small talk and smoked cigarettes and drank their beer and whiskey. All except Bea, who had the duty with Jimmy that night.

Frank wanted to talk about what he wanted to do with the Senator. Bea told him to shut up. Tom and Marla laughed. The lightning bugs came out and the yard was lit by the insects and the moon.

There were many changes that had been made at the Homestead. There were no more pigs. The kids hated them. Petunia had seen her last taste of root vegetables and flowers. Bea couldn't stand to butcher her herself and she sold her. Frank tried to chase the old boar out of the sty many times. The old tusk-less razorback kept coming back until Bea had the fence of the pig sty removed and the old boar couldn't find his home.

The small lots surveyed along the east side of the 800 acres had never been developed, except for the one small house that Al and Mary still owned. Mary and Big Al never visited in the last seven years. Big Al no longer called on the holidays, and the kids didn't think it would be right to ask Frank and Bea about their natural Mom and Dad. They didn't want to seem ungrateful, but the children still wondered about them.

The dairy was a large operation now. There were over 600 dairy cows on the property. The pine trees on the 800 acre homestead were all gone, as was the saw mill. The land was rolling pasture with one major stream that flowed into the woods to the north to feed the Tomoka River. There were deep wells and irrigation with water tanks and cow sheds interspersed on the land. Bea always reinvested the profit back into the business. The farm produced milk for a cooperative. Bea still made ice cream for a specialty market in grocery stores. The product was successful but the margins were slim and it was questionable if the dairy would be viable in the future. The grocery stores wanted to market their own brands and the stores were consolidating. There wouldn't be room for a small dairy operation offering specialty products.

Bea hated joining the cooperative but the wild fluctuations in the price of milk had driven most dairy farmers to bankruptcy and the farmers needed the price controls to maintain profitability. A big cooperative had the leverage that was needed as the grocery store chains grew. The O'Brien's could no longer depend on the Ormond Hotel and local businesses alone to purchase their milk. In fact the Ormond Hotel and the Florida East Coast Railroad were in trouble since the end of the war and now into the 1950s.

If you don't change and move fast you will be run over. That was the lesson in the fight with FTF. When the bottle of rye was empty, Marla helped Tom into the car. They drove south on US 1 to the Broadway Street bridge in Daytona, and then over to the beach. A neon sign proclaimed: "The World's Most Famous Beach," and they got a room rather than drive back at night. It was a seven hour drive to St. Petersburg. Marla didn't want to deal with Tom while he was drunk, particularly if he insisted for the entire seven hour trip that he was sober and he could drive the car.

Part V

Tom and Marla

Chapter 18
The Arm Wrestler

Before heading to the beach Tom was able to convince Marla to take him to a liquor store. There was one on Mason Avenue that stayed open all night. Daytona was a party town. The city had numerous clubs with bands playing Southern rock. The Almond Joys was the name of the favorite band at the moment. One all- night bar in the center of town was surrounded by all-night born again ministries that attempted with little success to quaff the thirst of the revelers with the words of the Lord. The City Councils of the cities surrounding Daytona passed blue laws and there were no bars or package sales of beer, wine and liquor. The cities were "dry". They offered a stark difference to Daytona, which was wild and garish, but advertised itself as a "family resort".

Marla had the wheel of the car since Tom ran over a curb on Highway US-1 and Flomish Road after they left the Homestead. Tom gave Marla directions to the package store and then passed out. Marla thought she should just go to the hotel or better still, just drive the seven hours back to St. Petersburg. But Marla was hooked. Tom wanted rye whiskey, Tom got rye whiskey. Marla would take Tom to the package store but Marla wouldn't go in the bar and make purchases alone. After parking Tom's car, a tapioca, very white, Chrysler Newport convertible, she shook Tom and slapped him in the face and finally aroused him by pinching the muscle in his arm.

He was asleep and then he yelped, "God that hurt."

"If you want another drink you will have to go in with me. I'm not going in alone and I'm not sitting in the parking lot with all these men milling about looking for a date."

"Ok, ok."

Tom was completely sober or acted that way. He was beyond drunk. He had so much alcohol in his system that he was sane and sober. He walked and talked straight but he was dead drunk.

The bar was named the Cypress Tavern and was decorated like a swamp. All the tables and stools and bar tops were made of cypress planks and cypress knees. Cypress knees are the root extensions the cypress tree sends up above the water in the swamp to help the tree breath. The knees of the tree can have odd and interesting shapes. The stumps were worth extra if they were in a recognizable shape. There was a stump that looked like the face of President Lincoln, complete with the top hat and beard. Someone said that that cypress knee was worth thousands.

The bar was lighted by Christmas lights intertwined with Spanish moss. Mirrors on the wall, particularly the mirror behind the bar, reflected the dim colored lights and the image of the grey/brown moss that hung on the walls. The cypress planks of the floor and the boards on the wall and knees, all the wood, had been shellacked to a high sheen and the wood surfaces also threw light about the room.

The owner of the bar was a world class wrestler. The first time you came in his bar you had to arm wrestle him at the bar. He never lost, or rarely lost. If he lost he threw the winner out and told him: "Don't come back 'til you learn some manners, ya, Bum. This is my bar. To be polite you're supposed to let me win." And the wrestler would laugh.

The owner's woman was the bartender. She was rough and ready. She sported a sawed-off shotgun on her hip. "I've never had a problem since I got my gun. I just tell them to take it outside and I pat this little baby and they're gone." The bartender patted her weapon as she explained.

Tom did his duty. He arm wrestled the owner and politely lost.

"Don't you want to feel my muscle, Little Lady?" The wrestler asked Marla and he flexed his biceps.

Marla deferred.

Tom purchased two bottles of rye. But then when he got hold of the liquor he became wobbly. Marla grabbed his arm and led him out the door to the car.

The owner and his lady watched them go out the door.

"Nice couple," they commented.

Like in a bad soap opera, Marla got in behind the wheel of the car and began yelling at Tom and banging her fist on the dashboard.

"That was stupid," she said.

Tom was drunk beyond oblivion and didn't have any control.

"How can you be so stupid?" she yelled.

It wasn't a question. It was the truth spoken to a stone.

***

Tom awoke staring into whiteness. He moved his head and heard the crinkle of crisp sheets. The smell was sweet and sterile. He was clean and his skin was smooth and nude. He had been bathed.

Marla was in an upholstered lounge chair seated on a large white towel. Nude. She was painting her toe nails scarlet red. Odalisque. She had her long blonde hair pulled back in a bun. Her eyes were blue/gray and her skin was tan, fit and firm.

There was cool air blowing through a vent high in the room. The ceilings were twelve feet high and white. The room was large and square. There was a large picture window covered with a white drape. The sun was low in the east and it cut through the sheer white drapery and washed the room with light that bounced off of the white upholstered furniture.

Tom could see or sense all this without moving his head, which hurt. He wanted someone to stroke his head so it would feel better. Tom closed his eyes and he passed out.

***

Marla donned a sun dress. It was linen and shoulder-less. Her painted red toenails deliciously stuck out of her sandals. Her fingernails matched her toenails and were scarlet.

"Scandalous," said the old woman pushing her granddaughter through the lobby in a buggy.

The front desk of the Whitehall Hotel was white as were the walls and drapes and upholstery. Marla was looking around in a daze.

"You look like you are expecting St. Peter," said the clerk.

"What did you say?" Marla's eyes blinked.

"How can I help you?" asked the clerk.

"Is there a doctor you could recommend for my friend?" Marla whispered.

"For your boyfriend?"

"Yes."

"We were worried about him."

The desk clerk gave Marla a card that he plucked from a small gray metal box under the desk.

"We are not recommending anyone." He handed her the business card. "We are only trying to help. We are not a hospital or sanitarium, you know?"

"Yes I know."

"I hope your friend gets better."

***

The doctor saw Tom. He suggested he go to a treatment center. Tom declined. He told the doctor he had never blacked out before. Marla said that wasn't true. This was just the first time she felt she needed to find him professional help.

"He is a very smart person. He is a lawyer. He helps people with very difficult, unique problems. I don't understand. He could be the governor of the state. How could he do this to himself?"

The doctor said Tom would survive this episode but if he continues he will have more episodes and eventually he will die from alcohol poisoning.

"He needs help. You won't be able to help him." The doctor turned to Marla. "You need help too. Buying him another bottle won't help him. He needs to take the first step. He needs to ask for help."

In his daze Tom listened and heard but did not ask for help.

The doctor left. Marla looked at Tom and went over and held him and said: "What am I going to do with you?"

Tom began to cry and she kissed his face dry. Then she laid him in bed and covered him with a clean sheet. She opened the drapes and could see the bright blue sky and the blue green Atlantic and the white hard packed sand on the shore with the cars driving slowly by. She removed her sun dress and sandals and loosed her long yellow hair. Her eyes were deep blue now. She climbed in bed with Tom hoping it would get better. Denying the truth of the matter, she held Tom tightly.

***

Marla and Tom stayed at the Whitehall Hotel for a week. Tom did not drink alcohol. They swam in the sea and walked along the beach. They talked seriously about their plans for the future. Tom asked Marla to marry him. She said yes. They drove back toward St. Petersburg. It was a long hot trip. Tom stopped in Winter Haven. The city was the half way point to home. They stopped for lunch. Tom ordered a beer. He drank it. Then he ordered a 6-pack to go. Marla said nothing. Marla drove the rest of the trip. Tom used a church key to pop the tops of the cans and he waxed eloquently about the future. Tom had Marla drop him at his apartment and let her use his car.

The day after they returned, Marla was not at work. Tom didn't see her again for five years.

Chapter 19
NASA

Marla had come to Frank and told him she and Tom had broken their engagement and she needed a job. As usual, Little Al was present during the conversation. Little Al suggested that they see if the US government would have a place for her in the new facilities in Brevard County. Frank agreed that that was an excellent idea.

The Barnes' company, CCC, had continued to purchase land to the south of its forest holdings in Volusia County. A purchasing agent for the new Federal agency, called NASA, was looking for a supply of milled lumber. The government offered CCC an exclusive contract obliging CCC to cut timber and mill it in a sawmill that would be constructed in Brevard County near the NASA spaceport. The lumber would be used for construction of buildings at the new space station.

CCC had a presence, an office for a timber purchasing agent, near the NASA property in a small town called Mims. Frank disliked the town because it was controlled by the Ku Klux Klan. The organization had murdered an NAACP recruiter and his wife by blowing the couple up in their house with dynamite in 1951. No one was arrested. There was no investigation of the killing by the local authorities. The FBI investigated but no charges were filed. The locals, white and colored, were in fear of the Klan. There was even a presence of the KKK at public gatherings. Cross burnings to intimidate locals were not uncommon. Frank did not want to support the economy of a town with leaders who were violent and could harm his workers. To further complicate matters, CCC's business for NASA was a federal contract and no racial discrimination would be condoned by the US Government.

Little Al suggested the fact the federal government would not condone discrimination could be CCC's excuse for integrating the mill. Further, if the US Government was there to watch CCC's back, then CCC would be safe to ignore the KKK. CCC would be protected by the FBI.

Frank smiled and shook his head. "You're right, Al, we should be able to put the US government between us and the KKK."

Frank and Little Al drove down to Mims which was located on US 1 and scouted for a site for a mill. They found a 25 acre plot that was high and dry and perfect for the mill. They spoke to a realtor and he knew the potential seller, on old family that was trying to leave the area. They executed an option on the mill land and entered into a contact to purchase another 17,500 acres of natural growth timber, mostly pine and cypress that the same family also was offering for sale. The acreage was contiguous to the new mill property.

Tom prepared the paperwork for the transactions for the purchase of the mill property and the timberland. By that time Marla was working for the US Government for NASA, but Tom was unaware that Marla was working for the government attorney who was handling the other side of the Mims' deal. Marla was able to remain in the background because she was executive secretary for the head of purchasing for NASA. She had interviewed for the job after Frank spoke up and recommended her.

It had been Little Al's suggestion that she apply for the job, as he reminded Marla numerous times.

***

Now, it was five years after Marla left Tom and St. Petersburg.

After the breakup, at first, she stayed in Ormond at Plantation #7 and learned how to make and market jams and jellies. She knew that Tom had asked Frank if he had spoken to her. She had asked Frank to not tell Tom where she was, at least for a while. Frank agreed. Then she got the job in Titusville with NASA's purchasing department. At first, Marla ran the office which was populated with attorneys and accountants. Then the agency head sent her out across the country to handle large contracts. Someone was needed to do background checks on the vendors and she was good at investigations from her experience working in Tom's law office.

Then Marla was back in Titusville at about the time NASA was finalizing work on the first manned space flights. She had been dating an Air Force pilot from the air base at Oak Hill. The fighter pilots provided air cover for Cape Canaveral and all of the government facilities in Brevard County. At least half of the employees in the county relied on the federal government for their pay check. The government had a big investment. It was concerned about security and protecting its property. Marla's pilot friend was part of the security team. He was dedicated to service and Marla realized that their relationship wasn't going to go anywhere. But Marla went to the best events as his date. Every politician in the country wanted their picture taken with an astronaut and there was a festive, exciting air to the place.

But after five years the pilot had transferred out to Omaha, Nebraska to a SAC base. He asked her to go with him as his wife and Marla thought about it, but said no. He understood. They wrote for a while but each of them went on with their lives. They had no contact after 1963.

***

Marla continued to see and keep in contact with the Barnes Family. She saw Frank and Little Al for business at the Cape. Every time she drove north on US 1 to Jacksonville or to Atlanta she stopped at the O'Brien dairy and bought an ice cream cone. She usually saw Bob or Jenny or Bea. There were picnic benches under an old large live oak tree in front of the dairy and they would visit and re-acquaint. She didn't see Jimmy. She had only seen him that one time at the party five years ago to celebrate CCC's victory over FTF.

Marla was told Jimmy had around-the-clock care now. Bob was at college at Stetson and he lived in a dorm. Jenny still helped Bea with Jimmy, but it was more that she paid attention to him and tried to coax him to consciousness. Frank and Bea and Jenny were lucky they had the financial and emotional resources to sustain Jimmy who was now in his twenties. Marla didn't think Jimmy would live much longer but she had said that for five years.

The Barnes Family members always kept Marla aware of Tom's activities. She knew that he was primarily working for CCC, as the family business grew from being a large timber owner in Volusia County to the owner of over 1,500,000 acres in the southeast US, and with international interests in the Caribbean and Central America. The work for CCC alone would keep a lawyer busy full time, but Tom also kept a criminal law practice and business law practice going in St. Petersburg. He had a staff of four legal secretaries, each handling specific areas of the law. He worked many hours, but in spite of that fact, he was able to keep all his clients happy. That is, except Little Al Barnes, who felt Tom had a serious drinking problem. Little Al suggested to Frank that they hire someone over in Daytona or in Jacksonville to handle their legal affairs.

"No," said Frank. "Tom has always represented the family fairly and competently."

Frank was comfortable with Tom even if he was a tippler. Alcohol didn't hurt his work or production. Frank didn't want to make a change, especially now, when the industry was changing and consolidating and CCC was going to have to become much larger or be bought out. CCC was the last large private company in the industry. Most companies the size of CCC were publicly traded and they had the ability to draw funds for expansion by issuing stock and bonds to the public.

If CCC needed a loan, CCC still had to deal with bankers and fund managers who were willing to take a chance with a company that was still owned by one family and operated by one family and controlled by one person, Frank Barnes. The Senator no longer handled day to day operations. Frank had convinced his father to place his ownership interest in a trust, and Frank was the trustee of the trust, Frank had full control of the Senator's 70% share of CCC, and Frank owned the other 30% of CCC outright.

Tom had argued that Frank should take CCC public to obtain the advantages the stock market would bring. Frank felt that he had enough scrutiny having his father looking over his shoulder. Frank did not want to deal with the Security and Exchange Commission (SEC). Besides, they all knew they were going to have to get much bigger by making a large purchase to double or triple the size of their timber holdings or they were all going to retire when CCC was bought out. If CCC was to be bought out and if it was purchased by a privately owned company, it would be a much simpler transaction if CCC were a private company and the sale would not have to be approved by the SEC.

Tom saw the sense of Frank's plan, just from the sake of its simplicity. But there were concerns about Frank's health. He had had a minor heart attack. Allegedly he was healthy. He was watching his weight. But his heart problem was still a concern. Tom hoped CCC received an offer to sell soon and they could fashion a stock trade of the private companies to accomplish the sale. Then they could retire.

Little Al did not want to give up CCC. He wanted to find more land they could purchase and a lending institution that would provide financing. Little Al had in mind that he would run the business. His first act would be to replace Tom.

***

It was at the time that Tom and Little Al were pushing their opposing positions regarding the future direction of the company when Marla mentioned to Frank she wanted to leave NASA. It was too big and too much bureaucracy and she didn't want to be involved in the "space race" anymore.

Little Al suggested to Marla that she return to St. Petersburg.

"Why?"

"You grew up there. You went to school there."

"What would I do?"

"You could go back to work at Tom's office. I was there last week and your desk is still empty."

"You're kidding." Marla blushed red in her cheeks.

"I asked Tom about the empty desk and he told me he hoped you would someday come back."

The little seed of an idea from Little Al took root. Marla couldn't think of anything else. She just kept considering the possibilities. She was not in a relationship or even dating. She still thought she loved Tom. She thought he loved her too. If she was making a break from NASA she could at least try to reestablish the relationship she had left five years ago. It had been her choice to leave. He didn't ask her to leave.

In the last five years Marla had established a life for herself on the east coast of Florida. She had purchased a house in Titusville. What to do? She decided to rent it. She took stock of herself and decided she needed a vacation, at least two months to regroup and refresh. She was still the beauty, the woman who couldn't enter a room without being noticed. She would think the matter of the change out fully. She would go to the south of France and consider her options.

***

At 9:00am Marla entered Tom's office building in downtown St. Petersburg. Tom was proud of the old building, two stories with Mediterranean accents. His office was on the second floor. There were circular stairs leading to his suite of rooms. The floors were covered with mission-style tiles, fired in California. The building was sturdy and well-crafted with stucco over red brick, and was featured in brochures the city printed for distribution to tourists and visitors of places to see for its early architecture.

When Marla entered the office after five years she was wearing her same linen sun suit with sandals she wore at the Whitehall Hotel. Her hair was loose but short, cut to the top of her neck. She had it cut in Nice, France. She was tan and fit from swimming in the sea on the Riviera. She had no tan lines. Her nails were scarlet.

She caused a stir when she took a seat at her desk. Just as Little Al had said, Marla's old desk was there as she left it. She asked the lady in the desk to her right how she could help.

"I'm the new girl," said Marla.

She was given a will to revise and she began work. As she was typing she noticed that Tom had opened his door a crack and was peering out. He closed the door when their eyes met. The office manager, Karen, came over to Marla's desk and asked her to fill out the employment documents, W-2 forms, et cetera. Karen said Tom would talk to her after they closed for the day. They needed to have a discussion regarding her salary requirements and such.

Marla continued to work. She was efficient and produced good work. She went out to lunch with the staff. They all got along fine. They were sitting at a table, cackling. Karen had been working there the longest and she worked with Marla before Marla left for NASA five years past and so they laughed about old times at the firm.

Marla had this way of gesturing with her fingers where she would softly touch the person she was speaking to. She acted as though she was so very familiar. She knew and understood you. That was the meaning of the touch. Marla fit right in like she had never been away—she was one of the gang.

Chapter 20
Tom's Criminal Law Practice

Marla thought it was kind that Little Al called her every day or two after she began working for Tom again. Little Al was 21 years old now. Marla thought he might be interested in her but he never asked for a date or said anything that would imply an interest in her sexually. When she asked, the staff at Tom's firm did not believe Al had ever had a date. Marla was 32 years old and there was a significant difference in their ages but Al was very mature for his age from a business perspective.

It seemed every time Al called the office he would ask to speak to her. He would ask how she was and he would ask about her family. Marla's mother and father lived in St. Petersburg. She had begun to work when she was just out of high school and she still lived at home. Marla was renting a house in the downtown area called the Old Northeast.

Then Al would ask about Tom. Marla thought it was a little funny that he would ask about Tom because Little Al spoke to Tom one or two times a day as it was.

Little Al and Frank were officers of CCC. Al was the President and Frank was the Secretary/Treasurer. Frank controlled all of the shares of CCC, and he appointed Al and Tom and himself as directors of CCC.

On most issues facing CCC, Frank received a thorough review because Al and Tom were normally on opposite sides of the matter. There was normally a good discussion before Frank broke the tie and chose a side. The difference between Al and Tom's thinking normally had to do with the education the men had. Tom as a lawyer was issue-oriented, and made decisions by isolating the issues involved and decided by answering the issue he identified as crucial to the question before them.

Al had deferred his schooling completely. He intended to follow Bob's footsteps by attending Catholic grade school and high school and then Stetson. But then after starting grade school, he didn't want to go to school. It was a waste of time he argued. Al was so stubborn that Frank and Bea gave in and agreed they would try home schooling. Frank and Bea taught him to read and write. Bob taught him arithmetic, algebra, geometry, trigonometry and biology.

Al's math skills, particularly simple math, were superior. He could add, subtract, multiply, and divide long series of numbers in his head by rounding off and he would come to an answer that was very close to being correct. Converting the trees on a piece of acreage into a dollar value was his specialty. He would estimate the number of trees per acre on the piece of property, and then by multiplying the estimate of the number of trees by the number of board feet that could be produced from the trees, and then estimating the grade of the timber and multiplying the price per board feet of the type and grade of the timber by the total number of board feet, Al would know the timber value of the trees on a parcel of land. Al got to the point where he could take stereo maps of property and from the aerial view depicted in the photographs he could determine the value of the timber plus or minus 5%. He obtained the value without even visiting the property. Little Al was so confident of his estimate that he would make a contingent offer for purchase of the land based on a calculation he would do in his head.

The bank would still require a timber cruise (a survey of the number of trees by type and grade) but the bankers came to rely on Al's estimate. The surveyors who actually counted the trees in representative plots on the property were nearly always within the five percent variant Little Al estimated by sight and by rounding the numbers in his head.

When Al made a decision in his role as a member of the Board of Directors of CCC, he had a unique process. Al wanted to know who he was going to be dealing with on the other side of the transaction. What was his character? Did he have a weakness? Would he fight for what he believed in? Were there things that were more important to the competitor than that he have a warm clean place to go to the bathroom? Did he curse? Did he speak behind a person's back? How did he treat his staff? Was he civil? Did he have a sense of humor? Did his opponent care about the problem they were dealing with? Was he fighting for his family or friends? Was his opponent healthy and physically strong?

Al felt most confident with a weak opponent, dealing with a person who did not have a dog in the hunt, no family or friends, who was civil and did not take the deal personally, and who was late for meetings—someone who had the smell of alcohol on their breath after lunch.

Al's concern with Tom was that he was inadequate and was missing the boat on some of the personal character traits that mattered to Al. Thus Tom was a risk to the people Al wanted to protect – Jimmy, Jenny, Frank, Bob and Bea – his family.

Al was an adult. Now 21, he was sure of himself. He had been Frank's advisor for 11 years. The advice was always practical and got to the quick.

Now, Al was looking to Marla to tell him when and if Tom slipped and made a mistake. If confirmed, Little Al would tell Frank, and Al expected that Tom would be gone. Al did not feel Tom had the same loyalty to the Barnes family as Al had. Tom was a good lawyer but he was not family.

***

The evening of the first day Marla was back working for Tom she was invited into Tom's office to discuss her duties. Tom told her what the salary ranges were for the staff and asked if she would stay in the middle range to begin with and he would move her up fast once the rest of the staff got to know her abilities. Tom admitted he couldn't pay Marla what she was worth.

Tom also wanted her to help him with criminal cases. Tom had a niche handling difficult criminal matters, murders mostly. As

Tom saw it they were pretty simple. The client had nothing to lose by going to trial. The State Attorney wasn't going to offer anything other than a long prison sentence or the death penalty, so the case was going to trial.

Further, the defenses were simple. Your client wasn't the perpetrator. Maybe he has an alibi witness—someone who says the client was somewhere else when the crime occurred. If he has no alibi and the State could show he was the killer, the argument was that the client was exercising his right to defend himself, or it was an accident or a mistake or an act under lawful authority. Homicide requires an evil intent. Was there premeditation, the act of a depraved mind or recklessness? If he was caught in the act and there was no issue of self-defense, then the argument was that there was provocation (wife in bed with another man) that caused temporary insanity. And last, if the client committed the crime and was not defending himself, and was not provoked and temporarily insane, then your client did not understand right from wrong and he could not appreciate the consequences of shooting the victim in the heart, and he was not guilty by reason of insanity.

Tom had a few current homicide files and he wanted more, particularly if he had someone as intelligent as Marla to help him work up the defenses of the cases. Tom gave the files he had to Marla to review. They could talk about the cases in a few days. He was going to be away in Atlanta with Frank and Al on business.

The files had been sitting at Tom's desk waiting for him to begin work. Tom had Marla sit at his desk in front of the files. Marla opened a file and began to turn the pages. Tom's room had heavy drapes covering blinds on the windows. The office was dimly lit. It seemed depressing with dark furniture and an Oriental rug. Tom went to the cabinet and took out a bottle of Johnny Walker Black. He poured a drink in a regular glass. It was about three fingers of scotch—four ounces. He dropped in a few ice cubes from the fridge.

"Drink?" he asked.

Marla knew Tom still drank though he didn't look like it affected him. He was six foot tall, thin, athletic, tanned and he appeared healthy. He had a full head of hair and was handsome. He had quit smoking cigarettes. Marla had thought about what she was going to say if she was offered alcohol in his presence. She had decided to live her own life like she had and not act in a way to please or displease him. Actually she would have liked a drink so she asked for a scotch, with water and ice.

"Why do you still take these criminal cases?" asked Marla. "You have been practicing fifteen years now. You don't need these clients."

"I don't know how long it will be before Al convinces Frank to hire someone over on the East coast in Jacksonville or Daytona or maybe Orlando to take my job. I thought I was going to be replaced last fall. Al and I had a dispute over the purchase of a sawmill. Really, I always defer to Frank and Al for purchases like that. It's a business decision. It is not a legal decision. If the matter regards an investment in a sawmill, Frank and Al know and understand what is best. It is not a subject in which I have any training.

"But Al was making a mistake," Tom continued, "and he knew he was making a mistake and he just wanted to argue with me and see if he could convince Frank he was right. He wanted to see if I would give up and just quit. He even said if I couldn't see his position was correct then I was not thinking straight and the 'alcohol had gone to my brain'."

"What happened?" asked Marla.

"Frank turned to Al and said 'Tom is right,' and that ended the argument."

"Maybe you are just reading something into it that's not there."

"I don't think so. Al took a position that was opposed by a highly respected timber surveyor and a banker and a tax attorney. He was baiting me—trying to get me to give in to his position. He didn't think I had any fight left in me." Tom swirled the liquid in his glass and took a sip.

Then Tom continued. "Al sees CCC as being his business, and he feels he is the only one who can run it successfully. At some point, Frank will turn CCC over to Al and I will be gone. I need to keep my options open so I need you to help me with these criminal cases. They are very lucrative. I didn't think I would be talking like that, worrying about money. But we have a lot of mouths to feed here. If I lost CCC's business I would have to let everyone go and I would have to work for someone."

"You always do fine," Marla reassured. "Even back when we first started you always had plenty of work."

Marla knew that Tom had always been concerned about going bankrupt. He remembered the Great Depression. Marla also knew that Tom was telling her that Al would try to find something that would help him remove Tom from the board of directors of CCC. She then considered Al's attention toward her. Al was not being courteous when suggesting she come back to Tom. It was not Al being thoughtful, but really it was Machiavellian. Al wanted Marla to provide him with the ammunition he needed to convince his father to fire Tom.

***

Al was waiting on the phone for Marla. He had a few simple questions about a trip the following week. The conversation was the same—about her, then her family and then Tom.

Tom had been right to suggest that Al was trying to use Marla to obtain information about Tom. Marla was careful to be truthful with Al because he was a client and Al had a right to know if Tom was doing or saying anything that concerned CCC. To that point in time Tom did not ever do anything to take advantage of a client and he was always truthful with his clients even if he upset them by being brutally honest. So Marla did not have anything bad to offer Al about Tom. But that didn't stop Al from calling and asking. He was nothing if not persistent.

Chapter 21
Henry T. Logan

The office manager, Karen, set Marla up in a part of the library and brought her the entire contents of the criminal files that needed the most work. Henry T. Logan was an alleged hit man for a new group of criminals selling literally boatloads of marijuana. They imported the drug from Central America, where it was grown. Possession and sale of the drug was not prosecuted in Central America at the time, but the possession and sale of the drug was a crime in the United States, and it was vigorously prosecuted because the drug was thought to lead to addiction to heroin. The penalties for possession and sale were severe. Possessing small amounts led to long prison terms. Police work was conducted undercover. Trafficking in the drug was lucrative. New combines of criminals formed which didn't involve the Mafia but instead involved a syndicate of young men and wealthy and otherwise legitimate business people. Some were from Florida.

Undercover police work was effective. The police picked the low hanging fruit for arrest and then by offering deals to the underlings worked their way up the ladder to the leaders and the money. As the gang's enforcer, Henry T. Logan's job was to interrupt the progress the police were making against the combine. As the police came closer to a top commander or banker, Logan would be employed to eliminate the threat by eliminating the informer who was aiding the police.

Logan's work was effective. Police investigations were being disrupted, and they ended with the discovery of the death of an informant. The cause of death was a single shot to the forehead with a .22 caliber long, copper clad slug. A .22 caliber pistol was the preferred close range weapon of assassins because the bullet is small and it deforms when it hits an object. The shot is quiet and there is easy access to cheap ammunition.

The police had collected slugs from the exploded brains of three individuals who were key witnesses in important prosecutions. The State abandoned the cases against higher ups (smugglers and money men), because of the death of their informing witnesses. Instead the police began to chase the killer, figuring if they could not eliminate the killer, they would have no witnesses to establish proof of guilt against the major criminals. Further, the police were finding there was reluctance on the part of the dealers they were able to capture to rat on other members of the organization, because of the fear they had of the enforcer.

Logan had been identified as the suspected killer in a shooting in St. Petersburg. The police found him in the Carolinas. At the time of his arrest, he was in possession of a .22 caliber pistol which was loaded with .22 caliber long, copper clad bullets. The police suspected they had their hit man.

While Logan was in jail in Columbia, South Carolina, Tom was visited by Logan's mother. She wanted to hire a lawyer for her son once he was brought back to St. Petersburg for trial. Logan had a lawyer in Carolina who was a well-regarded Carolina local. He was fighting extradition, trying to delay the trial in Florida by keeping Logan in Carolina and out of St. Petersburg. The trial had to be held in Florida, in Pinellas County, City of St. Petersburg, because venue was there where the alleged murder was committed.

Extradition could be waived and the prisoner could agree to be immediately returned to the court where the arrest warrant was issued. Otherwise, extradition could be a long process. The prisoner had to be taken before a judge in the jurisdiction where he was arrested and informed of the charge and advised that there was a warrant for his arrest in St. Petersburg, Florida and that the authorities in Florida were demanding his return to face charges. Logan had the right to local counsel, and he had hired an attorney. They were testing the legality of the arrest and they filed a Petition for *Writ of Habeas Corpus*.

The issues to be heard in Columbia were whether Logan was the same person named in the warrant, whether he was a fugitive, whether there was a charge or proceeding against him, and whether the warrant was in order "on its face".

Tom agreed to represent Logan in St. Petersburg and he had asked for and received a $25,000 retainer. The funds were deposited in Tom's trust account and as he or his staff worked on the case, funds were withdrawn from the trust account and paid into the office account to pay the staff at the law office for their work. The largest expense to date was for Tom's trip to Columbia to visit and interview Logan.

Logan had been in jail for a week. Tom brought his trusty transistor radio. The interview rooms at the jails were or could be bugged. A country music station provided sufficient noise to muddy Tom and Logan's conversation so they had privacy of communication. Tom kept no notes during the interview. He made copious notes afterward of what Logan said and what needed to be done to provide a defense to the charge.

Tom's notes in Logan's case said, "Delay, delay, delay."

The case would be very difficult to try for the defense. The evidence was circumstantial, but strong. The victim, a 25-year-old man, was shot at an outdoor rock and roll concert attended by 5,000 people in a waterfront park in downtown St. Petersburg. It was a wild and noisy affair with a colored singer with a band with horns and a driving beat. Allegedly, Logan walked up to the victim, smiled and raised the pistol and fired point blank. The victim turned his head before Logan pulled the trigger and the bullet entered the victims head just above the right ear. The victim crumbled into other people in the crowd, who thought there was a fight or riot. Everyone ran in a panic.

The newspaper had printed the police chief's prior warning that there could be trouble at the show because the band was said to stir up youth to violence. There were witnesses that put Logan near the scene of the shooting but there was a melee that resulted from the assault that developed into what became a riot and Logan and everyone had run. The only person left at the scene was the 25-year-old white male victim who was known to the police as being involved in the drug trade. The man had been shot in the head but was alive for a short while. The victim died at the scene without being able to identify his killer. The victim was found alone. He was armed with a small handgun (a "Saturday Night Special"), that was operative, and he was holding a baggie with marijuana in his front pocket.

The slug taken from the victim was determined by a police expert to have the same forensic characteristics as the slugs taken from the skulls of two other young white males who were killed in Steinhatchee, Florida. Those two individuals also had prior arrests for drug offences. The police also had a witness who alleged he was present when Logan was hired to perform the hit at the concert. Logan was alleged to have been hired by the twin sons of a State Senator from Hillsborough County (Tampa).

The twin brothers were last seen in Costa Rica after the alleged meeting between Logan and the brothers. There was reluctance on the part of the Police Chief to move forward with the case if it was based solely on the testimony of the informant who sat in on the meeting when Logan was hired to make the kill. The prosecutor also had Logan's girlfriend listed as a witness alleging Logan confessed to her. The Chief also believed they could obtain a conviction through the testimony of a firearms expert, who matched the slug from the victim with the slug from the gun found in Logan's possession at the time of his arrest.

There was important information the police were unaware of which Logan told Tom during the jail interview. Logan told Tom he had disposed of the gun he used to kill the victim by throwing it in Tampa Bay as he ran from the site of the concert.

"There was no way the gun found in my possession when I was arrested was the gun used in the killing." Logan emphasized by pounding his fist into his hand. The truth was that though guilty of the crime, this false evidence of guilt would provide Logan with a defense.

Tom explained to Logan that they didn't have time to waste. It was hard for Tom to believe the State's firearms expert was incompetent or lying. Logan told Tom that he knew Tom was a professional. Logan knew that he had to tell Tom the truth. Logan didn't intend to send Tom on a wild goose chase.

As they talked, Tom formed a belief that Logan's account that the gun in his possession at the time of his arrest was not the murder weapon was the truth.

Tom asked when Logan had purchased the pistol that was in evidence that had been tested by the police and was misidentified as the murder weapon.

Logan explained that after he dumped the murder weapon in the bay the night of the concert he had run to Columbia, South Carolina. Three days after the murder he had purchased another pistol, the same brand, make, and model, from a hunting and fishing store on the road coming into Columbia. It was a legal purchase. Logan did not have any intention to use the gun for his wet work. He bought it for his own protection. Logan explained there was a record of the purchase. The store had given him a receipt that he promptly lost but the clerk had told him, as a warning, that the sale would be recorded in the store's records. The clerk told Logan that people had complained about the store's record keeping policy and the clerk wanted Logan to know the police could obtain the particulars of the sale because the store had the serial number for the gun. Further, the store would advise the manufacturer of the sale and the name of the purchaser. Logan had told the clerk at the time of the sale that it was no mind to him.

Based on that information, Tom wrote a note on his "to do" list to hire an expert to check the findings of the expert in the employ of the police in St. Petersburg who was conducting the forensic investigation of the .22 caliber pistol. Tom also hired an investigator to do a background check on the informant, and also see what, if any, information they could get on the location of Logan's girlfriend. Logan was staying with her and her child at the time of his arrest, but now she was gone.

Logan knew that the girlfriend had spoken to the police. Logan knew the police in Columbia had threatened her with arrest for helping a fugitive escape justice. The police had attempted to record a conversation between Logan and the girl during a visit at the jail but Logan refused to speak to her about the crime. He was also smart enough to stay away from the other prisoners, fearing they would trick him into saying something that would be incriminating.

The police alleged that Logan made an incriminating statement to his girlfriend when he first arrived in Columbia. Logan confirmed to Tom that he had spoken to his girlfriend about the crime. The police said the girlfriend had been told by Logan that he was afraid he had "screwed up". He had been seen at the concert just after the victim was shot. The girlfriend had left the area after she talked to the police. Logan confirmed that what she had told the police was true and the girlfriend could put him in the electric chair. Logan said he didn't know where his girlfriend was now, but she had been married to a man in Guatemala and he thought she might be back with her former husband. The father of her child was the Guatemalan.

Without identifying the co-conspirators who had hired him, Logan also admitted to Tom that he had spoken to other members of the criminal enterprise and if they were so inclined they could testify against him, but not without incriminating themselves. He realized that as long as he was in jail, he was at risk of death from his co-conspirators. He wondered if there was something he could do or say to the police that would make a difference so that he could someday be free again. Tom said he would ask, but unless he would turn in someone at the top of the organization the police would not deal with him.

Logan said he did not want to rat on his employers.

Tom shrugged his shoulders. "What can I say?"

***

Marla had finished reviewing the file.

The last correspondence in the file was a letter from the extradition attorney who relayed that the judge in Columbia would be issuing his order on the Petition for *Writ of Habeas Corpus* within the week and Tom should be prepared to see Logan back in Florida soon.

Tom spoke to Marla on the phone the day after she completed the review of the file. Marla had a good grasp of the facts from reviewing Tom's file and his notes. The entire defense boiled down to a few scribbled notes. Tom had hired the firearm's expert and he had hired an investigator. Tom told Marla he needed her to set appointments with the men. Marla said she would do it.

Marla had those feelings again like she had in the past dealing with the Logan file. It was a rush, dealing with people at such a crucial time in their lives. Death by the State is an extraordinary remedy. The defendant draws some sympathy from the possibility of the penalty to be imposed regardless of his guilt.

Somehow, Marla blocked out any sympathy for the victim or felt that in this case the homicide was a business matter. The victim had turned on his employer and knew he could be killed for informing, and the rat had suffered the consequences.

Part VI

Little Al

Chapter 22

Peachtree Hotel – Neutral Territory

Atlanta, Georgia was the headquarters for most of the publicly traded lumber and timber companies that had assets in the Southeast United States. The Peachtree Hotel was the neutral site for meetings between timber companies if the matter to be discussed was confidential. Mergers and acquisitions were such topics.

Tom, Frank, and Albert had booked separate rooms in the hotel on the 23rd floor.

Little Al insisted he be called Albert. The formality was important to him even though everyone in the business still knew him as Little Al, and people who knew him for years messed up and forgot to call him Albert. But he had persisted and refused to answer to Little Al, even when Frank called him by the name from his youth. Albert was 22 and wanted a name that connoted his maturity.

The trio flew to Atlanta on Eastern Airlines in a Lockheed L-188 Electra. They flew out of Daytona and direct to Atlanta. Tom had asked the gate attendant the type of plane and when told it was an Electra he had a lot more questions. Tom hated to fly. He claimed flying was done with mirrors. "Nothing that big can get off the ground safely," he asserted.

The L-188 had suffered a series of three crashes between February 1959 and March 1960. The plane had four prop engines and was certified by the FAA as safe, even after the catastrophic incidents where all passengers and crew were lost. Tom had asked Karen when she booked the flight to tell the travel agent not to put the men on the Electra, but here he was at the airport and they were going to have to take the Electra or be late for the first meeting of the day.

Tom was assured by the manager for the airline in Daytona that the plane was safe. The manager admitted there had been a problem with the plane, but the problem was fixed. The FAA had required the plane to fly at a slower speed. The FAA was confident that if the L-188 was operated at a slower speed it would be safe, because the problem that brought the plane out of the sky was vibration and the vibration did not occur at the slower speed.

Tom was not convinced but he left it to Frank and Albert if they wanted to be delayed for the meeting. The pair was willing to take the Electra, but Albert commented that this was a bad start to the trip, and Albert looked at Tom. Frank told Albert to forget it. It wasn't Tom's fault and if Eastern was confident enough to put their pilot and crew in the plane he could fly with them.

The flight was miserable for Tom. He had a window seat and as the plane clattered over the Atlantic before heading inland, he watched out the window for two hours as the engines plowed through the clouds at 25,000 feet. Tom was tempted to have a drink to settle his nerves, but he didn't dare give Albert more ammunition. Drinking before noon would be another example why Tom should not be the Family's attorney. So Tom gripped the seat and held on.

***

The facilities at the Peachtree Hotel were first rate. The concierge personally inquired of both sides of the transaction after they were settled whether there was anything else that they needed.

The two parties were in a large conference room with a table 20 feet long and five feet wide. On one side sat the trio from CCC and on the other was the chief negotiator for Withlacoochee Lumber Company (WLC), a man named Gerald Brown.

Assisting WLC's negotiator were two lawyers (one tax attorney and one transaction specialist), a representative of WLC's Certified Public Accounting firm, and representatives who understood sawmill operations and lumber and timberland values and could read a timber map. In numbers, at least, the CCC team was outnumbered.

Albert smiled. He was proud that he was here with a place at the table where the destiny of the family would be determined. Albert was full of himself.

Tom and Frank did not see the negotiation as one for the heart and soul of CCC, but rather it was acceptance of reality. CCC had to get bigger or sell to the highest bidder. They were here in Atlanta to answer that question. Would CCC be a buyer or a seller?

Frank's plan was to present a list of all CCC properties and sawmills in the Southeast for WLC's consideration. Plantation #7 and the dairy operation and the land holdings in the Caribbean and Central America were not for sale, and WLC had no interest in obtaining those properties in any event. The plan was to show WLC what CCC had for sale, obtain a price, and then if the price was not fair, the trio would suggest that WLC sell some of their lands that were close to CCC's mills or to CCC's other timber land.

The first afternoon was a slog through surveys to confirm the size of the various tracts that CCC owned, and the age and type and grade of the timber on the property, and whether the timber would be difficult to harvest. Was it wetland, plantation, et cetera? Both sides were familiar with the other's property, but had specific questions. The sawmills were closed for maintenance and repair each year over the holidays and there were detailed descriptions and construction drawings of the work that was done to the mills in the last seven years, together with photographs and diagrams of the entire sawmill facility. With that information, WLC knew what the mills could produce and what shape the mills were in and what expense could be anticipated to keep the mills productive.

The CCC trio had determined a fair price for the timber on all 500,000 acres CCC owned that were in the Southeast US. That value was $150.00 per acre. The $150.00 price was an average price at which the land and timber would be sold, but only so long as the entire 500,000 acres located in the southeast United States was purchased. In other words, CCC wanted $75,000,000 for the land and timber.

"We'll think that over," said the WLC's Vice President. "We can meet again in the morning at 9:00am."

"That's fine," said Frank.

***

The trio had dinner in the hotel dining room. The specialty was fried chicken, with buttermilk biscuits, yams, and greens. All of the men drank sweet ice tea. Frank said he wanted to turn in early. Albert said he was going to take a walk. It was cold out. He had brought a sweater and he put that on under his coat and vest. Tom said he was going to review some paperwork and call the office.

***

When Tom entered his room he took off his jacket and tie and sat on the bed. He called the office, even though it was 8pm. He figured he would leave a message with the answering service, but Marla answered. She had just finished working on the Logan file. She was happy he called. She had a few questions. They talked. Tom told her he didn't want her to work so late. There was still time to prepare before the trial.

"What do you think of the case?" asked Tom.

"Well, it would be fine if there was no informer who says he was present when Logan was hired to commit the murder, and if Logan had not told his girlfriend what he did. Without those witnesses it would just be a battle of experts on the question of whether Logan's firearm was involved."

"What about Logan's statement that he had ditched the gun used in the homicide, and the gun he was found with was not purchased until after the crime?" asked Tom. "Do we have any information on that?"

"Strange, but true," said Marla. "I spoke to the salesman at the gun store in Columbia, South Carolina. The gun that was found in his possession when he was arrested after the murder, it's a different gun."

"I'm going to have to figure out the best way to use this information," said Tom.

"How's it going there in Atlanta?" asked Marla.

"Pretty slow. The delay in negotiations is making Albert nervous. He's very impatient. We are talking about a lot of money but to him it's just paper and nickel and silver. He doesn't have any intention of agreeing to sell anything. Albert's here to buy timber and he wants to cut to the chase. Anyway, you go home."

Tom hung up. On the table was a bottle of scotch whiskey and a bar glass. Tom poured two fingers of Johnny Walker Black and sat down and sipped the whiskey. After he finished, he took a bath and then poured a second drink. He read a magazine about golf.

"I wish I had time to play golf," he thought out loud. He finished the whiskey and considered pouring another drink but thought better of it and brushed his teeth and went to bed.

***

At 4:30am Tom heard a knock. He got up and went to the door, opened it a crack and saw Frank in the corridor.

"I need your help, Tom."

They went to Frank's room. Albert was sitting in a chair talking gibberish—a string of unconnected words.

"He's been like this since he came in the room a little bit ago," said Frank. "I don't think he recognizes me."

Tom went over and looked in Albert's face, and Albert spat at him and told Tom to get away.

"He knows me, damn it." Tom wiped his face and the trio sat looking at each other.

Finally Albert began to put words together correctly so they made sense, but the words were directed at Tom and they were harsh. Tom was not a member of the family and he was only looking out for himself. He was a drunk and he could smell whiskey on his breath.

Albert was paranoid and delusional, he thought he was home at the farmhouse and he wanted to talk to Bea, and then he began to talk to Mary Johnson, his natural mother. Albert claimed he could see Mary.

Tom told Frank they needed to get him to the hospital. Frank agreed and he and Tom dressed. Albert was still dressed. They got him in the elevator and downstairs. When the elevator door opened Tom took the bellman aside and told him they needed a cab.

"Be discreet," said Tom. The bellman understood.

The bellman hurried off and hailed a cab. The three men went outside and they got in the cab.

"We need a large hospital. Something connected to a university like Georgia Tech or Emory University."

"Right," said the driver.

Tom gave the bellman a $20.00 bill as he shut the door of the cab.

"What's wrong with your friend?" asked the driver.

"I think it's something he ate," said Tom.

Frank just sat there trying to comprehend what was happening. He remembered Bea telling him that Mary, Albert's natural mother, would sometimes babble, speak words out of context that made no sense. "God," he thought out loud.

Once at the hospital, Tom asked Frank to pay the driver. Tom got Albert in a wheel chair that he found by the ramp to the entrance door and rolled him into the ER.

"What's the problem?" asked the admitting nurse.

"I think it's psychiatric," said Tom.

The nurse pushed the chair into an examining room and began to speak to Albert. She got Tom out of the room and told him to stay with Frank. "The doctor will see you after he finishes his examination."

Tom asked Frank what happened.

"Albert came to my door and he was agitated. He said he wanted to leave. He said he didn't understand why we would sell all this land after it was so hard to accumulate. He got on you for not being loyal and claimed he was the only one who cared about the family, and he said I was disloyal, that we were all out to get him. Then he started to mush his words. They were just unconnected words and they made no sense."

"Ok, well he's in the right place." Tom looked at the clock. 5:30am. "Did you get any sleep?"

"I guess he came in at about four. I got five or six hours sleep. I'll be ok."

"How do you feel?"

"I'm ok, I don't feel weak, no chest pain."

"We may have to rent a suite at the hospital for the Barnes family," joked Tom inappropriately.

"That's not funny," said Frank. "What about the meeting set for this morning?"

"I could go in and tell them Albert is sick and that you took him to the hospital. Always tell the truth, you know, it sounds the most consistent. If they ask I can tell them he ate a bad oyster. You know they aren't going to offer any real money today. They are just probing us to see if we're desperate to sell. Maybe I can find out what land they would sell to us in Florida, and at what price. We know they have 45,000 acres near Jacksonville that's for sale. We could cut the timber at the mill in Fernandina Beach that's next to the paper mill."

"Yeah, and there is the 20,000 acres near Greenville and Lake City. We could use that as inventory timber for the mill in Baldwin, Florida."

"So, do you trust me to talk to these boys and see if we can buy a few sticks of wood?"

"Yes, I guess I trust you," said Frank. "I always have."

Tom got up. He got Frank's hotel key. Frank had all the paperwork in his room. Tom went out and got a taxi. It was the same driver.

"So, he was just dehydrated. No water and you hallucinate. How about that?" explained Tom.

"Damnedest thing," said the driver.

Tom gave the driver a twenty dollar bill.

When they got back to the hotel, Tom thanked the bellman again for his discretion. Tom went upstairs and got changed. He went to the meeting; explained what happened to Albert and Frank. He blamed Albert's hospital visit on a bad oyster. Then Tom listened to presentations by the lawyers, CPAs, and timber and sawmill experts as to why the CCC land wasn't worth near what the Barnes' family was asking. The offer that WLC would make for the timber and land was $112.50 per acre and they would pay for the sawmills based on the average value assigned to the asset by three appraisers.

Tom pitched a purchase by CCC of the 65,000 acres WLC owned near Jacksonville and Gainesville. The Barnes family would pay $112.50 per acre, $7,312,500.

The VP for WLC asked Tom if he was just trying to waste their time. "You know that land is worth $200 per acre."

"No, we aren't wasting your time. No more than you are wasting ours," said Tom. "We were hoping you would take the deal."

"We don't need money that bad."

"Didn't mean to imply that you did," said Tom. "Why don't we relax a bit?"

Tom took the men downstairs to the bar. "I'll buy," said Tom and he laid five $100 bills on the mahogany bar top. The men drank all afternoon and into the evening.

Before the evening was over the VP for WLC had asked Tom if the Barnes family needed an executive. He needed a job. The V.P.

didn't think WLC was long for the corporate world. The VP shared that if the Barnes would pay $125 an acre for the land in north Florida then he thought it would be a good deal. Tom said he would pass on the information, confidentially.

***

Once he was back at Emory University Hospital, Frank told Tom he had spoken to the doctors and they thought Albert was schizophrenic or had something close to that.

"It's a mental disorder," explained Frank. "He probably had a tendency to the disorder from his mother. She was a schizophrenic."

The doctors told Frank that the upset he had as a child with separation from his natural mother and father were probably part of the reason for him having the condition. The thing he was doing with his words that didn't make sense is called a "word salad", a sign of the disorder, according to the doctors.

Tom told Frank what had happened at the meeting with WLC, and later at the meeting in the bar.

"So, Albert was right," said Tom. "They were just trying to steal our land from us."

"Yes, Albert was right. What do you think about their offer to sell their land in north Florida to CCC for $125 per acre?" asked Frank.

"I think that's a good deal," replied Tom.

"Call that VP tomorrow when he's sober and see if they will send us a letter of intent to sell the 65,000 acres along with the latest timber cruises on the land? I will have to survey that land myself," said Frank. "Albert won't be working for a while. I think he wore himself out."

Chapter 23
Firearms Evidence

The firearms expert Tom hired was a retired FBI agent with 40 years' work experience. He had started the Bureau's forensics lab in Washington, DC. He had helped make cases against noted criminals such as John Dillinger, Baby Face Nelson, and Machine Gun Kelly. The expert was qualified in courts throughout the United States, and he had also testified in some of the US Territories such as Guam and Puerto Rico. He now worked as a witness for the defense.

To be allowed to testify as an expert, the witness has to convince the judge hearing the case that he has superior knowledge about the scientific evidence in the case. The expert has to show that the type of testimony he will give for the jury's consideration involves a recognized area of expertise. Fingerprint identification and firearms identification are two areas of expertise that, if the court can be convinced of the witness's competence, the expert is allowed to give opinion testimony and any conclusions he reached. In coming to his conclusion, the expert can quote statements by other witnesses, he can testify about the validity of the evidence in the case, and he can use statements of other experts in support of his opinion.

In fact, the expert is allowed to give ultimate opinions, such as, "Yes, in my opinion, this is the gun that fired the shot that killed the victim."

Once the witness is accepted by the court as an expert, the attorney who calls the expert has little to do. The attorney asks the expert to share his qualifications with the jury. The expert explains. Then the attorney asks what evidence the expert received. The expert explains. Next, the attorney asks what the expert did with the evidence, what tests or examinations were performed. The expert explains. Last, the inquiry is what were the conclusions reached in regard to the evidence?

In this case Tom's expert would first be asked about the manufacture of guns. That is, whether guns are required by law to have a serial number and that no two numbers are the same for the same make and model of gun. Also, Tom would ask if the serial number is placed on the gun by the manufacturer at the time it is constructed.

The expert would be allowed to refer to the sworn testimony of the clerk at the store where Logan purchased the pistol, to testify that the pistol was purchased after the date of the murder and the gun was in stock in the store since it was shipped from the manufacturer. The conclusion was that Logan's gun could not be the murder weapon.

The second area of inquiry involves identification of the murder weapon. The pistol is first compared to the bullet to see if it is the same caliber and then the rifling pattern contained in the barrel of the pistol is examined to compare the slug with the rifling. A cartridge can also be used for identification of a firearm but there were no cartridges found at the scene. The only evidence collected was the bullet from the victim's brain. Therefore the comparison Tom's expert would conduct was between the bullet and the gun.

The expert would explain that the way a bullet is matched to a particular gun involves the unique characteristics in the process of rifling a gun barrel. Rifling is cut into a gun barrel to cause the bullet to spin as it courses down the barrel after it is fired. A spinning bullet sails true like a spinning football. Without the spin the bullet would wobble through the air and would be inaccurate.

The rifling is cut into the inside of the barrel so that you have a high and low area. These areas are called the "land area" which is between two "grooves". The other fact that needs to be understood, besides the spin imparted by the land and the grooves that spiral through the barrel, is that the bullet is slightly larger than the diameter of the bore of the gun barrel. As a result the bullet is forced down the barrel by the exploding gas of the gun powder and the impression of the land and grooves are pressed onto the side of the bullet as the bullet is propelled down the barrel toward the target.

The expert examines the rifling pattern of the barrel of the gun with the impression the "land and grooves" made on the bullet. The expert first tries to determine if the number of land and groove impressions is the same on the bullet and in the barrel. Then the expert determines the direction of the twist of the bullet through the barrel to determine if the twist is to the right or the left. If the number of lands and grooves are the same and the twist is in the same direction, the expert measures the rifling impressions on the bullet. The measurement is in very small increments called micrometers, and they are measured by a device called a micrometer. What the expert measures is the widths of the lands and grooves of the bullet. If the widths of the "land and grooves" in the gun barrel and on the bullet are the same, this is a characteristic that the bullet was fired from the gun. Further, the pitch of the twist of the lands and grooves can be measured. How far did the bullet have to travel down the barrel to make a complete revolution? If the distance is the same, another characteristic has been determined to be similar.

Further, imperfections in the barrel of the particular gun can cause striations or scratch marks on the bullet. If you fire a bullet in the gun into a pool of water you will have a test bullet that you can compare with the bullet from the victim. Matching the striations or scratches on the test bullet with the same striations or scratches on the bullet from the victim can produce data to match the bullets to the same weapon.

All of these characteristics and whether there are similarities, when taken together, allows the expert to make an opinion that the bullet in the victim's head came from a particular gun or not.

In Logan's case, the gun could not have been used to murder the victim because it was not in circulation but was on the shelf in the store in Columbia at the time of the homicide. The expert could give his opinion as to how the police expert had made a mistake and misidentified the gun in Logan's possession to the bullet removed from the victim. The expert could point out areas of dissimilarity which were close to being similar, but not quite similar.

This testimony would lead the jury down a path to reasonable doubt. What Tom had to show the jury was that opinion testimony was only as good as the expert, and Tom was convinced that his expert was better by far than the police expert. Most times the defense in a criminal case involves the defense attorney pointing out that the State Attorney's evidence is weak or non-existent, or wrong. Tom believed that the testimony of his expert would raise a reasonable doubt that the police expert's opinion that Logan's pistol was the murder weapon was wrong—Logan's pistol was not the murder weapon.

***

Marla had also set a pretrial interview between Tom and the investigator.

The investigator was tasked with finding the informant and the girlfriend and taking their statement under oath if possible. However, neither witness could be found. Tom prepared a Motion to Compel Production of Witnesses to present to the court to obtain a Court Order that required the State Attorney (prosecutor) to produce these witnesses for a deposition. At the deposition Tom would ask the witness questions in the presence of a court reporter and the prosecutor.

To prevail on his Motion to Compel, Tom would have to show the judge that he had used best efforts to find the witnesses but that after reasonable diligence he could not locate them. Further, Tom would have to represent that he needed the testimony to prepare for trial, and to help find other witnesses for his client who might be identified during the interview of the informer and the girlfriend.

At the hearing on the motion to compel, the State Attorney admitted they had lost track of the girlfriend, but accused Logan of causing her to leave the jurisdiction of the court.

"What evidence do you have that the defendant procured her absence?" asked the judge.

The State Attorney began mumbling about the fact that Logan and the girlfriend had a "carnal relationship" and the court could assume, based on that relationship, that Tom was hiding the witness.

The judge looked at the prosecutor and then turned to Tom and asked, "Do you have any comment?"

"No, Judge," said Tom. "Except to say the statement is ridiculous."

The two attorneys then began to try to talk over one another and their voices were raised.

"Gentlemen. Gentlemen." said the court. "There is no jury here."

The men quieted down.

The judge ruled that if the girlfriend was not produced within 10 days of trial, that her testimony would be excluded from the trial. The informant was to be produced within 20 days after Logan had been returned from South Carolina.

"Your client should be back soon," commented the judge. "The Denial of his Petition for *Writ of Habeas Corpus* was in my mail today. We need to set this trial within the next 60 days. Are there any objections?"

Both sides made no objection and the matter was set for trial by jury, to begin on Monday in eight weeks.

***

Frank stayed with Albert in Atlanta for 21 days while his son was seen by doctors, and he was given medication to help Albert manage his illness. The new approach to treatment of schizophrenia was medication and psychosocial intervention. The doctors worked with Frank and with Bob and Jenny and Bea to educate the entire family as to what Albert's condition and prognosis were. All of the family was engaged and helpful. They understood that if Albert stayed on his medication and the family was supportive, he had the best chance to stay out of the hospital.

The doctors prescribed Phenothiazine because it worked with Albert's mother, Mary. The drug calmed Albert down and he wasn't so insistent that things be done his way.

There were other drugs in the pipeline, like Risperdal, but they were experimental. It seemed that Albert was responding to the intervention of his family. Albert admitted that he had visions and that he had heard voices all his life but he had been able to control them. The doctors felt that the pressure of the negotiations with WLC had put him over the top and he was unable to control his actions.

Bob was asked to come home and help with the business. Frank felt it was best if he and Albert continued to work together as though nothing had changed. Luckily, Albert understood and accepted the fact that although he would be given the chance to give his opinion on a business deal, the ultimate decision was left to Frank, Bob and Tom.

While Frank was in Atlanta, he spoke to the VP of Withlacoochee Lumber Company and they were able to negotiate a sale of WLC's north Florida property to CCC. Frank also established a relationship with a mutual fund, "Thompson's Timber Fund," that specialized in what the Fund called "timber banking".

Thompson's Timber Fund (TTF) purchased timberland and also lent its clients' money to land owners of timberland. Frank knew the owner of the fund. They had gone to school together at Georgia Military Academy.

Thompson's Timber Fund was asked to lend the money for the purchase of WLC land on short notice. The deal was closed successfully. Frank was impressed and wanted the mutual fund to review all of CCC's financing to see if re-financing with the fund made sense.

Part VII

Criminal Trial Work

Chapter 24
Logan's Trial

The Princess Diane Hotel was located in the city of Clearwater within a short walk from the Old Pinellas Courthouse. Clearwater was the county seat for Pinellas County, and it was about 25 miles north of St. Petersburg. Tom rented a room in the Princess Diane Hotel for the week whenever he expected that the trial of one of his cases would last a week or more. He did not want to be late for court if he got caught in traffic driving from home in St. Petersburg to Clearwater.

The Courthouse was stately, but too small. The jail was behind the courthouse and the County Commission was building a new multi-story facility to house additional courtrooms and space for the County Clerk, the Property Assessor and Appraiser, and Tax Collector, and room for the rest of the bureaucracy of the county government. The jail would be relocated to another site.

Clearwater had its icons. The old courthouse sat behind two large live oak trees that were probably each well over 200 years old. The county commission decided to remove one of the large, gangling limbs from the oak tree to the south of the courthouse. The large limb snaked back into the space dedicated for the new county building.

One of the judges who looked out at the tree from the window in his office was concerned. The judge took testimony on the issue of whether the tree would be harmed by amputating the limb. His ruling was that it would be damaged and the tree could even die. The judge ruled that cutting the tree would be a disruption to the court, and advised the Commission that its board members would be held in contempt if the tree was harmed. The Commission decided to re-conform the building to allow the tree limb to remain uncut.

There were two criminal court judges who could hear Logan's case. One was nearing retirement and the other was in his late 50's. The older judge was the jurist who had halted the removal of the limb of the oak tree. He was no one to mess with. Over the years, attorneys with big egos had attempted to push the judge around, to no avail. Tom had learned to be congenial and honest and live with the court's rulings. He would object in a timely manner to the court's ruling on the objection, and ask the court to note and rule on the objection. The judge knew when he was straying too far in favor of the State, and he would relent after he had made a series of erroneous rulings and would try to absolve his error by ruling in Tom's client's favor a time or two.

Over the course of a one-week trial, the jury would see the ebb and flow of the rulings and eventually the jury would pay little heed to the judge, who was biased in favor of the State. The jury would ultimately ignore the rulings of the court and determine for themselves whether Tom's objections were valid or not, and the jury would decide what the proper ruling should be and apply it to the facts.

A trial is not a real-life exercise. Only at a jury trial could a jury of twelve citizens hear testimony from a witness and then be told by a judge to ignore the testimony that the court says is inadmissible, and then after hearing the admonishment could the jury, in fact, ignore what was told to them on the witness stand. A jury would try its best to ignore what had been told to them by a witness, but it was a near impossibility. A trial was more like a play being acted out according to the direction of the court. It was a work in progress and was not necessarily a statement of fact.

In any event, a jury trial to determine life or death was heard by 12 members of the community who were 21 years of age or older and who were registered to vote. The exercise made Tom ill at ease. In order to be able to concentrate he moved into a room at the hotel and took his meals there. At trial he had the assistance of Marla and his investigator, Anthony Stewart. Marla stayed in the courtroom and then went back to St. Petersburg to the office at night. She went through the messages left for Tom at the office and decided what was important enough to bring to Tom's attention. They would meet in the morning for breakfast and review the messages. Then Tom would prepare for the day's work and Marla would call the office and forward Tom's instructions regarding the important messages that needed his attention.

Tom tried one or two jury trials a year. These were cases where there was no choice but to try the matter. The State could not let the murderer or rapist go free and the defendant would not agree to the imposition of the death penalty, so these trials were unavoidable. Other cases, where you could expect a sure trial, the defendant's reputation was at stake, so he chose to go to trial to clear his name.

The bias at the courthouse among the staff—clerks, bailiffs, deputies, investigators and even the defense attorneys—was that if the defendant was charged with the crime, he was guilty. That presumption of guilt pervaded the courthouse and the court and staff only gave lip service to the presumption of innocence. For that reason, on the defense, the voir dire, or examination of potential jurors, involved questions as to whether the juror had family or friends involved in law enforcement or the court system, or even if they knew a defense lawyer. Tom felt that if the potential juror was familiar with anyone in the court system they had a bias toward guilt.

The State, on the other hand, was concerned that some Communist would get on the jury, so they tried to remove or strike for cause any teacher or professor who might ever have taught or believed in the principle of the presumption of innocence. Tom always asked if a juror had served in the military, and if he was in the infantry, and if he felt the principles our forefathers fought for were still worth dying for. Most soldiers related to the idea that dying for freedom meant dying for an honest judicial system. Tom would fight to keep a foot soldier on his jury and most attorneys didn't understand why. It was because Tom felt the soldier would give the defendant the benefit of the doubt. And the soldier would apply the presumption of innocence to the trial, and until the presumption was stripped away by the evidence produced at trial by the State, this juror believed the defendant was not guilty. In short, a foot soldier learned to accept orders and the judge issued orders. One of the orders of the court involved the presumption of innocence and the soldier would follow the presumption.

Following the orders of the court kept the system honest. Tom had been told by an old-timer, that during the war American infantrymen were provided small books containing the U S Constitution. The soldier could read the document and know what he was fighting for.

Tom believed these principles himself, so they did not sound phony when he talked to the jury panel about them. The voir dire examination had few rules. The jurors were asked questions. Tom invited the jurors to ask questions and that always got a frown from the judge. Sometimes a juror would ask a question, but rarely. Ultimately, from the pool of 30 or so persons, 12 citizens of Pinellas County who were not familiar with the case, or knew a witness in the case, were picked to hear the death penalty case.

Generally, Tom chose teachers, former soldiers, people of color, newsmen, and beautiful women, those who had a college education, writers, artists, and the self-employed to sit in judgment of his client. He picked teachers and soldiers for the reasons previously stated. People of color and beautiful women were chosen because they knew and understood what it was like to be the subject of prejudice. The college-educated because over their college career they had received civics lessons the most often, and newspaper men, artists and writers because they fought for the principle of freedom of the individual every day. Finally, he chose the self-employed because they were independent and would stick to the rules for determining guilt or innocence and they would best apply the law to the facts of the case.

Of course, the jury Tom tried to choose was only based on Tom's guess of who the juror was and what they believed. Tom didn't really know.

Tom knew some very good attorneys who subscribed to the idea that the first 12 people in the jury box were as good as any 12 people they could choose. Choice was left to fate.

Usually the voir dire examination and the preliminary instructions began about 10:00am and ended in the late afternoon. By then Tom was exhausted. He had a nervous bladder and a tendency to vomit at least one time before he was relieved of the pretrial jitters. They had drawn the old judge and he would not let the attorneys pander in their questioning of the jurors.

Tom had met with Logan's mother in the morning. She appeared to be at ease. He had spoken to her the week before and explained what she could expect during the course of the trial. He explained the process of picking a jury and what he was trying to accomplish. Essentially he was trying to pick 12 jurors who would be fair and impartial to both sides. Tom explained to her, and again to Logan, that it was hard to do, but Tom felt if they could get six of twelve jurors who were not biased to the State they would have a chance.

Tom wanted Logan in a suit and tie, and he wanted him scrubbed clean, and he wanted him to have a fresh haircut. Logan resisted the haircut, but understood when Tom said, "I would hate to lose this case if your hair was too long. But I guess you would feel worse than me."

In court, Tom gave Logan a fresh pad of paper and a pen. "I want no talking, no grimaces, no facial expressions, and no outbursts. I need you with your best poker face." Logan was told to make notes. "I can't listen to you and the witness at the same time."

Logan followed all the instructions. His mother sat in the front row of the audience directly behind her son. She followed Tom's admonition that she and Logan were not to talk to one another. Tom explained to Logan that it was important for the jury to know that he had the support of family, and the three female members of the jury would want to know there was a mother who would feel the pain of the loss of her son to the electric chair if he was convicted.

At the end of the first day, Logan stayed in the holding cell just outside the courtroom. The cell had a combination toilet and water faucet, very degrading to the prisoner. The guards had left Logan a sandwich. He had not eaten it. The meat on the edges sticking out from the bread was a greenish color. The appearance of the meat made Tom gag and he understood why Logan did not eat the meal.

Logan changed his clothes, replacing his brown suit and white shirt and tie for his prison uniform of shirt and pants. He wore the same black shoes.

"Are you alright with the jury?" asked Tom.

"I guess. They all look pretty strict. None of them look like they want to let me go free if there is any possibility of my guilt," said Logan. "Do you intend to try to cut a deal with the prosecutor?"

"I would like to broach the subject. Maybe after tomorrow we will be in a better position to talk. Tomorrow we get all the technical testimony, identification of the decedent and your arrest."

"You spoke to my girlfriend?"

"Yes."

"What did she say?"

"She said pretty much what we expected," said Tom. "She said you came to Columbia because you were wanted for murder in St. Petersburg. She didn't say you confessed to killing anyone, only that you were on the run."

"Really, that sounds pretty awful," said Logan. "But that isn't what I told her. What I told her was worse than that."

"We have to just take the punches as they come and see where we are when the prosecutor has put on all their testimony."

"Okay."

"Let me have your clothes. Your mother is waiting for them. She will press the suit and wash your shirt. If you take the suit back to jail they will tie it in a knot before tomorrow and you will be in court in your prison uniform."

"Thank you for the help you are giving me."

"No problem. Opening statements are tomorrow. You need to take good notes," said Tom.

***

Tom met with Marla at Tom's hotel room. Marla briefed him on what was happening at the office. Everything was being handled. "Don't worry about it."

Tom asked Marla to be in court early for the opening statements. He wanted a record of what John Hale, the prosecutor, said he was going to prove in his case. If Hale exaggerated or if something Hale said he was going to offer as proof in the State's case wasn't proven, Tom would remind the jurors in closing argument at the end of the trial. Lack of evidence could be the basis for an acquittal-a reasonable doubt could form in a juror's mind if there was insufficient evidence.

Tom and Marla also discussed whether the investigator had been able to find the informant who allegedly said he witnessed the conversation where Logan was hired to commit murder. The State had not given notice they were going to call the man as a witness. Maybe the informant had turned and would testify for Logan and not against him. Or maybe the State just couldn't find him.

Marla would run down the investigator. She promised she knew it was important. It was one more thing Tom needed to have settled. Did he have to prepare for the informant's testimony or not?

***

John Hale took advantage of being the first person to introduce the jury to what the State claimed were the facts in the case. Because the State had the burden of proving Logan was guilty beyond and to the exclusion of every reasonable doubt, the prosecutor went first and he outlined the State's case by making an opening statement.

Hale described the statement as a "road map" to show the jury what the State intended to prove. The statement was long and involved, and Hale could not trust his memory so he read the statement to the 12 jurors who sat at attention during the first 10 minutes of Hale's speech. (It was more like a lecture.) Then after the first 10 minutes they looked down and crossed their arms.

The old judge began to rustle the papers on the dais high above the attorneys, the court personnel, and the jurors. "You might want to move this along, Mr. Hale."

Hale did not take the hint and he kept going, reading his speech. The judge stood up and began to roam around behind his perch and then went to the side door and said something to his secretary. The secretary came to the door and reached into the room with a gavel and handed it to the judge.

The judge went back to his chair and sat down. The jurors' eyes had not left the judge and they did not appear to have heard anything Hale had said.

Tom's turn. Tom did not discuss any facts in the case. He reminded the jurors that the defendant did not have to prove anything. The defendant did not have to call any witnesses or "put on one stick or shred of evidence". The State had the burden of proof. Tom reminded the jury that this was the law and it was what "we fought for in the long war in Europe and the Pacific. And it's what our boys are dying for now in Southeast Asia."

The jurors all sat up straight. Tom asked the jurors to listen carefully to all the evidence in the case: "The judge will tell you that you are to make your decision in this case from what you hear from the witnesses and the evidence presented in court. You are not to guess what the truth is, but you can use the evidence and your common sense to determine whether guilt has been proven beyond a reasonable doubt.

"Last," Tom said, "as jurors, you determine what the facts are and what is worthy of belief. You do not have to believe what a person says from the witness stand unless it is believable and makes sense."

Tom's opening statement took five minutes.

***

John Hale then called the State's first witnesses. He put on a few members of the outdoor audience at the concert where the shooting occurred. They were within a few feet of the victim when he was shot. The witnesses told how chaotic the event became after the shot was fired. There was blood and gore. This testimony woke up the jurors.

Tom asked these witnesses how close they were to the "victim". How many feet away?

"Just a few feet."

"Did you see the person who fired the shot?" Tom stood behind Logan.

"Yes," they said.

"Is this the man? Can you tell beyond a doubt?" Tom pointed at Logan.

"No," they said.

"Did the police show you a picture of my client?"

"Yes."

The witnesses all told the policeman who showed them the photograph of Logan that he was not the man who fired the shot.

Tom knew the answers these witnesses would make to these questions because Tom had sent his investigator, Anthony Stewart, out into the field to interview the State's witnesses. Tom would never have asked these questions if he did not know what the witnesses would say beforehand. Tom knew that the only thing the witnesses saw was the gun. They didn't see Logan's face.

Logan was identified at the concert by another witness who was not near the scene of the shooting but was over near the water in the Bay. The spot where Logan was seen was 125 yards from where the shot was fired. Logan was running and a police officer started to chase him but lost him near the old fishing pier.

When the police officer was called to testify, Tom asked the police officer why he chased Logan.

"Because he was running."

"Any other reason?"

"No."

"Was he identified by anyone in the crowd of 5,000 people as the one who shot the victim?"

"Not to my knowledge."

***

There was also testimony of the paramedics who rendered aid. They said the victim lived for about 12 minutes. They said the police tried to talk to him. They all asked the victim who shot him and he didn't say anything.

Tom asked if they found anything on the victim.

The attendants testified they found a large plastic bag with "plant material".

"Are you familiar with marijuana?" asked Tom, as he held up the baggie found on the victim for the witness and the jury to see. "Did it appear to be a baggie of marijuana?"

"Yes."

"Did you find a weapon?"

"We found a .22 caliber Saturday Night Special in his pocket."

"A gun and marijuana, is what you found on the victim?"

"Yes."

John Hale asked if counsel could approach the bench. The judge told Hale to speak from his table.

"Well, Judge, I'd rather speak with the court in private."

"Take out the jury," said the judge. When the jury was in the jury room the judge began to berate Hale for wasting the court's time. "What do you want?"

"At this time we are out of witnesses," admitted Hale.

"Who did you intend to call next?"

"The identification witnesses and the medical examiner. The witnesses are not available."

"How were you going to establish the identity of the victim?" asked the judge.

"We have to do the identification by fingerprints."

"No family in the area?" the judge turned to Tom and asked,. "Mr. Night, can you stipulate to ID?"

"Let me see the fingerprint cards, Judge." Tom reviewed the cards. The one card had the imprint of the fingerprints the medical examiner took. The other card was from the Florida State Division of Corrections, Davie Prison, Davie, Florida.

"If the cards are put in evidence and I can comment on the cards in my closing argument, we can stipulate to the identification of the victim."

The jury was returned to the courtroom and the judge addressed them, "Everyone was working while the jury was out of the room and the State and the defendant have agreed to the identification of the victim and these cards with the victim's fingerprints were placed in evidence."

Tom asked that the jurors be allowed to see the cards.

"Certainly," said the judge.

The jurors looked at the cards. One of the jurors pointed out to the other jurors that the one card came from the Florida prison system. The jurors used their common sense. The card proved the victim had been to prison.

The court recessed for the day.

***

The State Attorney had temporary offices on the second floor of a men's clothing store across the street from the old courthouse while the new courthouse annex was being constructed. The offices were only a little out of the way, so Tom walked there on the morning of the third day of trial. His intention was to speak to John Hale about the possibility of a plea deal.

Hale was in a bad mood. Tom could hear him yelling about the location of his trial notes. "They are on a special green colored pad."

Just as Tom told the receptionist that he could be reached at the courthouse in the attorney's lounge, Hale came into the re-

ception area and told Tom to come in. Hale was the Chief Assistant, which meant he had an office. The rest of the staff was in a
large room, sitting at desks trying to concentrate on piles of files.

"I wanted to see if there is any common ground," asked Tom.
"Can we negotiate a plea in this case?"

"If your client wants to plead guilty, it would be greatly appre-
ciated," said Hale. "We won't file the other two murder cases if he
pleads to this murder."

"If you had any evidence against Logan in those cases you
would have taken them to the grand jury," said Tom.

"Whatever," said Hale.

"What sentence would you propose to the court if he pled,
straight up to Murder One?" asked Tom.

"Death."

"There isn't much incentive there, John."

"Well, that's the best we can do."

Tom left the office wondering if Hale was crazy or overconfid-
ent. I will find out today, thought Tom.

***

By Wednesday of the trial week, any other case that was to be
tried was completed and the verdicts were in and the defendants,
if they were found guilty, were sentenced and in jail. The courthouse was relatively quiet. The jurors in the Logan case wandered
in the hall and they were rounded up by two bailiffs who got them
into the jury room and away from bystanders. Tom noticed that
the jurors were now acquainted and congenial. They were a good
group thought Tom.

Marla and Tom had a short chat. The investigator said he could
not find the informant, but he would keep looking. He did share
that Logan's girlfriend was being held in the county jail. The State
Attorney apparently was afraid she would run and hide if she was
not in custody.

The judge came in and spoke to the clerk. The judge's stump
was acting up. He lost his right leg in WW I and he suffered when

the weather changed. "I'm ready to start," said the judge to the bailiff.

The bailiff brought in Logan. His suit still looked good. The jury followed. They were greeted by the judge, who managed a smile. Everyone was seated and the judge turned to speak to Hale, and he wasn't present.

The bailiff went out the door after the prosecutor. A few minutes later Hale arrived. "Sorry," he said as he sat down and arranged his papers.

"Do you have a witness or does the State rest?" asked the judge.

The State called Detective George Randell. He testified that he was sent to Columbia, South Carolina to bring Logan back to stand trial. He also testified that he returned to St. Petersburg with a .22 caliber pistol loaded with copper clad, long bullets. Hale asked no further questions.

Detective Randell was the only Negro detective on the St. Petersburg Police force. Tom knew the officer was a favorite of State Attorney John Hale. Tom needed to handle the witness with caution because Randell had obtained his position as a detective through the influence of Mr. Hale.

Tom was concerned with asking the detective too many questions. Tom did not want to open a door that would allow Det. Randell to blindside the defense with testimony that would otherwise be inadmissible. Consequently, Tom asked no questions.

When Tom said "No questions," Hale was flustered and then he stood up and asked Randell, "Did you speak with Mr. Logan?"

Tom objected. An attorney can only ask questions on cross examination or on redirect about the particular subject matter the witness has already testified about. Since Tom asked Randell no questions, Hale could ask no questions.

Hale countered that he could re-call Randell as a witness later in the trial and besides, Hale said, "I just forgot."

The judge turned to the witness and told Detective Randell to tell the jury if he talked to Logan and if he did, what did Logan say?

"I asked Logan if he killed the victim and he said no," said the detective. "Then I asked him where he was the night of the concert and he said he was with his mother that night."

Tom was then allowed to ask Det. Randell questions based on the new testimony.

"No more questions," said Tom.

Quickly, Hale asked another question. "Why didn't you ask her if she was with her son on the night of the killing?"

Tom objected and the judge called the attorneys to the bench. The judge looked at Hale and asked him what the basis was for asking the question?

"Mr. Night opened the door to the question."

"I didn't open the door. Mr. Hale's question implies to the jury that my client has an obligation to call witnesses or prove he is innocent," said Tom.

"Mr. Night has listed an expert firearms witness," said Hale. "I'm not forcing him to call any witnesses."

"I haven't decided to call the expert. We listed the firearms expert because we might call him. We did not list the mother as a witness, nor did you. We didn't intend to call the mother as a witness," said Tom. "Besides, she can't be called as a witness, she has been in the courtroom through the whole trial to date and she has heard all the testimony. If she was going to testify she couldn't listen to what the other witnesses have said. That's 'The Rule.' "

"We are more than half way through this trial, Mr. Hale, and it appears you want to cause a mistrial," said the judge. The judge then turned to Tom and said, "You have three choices. First, if you ask for a mistrial, I will grant it. An appeal court may decide jeopardy has attached and the case will be dismissed with prejudice. It appears to me that the State intentionally caused a mistrial.

"Your second choice is that the defendant's mother can be called to testify as the court's witness and I will ask her if she was with her son at the time the victim was shot and killed. That is, does she provide her son with an alibi. In my opinion this option may make matters worse.

"Third, the trial will continue, and you can determine whether you want to call the defendant's mother during your case after the State rests.

"These are your choices," said the judge. "I will give you a minute to speak to your client."

Logan listened to Tom explain his choices. Logan asked Tom if he had talked to Prosecutor Hale about a plea bargain."

"They offered you the death penalty," said Tom. "The State made no offer except they won't charge you with any other criminal charges."

"How long will the appeal take to determine if jeopardy has attached?" asked Logan.

"A year," said Tom.

"Can I get bail during the appeal?"

"That is not likely. You will probably remain in jail here in Pinellas County."

"A lot can happen in jail waiting for a year."

"Yes, good and bad," said Tom.

"I want to go forward with the trial," said Logan.

Tom told the court.

John Hale objected and asked for a mistrial.

Tom objected to the mistrial.

Hale said Tom caused the mistrial and insisted that the court grant a mistrial. Hale's boss came in the door to the courtroom just as the judge did as Hale had asked, and granted the State's motion for mistrial.

The judge then had the jury returned to the courtroom and explained that the court was required by law to grant a mistrial and the case would have to be retried at another time. The jurors looked at each other and seemed to understand the State had done something wrong; probably because Logan was smiling. The judge thanked the jury for their service and adjourned the proceedings and left the courtroom.

Logan was removed from the courtroom by the bailiff and returned to the cell next to the courtroom. He glanced at his mother and smiled as he was cuffed.

Tom began to explain what had happened but Logan's mother understood. She thanked Tom for what he had done. She was relieved, she said, and left the courtroom.

Tom and Marla needed a ride back to St. Petersburg and Tom's investigator said he was going by their office. Marla and the investigator each grabbed a box of papers from the defense table. Tom continued to fill his large briefcase with his papers.

At that time John Hale and his boss came over to Tom and asked him to come with them into the attorney's lounge. Tom followed the two men and asked Marla and the investigator to wait for him.

***

John Hale and his boss wanted to talk about a deal.

"I'll listen," said Tom. "What do you propose?"

"Tom, your client is a very bad person and he deserves the death penalty. We believe that this is the third murder he's committed."

"So you say," said Tom. "I know what the witnesses say in this case and frankly, I am not impressed. If the evidence in the other two cases is as weak, you could lose all three cases."

"I know you think you have us," said Hale. "But we are right. Your man is the killer. We may have the wrong gun but we have the right man. All we have to do is win one case. We can bring the evidence in the other two cases to the jury's attention at the sentencing and your client will be on Death Row."

Tom said nothing. He knew what Hale said was true. (Similar fact evidence of commission of one crime was admissible to identify the perpetrator of another crime.)

"What we propose is a plea to Murder Two, with a sentence of 30 years. We will not pursue the other two cases."

"I'll speak to my client," said Tom.

***

Tom went back in the courtroom and told Marla to ride with the investigator and go home. "I will see you in the morning."

Tom went to the bailiff's quarters and asked to be put in the cell with Logan. They needed to talk privately. "No recordings," said Tom.

"He'll miss dinner," said the bailiff.

"No problem," said Logan.

Tom entered the cell with a pad and pen and said, "They are offering a deal. You plead guilty to Murder Two and you will be sentenced to 30 years. They will not pursue the other two cases."

Logan looked intently into Tom's eyes and quietly asked, "Did you ever find the informant? The man who claims he was present when I agreed to perform the hit?"

"No, my investigator is very good, but he found no trace of him."

Logan took the pad of paper from Tom and wrote: "You know that the State Attorney is not after me, they are after the twin brothers, the sons of the Senator from Hillsborough County."

"I don't understand," said Tom.

Logan wrote on the pad: "The State really wants me to testify against the twin brothers. Then the twin brothers will lead them to their father, Senator Frick from Bartow. Senator Frick controls the marijuana trade."

"If you will testify to that, I should be able to get you a much better deal," said Tom.

Logan wrote: "I know they would offer immunity if I would testify against the Senator and his sons, but I still will not testify against them even if I was freed."

"Why?"

Logan wrote: "They will kill my mother and my girlfriend."

"I understand," said Tom.

Logan wrote: "No, I don't think any promise the State makes regarding protection of me or the people I care for holds any water. I think I have to play this out to the bitter end through the courts. I have the money to pay you. You are doing a good job. I want you to keep working on my case. Will you represent me?"

"Yes," said Tom.

Tom gave Logan the pages of the pad Logan had written on. Logan ripped the pages into very small pieces and flushed them down the toilet in the cell.

The bailiff unlocked a side door and Tom exited the courthouse into the path through the construction of the new courthouse annex. He walked down the street to his hotel. He had a bellman help him get his clothes together and they emptied out his room and moved his belongings to the bellman's station. Tom tipped him $20. Tom intended to grab a cab and go back to the office for his car, but as he was about to walk out the door he saw the bar and tap room. The tavern was full of loud and happy people.

I'll just have one, thought Tom.

Chapter 25
You Dumb Fool

The room was cool. There was a breeze coming through the window and the white gauze curtains flittered on the window sill. Tom reached over for the phone and asked for room service.

"I would like coffee with Amaretto."

Tom had to repeat his request a number of times. He had a hard time being understood. His voice was hoarse and raspy. The person on the other end of the line was laughing.

Tom's pajamas felt scratchy – too much starch. I'll say something about the starch when they bring the coffee, thought Tom.

Tom tried to get out of bed but there were side bars and he couldn't find the latch. He tried to climb over the rails but he became exhausted. Tom laid back and looked around the room. There was an ottoman covered with white fabric in front of a large upholstered chair. On the ottoman sat a beautiful woman with short blond hair in an emerald green dress. She wore hose and high heels. Her legs were tucked against the ottoman. She looked stressed and almost in tears.

"Marla, is that you?" asked Tom. "Where am I?"

"You are in a mad house, you dumb fool."

"You're kidding."

Marla said nothing.

"I guess they aren't going to bring me the coffee with Amaretto," said Tom.

Marla cracked up laughing. They both laughed. Tom's laughter was deep. Marla's was full of tears.

The orderly responded to the mirth. It was unusual to hear laughter in the intoxication withdrawal ward of the hospital.

This was the first day Tom had been in shape to talk to Marla. Marla had visited with Tom every day for the last three days and she was heading in to the office so she was dressed for work. She and the Office Manager, Karen, had been practicing law since last Thursday in Tom's absence.

***

Tom had been found on the shore of Clearwater Bay, below the bluff. The police assumed he had fallen. Apparently he had left the bar in the Princess Diane Hotel and staggered about a mile to the edge of the bluff overlooking Clearwater Bay, and then tumbled down to the shore below. He was taken to Morton Plant Hospital. They thought he had broken every bone in his body, but the ER Physician noted only bruises. An ETOH test report showed a blood alcohol level of .32%. Tom was highly intoxicated, and he was put in a room to dry out.

Tom did not have his wallet when he got to the ER. He was recognized by one of the psychiatrists on duty. Tom had hired the doctor in a case where sanity was the issue.

The doctor called Tom's office and asked for the manager, and told Karen Tom was in the hospital in Clearwater. That was Thursday at 8:10am. Karen and Marla covered for Tom on Thursday and Friday.

Karen discovered that Tom's belongings and his file with confidential information was still at the hotel being guarded by the bellman who got the fat tip. Marla asked the bellman to put the luggage in a secure location. There would be another $20 tip when the file was retrieved.

On Saturday, Marla went to visit Tom in the hospital and gather his belongings. Marla drove to Clearwater in Tom's car, a 1955 Chrysler Newport convertible. The car had a soft white top and it was crème yellow. Marla loved the car. Tom rarely let her drive it. She put the top down. It was a beautiful Saturday-- blue sky, clear and almost balmy.

Marla got a lot of looks as she drove north on US 19 Highway.

She was still not prepared for what she saw in the hospital and it had been the same for three more days. Tom did not recognize her. The psychiatrist had advised her not to visit long. Tom lasted about a minute and then vomited into a can. There was a mattress that was covered with vinyl and a sheet, and the can. That was the entire contents of the room. There was an orderly that tried to help Tom catch the vomit in the can, but otherwise he had no assistance.

Marla's visit lasted about a half an hour. She talked to the doctor. She needed to know when she could tell clients he would be available. The doctor thought a week, but only if he quit drinking. If he started again he would be back in the hospital. The drunk would be in and then out of commission.

The question was whether Marla and Karen could cover for him if Tom was out of the office for a week or so. He never took a vacation and his clients knew that, so they would not begrudge a week off, thought Marla as she drove back after seeing him on the first visit. We can say he's on a trip. Marla drove back with the top up on the convertible. The sun was still shining but she was depressed.

Karen and Marla decided to move Tom to St. Petersburg to a more comfortable facility. They would pay the bill for a week. The women spent Sunday formulating their plan. It would be Marla's job to tell Tom their plan.

***

Back now to Monday, Tom was in the new digs, a clean, nice room with the white curtains and the ottoman and he was holding hands with beautiful Marla with the emerald green dress.

As they stopped laughing after Tom realized he was not going to be served Amaretto, Marla explained that she and Karen would keep the office running for a week. After that, Tom would have to be back to run the practice.

Tom would have to cure himself or more likely than not, he would lose his clients and die.

"You are too stubborn to listen to anyone but yourself," said Marla.

Marla's humble opinion was that Tom was, "Hiding some problem and you will not face it and talk about it. You are too lazy or too embarrassed, or too proud and so you drink."

"I don't think I can quit drinking forever," said Tom. "I stop, and then I start again."

"You only have to quit a day at a time," said Marla. "You quit smoking didn't you?"

"Yes," said Tom. "I quit smoking by staying drunk for six months."

Marla had typed the address of his new psychiatrist, and the number for Alcoholics Anonymous on an index card. She left him a copy of AA's book, "The Story of How Many Thousands of Men and Women Have Recovered from Alcoholism," Second Edition (1955).

"Do you have any questions?"

"No."

Chapter 26
AA

The AA meetings were helpful. Tom drank a lot of coffee and he inhaled a large amount of secondhand smoke. He was sorely tempted to start smoking again, but it had been so hard to quit that he was afraid to start again. Fifteen years after Tom quit smoking Camel cigarettes, he still smoked in his dreams and he could still smell the nicotine in the smoke. Tom wasn't affected that way by alcohol. He did not crave alcohol now that he had quit drinking for six weeks. In fact, he did not want to drink. His head was clear for the first time in years.

As Tom got older, the cases he handled became more complex. If you did not have a good basic knowledge of the law you would make an error, or you had to understand your limitations and find someone who had the expertise you lacked. But, either way, your head had to be clear to handle the case yourself or to find help to do the work.

Really, very few attorneys knew how to reorganize a railroad and those who had the grasp of the documentation that was necessary had to hire other specialists in labor law and union activities and god knows what other specialties in order to accomplish the task.

Tom did not want to represent a client who was too cheap to pay a reasonable price for the knowledge that was necessary to do the job right. A clause in Tom's retainer agreement (contract) stated that if Tom felt help was needed to successfully complete the job and the client refused to hire the help, Tom could withdraw from the case.

Life had become too short to spend it defending malpractice actions and testifying against old clients, thought Tom.

***

As time went by, Tom saw it was easier to practice law without a hangover. He was happy he had quit drinking, but he didn't tell Marla and Karen. He complained to them about how much he missed the drink now and again, and he would put an Irish lilt to his voice and tell a story about him being a young kid in senior high, drunk and on a bender, or in college or law school, intoxicated. Finally he realized that he pretty much stayed drunk for 15 years. So maybe he did miss it and maybe booze was in his bones like the nicotine in cigarettes. It was just subtler. He needed to remember the itch was still there. He had to avoid scratching it.

Meanwhile the life of his practice went on. He told the State Attorney that Logan wanted to proceed with his case and would not accept the plea bargain. The State filed an appeal of the Order Granting the Motion to Dismiss on the Motion for Mistrial. John Hale became very angry on the phone and told Tom he would remember his lack of cooperation. He also said sarcastically that he was sorry to hear about his accident. Tom mentioned the conversation to Marla and Karen. Marla said she had not heard any gossip from anyone about Tom falling off Clearwater Bluff.

"The police were the ones who found me after the fall. They took me to the hospital. If the police know, the State Attorney's office will know" said Tom. "I have to live with my mistakes."

***

Like a bolt out of the blue, Marla received a call from Frank Barnes. His father, the Senator, wanted to see her.

Marla borrowed Tom's car and drove alone across the state to Ormond, to the Plantation, the Saturday after the call. The Senator suffered from high blood pressure, diabetes, and old age (he was 75). When Marla first left Tom and came to the East Coast of Florida, she stayed at Plantation #7. She worked in the factory making jams and jellies and packaging the jars for shipment. She and the Senator had become good friends. The Senator thought it was more than that. He had feelings, rather, longings, or perhaps remembrances of time past when he could interest a woman. He felt he could still be of interest to Marla. Marla knew men and she was polite but kept her distance and avoided his advances.

To Marla, the Senator looked very old but brightened when he saw she had made the trip. He had problems with his legs but wanted to see Tom's car. They went outside. He asked for a ride. They drove north on John Anderson Drive to High Bridge and then over the narrow two-lane road through the briny headwaters of the Halifax River. They passed through Tomoka State Park and down River Road to Flomish Road. Marla stopped at the stop sign.

"Go ahead and make the turn," said the Senator, pointing the way. "We'll go visit Bea."

After making the right hand turn, Marla drove across US Highway 1 and then over the railroad tracks. The dairy was on the right. The building was huge. Milk was delivered to the facility by semi-trucks from across the state for processing. There was a rail siding and refrigerated freight cars were parked to receive the pasteurized product and deliver it throughout the country.

"Amazing," said the Senator. "This began with two cows in 1843."

They turned left off Flomish Road and followed a road through the woods to the farmhouse about a half mile from the turn. The house was the same. Jenny was on the porch.

"Hello, Grandpa," she said. It was like he was expected. Marla hugged Jenny. Marla had been Jenny's model for the modern woman. She had a job and her own place and she was free. That's what Jenny wanted. Though she still spent time with her brother, Jimmy, it was of her own choosing. Jimmy had round the clock care now.

The Senator wanted to visit and that meant seeing Jimmy too. He was his Grandfather. He thought, he's alive and that's about it. "Does he respond in any way?"

Jenny rubbed his forehead and Jimmy moved. "That's about it."

Marla thought there was a change in Jimmy's face when Jenny spoke. It was like a spark lit.

Bea came into the room and told everyone to get out. "He needs to rest."

Bea brought them up to date. Since CCC bought the 65,000 acres in North Florida, Frank, Albert, and Bob had been working out of Live Oak, Florida, re-orienting and modernizing the sawmill there to process the timber that would be cut off the new land, and cruising the land to determine what should be cut and when and what needed to be replanted. They were going to move some of the operations from Mims, Florida, north to Live Oak.

"They ought to buy a plane," said the Senator.

"They have been looking for a small plane," said Bea. "Albert says he won't fly though. That flight to Atlanta was his last, he says."

"How is Albert?"

"They changed his medication. He's taking Risperdal. It'd better than the Phenothiazine. That first medication caused him to gain a lot of weight."

"Did Bob finish school?" asked Marla. "He wanted to get a master's degree."

"Frank worked something out with the university so Bob can help out with our business and continue school. Bob studies what his professors suggest. He has decided on the topic for his thesis and he will give his dissertation in the spring. It will speak to issues involving the timber industry."

Jenny and Marla were together on the couch. "What are you going to do with yourself, Jenny?"

"I'm going to the University of Florida. I want to go to law school."

"You will have to talk to Tom about law school," said Marla.

"How is he? Anything we should know?"

"We are not together. We are best friends," Marla smiled. "He quit drinking."

"Great," said the Senator. Enough of the small talk, thought the Senator. "Are you going to feed us, Bea?"

They had dinner.

***

Back at Plantation #7, Marla and the Senator sat on the dock. It was being re-built to accommodate a river yacht. The yacht would take tourists on a cruise from the Daytona Beach Yacht Club to the plantation. It was about a four hour boat ride to and from. The destination was the Old House on the plantation and a tour of the bottling factory.

"It was my idea to enlarge the dock," said the Senator. The property was his prize. There was 250 feet of riverfront. There was a 15 foot high bluff from the river to the road in front of the Old House. The house was built on a prominence, probably an old Indian mound. Behind the house was the factory building and behind the factory was the grove. It had varieties of orange, tangerine, tangelo, grapefruit, fig, guava and many other fruits. The grove extended from the factory up a hill and over to A1A, the highway that fronted on the Atlantic Ocean. The sand on the shore at this location of the beach was burnished red coquina and mica and white sand. You sank to the top of your ankles in the sand and small shells when you trudged to the surf.

"You were always a good businessman," said Marla. "The plantation has grown. CCC would never have started without your sharp eye seeing that property in Volusia County. The company owns timberland and sawmills throughout the Southeast."

"The purchase of the Wetland was a good move," said the Senator. "Look Marla, the reason I asked you to visit was that I want you to move over here and run the plantation. I am going to have to go in a home soon. This diabetes is going to kill me. I don't eat right, still drink. If I go in a home I might make it to the end of my life without losing my legs."

"That's a lot to grasp at one time," said Marla.

"If you do this I will give you the Old House at the Plantation. I know you love it. You would live right here where you work. You would still be close to Ormond and Daytona. Maybe you could trap a man," he chuckled. "I wish I were younger. Please think about it."

"I will."

"You know Tom is really stupid to have let you go," said the Senator.

***

"Another rye whiskey and water?" asked the Senator.

"Maybe one more, but that's the last."

The Senator and Marla had sat up until the moon was high over the Halifax River. The west side of the river had mostly remained in its wild natural state but the developers were beginning to build houses along the riverfront. The Senator expected the developers would even take over the Bulow Plantation up north and build there. Bulow was an antebellum plantation. Construction began in 1821, and the owners grew indigo, cotton, rice and sugar cane on 2,000 acres. The plantation house was burnt in the second Seminole war and never rebuilt. The locals were trying to preserve the Bulow Plantation grounds and the ruins of the house and sugar mill vats and the red brick chimneys. The vats were part of the operation rendering the cane syrup into sugar crystal. The Senator had added his name to a citizen's petition to save Bulow for what good it would do.

"So, you are going to have to tell me the reason you want me to manage Plantation #7."

The Senator was not used to showing his cards so early in the negotiation, but it was getting late and he knew Marla wasn't going to believe it was only her good looks that got her the job. "You are going to save the family, is the real reason" said the Senator.

"How would giving me the Old House do that?"

"We need to separate this property and business from CCC. I intend to put this Plantation #7 property, except for the Old House that I will deed to you, and my stock in CCC, into a Trust. You will be the trustee and my children and grandchildren will be the beneficiaries of the trust. You will control the Plantation business. The Plantation business has no debt. It is my hope that you can keep it that way. The trust will avoid estate taxes. You will have full control over the trust. If a beneficiary objects to the trust they will be cut out."

"I will be Napoleon?"

"Exactly."

"You can't save the plantation forever."

"I know that, but I can give it some breathing room," said the Senator. "I can preserve it for a few more decades. That is my aim."

"Is it your belief that CCC will fail?"

"Yes."

"It is one of the strongest private corporations in the state," Marla contradicted. "How is it vulnerable?"

"Debt. Debt will take it down. The bankers almost got me. Tom saved us, or saved me from myself," said the Senator. "If he hadn't held off the bankers and slowly helped us sell assets and allowed time to refinance, we would have lost everything."

"What is the problem as you see it now?"

"The value the banks assign to collateral is too high. The banks just keep lending money. The value of the collateral is speculative. I don't believe the collateral will support CCC's loans if CCC has a problem with a reduction in cash flow from the sawmills. If we have a recession or people quit building houses and don't buy timber as they do now, CCC will not be able to make payments on the loans on CCC's timber holdings."

"And you feel the banks will wrap their tentacles around your plantation if it's not separated from CCC."

"Exactly. Bea understands. She has kept the 800 acre homestead and her family house separated from all the other businesses including the dairy."

"The dairy is in debt?"

"The dairy and the processing plant are all but owned by the banks. Bea almost lost the dairy last year. She needs to sell it. A cooperative will buy it but she won't sell. The processing plant can't make money because it has to buy the milk at prices set by the Federal Government. If a co-operative owned the dairy they would process their own milk. The dairy operations would be an expense added into the cost of the co-operative's milk."

"If I remember, the dairy used to process its own milk from the cows on the homestead," said Marla.

"They still do, but Bea let the operation get too big. They bring in milk from all over the state. The more milk they process, the more money they lose. The margins are too small. They are barely breaking even now, but the dairy is regulated by the banks and it is destined to fail. Her operation is on a 'lock box' now."

"What do you mean?" asked Marla.

"All of the receivables from the two million dollars a food chain pays for a month's supply of milk to the dollar a customer at the dairy store pays for a single ice cream cone is put in a bank account controlled by the banker. The account is the lock box. The banks control the money the dairy receives from all sales and decides how much it will pay toward the cost of operations. Interest is paid to the bank first. The bank always comes first. The debt keeps getting bigger."

"I get it, the bank is sucking all the earnings from the business," said Marla. "Why won't Bea sell the dairy to the co-op?"

"She goes there every day. She inspects the operation and reviews the receipts and talks to the bank overseer. She has done this for many years. Frank and Bea have never taken a vacation. She goes in every day for the boy."

"You think it's for Jimmy?" asked Marla.

"She thinks if she loses the dairy that Jimmy will die."

"It's all based on superstition?" asked Marla.

"Exactly, it makes no sense. But it's the same with Frank. He just keeps doing the same thing. He keeps buying and building. But what is happening to the dairy could easily happen to CCC. It's just a bit of a different variation of the same story. Bigger is not necessarily better. If the value of the timber lands deflates, CCC will bankrupt."

"And you feel that if you are gone and Frank controls your plantation he will use it as collateral for CCC's loans to try to save CCC, and if CCC bankrupts it will take the plantation with it."

"You understand. I have tried to explain it to him but he won't listen."

"So you expect me to push back against Frank?"

"Yes, you can do it." The Senator tipped his glass and took the last swallow of rye whiskey.

***

As Marla listened to the Senator she remembered that when Tom worked so hard years ago to save the Barnes family from bankruptcy, the problem was that the Senator couldn't stop buying. Now apparently it was his son who was on a tear. Or maybe Frank didn't see what he was doing. Marla would talk to Tom. She would have to talk to Tom to tell him she was going to take the Senator's offer.

She felt it was the opportunity of a lifetime.

Chapter 27
Marla Moves to the Plantation

On her return to St. Petersburg, Marla set a time to speak with Tom to discuss his future without her as his trial assistant.

Tom had two active homicide cases. Marla had worked one of them up for trial, identifying witnesses, setting depositions, and anticipating the need for expert witnesses. The other case was more recent and no work had been done on the file. Neither of the cases had a trial date set so Tom would be able to work with the court to get the time he needed to prepare. Both of the cases were heinous. One involved a young parolee from New York who had allegedly killed a local lawyer, beating him to death with a fireplace poker.

The other case involved an old drunk who allegedly drowned a woman in Mirror Lake. Tom was a peripheral witness in the drowning case. He had been in the library looking out the window of his office and he saw the police activity at the lake when they hauled the woman's body out of the water.

Marla had also worked with Karen on CCC's files. These files involved business, real estate, contracts, and commercial litigation. Tom was going to have to get more help for Karen when Marla left. Tom paid well but he hated to make a new hire. It took a while for secretaries to understand him. He talked in code and expected his workers to know what he was thinking. In court, Tom concentrated on his words and spoke in clear, precise sentences. When Tom was in the office, he was careless with explanations and words and sentence structure and said, "You know what I mean," a lot.

In the office it was all about Tom, except he didn't ask his staff to make his coffee or lie for him.

***

"I hear you are going to move to the East Coast and run Plantation #7," said Tom as Marla set her bag down at her desk. He smiled as Marla's cheeks reddened. Tom was not happy to see Marla go. Frank had called him and told him what his father was doing with the plantation. Frank asked if Tom could represent the family in the matter and Tom said no. "You will all need separate counsel. I would have a conflict."

Tom was conflicted about dating Marla and her being an employee and the fact they did not marry, but that was just the way it turned out.

Marla didn't have a chance to get advice from Tom about her move to Ormond. The decision was kind of forced on her, but Marla did have a chance to talk about the Senator's concerns about CCC overextending itself.

Tom listened as Marla restated the conversation she had with the Senator as they drank rye whiskey sitting by the river.

"The Senator is one to talk about the evils of debt. He almost bankrupted CCC ten years ago," said Tom.

"That's what I remembered," said Marla.

"I don't think the Senator understands what Frank and Bob are working on."

"Tell me."

"When Albert was in the hospital in Atlanta, Frank negotiated the purchase of 65,000 acres of land from Withlacoochee Lumber Company (WLC). He knew about an investment fund that was loaning money to timber property owners and the timber industry. Frank met with the owner, Thomas N. Thompson. They knew each other from school. They were roommates at Georgia Military Academy. The fund loaned the money that allowed CCC to purchase the WLC land. Frank is convinced this fund is the future in financing for the timber industry. Frank feels the banks do not properly collateralize timber. They do not give the owner of the land credit for the growth of the trees."

"I don't understand," said Marla.

"Really, I don't either, but I'm just a lawyer," said Tom. "What they are saying is that there is a value component in timber that is not recognized. The timber is alive and it grows. In the industry, timber is called fiber. Each year the timber, through growth, produces more fiber. The trees get bigger. The timber owner only sees the profit from the growth when he cuts the timber and sells it. What the fund is willing to do is give the timber owner a credit for the growth each year against interest owed on a loan on the timber land. Then, when the timber land is sold the fund is paid the amount it lent in principle plus the interest on the loan. So if you borrow a hundred dollars at 5% interest and the timber grows 5% a year you are only required to make principle payments on the loan and the interest is paid to the fund when the property is sold. The interest is deferred."

"What if the property doesn't bring a price high enough to cover the balance of the principle of the loan and the deferred interest?" asked Marla.

"I know," said Tom. "That's only one of my problems with the concept. I have been trying to talk Frank and Albert out of this. They want to refinance all their loans with the Fund. Bob understands there is real risk in this proposition. Albert thinks it's great, but what can I say, he's on medication. Frank just wants to quit fighting with the banks. He doesn't feel like he ever gets ahead. He is getting a lot of pressure from Bea to do the deal so she can use some of the new all-encompassing loan from Thompson to refinance the dairy."

Marla got up from her seat and went over to Tom and gave him a kiss on the forehead. "Well at least you still have your hair," she said. "I will probably be talking to you. You can call me at the plantation. I'm going to put my office in the library in the Old House."

***

When Marla left, Tom was feeling sorry for himself. He kept a bottle of Johnny Walker Black in the bottom drawer of his desk. He pulled it out and began to twist the cap. This would be the first drink since he left the hospital after his fall off the top of Clearwater Bluff. The cap was still sealed with a paper tax receipt glued on at the distillery to pay Florida's alcoholic beverage tax.

Tom pulled the bottle to his chest with his left hand and began to twist the cap with his right hand but the cap appeared to be stuck. He twisted with all his might but could not remove the cap. To get a drink he would have to break the neck off the bottle and risk drinking scotch laced with slivers of glass.

"The hell with it," said Tom as he put the bottle back in the drawer.

Tom opened the Logan file to see where things were at on the appeal. Marla had interviewed a young attorney named Roger Adams to do the basic research and rough out the defense brief in response to the State's brief to overturn the dismissal of the murder charges. The State Attorney had lost the case. At a short hearing the judge ruled that the prosecutor had committed intentional error, causing the court to grant the mistrial. The judge found the State was attempting to obtain a continuance of the case after jeopardy attached through the motion for mistrial. That tactic was impermissible. The judge had set bail for Logan on the charge in the amount of two million dollars pending a ruling by the appeals court on the order dismissing the homicide charge. Logan couldn't post the bond but he was feeling better about his situation. Logan told his mother to pay Tom's firm another $10,000 for the work necessary on the appeal.

Tom hired Roger Adams to help with the appeal. Tom hated appeals and had tried to convince Logan to hire someone who specialized in appeals. Tom even threatened to withdraw, but Logan insisted. "No, I need you to do this."

Tom told Logan he would hire a young lawyer to help. Logan said he did not care who Tom hired so long as Tom was the lead attorney and he had the ultimate responsibility for the argument that would be made to the appeal court on Logan's behalf.

Roger had completed the response to the State's argument. Tom read all the cases Roger used in his argument. Roger's work was superb. Tom buttonholed two criminal lawyers who he respected and they agreed to review Tom and Roger's work. The attorneys blessed the legal product and the brief was hand delivered by Roger to the clerk of the Appellate Court on the last day for filing the response, at 4:48pm – 12 minutes before the clerk's office closed.

***

As soon as Logan's appeal was filed, Tom received notice that the Jasper Lee Smiley case was set for trial. This was the case involving the intentional drowning.

Jasper and his girlfriend Betty Jane Smith were a sad case. The pair was in their 70s. They were alcoholics living on monthly government stipends. They lived in a garage apartment near City Hall in downtown St. Petersburg. The garage apartment had been built without a permit and did not meet code. It seemed like there were thousands of these illegal housing units in St. Petersburg. The apartment Smiley rented was sparse and bare but perfect for winter visitors trying to escape the blizzards up north.

Betty and Jasper were a nice couple when they weren't in a fight after drinking too much. According to the neighbors, Betty was the mean one who picked the fight, yelled and screamed, and then brought it outside to the alley where she demeaned Jasper to the neighbors by listing Jasper's short comings. Her final insult usually involved a curse upon Jasper and his family.

But no matter what she said Jasper always walked away.

Allegedly, after one of these harangues, Jasper hit Betty in the head with a blunt object and dragged her down the alley and across Mirror Lake Drive. Then he threw her in the lake, where she sank and ultimately drowned after her head was held under water by her assailant.

There was no witness to the event.

But Jasper was the natural suspect. He had the motive to kill Betty. Betty was a harpy and she finally pushed him too hard.

Jasper was interviewed by the police after a body floated up from the lake and was identified as that of his girlfriend. Jasper was polite and answered all the questions put to him by the detective. He did not admit killing Betty, although he admitted she made him so mad that he sometimes considered the possibility that he would hit her. He did not remember striking her. But he might have done so. He was not sure.

None of the neighbors heard or saw the crime or observed any efforts that had been made to conceal the crime. There was no evidence of a fight in the couple's apartment. There was no weapon found, but Jasper had scratches on his face and chest and the police found a wet T-shirt and shorts in the bathroom in the garage apartment. Jasper told the police he thought he had done some yard work for the man up front. He thought he may have gotten the scratches on the purple-flowered Bougainvillea plant he was asked to trim. Jasper thought he had gotten the T-shirt and shorts wet in a rain storm.

The police saw the evidence differently. The scratches on Jasper's chest came as Betty was desperately trying to survive and Jasper's clothes became wet when he forced her head underwater to drown her.

When asked directly if he killed Betty, Jasper equivocated and said, "I don't think so."

As soon as Jasper's son's check in the amount of $25,000 cleared Tom's trust account, two days after Jasper was arrested, Tom went for a visit at the jail with his investigator, Anthony Stewart. Tom got the same responses from Jasper that the police detective had received. Jasper did not know what happened to Betty. He admitted he had many reasons to kill her. She treated him badly and called him out when he was bad and embarrassed him in front of his neighbors. But otherwise, Jasper said he didn't think he had it in himself to commit a murder, even when the victim was as foul and mean as Betty.

After the interview, Tom had his client give his investigator the names and addresses of all the neighbors who had witnessed the activities of Betty and Jasper in the year leading up to the discovery of her body in Mirror Lake.

Tom's impression was that the State could not prove the charge the Grand Jury brought against Jasper, which was Murder in the First Degree. Tom didn't believe a jury would convict Jasper of that crime. Maybe the crime of manslaughter would be appropriate, but from what he heard, Tom thought that maybe the jury would thank Jasper for releasing the world from the shrew.

Tom had another client early in his career with a similar situation involving a mean victim who terrorized the defendant. The client and three buddies were playing cards outside in the sun near the Snow Peak Soda Fountain on 22nd Street South. The jury knew this area was in the heart of "Colored Town". One of the players began to berate Tom's client, then pulled a small gun and began shooting. The shooter missed and the client ran home and got his rifle and shot and killed the other man about an hour later. The client claimed self-defense.

The State said he couldn't wait an hour to shoot the man, and besides he should have called the police and not taken the law into his own hands. The client claimed the now dead man would have killed him eventually, and he was defending himself from the future attack. Tom refined the argument and told the jury that the attack was "preemptive in nature". The State objected and argued to the jury that there was no such defense as preemptive attack. The all-white jury disagreed. They were convinced the South Side of St. Petersburg was a war zone and that "self-defense" could be stretched a bit. The jury found the client guilty of manslaughter and the judge gave Tom's client five years.

Tom felt a jury would see Jasper's case in a similar vein. Jasper didn't have a true defense, but he had a good argument that he was provoked by the victim. Tom felt the jury would reduce the charge so the judge could not impose the death sentence or a mandatory 25-year sentence on his client for Murder in the First Degree.

That was Tom's plan. He would also ask Roger to help him with a motion to be presented to the court after the State rested their case. Tom didn't see there was any evidence of premeditation. Tom liked Roger. Maybe Tom would replace Marla with an associate attorney. Roger was the perfect candidate.

Chapter 28
Jimmy Passes

The Old House at Plantation #7 had a zinc roof. The roof extended over the eaves of the main house and covered the porches that surrounded the home. The house was built in the early 1880s by a family that planted the orange grove and then went bust and returned north. The Barnes family had taken over in 1902 and filled the large two-story house with heavy upholstered furniture, and books and mahogany flooring, and solid wood tables and chairs, cabinets and desks. The ground floor contained the parlor, the library, the dining room, and kitchen. However, most of the living was done on the porches, which were screened to keep out the insects but allow the cool breezes from the river to flow into the downstairs and up to the second floor where there were four bedrooms and three baths. One bath had a barber chair.

Marla stayed with Bea and Frank at the farmhouse until the Senator was able to move to the nursing home. It took him a few weeks. He was procrastinating, hoping he did not have to leave his home, that a miracle would occur and his diabetes would be cured. But when a new foul-smelling sore erupted on the inside of his left ankle, he knew it was time. He had a small writing desk and a chair that he would carry to the nursing home. He intended to write his life's story. He had an old Packard four-door motor car that he loaded with a few things and he was off.

Marla filed the deed titling the Old House in her name with the Clerk of Court for Volusia County. It was official, she now owned the house. Marla moved in and set up her office in the library. Tom had given her a desk and chair from his law office. She went to work managing the affairs of the Plantation and the Trust that controlled the land and business. Marla knew Frank and Bea as Tom's clients. Now she was involved in their business and she wanted them to be comfortable with her.

Frank, Bob and Albert were gone most of the time, overseeing the various pieces of land and the mills scattered throughout the southeast United States. Marla saw that no one was handling their travel and itineraries. Making travel plans was simple for Marla; she had handled that duty for Tom. So Marla added the men's travel plans to her scope of work. She could do it by phone. By handling travel, Marla knew what the men were working on, the problems they were having with particular operations, and how long they were going to be needed at a particular location.

Marla also made sure she saw Bea and Jenny once a week.

Bea was an open book and immediately began to unload her worries and concerns for her family and her business. Bea realized the dairy was dragging the Homestead down financially. She also knew what needed to be done to resolve the problem. She had to get rid of the loans owed to the bank. To accomplish that, she needed to sell the dairy to the co-operative.

Marla did not share with Bea the secret Tom had revealed, that Bea wouldn't sell the dairy because Bea believed the dairy was Jimmy's source of life. Marla did not push Bea for information. She just listened and if she could help, she offered her help.

All of the family began to rely on Marla. In particular, Bea relied on her. Bea was worried. Marla told her to be patient. "Everything will work out."

***

Jimmy passed seven months after Marla had moved to the East Coast of Florida. Though emotionally drained by the death, Bea was able to participate in the funeral and the viewing and graveside services. The local Catholic priest officiated. Jimmy had been baptized in the church. He had received Extreme Unction when he was born and the priest was able to arrive at the farmhouse just in time to give the Last Rights again before Jimmy died in Bea's arms.

After the burial, when Bea was home alone after Frank had left the house the first time on business, Marla received a phone call from Jenny.

"Mom has fallen out," said Jenny.

Marla understood that to mean Bea had fainted. Jenny did not drive. Marla drove to the farmhouse and transported Bea and Jenny to the hospital in Daytona. The doctor gave Bea a sedative. Marla knew Bea would need more than a pill. She contacted Frank and told him Bea had seen the doctor and Marla needed to speak to him privately. Once he was back home, Marla told him the doctor recommended that Frank spend time with Bea, maybe take her on a trip and get her out of the farmhouse and away from the dairy.

Frank talked to Tom and they made plans for Bob and Albert to work together maintaining CCC while Frank and Bea traveled. Tom was to contact the milk co-operative to see if they would purchase the dairy. Tom was to try to sell to the co-op as soon as he could arrange a sale. Meanwhile Jenny would move to the Old House at the plantation with Marla until Frank and Bea returned.

***

The Medical Committee of Halifax District Hospital met to discuss the case of Jimmy Lee Barnes, who was born in 1936 and died on October 31, 1966. The pathologist who conducted the autopsy described an individual who was emaciated and appeared to suffer from starvation. The cause of death was listed in the following order:

"Cardiac Arrest, Myocardial Infarction, malnutrition, Failure to Thrive."

The purpose of the meeting was for the medical committee to confirm the diagnosis and cause of death and determine whether the matter should be referred to the State Attorney for further review and prosecution as a homicide. The pathologist was new to the medical community in Daytona Beach and he was unfamiliar with the case of Jimmy Lee Barnes.

"Jimmy has been my patient for over ten years," said the General Practitioner sitting on the board. "He has always presented in an atypical manner. His mother was 15 years old when Jimmy was born. He was born breach and he was deprived of oxygen during birth – strangulation with the umbilical cord. The obstetrician attempted to use forceps to speed the delivery and the forceps damaged Jimmy's spine causing paralysis to his extremities. The lack of oxygen caused cerebral palsy. Dr. Michael, who saw him from birth until he referred Jimmy to me, was unconcerned with the diagnosis of Failure to Thrive, although we both thought it unusual. Both he and I had visited the Barnes home, which is on one of the last old homesteads in Volusia County, and we felt Jimmy was well cared for by the father and mother. Actually we thought they went overboard in their care. We felt if he was in any other home he would have died very early in life, probably in infancy."

"I am concerned that this patient is a victim of abuse," said the pathologist. "There are cases being reported of Munchausen Syndrome by Proxy, where a caregiver fabricates health problems in those in their care. I wonder if that could be the case here."

"Jimmy Lee Barnes suffered a heart attack and cardiac arrest. He was not poisoned or suffocated nor did he suffer an acute physical injury," argued the general practitioner. "He was not a victim of a mother's psychosis. Bea Barnes is not psychotic."

"I agree that the case is unusual, but the mother was very caring and wanted her child to be normal. She even provided the deceased with companionship. The family adopted three other children. The interaction with those children was normal given the fact that Jimmy never walked or talked or functioned much beyond that of an infant," said the pediatrician. "Further, if this was a case of child abuse, you would see signs of the abuse in the other children, and that was never reported."

The fact there was no abuse reported to the other children took the air out of the allegation.

The chairman of the committee asked if there was any more comment. There was none. "Does anyone want to add a diagnosis of death by homicide to the death certificate?" asked the chairman of the committee.

There was no motion.

"Then the matter is closed," said the chairman.

***

The Senator's left big toe became a concern soon after the sore on his inner left ankle began to fester. The Senator did not trust the doctors in Daytona and he wanted a second opinion. He asked Marla if she would drive him from his nursing home to the specialist in Jacksonville for an exam.

Marla agreed so long as Jenny could go too. She wanted Jenny to drive. She didn't get much practice driving from the plantation to school and back. A long trip at high speed on US 1 was an experience she needed. The Senator wasn't so sure he wanted her driving his Packard. The car, though old, was immaculate and dent free.

"We will drive you to the doctor but you have to abide by my conditions," said Marla. "Jenny has to drive and you can't tell any of your ribald jokes."

The Senator agreed. He was very concerned about his toe. Really, it was his whole foot that looked diseased. Both wounds smelled. The doctors in Daytona had been chipping away, debriding the infection, but it seemed like something more dramatic needed to be done to clear up the wounds. The problem was that the circulation to his lower extremity was insufficient to bring oxygen and healthy blood to his left foot. As a consequence his foot was dying. The Senator knew that if the rotting foot was not removed he would die from sepsis.

***

The situation became obvious as the trio began the drive north. The smell of the wound permeated the car and they had to drive with the windows down.

"Sorry," said the Senator, who sat in the back seat with his foot elevated.

The doctors in Jacksonville were hopeful after the initial examination and blood work and x-rays, but said he had to stay in Jacksonville in the hospital and they were probably going to need to remove the big toe. But first they wanted to begin a course of antibiotics that were new and very expensive.

Marla had the sense to bring checks to prepay the hospital and doctors. Marla arranged with the hospital to have a private phone put in the Senator's room, and she ordered the Jacksonville Herald and the Wall Street Journal to be delivered to his room daily.

Marla explained to the Senator that Bea and Frank were gone and that Bea needed rest. "Do you want me to bring them back home?"

"We'll wait and see how this treatment plays out and then bring them home if it gets much worse," said the Senator as he patted the sheets on his bed with the palms of his open hands. The Senator was trying to be brave but he was worried and he wanted Frank close now, but he understood. "I know Bea needs some time after Jimmy's death." he said.

Marla called Tom and Bob. Bob said he and Albert would be working in the area near the hospital. They had to stop in at the CCC sawmill near Baldwin and they would drop in a day or two at the hospital. All of the Senator's legal affairs had been put in order when Marla was brought on as Trustee.

Tom was still working on the sale of the dairy to the co-op. Progress was being made. Tom spoke with Frank every other day and he would break the news about his father's medical condition and keep him informed as conditions warranted.

The Senator's condition seemed to stabilize once the antibiotics grabbed hold. The doctors then began to debride his foot and apply skin grafts. Treatment would be long and painful. The Senator was uncharacteristically patient.

Marla didn't feel any pressure at the plantation. The workers had been there for many years and each knew their job. They knew the Senator was ill. They also knew he had made provision for the continuation of the business. They wanted to keep their jobs and make the plantation continue to be a success. So they did their jobs and Marla had time to help the Senator. She kept the Packard. It was an asset of the plantation Trust, so as the Trustee, she could use it. She was confident letting Jenny drive her little car, a Ford, so they were able to manage their transportation needs. Jenny was like the little sister Marla never had. It was fun being with her and she had a feeling of accomplishment giving her direction for her life.

Jenny still wanted to go to the University of Florida in pre-law. They visited the school and spoke to an administrator and two law professors on one of the trips to visit the Senator at the hospital. The scholars talked like Tom, Jenny thought. They had the same way of thinking through a problem which was logical and quick. Jenny liked that. They brought an admission application back to the Old House and completed it and mailed it to the admissions department at the university.

***

Three weeks after the Senator was in Jacksonville, Marla made her routine daily call to the Senator. A nurse answered and said he was in surgery. It was not an emergency, she explained. They were trying to debride the wound after the removal of the big toe and place another skin graft over the wound on the toe and the one on the inner ankle.

"Do I need to be there?" asked Marla.

"No need, the surgery is being done with local anesthetic."

Marla thought about it after they hung up and decided to drive north as soon as Jenny returned from school. They arrived in Jacksonville at about 7:00pm. They went to the room and were told to wait outside the surgical suite.

"I don't think this is very good," said Marla.

"You're right about that," said Jenny.

Marla sent Jenny to the pay phones with a couple of rolls of quarters and told her to call Tom and have him call the boys and Frank.

The doctor came out after about two hours and advised Marla and Jenny that the Senator had a heart attack as they were operating and that they could not save him. Marla thanked the doctor and she called Tom.

"He's gone," she said.

"Are you going to bring him back to the plantation?"

"We'll see what Frank wants to do," said Marla.

Part VIII

Mortality Brings Change

Chapter 29
The Senator's Funeral

The Old House was spic and span, cleaned top to bottom to receive guests for the funeral services of Senator Francis Aloysius Barnes. The work in the processing plant was suspended and the citrus grove closed, and the operations of CCC were reduced to a minimum so the workers could attend the services. The Senator was not affiliated with any church or denomination. In fact he never entered a church, synagogue or temple except when he was campaigning for office, and that was years ago.

Bea enlisted the Catholic priest who had officiated at Jimmy's funeral to say prayers at the grave site that was to be located on the property of the Old House on Plantation #7. The Senator's specific request to Marla was that the Senator was to be buried on Marla's property. Marla wasn't sure it was legal, but the sheriff of Volusia County and most of the judges would be at the service, and they could object if they wished. Marla had no objection to the Senator being buried in her back yard. In fact, if the county did not object, she would be buried there too.

Before the Senator's bad toe was removed, he had written notes and instructions to Marla as to his wishes. First the Democrats were in power in Tallahassee and he did not want any State Official specifically invited to the funeral. The Senator was a Republican and he couldn't abide having a Democrat drinking his whiskey at his funeral and wake. If Democrats wanted to come, they could, but no Democrat was to be given a special invitation.

Second, he wanted the house to be open and anyone who wanted to stop by would be welcome. Marla was to put an ad in the News Journal obituary section to that effect. Last, there was a list of names of people who were to be called and invited, although the Senator realized that many of them were probably already dead and buried. These were all friends, most of them were old political comrades who had helped him win election before the Democrats took over and seemed to never let go. The Senator had never gotten over losing an election and once he lost and was "rejected by the people," he would not stand for election again.

Marla told Frank and Bea about the instructions. There was also a will that was in a sealed envelope. The envelope had further directions that the will was to be delivered to Frank "when the time came". Marla figured that was now, since the Senator was dead. Frank said the family would get together with Tom and Marla the day after the funeral and wake and review the will.

Frank was confused about the will since the Senator had established the Trust and Marla was the Trustee and controlled Plantation #7. The Senator also personally owned 70% of the stock of CCC and Frank thought the will may concern those shares. Tom did not know anything about the will because another attorney had been hired to prepare the document.

"I'm just your attorney," Tom told Frank when he was asked about the will. "What do I know?"

***

Able Catering was hired to handle the food and beverages for the wake. Marla told Mr. Able to figure what he would normally need to satisfy 1,000 people and then double the order. Mr. Able followed those instructions. When it was all said and done, Mr. Able still barely had enough to feed and sate the thirst of the crowd of 1,500 who made the trip to the funeral.

When guests arrived at the home they were greeted by the Senator. The Senator's body had been placed in his coffin on the large table in the dining room. The lid of the coffin was open so the Senator could "view the festivities," as his instructions dictated. Some who looked at the body among the knot of people streaming through the dining room thought the festivities were odd. The Senator's old friends thought the display was just like the man—irreverent.

The prayers were said outside in front of the Old House. John Anderson Drive was blocked off for the service and then, as the Senator had instructed, the guests flowed through the house, past the coffin in the dining room and then they were given a libation in the kitchen and directed out the back door to an old live oak tree with a hole dug in front of the tree. Once everyone was outside, the casket was carried to the grave, lowered by rope into the ground and the hole was filled with dirt while the crowd sang, "Amazing Grace".

Then the party began. Jenny tried to keep the men from putting their drinks on the old furniture but Marla ran her out of the house and told her to mingle.

"These will be your clients once you graduate from law school," said Marla.

Jenny got in the swing of things and began to introduce herself and began to understand how the Senator had fit in the lives of the guests. She snuck a glass of red wine and enjoyed it thoroughly.

Frank, Bea, Bob, and Albert had staked out a section of the front porch and they greeted visitors as they entered the Old House and proceeded through the living room to the dining room for the viewing and then into the kitchen and out the back porch to the oak tree and the grave. Most people just said hello. The visitors did not know Frank as he and Bea married so young and moved to the farmhouse and concentrated all their efforts on Jimmy and the dairy, and then on the three children they adopted. But all the visitors knew the Senator and were there to pay their respects and quench their thirst.

As the gathering swelled to a count of over 1,500 souls, Marla instructed Tom to drive into Ormond and buy at least five more cases of liquor.

Tom was antsy with all the booze swirling about and he had become sorely tempted to drink. He looked at the trip into town as a way to tramp down the desire for "just one drink". Marla told him to take Albert to help. Marla knew Albert would keep an eye on Tom and make sure he did not stray and find himself in a bottle at the end of the day.

***

The event was successful, well attended and there were no fights. After the last die hard was ejected, the family gathered in the parlor of the Old House. They were tired but laughing, relating some of the stories they had been told by the guests about the Senator in his younger years.

It was late now, but Frank decided to have Tom read the will. They called the meeting to order. Everyone agreed Marla should be present. She was almost family and in any event she would be affected by whatever was contained in the will, and Tom was there and he could explain it.

The will turned out to be a pour over will. The Senator transferred all his assets including the 70% ownership in CCC to the Trust controlled by Marla, not to Frank as had been anticipated. The will also identified an asset that none of the family or Tom or Marla were really familiar with. The Senator had purchased a company called Belize Resources for $250,000. There was a brief description of the asset in the will. The family was aware Frank had purchased 600,000 acres of land in British Honduras. Now they found out he also controlled licenses to remove timber, naval stores from pine trees, and gum resin from the sapodilla tree in the Central American country.

The effect of the devises to the Trust was to make Marla the primary decision maker for the family so far as CCC was concerned. Before the Senator died, he had deferred all decisions regarding CCC to Frank, and Frank had 100% decision making authority but only "until the death of Francis Aloysius Barnes". Frank had assumed that at his father's death all the CCC stock would be devised to him. The way the will was written, Marla would control the Trust, which would mean Marla controlled 100% of Plantation #7 and 70% of CCC. The only assets Marla did not control were the Homestead and the dairy, which were owned and controlled by Bea, and the 30% of CCC controlled by Frank.

Although Marla controlled a majority interest in CCC and the Plantation through the Trust, she was not a beneficiary of the Trust. The beneficiaries were Frank, Bea, Bob, Albert and Jenny. Each of the Family members was a 20% beneficiary.

After the will was read, there was a lot of uncomfortable movement within the group. The body language showed frustration. Tom knew someone would say something stupid that they would regret later and he suggested that they all go home, think over the effect of the will, and revisit the matter in a week. They all agreed.

Chapter 30
A Fly on the Wall

Jenny, Tom and Marla sat in the parlor of the Old House as the crew from Able Catering tried to retrieve all of their bar glasses and pick up the trash at the plantation. Frank, Bea, Albert, and Bob had driven home to the farmhouse. Tom asked the cleaning crew to concentrate on the parlor so they could close the doors and have some privacy. Marla told Tom to just relax and sit down.

"You are getting to be an old man, Tom. Leave these people to their jobs."

"Why do you think the Senator transferred all the stock to the Trust to Marla's control?" asked Jenny.

"He didn't talk to me about it," said Tom. Tom was visibly put out that he was not consulted.

"I think he had his reasons," said Marla as she picked up all the ash trays in the room and put them in a box and gave them to the custodian. "I can't stand the smell of smoke."

"Well, whatever his reason, I don't think he made Dad or Mom or the boys happy. They looked shocked," said Jenny. "You were smart to suggest that everyone go home and think things over before they opened their mouths. I thought Albert was going to say something. He got all red in the face."

"It will be an interesting ride home for those four, that's for sure."

"As soon as the caterer has the downstairs picked up we can talk. I can't believe how many people showed up," said Marla.

"Do you want me to help the crew?" asked Tom.

"Sit down, Tom."

***

Frank pulled the car into the driveway and let everyone out. Bob helped his Mom in. The living room was full of suitcases and a trunk of clothes. Frank and Bea had made it as far as Grand Rapids, Michigan, on their tour of the boundary of the United States and Canada when they were contacted by Tom and told that the Senator had died. They went to Chicago with the rental car and shipped the luggage back by rail and flew from Chicago. They got home before their luggage and the luggage had been delivered while they were at the funeral service and now it was in the living room.

Frank would not let his sons talk about the news in the will during the ride home. Bob and Albert instead talked about the stock car races on the South Beach in Daytona. This was the last year for the auto races on the beach. There was a new track that was built west of Daytona on US Highway 92, on land the Barnes family sold to the race car company, NASCAR.

Once home, Albert was anxious about the fact that there would be a change in control of CCC.

"We don't know that it will make any difference in our lives," said Bob, laughing. "In fact, as I see it, we are still the beneficiaries of the Trust, so we get the money without the hassle of working."

"I don't think that is what the Senator had in mind," said Frank. "He was telling us he didn't think we were going in the right direction. He thinks Marla will move the company the right way. I'm willing to think it over. Dad's death gave us a reprieve. We can think it over and see what our options are."

"Ok," said Bea, "time for bed."

Bea followed Albert upstairs and into his bathroom. It had been her practice to give him his evening dose of Risperdal when she was home. She went to the medicine cabinet. The pills were in separate pieces of foil in a package. It didn't look like Albert had been taking his medicine since she and Frank had been traveling.

"Have you been taking your medicine?"

"I don't need it anymore. I feel fine," said Albert.

"Did the doctor tell you that you don't need to take it?"

"No, I just feel so much better without taking it. It makes me fat."

"No it doesn't."

"I'll never find a girl if I'm fat."

"You're beautiful Albert, and the smartest one of the bunch. You'll find a girl." She hugged him. "Let's take that pill." She poured a glass of water and gave him the pill and the glass.

Albert took his medicine and said, "Thanks, Mom. I'm glad you're back. Bob is a terrible cook."

When Bea went downstairs, she said nothing to Frank about the fact Albert had not been taking his Risperdal for the schizophrenia. She told herself she was right about the trip. They should never have gone on vacation. She was needed at home.

***

Jenny had fallen asleep in the large upholstered chair in the parlor. Her feet were up on an ottoman and Marla had covered her with a blanket. For mid-Florida in the fall, it was chilly. Tom had put a few logs on the fire and was coaxing coals from the logs with used paper napkins from the wake. The logs finally caught and the parlor warmed quickly.

Marla was on the couch and Tom moved over to sit next to her. Marla looked at him. Tom understood the look and moved and sat in a chair by himself.

"There are three entities the family is involved with. The dairy operation, the plantation and the timberland," said Marla.

"Correct," said Tom.

"Of the entities only one makes a clear profit and that is the plantation."

"Correct, the dairy is close to bankruptcy. The bank expects the dairy and the milk processing plant to be sold to the milk co-operative. That will leave the homestead land and the farmhouse free and clear."

"Would the homestead be profitable if it kept the cows and milking parlor and operated as a dairy and became a member of the co-operative and sold its milk through the co-operative like all the other dairies? I mean, they would keep the dairy but sell the processing plant," said Marla.

"I don't know. I think it would as long as it didn't have the expense of the large packaging plant and the operations that produce the milk and cream products and then loads the containers on the freight cars and semi-trucks for delivery throughout the South. The problem with the dairy is that it got too big and Bea couldn't handle it. She was good at paying bills but she couldn't run a factory and manage a wholesale operation to sell all the product. And then there were the price controls on the milk imposed by the government. That was the last straw."

"So you think it's possible that if the factory operations, sales and shipping functions were eliminated, the dairy-just the acreage, the cows and a milk parlor-would be profitable?" asked Marla.

"I think so. Frank will know the answer to that," said Tom.

"Let's discuss the timber operations. CCC – describe what it is."

"CCC began as about 40,000 acres of land with a sawmill near Deland. Then CCC entered the government contract to produce lumber for the spaceport. CCC purchased the land and established the sawmill in Mims. Then over time Frank purchased timberland throughout the southeast. He always had good lines of financing, since his father relinquished control to him after the Senator got into credit problems. Frank always presented the banks with a plan that shows exactly how he intends to pay the loan off. The banks trust him and they loan him what he needs."

"Is CCC sound?"

"Frank and Albert think it is. Bob and I think it is stretched thin and if there is a downturn in the economy that affects home building in the northeast, CCC will be in trouble. CCC entered the government contract with NASA, which was very profitable. Since then, CCC has relied on the home building industry for sales and profit. CCC ships its timber to New Jersey and then it is allocated among large builders like Levitt Homes, which builds track homes in the suburbs in the North. CCC is able to provide factory pricing and CCC's business model is the standard in the industry."

"Your concern is if there is a recession it will affect home building and then CCC could fail?" asked Marla.

"Correct. America's core economy depends on the production and sale of homes, cars and appliances. If there is a recession, any company involved in those industries will be hurt first and longest. To prepare, CCC has to get very small. I would say no bigger than the Deland and Mims operations plus the new north Florida operation, because those operations are not dependent on the American consumer, but mainly on the supply of lumber to the government. If CCC does not get small, CCC has to become very big."

"Why big?" asked Marla.

"If a company is biggest, the nation will most likely not allow it to fail. All of the other major industries and the government will prop it up."

"Can CCC become the biggest, a necessity for the US economy?"

"Frank and Albert think so. Bob and I do not," said Tom.

"How long do we have?" asked Marla.

"Not long," said Tom. "You do not have time to grow CCC into a position of power where it is immune from a recession."

"Are there any other markets besides home building and the government?"

"Bob thinks the bird watchers may want to buy some of the land," said Tom.

"Do you mean conservation and environmentalists?" asked Marla.

"Yes, the conservationists are looking at wetlands in the southeast. To me that's swamp land. Most timberland has some swamp so some CCC property would qualify as environmentally sensitive land," said Tom.

"What about the British Honduras Company? What is that all about?" asked Marla.

"We'll have to find out," said Tom. "I think it's probably one of those things the Senator did when he was three sheets to the wind. But you never know."

"Well, I think we need to meet with the family as soon as possible. Can you stay this week until we agree to a plan?"

"Yes," said Tom. "The Senator was right putting you in this position. You can break the tie on CCC and push through the sale of the dairy to the co-op. If that is what you believe is best. It will be your decision."

"Help me get Jenny upstairs. You will be down here on the couch."

"That's too bad," said Tom.

Chapter 31
The Director's Meeting

The notice for the consolidated meeting of CCC, Plantation #7, and the homestead/dairy was delivered by courier to comply with the notice requirements in the corporate bylaws. Marla had asked Frank and Bea if they could use the dining room in the farmhouse to conduct the proceedings. Bea thought a meeting at the Homestead would be appropriate because that is where the business interests of the family had begun.

The conversation with Bea helped Marla anticipate the mood of the members of the family. Bob and Frank were open to any new ideas. Albert wanted to hold what they had and build on what existed. He was consistent in his thinking, at least, thought Marla. Bea assured her that Albert was taking his medication. Marla thought about excluding Tom, Bob, Jenny and Albert from the meeting, but she was afraid Albert could become more disruptive outside the meeting than in.

Marla had typed out an agenda and she had her presentation typed into an abbreviated form. She copied her talking points so they would be available for discussion.

***

The meeting opened. Bea gave a little speech about the importance of cooperation and attention to everyone's ideas and point of view. Everyone was polite and listened.

Frank said he thought that his father was trying to be helpful placing his CCC stock in the Trust. He felt the family had been hitting a wall and needed some new ideas, but asked that Marla take advantage of the ground work that he and Bob and Albert had already plowed, so they would not repeat the same mistakes or waste time.

Albert wanted to say that he was sorry his grandfather had not chosen his father to be the Trustee. He was concerned that Marla would not be able to understand the business, but he had promised his father that he would give Marla a chance.

***

Five hours later the family had agreed with the following business plan:

1. The family was to explore all possibilities of sale of all timberland except the land in Deland, Mims and Live Oak. The properties CCC would retain were not dependent on the home building industry in the Northeast US for sales. CCC would continue to operate the sawmills and the trucking and logistic systems that delivered the finished lumber product to New Jersey.

Once the anticipated recession occurred, they would revisit the purchase of timberland in the Southeast using the cash they had acquired from the timberland sales. They could possibly find some good bargains in a recession. For the present, CCC would try to save as much cash as it could, to weather the storm.

2. Bob would explore sales of environmentally sensitive lands to conservation interests and try to identify any endangered species, rookery, migratory flyway, or animal habitat, that existed on the land that would be of particular interest to the environmentalists. Albert was to use his skill to re-analyze all CCC lands to determine what CCC land was swamp or wetland that could be animal habitat or watershed. Marla was to re-establish her contacts with the US Government to see if there were any other government contracts CCC could bid on so they could diversify their sales for the product CCC was producing in its sawmills in the Southeast.

3. CCC would be managed by Albert and Bob and Marla jointly, and they would meet weekly. Everyone agreed that CCC could

bring the family down. They had to reduce their exposure to debt. At the time of the meeting, CCC owned 500,000 acres of land and owed $100,000,000 to the banks.

4. Tom would go to British Honduras and see what "Belize Resources" was and if it was worth anything.

5. Frank would manage the homestead and the dairy. He would try to determine if the farm acreage and the herd of Milking Devon cows and the milking parlor could be spun off from the dairy, if that business unit would be profitable long term, and if the cooperative would purchase the processing and logistic assets only. They agreed that would simplify the co-op's due diligence and hopefully speed up the closing of the sale. It seemed like the bankers were delaying the sale to allow the bank to collect interest and fees from the operation now that the bankers knew there was a probable sale and their loans would be paid in full.

6. Bea would manage Plantation #7. She would work on improving the tourist trade by inviting more boat traffic to the riverfront. Otherwise she would make no changes without approval of the board.

7. The accounting for all three businesses would be handled by the same firm and the CPAs would produce a consolidated statement for information purposes so the board would not delude itself as to the viability of the overall business plan.

The meeting was adjourned.

Bea had fixed a roast with oven baked potatoes and greens. The group ate wholeheartedly.

***

The first trial for Tom's associates went quick.

Tom's new associate, Roger Adams, had addressed the court. Now, it was the State Attorney's turn.

"So, Mr. Hale, how do you respond to Defense Council's argument that the State has failed to offer any proof of premeditation in the case against Jasper Lee Smiley?"

"Well, Mr. Adams is just wrong. If you consider the testimony of the Medical Examiner, the victim in this case was drowned. A human being does not drown quickly, it takes some time. The Medical Examiner testified it would take a matter of minutes and during that time; the defendant would have to struggle with the victim, holding her head below the water so she could not breathe. There was also testimony that the defendant had scratches on his face and arms, and the victim's fingernails were broken from her efforts to survive the murderous assault. The court should be reminded; Mr. Smiley had numerous deep scratches on his arms and shoulders. The defendant would be aware of the victim's distress and her fight for oxygen for a period of minutes and he would know he was in the process of extinguishing her life. Thus, the manner of the death is evidence in itself that there is premeditation. Ample evidence of premeditation," said the prosecutor, John Hale.

"I agree there is sufficient testimony in the record for the case to go to the jury for a decision on the element of premeditation," ruled the judge.

The judge looked around on his desk for his book of jury instructions. He then turned to the defense table and said, "Mr. Adams, I will give you a few minutes to decide if you will call any witnesses. Court is adjourned for 15 minutes."

The courtroom emptied. Tom, Roger and Mr. Smiley sat at the defense table with the sheriff's deputy a short distance away, yet out of ear shot.

"I think we should put Mr. Smiley on the stand," said Roger.

"I don't think so," said Tom.

"He says he will testify that he didn't assault or strangle Miss Smith."

"If Jasper testifies he will be subject to cross examination by Mr. Hale, The detective testified he told the police he 'might have' committed the assault. Hale would make a liar out of our client."

Tom turned to Mr. Smiley. "Do you want to take the stand, Mr. Smiley?"

"Well, no I don't. But I will if I have to," said Mr. Smiley.

"You will have to tell the truth if you take the stand," said Tom.

"Will they ask me if I killed Betty?"

"Yes they will," said Tom.

"Then I don't think you should put me on the stand."

"Why?"

"As the trial has gone on, I have been remembering things better and I believe I killed Betty. At least I remember hitting her in the head and dragging her to the water. I don't remember pushing her head under the water, though. I don't think I had it in me to drown her."

Tom looked at Roger.

"Ok, we can't put him on the stand," said Roger. "I agree."

"Roger, when the judge comes in just tell him the defense rests," said Tom. "Are you ready for your closing argument?"

Roger nodded and looked at the pages of notes in his hands. Tom took the notes from Roger.

"Don't use notes. Speak from your heart. Go to the bathroom and wash your face." Tom wondered if he should let Roger present final argument to the jury. He has to learn sometime. Sink or swim, thought Tom.

***

Roger's closing argument:

"Members of the jury, Mr. Smiley thanks you for listening to the evidence in the case.

"The judge will tell you, as he has done a number of times that the State has to prove Mr. Smiley unlawfully caused the death of Betty Jane Smith, and the State has to prove each element of the crime of Murder in the First Degree beyond a reasonable doubt. Further, the State has to prove guilt through evidence presented in trial. You cannot speculate or guess Mr. Smiley is guilty. It must be proved to your satisfaction by competent evidence that he is guilty.

"But what has the State offered you as evidence? Did anyone testify they saw Mr. Smiley kill Miss Smith, or that they saw him touch her or did they present evidence he was even with her? No they have not.

"The State is trying to prove Mr. Smiley killed Betty Jane Smith simply because he had a motive. The motive was that she was mean to him the day of her death. But neighbors, who testified to the fact that she was mean the day she was killed, also testified that Betty Jane Smith was a mean, awful and harsh shrew. The neighbors said she was that way every time she drank, and she drank every day.

"And remember, the neighbors testified she wasn't just mean to Mr. Smiley, she was mean to everyone when she drank. So does Miss Smith's personality offer a motive to Mr. Smiley to the exclusion of all other people who may have come into her presence on the day she was killed? Of course not. Use your common sense. The woman appears to have been so vitriolic that no one could stand her. Sorry to say, that was the testimony.

"What else has the State presented to you to prove that Mr. Smiley and no other person on earth murdered Betty Jane Smith? The State points to the scratches found on his body and the wet clothing in the bathroom. The question for the jury is whether the scratches and the wet pants and shirt prove guilt to the exclusion of every reasonable doubt."

"On cross examination we asked, and the police admitted, that it rained the day Miss Smith's body was discovered. Mr. Smiley told the police his clothes got wet in a rainstorm when he was doing yard work for his landlord. Therefore the wet clothes have an innocent as well as a guilty connotation. The clothes became wet when Mr. Smiley strangled Betty Smith or they were wet by the rain. Either explanation is reasonable.

"But by law if both explanations are reasonable you have to give Mr. Smiley the benefit of the doubt and find that the clothes were wet by the rain shower.

"The landlord also testified that he asked Mr. Smiley to cut back the bougainvillea bush in his front yard. The landlord testified he asked Mr. Smiley to cut the bush because it had so many thorns and he did not want to be scratched. Mr. Smiley told the police the scratches on his arms and neck came from the thorns on the bougainvillea. Did the State offer any explanation that Mr. Smiley's statement was false? Is the explanation for the scratches on Mr. Smiley's arms and neck reasonable? If it is reasonable you have to give my client the benefit of the doubt.

"Last, the State argues that Mr. Smiley admitted he killed Miss Smith. But is that true or did he merely raise the question that he may have killed her? Does his statement that he 'might have' killed Miss Smith offer proof beyond and to the exclusion of every reasonable doubt that he killed her or only that he might have killed her?

"We would argue that if Mr. Smiley's statement only raises the possibility that he killed her and does not exclude the possibility that someone else killed her, then in that event, that you should find Mr. Smiley not guilty because the crime has not been proven to have been committed by Mr. Smiley beyond a reasonable doubt."

"Thank you for your attention."

***

Tom and Roger and Jasper were sitting at the bar at the Princess Dianne. The barman brought Tom the phone.

"She says it's Marla," said the bartender.

"Marla. Is that you?"

"How did it go?"

"Here," Tom handed the phone to Jasper.

"Hello, this is Jasper."

"Who?" asked Marla.

"Jasper Lee Smiley, I'm Tom's client."

"Were you found not guilty?"

"Yep."

"Tell Tom to call me later," said Marla. "Tell him to stay sober."

"Yes, ma'am," said Jasper.

Part IX

Marla's Reign

Chapter 32
Corporate Action Recorded

It had taken three weeks for Marla, Bob, and Albert to complete their assignments for CCC.

Marla had contacted her former boss, who was the head of procurement for the US Government in the Southeast US. She was told the Southeast and the Northeast were awash in building materials made of pine timber. There were some contracts in the Northwest where the market was still tight. China and the US military in Viet Nam were competing for timber from the old growth forests in Washington and Oregon. In the Southwest, including Arizona and New Mexico, there was a brisk market for 2 X 4's and 2 X 6's to construct one-story houses. These two western states were the newest members of the Sun Belt, which was popular with retirees. There was no central purchasing hub in those states, however, to which CCC could make deliveries of timber supplies. Otherwise, the government was not looking for wood in excess of its present contracts. Marla was relieved when she was told by her government contacts that the timber contracts CCC held in Mims and Deland would be good for many more years.

Marla was given a tip that the government was dissatisfied with the timber supplier for the Oak Ridge Facility in Eastern Tennessee. Marla immediately bid on that contract and CCC was awarded the contract. The CCC sawmill near Savannah, in Riceboro, Georgia, could supply the Department of Energy facility in Tennessee. The Riceboro plant was one of the sawmills that Frank worried CCC would have to shutter. That mill provided 75 good-paying jobs to the middle of Georgia. Georgia seemed to be going into recession and Riceboro was happy to keep the jobs at the mill.

Over breakfast of eggs over-easy, country ham, grits, and wheat toast with guava jelly, (served up by Jenny), Bob, Albert, and Marla sat down and conducted their meeting.

Albert always went first. He had reviewed all of the stereo photographs of the CCC timber lands. He broke the land into categories. 1. Pine upland, 2. Pine Plantation, 3. Wetlands, Natural Growth. 4. Hardwood, and 5. Cypress.

Albert also had a special designation for "Open Water," that included oceans, rivers, streams, ponds, lakes and swamps. Albert had also searched for parts of the wetlands that abutted or were contiguous to park and recreation, or preservation, or environmentally sensitive lands. An example of the latter was a CCC property that was shaped like a perfect circle with a ten-mile diameter. The property was swamp land full of mature virgin cypress and hardwood. The land was underwater all year long. It was not dependent on rain but was fed by a wide stream that kept it wet and nourished the trees. Geologists identified the hole as a crater left from the collision of an asteroid with the earth.

A group from the Audubon Society wanted the property because there had been sightings of Ivory Billed Woodpeckers in the swamp. This bird was the most magnificent bird in the swamps of the Southeast and was thought to be extinct. Once there were thousands of the large birds, but then one day, as the last old wood swamps was cut of their mature virgin cypress and hardwood, the Ivory Billed Woodpecker was gone.

Albert found numerous references to the ten mile crater in ornithological journals. The bird watchers had been unsuccessful keeping quiet their desire for the property. There were numerous sightings of a pair of the birds by amateur birders in this swamp. The University of Arkansas sent a team to try and photograph the birds to assure the birding community that they were not extinct. The two-person team stayed in a blind in the middle of the swamp for two winters after the leaves from the cypress and bay trees had fallen. Because the trees were bare in winter, that season would be the best time to record evidence of the birds.

The scientists both claimed to have seen the birds, but were unable to obtain a photograph. They did sight a number of Pileated Woodpeckers that were probably the source of some of the sightings by novice birders. But the Pileated Woodpecker, though similar to the Ivory Billed, was smaller than the Ivory Billed bird and the coloration was different. An expert would not mistake an Ivory Billed for a Pileated Woodpecker. According to Albert's research, there was an effort by the society to set aside enough money to buy the ten mile swamp on the chance the bird was still alive, and to give nature or science a chance to save this beautiful bird.

Marla was familiar with the ten mile crater swamp. The Senator had told her the land was special, and they should not cut the trees, and they should hold it. The Senator told Marla that she would know when to sell it. He told her it had an intrinsic value far greater than the value of the trees and the dirt. Marla now understood what the Senator meant. She asked Bob and Albert if she could explore the sale of the property. It was ok by them.

Marla also explained the information she had from the successful bid from Oakridge.

"Great news," they said.

Bob thought maybe they should open a sales office and send out representatives searching for new buyers rather than waiting for the buyers to knock on CCC's door, which was the typical marketing approach in the industry. Maybe they could even advertise in newspaper classifieds. An apartment complex would need truckloads of timber. The contractors for big jobs were from the main cities in the South, and they bid jobs in big and small towns. The trio decided to send Bob on the road to see if these contractors would buy direct from the mill. CCC could offer a discount for these sales.

When Jenny said lunch was ready, the trio saw they had been at it for six hours. Bob and Albert had to leave early. They had free tickets to the stock car races on the beach and it would take an hour to drive there.

"No time for lunch." They were off.

Marla coordinated the ideas that were discussed, put them on paper, and sent them on to Frank, Bea, and Tom. In the letter, she advised that she was going to contact the Audubon Society and the scientists who sat in the blind the last two winters waiting for the birds to appear. Those would be the best sources to drum up a buyer for a sale of the ten mile swamp.

Marla also advised about the bid at Oakridge, that the contract would keep the Riceboro, Georgia, mill busy for two years. She reported that on Bob and Albert's advice, that she would have Bob concentrate on factory direct sales in the South to large building contractors. Albert would work with her doing research.

***

The Beach stock car race was held once a year on A1A near Ponce Inlet, south of Daytona. The race organizers created an oval track by running the cars on A1A south for two miles and then the race cars came to the south turn that took the cars to the beach and the cars ran on the beach north for two miles and then came to the north turn that the cars took to connect to A1A and then the race was headed south again. Thus by incorporating the road, the beach and two turns cut through the sand dunes there was an oval-shaped race track. The cars were allegedly "strictly" stock cars, but the drivers and their friends souped the cars up. The cars were nothing like a car you could purchase on a show room floor. This was the last year the race would be held on the beach track. In the future, it would be held on a tri-oval shaped track built near US Highway 92 in Daytona.

Bob and Albert enjoyed the excitement of the race. Frank normally went with them, but not this year. Spectators could watch from the north or south turn where the promoter erected temporary stands. Otherwise, for a flat fee ($5.00), you could scramble into the palmetto scrub and sit in the sand dunes and watch the race.

Some fans would watch from the side of the track. The cars could reach speeds of over 100 mph in the straightaway on A1A and viewing the race from that vantage on the side of the road was discouraged.

You couldn't spectate properly without a beer, and the concessions made excellent money selling long neck bottles of Buds and Millers from 55 gallon drums filled with chipped ice and loose bottles of beer.

Drinking alcohol brought brazen activity. Women were hooted by men to remove there tops and expose their white, shiny breasts before re-covering their bodice and pretending to be embarrassed.

Bob and Albert sat in the sand dunes. From the dunes they could watch the action on both straightaways, and if there was a crash they could run and get a good look. The purpose of the race on the beach was sex, thrills, and the possibility of death. The raw experience and excitement spectators felt on the beach race track was never fully replicated once the race was moved to the modern asphalt tri-oval track, in most people's opinion.

Most of the race drivers were from the Southeast US. You didn't have to be the biggest guy or in shape or coordinated to drive a race car. All you had to do was be willing to dare fate and push the accelerator pedal to the floor board and never let up. You had to be crazy.

Some of the drivers were natives of Daytona, or were from the South, but moved to Daytona, because that's where the modern race car was being engineered and manufactured. There were speed shops throughout town where mechanics and tinkerers were exploring how to get the most from high-test fuel, oxygen, and a spark to ignite and push rods and pistons in a 425 cc block of metal to generate faster and faster speeds.

The big three auto makers were involved. The auto industry understood that hormones in men and women in the USA were stirred by speed, and also by the style of the GTO, the Mustang, and the Road Runner, and that the American youth knew the names Petty and Roberts. The men were heroes.

Bob was three years older than Albert and he was more mature than Albert, and Albert, because of his mental disease, had a strange way of viewing things. Sometimes, Albert would say something that would be misunderstood by people who did not know him.

Sometimes, Albert became loud and repeated himself when he was agitated. When a big drunk bumped into Albert in the dunes, Albert had one of those episodes. Bob pulled Albert away from the man who was looking for a fight. Bob intervened and advised the big man that Albert didn't mean anything by calling him a "big ugly brute".

"He's going to pay," said the man, who was the epitome of the big ugly brute one met in Daytona.

The man's friends also intervened and tried to pull him back, but he kept coming forward against the weight of his friends, who were holding onto his shirt and pants.

About then a girl flashed her bare breasts and someone got the brute's attention.

"Look at those boobs," and Albert and Bob were free of the danger.

The big brute was danger in the dunes. There were no police assigned to control the crowd, which was the main reason Bob wanted to stay in the temporary stands at the south turn. Bob got Albert away and they went down to the track and watched the brass band, and mingled with the crowd among the race cars that were parked on the track waiting for the parade of the cars and the green flag. A few of the drivers wore seat belts and some wore football helmets. It would be different at the new tri-oval, the drivers would have to have roll bars, and safety features would be strictly enforced.

It would be expensive to race in the future. This might be the last race in Daytona for many of the drivers. Every driver wanted to be enrolled on the list as a man who raced at Daytona, so the field was large and it would take five qualifying races of at least 20 cars per race to determine the cars that would race in the grand finale.

Bob was able to convince Albert to sit in the stands. Bob promised Albert one beer. Albert was of legal age (21), but the doctors and Bea discouraged him drinking because of his condition.

The elimination race began from a moving start. There was a pace car, and the 20 or so cars lined up behind the pace car and followed the pace car around the track for one lap. Then the pace car pulled off the track and the cars were off for the first five lap qualifier. There were no wrecks in the first qualifier. In the second qualifier there was a big crash on the beach just out of the south turn. The wreck occurred right in front of the Barnes brothers as they sat in the stands.

One stock car turned over one and a half times and landed on its roof with its tires spinning. A crowd of men went to assist and pushed the car over on its tires and the car sped off. Bob had a hard time convincing Albert to stay in the stands and not go on the track. The cars didn't seem to stop for anything or anyone, even if there were fans on the race track trying to right a racing machine. After being turned over, the car that had wrecked stayed in the same lap as the other cars but was not able to place in the top four cars in the qualifying race and missed out on making the cut for the 20 car field for the 100 mile, 40 lap grand finale race, which was called the "Grand National Race".

Albert convinced Bob to buy him another beer before the grand finale. There were many people milling about. Bob told Albert to stay in the seats. He had paid extra to keep them out of the trouble in the dunes. It was hard to find someone if you separated.

Bob would buy Albert another beer if he would watch the seats. Albert promised he would stay in the stands.

The promoter had announced there were 11,347 fans at the race. That was the largest gate ever. There were people holding pennants and flags. Some of the drivers had their family members selling autographed, glossy, black and white photos of the driver next to his car. The racers did this for extra money. They had to pay for the car, the tires, and the special racing fuel, and most drivers lost money every time they participated in a race if they didn't have a sponsor, like Ford, Mo Par, or Delco.

The purse for the race for the winning driver was $10,000. Only one man would be paid. There was no runner-up prize. It was just like in life—winner takes all.

The grand finale was a long distance race. A driver had to stay out of trouble on the track and also coax his car through a race that combined a road race with a steeple chase over hard packed sand with dips and pot holes. The favorite racers were a local boy named Roberts, and Petty, from the Carolinas. Roberts drove a red Pontiac and Petty drove a powder blue Plymouth. Their cars were the fastest and they were the best built. They said the Petty Family returned to their home after every race and tore down the car and rebuilt the racer from the ground up and replaced any part that was broken or worn.

Bob walked past both of these cars as he went to and returned from the beer truck. He took a minute to look into the cars and the drivers were sitting inside and talking to the fans, who wished them luck. Roberts was selling his glossy print and Bob bought one for Albert.

When Bob got back to the stands with the beers, Albert was gone. The lady in the seat near theirs said Albert said he was going to the rest room (an open trench behind a sand dune), and he would be back before the race began. Bob knew Albert was back in the dunes. He guessed Albert had become excited watching the wreck in the south turn and he didn't want to be restrained by having to remain in a seat in the stands.

Before the Grand National Race began, Bob convinced the lady in the stands to hold the beers and the photograph, and Bob headed across the track and climbed the sand dune. The dunes supported a field of sea oats, saw palmetto, agave and Spanish bayonets. The plants held the dune in place if the storm surge of a hurricane hit the shore, but the vegetation could not overcome the trampling it was receiving from 11,000 race fans. Once Bob got on the top of the dune about 15 feet above the road grade of A1A he was able to see the large number of people in the crowd and realized he would only be able to find Albert with a lot of luck.

Bob approached the issue logically. What would interest Albert? He would want to see the site of the car wreck on the beach in the south turn. Bob headed that way and as he kept a sharp look out for Albert, he saw the big ugly brute with his friends harassing a young girl and the girl's male friend. Bob hoped these folks stayed where they were and he could get Albert to go in the opposite direction.

When Bob got to the south turn there was evidence of the crash; there was a green fender from a Hornet Motorcar and there was the smell of gasoline and the sheen of oil on the wet sand. As Bob inspected the area, a group of cars came out of the turn and Bob realized he was on the track. The cars missed him. These were the slow cars and they were about to be lapped by the leaders. Bob ran to the ocean and got in the surf up to his knees. He figured if he was in the Atlantic Ocean he was safe. Bob faced the track and watched as about 10 more cars drove by. He watched as they made the two mile distance up the beach until they turned off the beach and could no longer be seen.

Bob retreated back up the dunes and took off his shoes and socks and rolled up his trousers. It was chilly, but sunny. The races during speed weeks were run in February now. It was better for the cars, preventing overheating engines. Bob continued to search and then saw a crowd of 35 or so people. He headed that way and heard the loud voice of his brother, yelling, "Bob, Bob."

Albert was in the clutches of the brute, but the brute was trying to pull away. Albert had the brute by the testicles and he held on and squeezed and pulled for dear life. The brute was finally able to get lose with the help of a friend. He crawled backwards and got on his knees and reached in the front pocket of his lose canvas slacks and pulled out a small Derringer pistol. Albert did not see the gun, but Bob did.

"He's got a gun," said Bob.

"Go ahead and shoot," yelled Albert as he turned to look at the gun. Albert always said the inappropriate.

The gun fired and the single bullet took an upward trajectory. Bob could feel the slug pass through the air and Albert felt the slug hit the top of his left shoulder. The crowd in the vicinity of the fight hushed after hearing the explosion of the .45 caliber shell, and everyone looked to see if they were hit.

The only person who was injured was Albert. Bob saw blood spurt from his shoulder and he pushed his socks into the wound to stop the bleeding.

Two of the men wrestled with the brute and got the gun.

The brute ran away but his friends stayed and waited for the medic to work on Albert's shoulder. The medical work was just part of the sideshow.

Later the police came and the brute's friends gave the police his name.

"What an idiot," they said. "He jumps this guy and loses the fight and tries to shoot him."

It was an open and shut case of self-defense. The crowd all turned on the brute, forgetting they had egged him on all day long.

In all the excitement of the shooting, no one saw the finish of the race.

"Who won the race?" asked Albert as they drove home. Bob didn't know.

***

Worse than facing the police, Bob and Albert had to face Bea and Frank. Their parents had not wanted them to go to the race. If anything bad happened, it always happened to them, or so they thought. And it was Bob's fault. He was older and should have stayed with Albert.

"It was my fault, Mom," said Albert.

"You could have been killed," said Frank.

Bea wanted Albert to move into Jimmy's room because of his injury. "I'm afraid I will lose another one of you. We lost Jimmy and the Senator. Bad news comes in threes."

Albert refused to move into Jimmy's room.

"It's just a flesh wound," said Bob. "I'm going to move in at the plantation."

"No," said Frank. "You may be needed here."

The next day, Bea received a call from the police. They wanted Albert and Bob to come into the station. The brute and his friends had had a change of heart and wanted Albert prosecuted for battery on the brute.

Tom was called and he went to the police station with Albert and Bob. Both brothers were upset that they had to go to the police station, and they were concerned that they could be arrested. Tom asked them to trust him. He did not believe they were in jeopardy. It was difficult for Albert to trust Tom. Tom asked the brothers to say nothing unless he told them to speak, and to listen carefully to what the detective had to say.

After Tom listened to the police explain how bad the brute felt from the injury to his "manhood", Tom showed the police the photo of the bullet wound to Albert's shoulder, which looked worse than it was.

The brute also had a criminal record for fighting and brawling, and public intoxication and assault. Tom had a copy of the rap sheet, which he shared with the police.

Tom left the FBI rap sheet and the photos of Albert's shoulder with the police, and told the lead detective that he would be happy to speak to them in the future if they needed more information.

The three men walked out of the station. The reaction of the men was telling.

Albert said, "Thank you for speaking up for me," and he shook Tom's hand.

Bob said nothing to Tom and had no visible reaction. The police had done their job. Tom had done his job. Enough said.

Tom was oblivious. He was trying to figure out in his head who would pay his fee. He decided to let Karen sort it out.

Marla paid the bill.

Tom never heard another word from the police.

Chapter 33
Creative Thinking

Tank cypress, deadhead logs, and pecky cypress are as expensive as mahogany. Tank cypress and deadhead logs were found sunk in rivers. Loggers used rivers to float rafts of logs to sawmills at the turn of the last century. In the 1800s and early 1900s sawmills were constructed near rivers, and logs were cut near the river and floated to the mills. Some of the logs snagged on the bottom of the river, sank and stuck in the mud in the bottom. Because of the logs' chemical reaction to being submerged in the water, the lumber cut from the dead head logs were immune from rot. The tank cypress also had a purple hue to the wood that was desirable to home builders to cover interior walls in residences. Pecky cypress was desired by decorators because of the natural grain of the lumber produced from logs that contained the "pecky" feature in its grain.

Over half of CCC timber properties had long stretches of river that had been employed by loggers to transport logs to mills. Those rivers had logs sunk in them that had value if they were removed and cut into timber. Those logs also were a navigation hazard to recreational boaters and to navigation for commercial purposes, so the government felt loggers did society a favor removing the logs from the water ways to open the river for commerce and recreation.

While Albert's shoulder healed up, he and Jenny worked in the office at the plantation trying to put together a team of loggers who knew how to grapple the sunken logs out of CCC's riverine corridors. Tom was asked his legal opinion as to the ownership of the logs. Finally, Marla got on the phone to determine just how big the market for the logs would be and where the market was located.

Tom's opinion was that if the river was navigable under Federal law, the river and the logs belonged to the federal government. Marla was used to dealing with the Federal authorities so she would find out if CCC could get a contract to remove the logs. The other river water that was deeded to CCC, for which no state or local government exercised authority, would be CCC's to harvest so long as CCC owned the deed to the river. But Tom was not sure, because there was no legal precedent in the matter and Tom said so in his opinion letter.

Frank said it was a business decision regarding whether to salvage the logs. Essentially, the logs were very valuable and would be inexpensive to remove from the river, and CCC had idle time in its sawmills to cut the timber. They were in a recession. Marla identified a strong market, so they should proceed. Bob agreed, and Jenny and Albert began the operation. It was very successful, resulting in gross profit of just over three million dollars the first year.

Marla knew that the number of logs they could harvest was finite, and the market would become saturated over time with land owners who would imitate CCC and put the logs they pulled from their water on the market, so CCC did not rely on this specialty item for a permanent stream of cash.

But harvesting and cutting this timber was one of the business propositions that allowed CCC to keep its operations profitable, even though the country was definitely deep in a downturn.

CCC also was successful selling manufactured lumber to contractors on a factory direct basis. CCC became the wholesaler and offered volume discounts. The CCC sales force worked in all major US cities and more than paid for itself by generating additional orders for timber.

CCC also added new operations to their sawmills. CCC began to produce plywood where it had land with large diameter at breast height (DBH) timber that could be lathed into veneer. Plywood was made by gluing the pieces of veneer together to make a "board" that was 4' X 8', and the panel was used in construction for sheathing walls and roofs and floors. There were other variations on the 4' x 8' template that were made of wood chips and slivers of wood glued together sometimes called "Aspen Wood". CCC did not venture beyond the addition of the plywood mills where CCC had large DBH trees located on their nearby timber holdings. The Aspen wood mill was too risky.

Marla and Frank also were aware that the timber industry's future included the production of manufactured strand board and structural beams made of pieces of wood fused together using heat and pressure and glue. It was Marla and Frank's intent to participate in the changes in the industry where CCC could find a niche, but otherwise avoid manufacturing and concentrate on growing timber and fiber for the manufacturers.

By being careful, selling mills and property where it made sense, CCC was successful and able to outlast the nationwide recession. Further, the fact that Frank was able to quickly sell the milk processing plant to the co-op and retain the dairy farm operation, released all the CCC operations from the debt of the milk processing plant that was strangling the entire operation.

In fact, CCC was making a good profit, and Marla began to shop to purchase timber acreage. CCC was a buyer in a down market. Marla received solicitations daily from timberland owners wanting to sell. However, Marla saw nothing she thought was worth buying. CCC was not spending every spare dime making mortgage payments to the bank. It was holding cash. It was better to retain cash for an emergency than buy more land.

***

Tom knew he was expected to head for British Honduras. He was able to obtain a response from corporate council for Belize Resource, Ltd. The attorney's name was Herbert John, Esq. He had no International telephone service but he did have a telex communication system, which was similar to a telegraph. A telex user could communicate by a special typewriter connected to a communication cable that ran underwater from the USA to Central America. The cable was operated by Western Union. The machine allowed Tom to communicate internationally regarding the assets and operations CCC owned and operated in the country. It appeared that most of the land was near the coastal plain south of Stan Creek. British Honduras was a small country and its population center was in Belize City. (See map 10) The land to the south was sparsely populated and there was little water that was fit to drink.

The one advantage an American had operating a business in British Honduras was that the official language was English. Tom decided that he needed to visit the country, and he made arrangements to fly there as soon as his remaining murder trial concluded.

***

Michael Grant was 22 years old. He had hitchhiked to St. Petersburg from New York State on his release from Attica State Prison. There had been a riot at the prison two years earlier, and he had an extra two years added to his sentence for allegedly participating in the riot. The only "criminal activity" he engaged in was not remaining in his cell and having been dragged involuntarily into the prison yard, stripped and beaten during the melee.

Grant was a burglar, though not very proficient. By the time he was 18 he had been convicted of committing over 25 daylight, residential burglaries. He had been before the juvenile judge so many times the judge knew his middle initial ("C" for Charles). The judge was sick of him and couldn't think of anything to say to him except: "I sentence you to five years at hard labor."

Attica was for hardened criminals, not 18-year-olds. The system was overrun with criminals who were sentenced for weapons and drug charges. The legislators had discovered mandatory sentences were popular with the voters. But the government failed to provide funding for the new jails needed to house the extra inmates these sentences produced. Therefore, state prison was overcrowded and dangerous.

Grant learned quickly how prison worked and how he could protect himself, and he did what he had to do to survive. In fact, Grant's boyfriend had some influence and Grant landed a job in the library. Grant did research for the writ writers, inmates with legal knowledge who were filing court papers and appeals for other inmates. Some of the writ writers were lawyers who were in prison, most of the time for stealing from their clients.

After the riot Grant served his sentence plus the two additional years for attempted escape. He was released and given $100 and a fresh set of clothes.

Grant and another inmate who was released that morning walked down the road and made it as far as an inn. They rented a room and went to the bar. They had a few drinks and hooked up with two girls and they became friendly. So far as women were concerned, Grant was a virgin and after they were in bed nude he became so excited by the feel of a woman that he reached climax in two strokes.

The woman, named Frankie, laughed. Grant was embarrassed. They tried it again. The experience was pleasurable. Grant thought it was ok with a woman, but he wasn't convinced, so he kept trying. He and Frankie tried all night. Early in the morning, Frankie and Grant snuck out of the room, leaving their partners in bed. Grant stole the man's money, bought a baggie of pot, and they headed out in the dark to hitchhike south. It was winter and cold in New York. The girl had family in Florida.

The first ride got them to Atlanta. They were high on pot the whole way. Frankie drove, and Grant and the car's owner lay out in the back seat giggling and playing. Frankie was upset that Grant ignored her. When they stopped in Atlanta, Frankie stole the car and left the men at a truck stop.

A day later, Grant left the car's owner and headed south alone. He hitched a ride to St. Petersburg and arrived in the daylight hours the next day. St. Petersburg was warm and sunny.

Grant found William's Park downtown near the bay. He was told "his kind" belonged near Spa Beach. As he walked along the road in the downtown near the waterfront parks, Grant got a little male attention and a ride to the beach. There was a sandy shore and cabanas and people lounging in chairs under boldly colored umbrellas. The canvas slapped in the wind.

Grant checked his resources and felt he had enough money to rent a blanket and a towel and he laid in the sun. His pure white torso had not felt the rays of the sun in a cloudless sky for seven years. It was freedom and exhilaration, and then he was asleep.

At 5:00pm the towel boy collected his towel and blanket.

"Can I rent them for the night?" asked Grant.

"You 'crazy, you can't stay here on the beach tonight."

"I don't have a place to stay."

"Go sit on a bench in the park. Someone will take you home."

There were green benches in the park and a restroom they called "Little St. Mary's". A group of young men in their teens, who were mostly freckle faced and skinny, were sitting on the benches with their elbows on their knees. Grant watched the action. Older men would partner up with a boy and go to the men's room for a tryst. One boy seemed very popular and efficient. He would be in and out of the toilet in a flash. Maybe he's selling drugs, thought Grant.

The boy, named Arthur, was friendly to Grant and helped him break the ice with the locals. He arranged for Grant to have a couple of dates in St. Mary's. But Arthur told Grant he had to give him a cut of the fee for the assignation.

"I don't do nothing for nothing," said Arthur.

"Don't you mean 'something for nothing'?" asked Grant, as he gave Arthur a dollar.

"No, I mean nothing for nothing. I would be here anyway. What I do for you is nothing."

Too confusing, thought Grant. He was messed up.

Arthur changed the subject. "Where are you staying tonight?"

"I don't know," said Grant.

"Wait until it's dark and we'll find someone who will take us home with them."

"I'm going to sleep," said Grant as he stretched out on a bench. "Wake me when it's time to go."

Later, after midnight, after the cops had rousted the boys from the benches and the bushes and the door on Little Saint Mary's had been bolted shut, Grant and Arthur went with Arthur's friend Neal to Neal's house on the Southside.

Arthur gave Grant a pill "for energy" as they rode in Neal's Mercedes-Benz, four door sedan (low and sleek) to Neal's house. Grant remembered the front door of the house was painted red and the house had an oriental motif. Otherwise he could remember nothing. When he awoke he was alone and in custody at the St. Petersburg Police holding facility and his head hurt. There was blood on his hands and blood was crusted in his fingernails. Grant smelled like he had been in a fight.

A detective tried to talk to him for hours. Grant told the detective he wanted a lawyer. Grant refused to cooperate in any way with the police, who took his clothes and samples of his blood and photographs of the cuts and bruises on his face and chest.

"What am I charged with?" asked Grant.

"Murder of some guy named Neal O'Day," said the bailiff.

"I didn't murder no one," said Grant. The next morning, he went before the judge and again he refused to talk. The judge sent him to County Jail.

After the hearing the judge called Tom and told Tom he was appointing Tom to represent Grant. Tom said he refused to take another murder case where he wouldn't be paid.

"Give this case to someone else. I can't afford it."

"If you don't take the case I will send a grievance to the Florida Bar. You have an ethical obligation to take the case," said the judge.

"Will I be paid?"

"The County can pay $1,500 toward costs. That's it," said the judge.

"It really isn't right that the state and the courts can force me to take a client who can't pay a fair fee for my services."

"You can file an appeal." The judge was laughing. "Tom, you are rolling in dough. Just put this case in the queue at your office. I hear your girl's do all the work on the cases anyway. This defendant is just another low-life faggot who killed his trick. The case will be a no-brainer. You will make money on the deal."

"I will need Xerox copies of all of the police reports and Pinellas County will have to pay the fee and expenses of my investigator," argued Tom.

The judge agreed. Anthony Stewart, a former police sergeant, worked for Tom as his investigator and the judge agreed to appoint him if Tom took the case.

"Ok," said Tom. "I'll do it."

***

Tom went to the Police Department to speak to Grant that afternoon, accompanied by Anthony Stewart. Grant was cooperative with Tom. He told Tom what he remembered, which was very little. The best Grant could figure was that he had been drugged by his friend Arthur when he was in the Mercedes.

Tom then read the police report out loud to Grant and Anthony Stewart.

According to the police, Neal's boyfriend came home and was confronted by the sight of Grant in bed with Neal. There was a loud fight which alarmed the neighbors and the police were called. The police found Neal dead, bludgeoned to death with a fireplace poker. Grant was unconscious and wounded. Neal's boyfriend was also injured. There was no sign or mention of Arthur in the police reports.

Neal's boyfriend, Simon Marks, was a bank president. Neal was a lawyer. The police all got a big chuckle at the expense of the legal community, Tom figured.

Tom told Anthony Stewart to find and interview Arthur.

Grant said he had a friend. He asked Tom to call his friend in New York. "He will help me," said Grant.

"You need money to pay a lawyer," said Tom.

"You will be paid," said Grant. "Just call my friend."

Tom explained that Grant was not to talk to the police or any inmate about the crime. Tom told Grant he would contact him when he found Arthur. Tom also explained he had to be out of the country for a day or two. He told Grant about Roger Adams, Tom's partner.

"You can talk to Roger if I am gone," said Tom.

Part X

Marla and Bob

Chapter 34
Savannah

Bob Barnes had never sold any product of any kind, but Marla had. Therefore, he spent time with Marla at the plantation for an education in marketing. She had experience in sales, particularly in the sale of large quantities of goods for large amounts of money.

To accomplish a timber sale, Marla suggested to Bob that he needed to present CCC's product in an honest way to a buyer who needed the product; otherwise, you were just wasting time. Using these simple suggestions, Bob became adept at selling wood and finding purchasers for CCC's product. He had a handle on all the product lines available at all of CCC's mills in the Southeast, and he could schedule a delivery of the product quickly and guarantee delivery within a three-day window. CCC was able to guarantee delivery because CCC still owned a fleet of trucks that were coursing throughout the Eastern US, making deliveries of timber to regular long term customers who were under contract.

Eventually, Bob hired a sales team.

Bob's sales team was on the phone from 7:00am to 5:00pm daily EST and Central Time, making cold calls to develop leads, and Bob scheduled appointments to make personal contact with potential buyers. Bob would be on the hunt for business during the week and fly back to Jacksonville on Friday evening. After the weekend, he was back in the plane to the Northeast and Central US on Sunday afternoon.

Marla tried to arrange to pick up Bob at the airport, and deliver him back on Sunday. Bob stayed at the Plantation. Jenny was home from the University of Florida most weekends, and Albert, Frank, and Bea would drop by, so every weekend brought a business meeting.

The group could see that the economy was in a recession, but they were staying ahead of the downturn. CCC had not had to close any mills and the timber harvesting and planting programs established by Frank continued. Frank was still getting inquiries from the president of Thompson Timber Fund about refinancing all of CCC's remaining debt with the Fund. Frank had explained the change in leadership at CCC, and Mr. Thompson wanted to meet with Marla at his offices in Savannah, Georgia.

"I don't want to encourage the man," said Marla. "We don't need to borrow any money."

Bob said he had to be in Savannah the next week, and they could fly in and meet with Thompson. Frank encouraged a meeting and it was set for Friday, and the pair could fly back to Florida that afternoon.

***

Thursday evening, Bob met Marla at the airport. Savannah was an old Southern City that was being rebuilt, preserving all the old buildings. Factor's Row and the City's squares had been preserved and replanted and repaved, and the old iron fountains in the squares had been re-constructed.

Many of the old homes had been preserved, and were refurbished as bed and breakfast hotels. Other houses were now corporate offices for corporations that had operations in the South. Thomas N. Thompson's timber fund was one such firm.

Marla booked two rooms in one of the nice hotels, and had reservations for dinner that night at an eatery down the street that was close enough to walk to. The Fund's office was across the street from the hotel on Bull Street near Lafayette Square

Thursday evening was cold, clear and crisp. A brisk walk to the diner, and then a short conversation in the parlor with a cup of chamomile tea, and the pair were tired from a long week and they were asleep in their separate beds.

***

The next morning over breakfast, and while they waited in the parlor of the hotel, Bob and Marla had a chance to talk.

Marla was interested in what Bob wanted out of life. He said he didn't know. He was just being pushed along, controlled by his environment. He had gone to Frank's school. He worked for the business owned by the CCC Trust. He had tried to help his brother and sister. Now he was 26 and he never thought much about what he should do with his life.

Then it was Bob's turn.

"Is this what you want?" asked Bob.

"I had wanted a family and children, but that's not likely now that I am 38," said Marla. "But I am very satisfied to be in this business with your family."

"Do you feel you are in control?" asked Bob. "You never give orders."

"I've never had to exercise control. Your family has been very kind. I haven't had to exercise my authority."

"Would you?"

"Yes, if I thought I was right and the family was wrong, and the issue was important. Then I would pull rank and exercise my authority under the CCC Trust," said Marla. "You have to remember that my responsibility is to the beneficiaries. The beneficiaries are the members of your family. The family is my responsibility."

***

Thomas N. Thompson was a big man, tall, with a barrel chest and loud voice. As Bob and Marla waited in the reception room, they could hear him ordering the staff to do this and that. If this was a show for his guests it was not making a good impression.

Neither Bob nor Marla raised their voices when they were giving instructions to their employees.

Bob and Marla were moved from the reception room into Thompson's office. It was a room that fit Thompson's personality. It was large with photographs of Thompson shaking hands with smiling political figures and other important people.

"So how can I make you happy? Can I give you some money?" said Thompson, as he sat in a big leather chair behind the desk. Thompson ignored Marla and continued with his pitch. "Bob, I have been talking to your Dad for a year now, and have only been able to make one loan on that sale from WLC to CCC. We need to do some more business, Bob."

"Well, we are here to understand the Fund's program," said Bob quietly. "How are we protected if the Fund has a call for cash from its investors? We are worried about the lack of liquidity of the fund."

"I will personally guarantee that your loans will not be called due if there is a liquidity crisis," said Thompson with a sincere face.

"The fund loaned CCC $7,500,000," said Bob. "As I understand from our attorney, if the Fund had to call the loan because the investors in the fund wanted their money back, the Fund could call our loan and we would have to repay the Fund in 30 days. If we could not pay, we would lose our land. That is not reasonable or acceptable."

"I don't think your attorney knows what he's talking about," said Thompson. "CCC would be protected. I know your dad. Frank and I were roommates in school."

"Look, if you say my attorney is wrong after he's shown me the language of the mortgage that states he is correct, then neither my attorney nor I are able to understand this obligation. If we can't understand the plain meaning of the words of the mortgage, we will not do business with you."

"If you didn't want to do business with the Fund, why did you borrow the Fund's money to buy WLC land?" asked Thompson. "Obviously, we were an acceptable risk a few years back."

"It was a business decision that my father made before CCC was restructured," said Bob. "We will honor that decision and pay the loan according to the terms of the note and mortgage, but we will not increase the debt owed to the Fund."

"What would happen to CCC if the loan was called today?" asked Thompson.

"My attorney says CCC would have 30 days to repay the money we borrowed."

"How would you come up with seven million dollars in the middle of this recession?"

"You need to believe we could," said Bob.

"Well I do not think you can pay the Fund," said Thompson, who then sat forward with his hands on his desk, then he paused and said, "I think we got off on the wrong foot."

"I think we had an honest discussion and we thank you for your time," said Bob, staring back at Thompson.

Thompson turned his attention to Marla. "I didn't mean to upset you, little lady. Are you Bob's wife?"

"No Sir, I'm not his wife."

***

The couple picked up their bags at the hotel and caught a cab to the airport. They missed the plane and sat in the lounge to relax with a glass of sweet tea. They had an hour to wait for the next flight.

"You believe that man won't call the loan?" asked Bob. "He's a shark."

"I bet the notice requiring CCC to repay the mortgage to the fund will beat us home," said Marla. "He's trying to trap us. Force us to accept the Funds' debt. It's very dangerous."

"Have you made arrangements for repayment of the loan to the Fund?" asked Bob.

"We can go to savings and pay off the loan to the Fund, but we will not have much in cash reserves. We will have to find someone to loan CCC a million dollars or so on a short term basis to maintain cash flow."

"We need to let this play out," said Bob. "If Thompson calls the loan, we need to show Dad the notice of cancellation of the loan, so Dad can see just how dangerous this short term financing can be."

"Agreed."

***

Four hours later, Bob and Marla were at the airport in Jacksonville and Frank and Bea were at the gate to meet them.

As soon as they were in the car, Frank handed Marla the telegram from Thompson Timber Fund that stated their loan from the Fund had been cancelled and repayment was due in 30 days. Frank had received the notice just before he and Bea left to come to the airport.

"Are we in trouble here?" asked Frank.

"No, Marla has set aside the cash needed to pay off the Fund. The Fund could ask for their money back at any time. It's like a 30 day note. We have the cash to pay the Fund."

Marla let Bob explain. He understood better than her how to deal with Bea and Frank. Marla watched the scenery. They were passing through a small Polish community. It had only two buildings—a church and a bar—something for the spirit and the heart. Marla was relaxed. It was obvious to her that Bob was the right person to run CCC. Marla considered that this was the Senator's idea. The person best able to operate CCC would show themselves as difficulties arose.

That night Bob and Marla were alone in the Big House at Plantation #7. Bob built a big fire and they sat in the parlor and talked all night about CCC. Neither one felt tired, they were wide awake.

***

The following Monday, Marla called CCC's primary lender, a commercial bank in Orlando, Florida. When she asked about a one year fixed-rate loan on the 65,000 acres in North Florida CCC had purchased from WLC, she was surprised to learn that the value of the land had increased from 7.5 to ten million dollars since the purchase. The commercial bank would be happy to make the loan even in the recession. There was sufficient collateral.

Marla told Bob, Frank, and Albert about the conversation with the banker. The family didn't think it was correct that the value of the land had increased 50% in the middle of a recession. Albert was asked to research the Grantor/Grantee indexes to determine the names of the purchasers and sellers, and cost of sales of large timber tracks in Florida and Georgia during the last 12 months.

Albert reported back that there were numerous sales; more than they thought would be normal, and it appeared the same parties were involved buying and selling the same property. Albert identified one property that had been sold four times in a year, each time the sales price increased five or ten percent. It looked like the buyers and sellers were "churning". The sales were artificial.

Albert also reported that property appraisers were picking up those sales in their research to value timberland, and were including them in comparable sales and consequently, the value of all timberland in Florida and Georgia was increasing in the recession. It was also strange that most of the lenders for the loans for the purchases were offices of the Farm Credit Bureau, which was only allowed to make loans for crops and farm equipment. Farm Credit was not supposed to loan on land purchases or make long term loans.

Tom's take on these sales was one of two things. First, it was like a game of musical chairs. The participants were acting honestly and were good faith buyers of property with ever increasing value. If that was the case, since the country was in a recession, the increase in value was false; it was a bubble that would burst at some point. Second, the participants were using the sales to generate funds for the operation of their businesses during the recession, and what the buyers and sellers were doing was illegal.

Frank was concerned that CCC hold all its property at book value (the value CCC paid for the land), and CCC should not participate in the artificial inflation of land values by repricing its land or by buying or selling into the market for timberland. The market was now becoming hot with many more sales than normal. Frank agreed with Bob that whatever the cause, the bubble would burst and the companies that made purchases at inflated prices or who borrowed to make the purchase, expecting to resell the property at a higher price, would become bankrupt once the bubble burst.

***

Marla and Bob discussed their view that timberland was going to experience a major deflationary event. They were right to stay liquid and also avoid debt, but there was opportunity just around the corner. After the land devalued and reached bottom, CCC should be prepared to buy. They needed to find a good source of long term financing so that CCC could be one of the companies that would purchase the devalued land and participate in the rebound of land values as the market came back in the future.

Had they forgotten the Senator's warning about the evils of debt, thought Marla?

Chapter 35
Belize City

Eastern Airlines had a connecting flight to British Honduras through Miami on an airline called TAN. Tom researched TAN and found little information. It had a small fleet of Boeing 707-120 jets. The planes were earlier, shorter length models, with four jet engines. The planes were reliable. The planes had been in the air a number of years. Boeing had had time to work all the bugs out.

TAN flew to Belize City, the capital of British Honduras, on Mondays and Wednesdays, and returned to Miami on Tuesday and Thursday of the same week. There were no other flights unless you had a private plane. Tom's plan was to fly out of town on Monday and return on Thursday. That would have him back in time to have a week to prepare for the Michael Grant trial.

Preparations for the Grant defense case were moving along well. Anthony Stewart, the investigator appointed by the court, had found the witness, Arthur, and Tom and the investigator had interviewed him. Arthur claimed that he was present at Neal's house with Grant the night of the murder. Neal and Grant went in the bedroom and later Simon Marks, the banker, who shared the house with Neal, came home. Marks became enraged when he found Neal in bed with Grant and he attacked them both with a poker from the fireplace. Arthur ran away when the men were fighting. He was afraid to go to court, but agreed he would testify. Tom gave the State Attorney notice that Arthur was a defense witness, and the State Attorney had set Arthur for deposition. Tom set the banker for deposition the day after Arthur's statement was to be taken. Both statements would be taken on Tom's return from Belize.

Tom was worried Arthur would run again, but Tony Stewart was keeping in touch with Arthur, and he would transport him to the deposition. Tom felt he could relax on his trip. Marla knew he would be out of pocket. There was no phone service, only the telex. But Marla would be ok. She worked well with his partner, Roger, so Tom felt he had his bases covered.

***

Tom was persnickety, and no more so than when packing for a trip. Tom had a fear that he would not find potable water or food that would be edible in British Honduras, so he packed a small locker with canned meats and jelly, and crackers and snacks. He figured he would not starve if he had American, ready-to-eat foodstuffs. He also brought too many clothes. He had one suit for the day and one suit for evening wear. He did not know that a pair of slacks and a guayabera (like a sport shirt), was standard dress 24 hours a day. He wasn't going to take chances and be underdressed.

The Eastern flight from Tampa to Miami was very smooth.

Tom had complaints as soon as he boarded his connecting flight to Central America. TAN's airliner was dirty. There was a three person cabin crew with a navigator and pilot and co-pilot on the flight deck. Tom peeked into the cockpit. The flight crew seemed sober. They were speaking the King's English, and probably received flight training in the RAF, thought Tom.

The plane was full – 140 passengers. Most of the passengers appeared to be poor. The women were dressed in un-ironed cotton dresses. They had large black purses and paper bags in their hands and bags under the seat. Everyone was holding as many items in the bags as they could. They were probably hoping to pay for the trip by re-selling the contents of their luggage when they landed. Tom understood used goods were not subject to tariff or duty, and the tax in any event was only 5% unless you imported electronics, like a transistor radio, which were taxed 50% of the cost of the device in the USA.

The men on the plane wore straw hats, even when they were in their seats. They wore short sleeve shirts (guayabera), untucked, outside their cotton pants. Everyone wore closed-toed shoes with socks.

Tom stood out in his Wolf Brother's suit and tie. He was surprised by the dress of the passengers. Flying in an airliner was an event, like church or going to the department store. You were expected to dress up and be on your best behavior. At least that was Tom's view.

***

The flight out of Miami was scheduled to last three and one half hours. They had to fly around Cuba as Castro would not relinquish the use of Cuban airspace to the Americans or their allies since the dictator had joined forces with the USSR.

Surprisingly, Tom slept after takeoff. He hated flying.

The clouds had built up after the pilot turned the plane to the west. As they headed south after passing the Western tip of Cuba, the vibration began. There was no first class seating, but Tom sat in front in the first row so he could stretch out. He was in an aisle seat.

When the vibration became a sideways shake and then a big bump, Tom was forced awake and out of his seat like he had fallen 100 feet. He awoke completely as he flew into the air and his head hit the luggage compartment. Then he slammed down again into the seat and grabbed his seat belt and locked it. The cabin crew was yelling at the passengers to buckle their seat belts and stay seated. All cigarettes were to be extinguished.

Tom was looking into the faces of the two stewardesses, who were struggling into fold down seats pointed toward the passengers. They were flying backwards. The thought of it made Tom wretch. He swallowed as the plane took another swoon and was then snapped like the crack of the tip of a whip as the wings caught the air. The pilot tried to escape by climbing but it was no good—the plane began to stall. There was a great whooshing sound, like the sound of water beating on a car in a carwash. It was wind shear. The pilot tried to dive and he was able to maintain control but as he leveled off the plane hit more turbulence.

"Really, this is unacceptable," Tom stated to the stewardess who was being whipped about because her seat had no arms or sides. She was trying to dig her long high heels into the short loops of the carpet on the floor to gain traction from the bucking bronco of a plane. The lady was terrified as was Tom, but she's supposed to show no fear, thought Tom.

And then it stopped.

The passengers wiped the tears from their eyes and sighed, and the pilot got on the speaker and downplayed the incident as being a "little rough air," and advising the passengers to keep their seat belts fastened securely, and no smoking until they landed. Everyone could smell gas. Something caused a leak. Hopefully it was actually only the smell of chemicals that had sloshed about in the toilets. That is what the attendant stated.

After the pilot spoke, all the passengers applauded except Tom, who considered having a drink. He had been on the wagon for almost three months since his last embarrassing bender. He had fallen out at a bar in front of a judge; split his head open, and was carried to the emergency room for stiches.

Tom knew if he drank just one scotch he would miss all his appointments for the week. Tom was still trying to woo Marla back, and he couldn't fly to British Honduras and make a fool of himself and disappoint Marla. And so he suppressed the desire for a Johnnie Walker Red, two ounces with ice and water.

***

CCC owned the stock of Belize Resources Ltd., which was deeded to CCC when CCC purchased British Trading Company, an enterprise that had been granted the monopoly in all the timber resources in the Central American country by the Queen of England over 200 years ago. Because it owned Belize Trading Company and Belize Resources, CCC had been granted the 600,000 acres of land in the Southeast of the country, together with what was now the largest steam operated sawmill in Central America. The company also owned the chicle concession. Chicle (as in Chiclet) was a resin collected from the sapodilla tree. Chicle was processed into chewing gum. Belize Resources had assigned its rights in the sap to chewing gum manufacturers in Britain and they harvested the sap from the sapodilla trees using native climbers called chickleros (really!) and Belize Resources was paid a royalty per pound for chicle that was collected.

By owning the timber rights, Belize Resources also owned the products produced by the Honduran pine (like a slash pine tree in the USA). Those products included the timber, pine sap, pine resin, turpentine, and naval stores. Further the company owned what remained of all the exotic wood in the country. That is, all the mahogany and ebony that remained on the lands owned by the government—what little there was.

After his wild plane ride, Tom was happy to sit down in the British Club located near the airport. The club was a worn out building near the polo grounds, the soccer pitch and the horse racing track. All of the three sporting venues that were exclusively used by the British ex-patriots had been abandoned. Most of the ex-patriots had moved to other British colonies for work or cheaper living since Britain advised it was giving up the colony and British Honduras would become independent.

The man who met Tom at the airport managed Belize Resources. His name was Monte Styles. Before this day, he had been the person who authored a series of keystrokes on pages of paper that unrolled from the Telex machine in the business office at Plantation #7. The Telex messages from Styles were normally a plea for money to be wired to the business account in the Barclay's Bank of Belize City to cover an overdraft at the bank. Marla had become concerned because the amount requested had doubled to $10,000 this last month. Marla had really pressured Tom to make the trip to investigate this CCC asset quickly.

So, here was Tom sitting at the British Club with Mr. Styles, the manager. Tom was watching him drink whiskey while Tom drank club soda with a twist of lime. They were eating Shepherd's Pie. It was bland and tasteless. Styles suggested Tom use a bit of Malinda's Sauce to spice it up. Using the Malinda's was the best advice Styles gave that day, as it did spice up the dish.

Styles announced his retirement during the meeting, but not before he all but admitted there were irregularities in the books, or rather, no one was keeping the books reconciled and the bank had advised that it would only cover payroll for the next month.

The bright spot was that the last of the mahogany logs had been floated down the Old Belize River and had arrived at the mill, and were presently being pulled up the ramps at the old sawmill to be cut into cants. "Cants" were the result of the first raw cut of the large logs. The timbers were cut into sizes that could be more easily stacked and transported and then re-cut in a smaller finishing mill. The cants were stacked on a barge and floated out the mouth of the river on the barge and then loaded on ships for England. The terms of payment were FOB (payment had to be made when the lumber cants were on board the ships). Styles reckoned that the payment would occur in the next week. At that time there would be $150,000 paid into the Barclay's account for Belize Resources, and the company "would be flush".

Other information from this meeting included the fact that the reason the company had been sold so cheaply, about 45 cents US per acre for the raw ground, and with personal property assets at no additional cost, discounted to no value, was that the British Government announced it was ready to abandon the country, and the chicle royalty was worthless because science had determined how to make the gum synthetically.

"It appears there is nothing that can't be made from plastic by a chemist," commented Styles, enjoying himself as he heaped more bad news onto Tom's shoulders—bad news that Tom would have to carry back to Marla.

Tom decided that he needed to change the signatories on the accounts and took Styles with him to the bank, ostensibly for an introduction to the bank manager. "But while we are here, we need to take your name off the accounts as you are retiring, and we need to replace the persons who control the account. CCC in the USA will control the account," Tom announced to the bank manager.

Styles had no objection. He had already fattened his wallet while he was in charge of the company.

***

Tom next met with Mr. Johns, Belize Resources' local attorney, and got a quick lesson in corporate law and some good advice. "I knew the Senator. He enjoyed visiting our country. He acted like he was our father. He was unrealistic."

"Yes," said Tom as if to say, "Tell me something I did not already know."

Mr. Johns was an old man. He had been educated in England at Cambridge. He was married, church-going, and had three children.

He reminded Tom that their conversation was confidential. They were both attorneys representing Belize Resources. Mr. Johns wanted to be assured Tom understood the concept of confidentiality and privacy, so he could be totally honest.

"We are a small country," said Mr. Johns. "The British want out, except for a military presence for their Air Force. They will encourage the local leaders to form a parliamentary government and then transfer power to the new government, retaining only limited power, as the country will remain a protectorate. The locals will be jealous if your foreign US company owns 600,000 acres of our land. Belize needs to be owned by our countrymen, not by CCC."

"Do you have a buyer in mind?"

"I will deny it if you repeat it."

"Then don't tell me," said Tom. "I only need to know what they will pay for the land."

"They will pay $1,000,000 US dollars, half at closing and half in 10 years, secured by a note at 10% interest."

"I would have to discuss this with Marla. I would have to do that in person. I won't use the Telex or everyone will know what we are discussing," said Tom. "My client will want to know why the buyer is so generous. The Senator only paid $250,000 for the entire company."

"These are dangerous times," said Solicitor Johns. "It would be smart to own a large part of a country if through that ownership you could encourage the country to flourish as a democracy, rather than to allow Belize to flounder and become another Cuba. If the USA controlled the 600,000 acres of land through local citizens of Belize, it could exercise some control over the new government."

"I take it that the note would be secured indirectly by the full faith and credit of the United States?"

"Yes, the Chief of Staff of the US Embassy in Belize is retiring. He intends to stay here in this country and will be a member of the Board of Directors of the new Belize Corporation that will own the land. He and all the other members will sign the note. They will be personally responsible for payment."

"Does the new company intend to use the licenses for the pine timber on the land or the pine stumps or resin or sap?"

"No. The new company would be more interested in a stable country than in a forest of Honduran pine trees," said Mr. Johns. "In fact, the new owners would encourage foreign investment that employs the resources of the country to offer good jobs to the people of Belize. If CCC intended to hire citizens of Belize to run the operations in Belize, CCC would be able to retain control of the licenses and leases."

"How do you know all this to be true?"

"I will be part of the new government and I will be part of CCC's company—Belize Resources."

"You can guarantee control of the government?" asked Tom.

"Yes, we can. At least I can guarantee the first government, which will be appointed by the British and which will be in office for four years, and then there will be an election."

"Worse case we are paid $500,000," said Tom.

"Correct."

"Best case we make some money and are good US citizens and we act as partners with the CIA and help stabilize the Caribbean."

"Correct."

"But you will deny anything that we said here today if I repeat it?"

"Correct," said Johns.

"Let me send a Telex to our client to tell her everything is settled. I will be vague and say that I will explain fully when I return to the States. Then, after the Telex, I have to return to the airport to collect my luggage," said Tom, as they left Mr. Johns' office. "TAN lost my baggage."

In the reception room, there was a man making a payment to the receptionist, and he was taking a receipt.

"Tom, this is Winston Grey," said Attorney Johns. "He can drive you to the airport. He has a truck and he can bring your luggage back to the hotel."

Winston said he would be happy to oblige. He had a very unusual soft, low voice. He was odd looking, short and squat. He had a nice smile and a good, firm grip when he shook hands. Winston said he would be happy to take Tom back to the airport. Tom wanted to see if he could fly back early. Winston said if he couldn't get a flight he would show him the sights.

***

The return trip to the airport was quick. There were no cars on the road. There was no reason to go to the airport because the last plane, operated by TACA, had left for Miami. Tom missed the flight. There would be no plane heading south until Thursday.

Tom had four suitcases plus a brief case and the food locker. Everything was located by the airline employees, except the food locker. Tom complained. The custom agent who spoke perfect English when Tom entered the country could not understand that it was a problem that Tom's food was missing.

"Why would you bring food into the country?" asked the agent. "Don't you trust our food? Do you think it's not healthy?"

Winston told Tom to forget it. The food was gone. It was probably divided up amongst the workers at the airport. Tom understood that he was starting to make a scene and this was not his country. He didn't want any trouble. Tom went to ticketing to see if he could return on an earlier flight. The planes were all full and there was no likelihood that standby was available. He would have to wait until Thursday. Tom was concerned that he had no control. In the States, the economy always gave its citizens choices. Here in this backwater, Tom had no choices and no control.

"You might as well relax and enjoy yourself," said Winston. "I will take you to see the sights, if you like."

***

Winston liked to talk. He drove to the north to his ranch, passing by pastured cattle land on rough roads. He talked all the way in his soft girlish voice. Then after a snack at the ranch and small talk with his manager, Winston pointed the truck north to Orange Walk District, and then on to the sugar cane fields and the sugar processing plant.

At the sugar plant the owners had installed a boiler system to produce steam from bagasse. Bagasse was the fiber that was left over after the sugar cane stalk had been squeezed of its juice. The crushed stalks were chopped into small pieces and fed into the boiler as fuel to burn and heat water, and produce steam that ran a dynamo that produced electricity for the plant and the company offices and the homes for the workers who lived on site. The bagasse plant was the pride of the country. It had been built by Cuban engineers using Soviet technology. Tom began to understand the American government's concern for the potential loss of the hearts and minds of the citizens of Belize to the communists.

Not too far north was the border with Mexico. Tom was interested in entering another country to have his new passport stamped but Winston said no. He didn't really explain but it wasn't Tom's truck and so Tom did not object. Tom thought perhaps Winston would not be welcome in Mexico. What Tom could see of Mexico from the road was that the bridge over the river that divided the countries was in disrepair and the street on the Mexican side was dusty and the buildings appeared to have not seen a coat of paint in many years.

The pair drove south on the Northern Highway and back to Belize City by way of Belmopan. This small village was to become the new capital of the country if the country was ever released by Britain. Winston had misgivings about Belize becoming a protectorate and losing its status as a part of Britain.

Winston was originally from the Bahamas, and he was forced to leave the country. He didn't explain why, exactly, just that it was not pleasant and it was costly, and he did not like Belize as much as he liked the Bahamas.

***

Back in Belize City, Winston asked if Tom wanted to eat. They were hungry and they went to the beach for a steak at Tom's hotel, The Governor. Tom checked in and felt relief once his luggage was in his room under lock and key. The steak was very good. Winston said it was local, raised on a ranch near Winston's. They began to talk about farming and Winston became upset about government interference. The District had refused to allow the cattlemen to eradicate the jaguar, "el tigre". As a consequence, the jaguars were taking many cattle, particularly the calves.

Winston had no qualms about the jaguar living in the mountains in the Coxcomb Basin, and south of the Hummingbird Highway, but to restrict hunting the big cats in the prime pastureland of the country was not good business.

Tom and Winston sat and talked after dinner. Tom had finished his business and wanted to see more of the country. Winston was happy to oblige. Tom took a chance on a glass of Belican Beer, locally brewed and dark like Michelob. It had a good biting taste. Winston would show Tom the Belican brewing plant tomorrow.

The men kept drinking and talking. They ended up at a brothel in the city, away from the beach, on the Belize River. Winston invited Tom to partake. He said the girls were from throughout Central America. They were mostly farm girls. They were cheap and clean; government inspected, and thus double the price of the women you would find for sale on the streets. Tom deferred, at least not in the rooms of the brothel. Winston agreed. "We might be photographed while we are in the act."

Winston convinced Tom to take a woman to his hotel. After dropping him and the lady off for the night, Winston left and promised to return in the morning.

***

In the night, very early, the girl awoke and stole all of Tom's cash except his traveler's checks, and snuck out the door. She had not earned the money. All Tom was interested in doing was drinking. Somewhere he had gotten a bottle of scotch.

Now there was hammering on the door. Tom opened the door, and two men with badges, but in civilian clothes, entered the room and looked through the room. The room was in disarray. There was a broken glass. There was drink spilled on the floor. Tom had a cut on his hand and a towel covering the wound.

"Where is the woman?" the men asked.

"There is no woman," said Tom, as he lifted his arms and gestured around the room. Tom was still dressed. He went in the bathroom and vomited. The men had him take his wallet and passport off the bureau in the room and they took him to their car. This was where Tom's memory became vague and he lost control. Tom remembered he was taken to a doctor's office in the City. He was placed on a bed. The following day he slept through.

No one in Solicitor John's office knew where he was. They sent a driver to Winston's ranch. He claimed he did not know where Tom was. He said he came to the hotel on the beach to take him out the next day, but Tom was not in his room. The hotel employees claimed no knowledge of Tom.

Tom remained at the doctor's office. When his traveler's checks were exhausted the doctor released him and had him driven to the Hotel Governor. It was Thursday. Tom cleaned and shaved with his own razor. He went downstairs and took a cab to the airport. He got on his flight and flew back to Miami, then Tampa. He got in his car and drove to St. Petersburg and was home.

He never mentioned his misadventure, primarily because he could not remember much of what occurred after he began drinking the scotch.

That was absolutely the last time this would happen to him, he vowed. He would never leave the USA without being in control. Tom felt he lost control when he could not leave Belize when he wanted to. He was at the mercy of others. He was vulnerable. He could have been killed.

Chapter 36
The Lie

During the plane trip back home, Tom Night composed his notes from the trip and his impressions from speaking to Attorney Johns, Mr. Styles, and Winston, into a memorandum. The facts of the memo were mostly from a travel folder and newspaper articles, but not his personal experience. The memo was a lie to cover the fact that Tom had spent the majority of his stay in the hospital after an alcohol induced blackout. As Tom scribbled these notes, he was drenched in sweat. Tom's secretary, Karen, could read his chicken scratch and she typed the memo. The following was the result:

> Actually, Belize should have been called "Florida" because Belize is always in bloom. It has two seasons – wet and dry. In the dry (winter) season, the weather is more humane because it is less humid, but it was still hot.

> The small country is nestled below Mexico, on the Yucatan Peninsula. It is east and north of Guatemala. Belize is about the size of Vermont; it has about 300,000 people and about 70,000 people live in Belize City.

> Belize borrowed its bureaucracy and parliamentary system with its prime minister and appointed cabinet from the British. In 1964, Belize claimed it won its independence, but in my opinion the British had wrung the country dry, and the British abandoned

Belize as a colony. Belize will remain a Protectorate of Britain. Through the agreements that will flow from the Protectorate, the British will have what they wanted – a military foothold in Central America that allows the English to fly in an hour by Harrier jet to its other interests in the Caribbean. The British Air Force has a base at the International Airport in Belize City.

I feel the multinationals abandoned Belize when it claimed independence. For a hundred years, chicle, a product produced from the resin of the sapodilla tree, was processed into chewing gum, but chicle has been replaced by a synthetic. The market for virgin pure stumps and naval stores is still viable but weak. The last, large, tropical timbers in the jungles that were privately owned, had been cut by the Mennonites, who established a colony in the highlands in the west near Guatemala, in the land known as the "Spanish Lookout". Some timber taken from government lands was last processed at the steam sawmill on the Belize River near the airport in the 1960's. The sawmill is now abandoned. The workers left the large factory building, throwing their wrenches and tools to the ground. When I visited the steam sawmill, the tools still lay where they were thrown. There was a caretaker at the sawmill, who now herded goats on the property, and so its ten acres were strewn with black goat pellets. The only multinational who maintained its operations was a confectioner, which had a forest of cacao trees. This operation was serviced by a village that the company supported.

When the multinationals left Belize, they sold their rights and licenses to harvest natural resources that were granted by the government. The entities that obtained the licenses paid mere pennies for the license. However, the assignment of the license had to contain a clause that relieved the multinational of any responsibility it had assumed when it obtained the right to strip the country of its resources.

The shareholders of Commercial Carriers Corporation (CCC), unknowingly obtained many of these rights and licenses through its purchase of Belize Resources. An audit of the rights is being conducted by Attorney Johns.

When Belize gained its independence, the country had high unemployment, but unemployment statistics were skewed to the upside because any Belizean who worked at all, even cutting a yard on a regular basis for a few Belizean dollars, was counted as among the ranks of the employed.

Although there was high unemployment, the people of Belize City all acted like they were employed. At 8:00am Central Time, it seemed the entire population got out on the streets and mingled with the few cars and trucks on the road. The unemployed marched into the city's core with the people who were employed, and then the unemployed loitered on the streets. Some hawked a few meager items to tourists – post cards, a carved mahogany dolphin. The citizens looked for the opportunity to earn a few pennies. Though they had no jobs, everyone seemed to have a place to sleep and there was fruit in the trees, so they lived. Everyone had support from family.

When a commercial plane arrived, a mass of entrepreneurs with their wares – carvings and food stuffs – mostly tamales – swamped the few visitors as they were insulted by the heat and humidity after leaving the air conditioned custom house.

Most of the arrivals were business people, but there were a few tourists who arrived to tour the Mayan ruins or to visit the Cayes, (the name for the barrier islands off the coast). Canadians had recently discovered an extensive system of Mayan ruins and a few tourists from Canada had heard about the discoveries, and they visited. Divers and fisherman flew in and then went to the Caye. A few knew about and visited Blancaneaux Lodge in the Mountain Pine Ridge. Otherwise, tourist venues have not yet been established.

To be a tourist destination, the venue would necessarily have to be safe, and therefore the government would have to separate the tourists from the locals and provide a secure walled environment. Most tourists do not desire to see beggars plying their disease or deformity for profit. I experienced the beggars in person. The beggars' solicitation was not mailed in a clean envelope from a non-profit agency. Pleas for money came with the rap of the stump of an elbow to your back while you were stopped to observe an Indian without legs seated on a mat who had grasped your ankle. The beggars, though, were being run out by the drug addicts, who were more troublesome because they had a good pair of legs and you were unable to gain any distance from them by walking away. You had to listen to their pleas as they followed behind. "Man, I am hungry. I am sick. I need a meal. I will work for you. I will come with you. I will stay at your doorstep". They said, "I will be your slave for a dollar."

A tourist venue would necessarily avoid the city dump in Belize City that was established behind the grave yard. The pickers and the diggers and the dead all vied for space and peace. A tourist wouldn't shop at a hut on the road that has little inventory and a strange mix of merchandise – hair picks, a lipstick, moon pies, syrupy pink colored drinks, Coke, rum and the local beer. The shops were an excuse for the beer named "Belkin", which was quite good.

In Belize City, tourists wouldn't walk on the roads because the road was the sewer and the fish market near the swing bridge smelled putrid.

In fact, to establish a tourist venue in Belize, you would necessarily have to avoid Belize City. You would need to bus the tourists from the airport to a location outside the city to a walled enclave with private police. You would have to satisfy government officials with gifts and offer minimal work to the locals, and closely monitor them. The optimum would be to build a private pier out into the sea as a dock for an ocean liner, or use vessels to transport tourists from ship to shore. The tourists would then pass through a duty free bazaar with crafts and tobacco and rum that led to a transfer facility. The tourists would then be bussed to a tourist activity. You had to lure tourists from the liner with a safe experience; tourists would not pay for the experience of the native Belize. Few people in the civilized world knew Belize existed. Some may have heard of it when it was called British Honduras. But they would as soon believe it was in Africa as that it were in Central American, and they had no reason to visit.

It would be best to avoid all the unpleasantries of Belize City by renting a car or hiring a cab and driver. The harassment on the streets by the addicts is bad. When I was in the city I took private transportation even if I only had to go a block. This was true except in the early morning. To get a grip on myself and free my mind I got up at dawn and ran from the hotel out to the light house along the sea to the river, then past the Belize City sawmill to the airport, and then reversed this route. The trip is 5 miles and takes 50 minutes. I am back in time for a shower and breakfast at 7:00am. When I ran, no one was on the street. The addicts were huddled back under the stilts of the buildings as I jogged by. Later, at 8:00am, the citizenry was on the streets and I was in a car.

Most of the core area of Belize City is at or below sea level. It seemed that any ground that was not paved was home to hordes of large fiddler crabs. They were black, with one large, bright orange pincher claw. The city straddled the Belize River, which ran into the sea. There was a harbor at the mouth of the river, but it was very shallow and filled with sediment. Larger boats and ships had to launch their cargo or passengers from out at sea and deliver them to the harbor. Had the country maintained and repaired the dredge it owned, the harbor would be deep and accessible. But the dredge was a wreck.

Housing in the city was generally built on stilts.

Most living areas were 8 to 12 feet off the ground, stacked on concrete pilings. The living quarters were built of poor quality wood that looked like mahogany when it was first cut, but had no resin and faded quickly and rotted away, unless the surface of the wood was covered with varnish or paint.

Few citizens painted their houses so they began to rot immediately from the sun and rain.

The coast of Belize was susceptible to violent low pressure storms. Most of those storms, though they were as strong as hurricanes, were unnamed. Hurricane Hattie was the exception. The storm was named and notable for causing great death and destruction. Most of the population lived in Belize City at the time and most of the housing in the city was lost in this storm. Afterward, a decision was made to leave the coast and move the city inland to Belmopan.

A new capital will be constructed in Belmopan on the plateau west of the center of the country. Much of the construction of the government facilities will be funded with loans from the World Bank. The loans are expensive and the terms dictated by the World Bank force concessions from the government to conduct its affairs in accordance with its dictates, essentially, the country was to renounce Communism.

Belize has little money to repay the loans from the World Bank. It had natural resources that were of value but there was little competition for the resources. It had no heavy industry; it had no significant agricultural products for export – and therefore it had no collateral and it could not borrow from International Banks. The country could not afford an infrastructure. Belize City seemed to become like its beggars. The Japanese engineered and rebuilt a bridge that had collapsed. The Canadians brought portable water to households in sections of the city. Otherwise, if not donated by the world, the people did without and poached what little the British had left behind.

In my opinion, the new country is the perfect partner for drug trafficking. It is close to production centers in Columbia, Ecuador, and Peru. The drug industry was a corrupter of countries large and small. The US dollar is openly used as the primary medium of exchange in South and Central America, and even though there were laws against it, local currency was openly traded for dollars. As a result, the local currency collapsed in value against the dollar on the street, and the local currency was not used in any transaction that involved more than the cost of the purchase of a beer.

In my opinion it was probable, more likely than not, that any business transaction funded in dollars was at least tainted by drug money, and that any income received by a citizen of Belize was directly earned from, or was subsidized by, the drug industry. In this way, economically, drugs corrupt all human activity in Belize.

Belize was close to demand centers in the US, Canada, and Europe, and could transfer the product to those markets easily. So Belize, by its location, and the weakness of its government, will become a prime distribution link for the narcotics industry. This is my opinion.

And even though the country was awash in US dollars, the infrastructure of the country is non-existent and decrepit, because the government could not directly tax the drug industry without recognizing it and legalizing it. If the government legalized the industry, the government would become a pariah. It would lose its loans from the World Bank and its contacts with legitimate banks. The government did obtain tax revenue from the drug industry by taxing the goods imported with drug money. But imports were smuggled into Belize because the citizens involved in the import of legitimate trade goods did not want to reveal their new found wealth, as the wealth would cause suspicion that the person was involved in illegal activities. So, the citizens did not share their wealth with the country, but instead established private bank accounts in Miami, Panama, the Caymans or the Netherlands Antilles.

The drug industry is a waste. It fails to produce a life sustaining product. It ultimately provides pain and death. Sad to say, I indirectly represent those involved in the drug industry, if only in relation to their legitimate operations.

I am like the criminal lawyer who would represent a bank robber, but would refuse to take his fee in cash wrapped in a bank wrapper, because the cash was too recently stolen. The fee had to age a bit. It had to be laundered through another legitimate business before I would touch it.

/S/ Tom Night

Tom failed to mention the fact he was in a hospital for three days, or the misadventures he had with the police. Tom had Karen type the memorandum and mail a copy to each member of the Barnes family to show them what he had accomplished and learned during his trip.

This is the first time Tom was professionally dishonest with a client, and misrepresented himself and lied.

He had lost control of himself in yet another way.

Chapter 37
Bob and Marla

Bob and Marla had been sharing the same bed for about a month. Only Jenny knew. They didn't hide the fact from her when she came home on weekends from the university. Jenny felt the relationship was their own business and she would not reveal it without their permission. Bob was still out on the road most weekdays, but they had hired a new sales manager who was able to do Bob's job on the road, and Bob spent more time at Plantation #7.

Bob and Marla were working many hours, and CCC was outstandingly successful. It became a prize for some large conglomerate to pluck.

Marla began to receive feelers from JRD Corporation, a large, publically traded company with headquarters in the Northeast. JRD had various divisions, including electronics, defense, heavy manufacturing, banking, health care, and building products. CCC would be a perfect fit for JRD's building products division. Marla and Bob kept the information to themselves. They let the matter play out.

JRD worked fast. The CEO had the power to decide the matter on his own with the concurrence of an executive committee of the Board.

JRD was not interested in the homestead, the acreage, or the licenses and leases in British Honduras, or in the businesses comprising Plantation #7. But JRD wanted all of CCC's timberland, mills, sales and logistics' operations. JRD would not want CCC to compete with its building products division. Marla, Bob, Albert, Bea, and Frank would also be required to sign personal non-compete agreements.

Tom was in British Honduras when JRD made its initial offer to the family. James Reynolds, the CEO and President of JRD, personally presented the offer at the plantation. He flew to Florida in his private jet, a brand new Boeing 727-100. The jet was outfitted with all the accoutrements of corporate power. The Daytona airport had not seen anything so majestic. The air traffic controllers were impressed by the JRD plane.

The family listened to the offer. No one from Tom's office was involved. Bob brought in one of the partners in a large law firm in Atlanta for advice on the sale. It was obvious Tom had been drinking heavily before he traveled to Belize and Frank agreed to hire the attorney from Atlanta. Tom was unaware of the potential sale to JRD.

The offer was a cash offer net of debt and taxes. The offer was $70,000,000 for all assets of the CCC Trust, mills and timberland, and sales and logistics.

The family, including Marla, huddled together in the parlor of the Old House while the President of JRD was given a tour of Plantation #7, including a stroll through the grove and on the beach. The president walked over the sand dunes to the ocean, he was impressed by the large swells of surf that were coming to shore. There was a wind out of the west that would pick up the swells as they came into the shallows and the face of the wave would flatten and then the top of the wave would tail off into a mist behind the wave. There were men and boys riding surf boards, and the President felt their exhilaration as they slid down the face of the wave. The athletes were walking back and forth on their surf boards to position themselves for a better ride on what appeared to be perfect waves. Mr. Reynolds would be happy to have stood in the sand and watched the waves and surfers all day.

***

The parlor was warm. The excitement caused by the offer, so much larger than expected, made the occupants of the room flush; their cheeks reddened.

Frank had a pad. He had marked it with a line followed by an "X". Below the line were six names: Frank, Bea, Bob, Albert, Jenny and Marla.

There was one other line below those names and on that line was Tom's name.

"These are the people who should share in the reward of this sale, in my opinion," said Frank. He looked around the room. There were no objections.

"I think the managers of each of the sawmills and timber lands should receive a reward for their service, depending on how long they have been with CCC," said Bob.

"First, is there any discussion about the first six names?" asked Frank. There was no discussion.

Frank wrote in the figure $10,000,000 in each of the top six lines.

Is there any disagreement with that amount?"

There was none.

"How much for Tom?" asked Frank.

"Five million," said Bob. "He does not deserve a full share."

"The last five million will be needed for closing and the balance can be paid to the managers and any others who have been particularly helpful obtaining this offer. Is there full agreement?" asked Frank.

Everyone nodded. The lawyer from Atlanta hand wrote the agreement and everyone, the Trustee and the beneficiaries of the CCC Trust, signed the paper.

Chapter 38
Back to the Salt Mines

It was two weeks after Tom returned from British Honduras before he and Marla could meet in person. By then the statement of Arthur had been taken by the State Attorney, and the banker's deposition had been taken by Tom.

Neither the State Attorney nor Tom was satisfied because Arthur and Simon Marks, the banker, refused to answer certain questions unless they were granted immunity. Arthur refused to answer whether he was engaged in the possession or sale of illegal drugs and that he offered Grant to men for sex. Arthur did testify that the banker came home to find Grant and Neal in bed; became enraged and the banker attacked Grant and Neal with a poker, at which time Arthur ran away.

Simon Marks admitted he was Neal's roommate and that they owned the house in which the death occurred, together. Other than that, he would not answer any questions, claiming his right to remain silent under the Fifth Amendment to the US Constitution.

The State Attorney knew he would look stupid trying to convince a jury that Arthur was lying and that Grant was the assailant and not the victim of an attack. The State Attorney made an offer to Grant of a plea bargain to the offence of prostitution, and assault and battery. Grant agreed to a sentence of one year in the County Jail. Simon Marks' attorney was able to convince the State Attorney that, even if Arthur was telling the truth, the banker had been temporarily insane. The banker faced no charges, however, his reputation was ruined and he left town.

Tom, Roger, and Grant were pleased with the result. Tom and Roger were also pleased with the fact they were paid the standard fee of $25,000 to defend a murder case by Grant's friend in New York.

***

Tom's office was still in an uproar after the various proceedings involved in finalizing the Grant case.

Marla entered the office late in the afternoon. The staff greeted her. She was no stranger. She had been to St. Petersburg a number of times over the last year trying to help her mother since her Dad passed. Marla was ushered into Tom's office for their meeting.

"You first," said Marla. "What happened in British Honduras?"

Tom began by saying they had received an interesting offer for sale of the 600,000 acres in the country, allowing CCC's foreign corporation, Belize Resources, to continue to own and operate businesses under the licenses and leases granted by the government. The leases would be guaranteed for four more years.

"How much will they pay?"

"They will pay one million US, half down and half in five years, with interest on the balance at ten percent per year. So we would receive $50,000 per year while we wait for the final payment."

"Do we have any security?"

"You will have a note signed by prominent citizens of the country. One of the signatories will be the Chief of Staff at the US Embassy in Belize City. He's retiring and will be staying in the country working on improving the land owned by Belize Trading Company. Essentially, the land is barren, with some forest, but mostly its wiregrass and swamp," said Tom.

"Your notes said this has something to do with the CIA?" asked Marla.

"I think so, but we will not be involved in any of the shooting," joked Tom. "The US is trying to obtain a foothold in the economy of the country."

"The Senator mentioned something about his dealings with the US Government in Central America," said Marla. "I thought he meant his dealings with the foreign governments, not the CIA."

"Apparently, our government wants to use ownership of this land to stabilize the country. Britain is abandoning the country and the USA is worried about Cuba."

"But to the CCC Trust, this is just a sale of its real estate holdings in the British Honduras?" asked Marla.

"Correct."

"This is a can of worms," said Marla. "I read your memorandum about Belize. We should sell the land and get out with as much as we can of our investment."

"That's a good business decision."

"Thank you for your confidence," said Marla. She was short and snippy.

"I will send a Telex to Mr. Johns. He brought the deal to CCC." Tom went to the liquor cabinet. He had not stopped drinking since his trip and his black out, but he was back to limiting himself to two, two ounce drinks a day.

Marla looked Tom in the eye. "I know what happened to you on your trip."

"What?"

"You ended up blacked out and were treated in a hospital," said Marla.

"Whatever," Tom wasn't going to deny the truth at this point.

"Whatever indeed, while you were laid out in the hospital I sold most of the assets of CCC Trust," said Marla. She pushed a copy of the agreements with JRD Corporation and CCC Trust to sell all the mills and timberlands, and the settlement agreement between the beneficiaries and the Trustee to divide the proceeds of the sale in front of Tom. Tom inspected the documents of sale.

"Seventy Million Dollars, net. That is unbelievable," said Tom. "It's good I was in the hospital. I would probably have convinced you to take much less," he said, sarcastically.

"Do you see that you are paid five million dollars?" said Marla.

"Yes, it's very kind," said Tom. "But why didn't you call me? I'm your attorney."

"You are our drunk attorney." Marla could have said much worse. The truth was that Tom only remained as the attorney for the CCC Trust after the debacle in Belize because Frank refused to fire him.

"That's a little cruel. I've been with CCC through thick and thin, mostly thin." Tom began to tear up. "What about us?"

"I have been dating Bob."

Tom took a sip of his drink. "Ok," he said. "You are dating Bob." Tom considered the fact.

"I don't know if anything will come of this new relationship but you and I were going nowhere. I can't chase you from one sanatorium to another."

"Is CCC going to fire me?"

"CCC has been sold. After the sale there will be some odds and ends left over called CCC Trust, but CCC Trust will only be the plantation, the homestead and what's left of British Honduras after the sale. I think Bob should take over and you deal with him."

"What are you going to do?"

"I will probably look for another job. Maybe I'll ask JRD Corporation for a job running the mills and timberland we sold them. They need an experienced manager for the Timber Division of the conglomerate."

"You could come back here to the law office," said Tom, knowing Marla could do much better than that.

Marla ignored Tom's offer to return and tried to change the subject. "In the last year, my father died, and now I have to make arrangements for mother. I intend to take her to the Old House at the plantation."

Tom persisted; "If you need help, I can help you," said Tom. "I would pay you a lot to run the office."

"Tom, didn't you see that I am finally being paid what I'm worth? Did you read the settlement agreement?"

Tom picked up the agreement again. It was then that he saw Marla was being paid $10,000,000.

"I guess you don't need me," said Tom, trying a play for sympathy.

"We'll stay in touch, but for business only," said Marla.

***

The office was dark after Marla left, except for a light in Roger's office and the one in Karen's room. She was now the office manager and the bookkeeper, and she handled the CCC account.

Roger entered Tom's office after knocking. The room was dark except for the light filtering in from the street.

"Would you like a drink?" asked Tom as he flipped on the light.

"Sure," said Roger, as he accepted a glass of scotch from Tom, two ounces, with water and ice. Tom refreshed his glass with a splash of scotch.

"Marla just informed me that CCC has sold all its timber assets to JRD Corporation," said Tom.

"Does that mean we will finally get paid?" asked Roger.

"We get five million dollars."

"We aren't owed that much. Karen and I were just going over our receivables. CCC owes a lot. It owes over $350,000."

"How did their bill get up so high?" Tom was surprised. "Haven't they been paying us right along?"

"No, we thought you had some special arrangement with Marla, and we knew CCC was going through some hard times with the recession, so no one asked."

"Well, the recession is over. Look." Tom gave the copy of the agreements Marla had left Tom, referencing the sale. Roger read through the papers.

"I don't think it would be right for the firm to receive five million," said Roger. "That's your money."

"What if we used part of the money and settled up with CCC. What if the firm was paid half a million dollars to cover CCC's outstanding bill?" said Tom.

"Sold," said Roger.

"We won't be getting that much work from the CCC account in the future since they sold their timber and mills. The extra money over what they owe will hold us over," said Tom.

"You don't have to worry about having enough work, we are picking up a lot of criminal referrals," said Roger. "You won't believe the latest homicide."

"Tell me about it," said Tom as he stared into his glass of whiskey.

"Well," said Roger, and he began yet another tale of woe:

"A man and his wife were in their bedroom arguing about something. They begin to tussle and roll around in the bed. They fall off the bed and the man injures his head. The woman realizes he's bleeding pretty badly. Did I tell you they were both nude?"

"No."

"Well they were nude. The fight is over. According to the man, who is our client, they are going to kiss and make up. The woman goes to the bathroom to get a towel to stanch the client's head wound. Oh, and they had been drinking. Did I tell you that?"

"I assumed they were drinking," said Tom.

"Well, they were drinking," said Roger. "And the man falls asleep or passes out while he's waiting for the towel. Later he wakes up with a terrible headache and starts to look for his wife."

"And?"

"He finds her in the bathroom sitting on the toilet and she's bled out, literally she has bled to death on the john," said Roger. "So what do you think happened?"

"She had a ruptured vulva artery, is my guess," said Tom.

"How did you know?"

"She got the rupture when they were fighting. He probably kicked her. If she had not sat on the toilet and instead if she just crossed her legs she would not have bled at all. A doctor at the ER could have repaired the wound. What is our client charged with?" asked Tom.

"Murder One."

"It might be manslaughter. A death as a result of mutual combat, a sudden quarrel, but more likely it was just an accidental death from a fist fight or scuffle," said Tom. "What did our client tell the police?"

"Nothing. He called his attorney's office before reporting the crime to the police. After talking to his lawyer, he was told to call us. We told him to call the police and report the death. We told him not to say anything else. If the police wanted to interview him he was to ask for a lawyer and give them our phone number. We would come right down to the police station."

"Did he call?"

"No. The police took him to court and the judge released him on $50,000 bail this morning," said Roger. "And get this, he posted a cash bond. He didn't need a bondsman. He has plenty of money. He will be in tomorrow morning, first thing."

"Great," said Tom. "We need to send Anthony to the house to get pictures of the bedroom and the bathroom. Make sure there is a picture of the toilet and one of our client's head with the wound."

Roger looked at Tom and the drink in his hand. "Will you be here tomorrow?" asked Roger.

"Yes, I will be here and I will be sober," said Tom.

Chapter 39
Corporate Marriage

The president of JRD was impressed with Marla. She had done well closing the sale of CCC assets, and had gained a tidy sum, making her one of the wealthiest women in Florida. A further distinction was that her wealth had not come from the efforts of her husband.

To James M. Reynolds, the President of JRD, Marla was a prize. He waited for the deal with CCC to close, and then he went forward with a full course press trying to woo Marla. But, first the President had to destroy the relationship between Marla and Bob. It didn't take much of a push. The pair's relationship had become stressed during the process of the sale of CCC. Marla and Bob competed over who should handle the sale, and Marla exercised her ultimate authority and took control as the Trustee of the CCC Trust.

After that, Bob had found reasons to remain at the Homestead with his parents and Albert, and out of Marla's bed. But he hadn't forgotten the pleasure she gave him. He did nothing but talk about Marla when he wasn't working building another empire, this time in lime rock and cement.

Florida needed roads. For roads, the State needed road base, lime rock. Bob and Albert quickly learned the industry and bought a small paving outfit in Daytona that had a sales office in Tallahassee. They named the company Barnes Lime Rock.

They hired a lobbyist to follow the road building appropriations in the legislature. They bought equipment on a tear so they could build roads where the legislature wanted them. They bought lime rock pits just where they were needed to provide material for roadbeds and bought asphalt road topping production machines, and the thick asphalt petroleum product for the road covering from importers in Tampa. They would be a great success, they hoped. They didn't tell Frank or Bea the cost of operations.

Regarding the other assets, all agreed that Tom was to handle Belize.

Marla could run the plantation if she wanted, or let Frank and Bea run the operation.

"Hell," Bob said, "the dairy and Plantation #7 run themselves. They have no competition."

Albert agreed. "Let Frank and Bea run them both."

***

Frank and Bea still loved the dairy, particularly now that the headaches and debt of the processing plant had been sold to the co-op. They drove to the small dairy each day, which had been cut out of the sale to the co-op, and they had an ice cream while they reviewed the receipts and the bills. They talked to the workers and responded to their worries. They opened a small store, selling milk and creams and other dairy products on Flomish Road where the old dairy store had been. This time they designed a drive-through operation so shoppers did not have to get out of their cars. The problem was that the drive-through concept was so popular that the cars backed up onto Flomish Road around 5:00pm, as workers were heading home and needed to stop for milk. First, they hired a policeman to direct traffic. Then, they had to hire attendants who would bring the milk to the cars to move the cars through the drive-through quickly.

Then, as word spread of the convenience of having an attendant come to your car, saving you the inconvenience of leaving your car, the business was full of customers all the time. Frank and Bea added lanes for more traffic.

Then they opened other outlets in cities in Volusia county, and then in Orange and Polk and Hillsborough and Pinellas Counties.

They had a business presence all along the I-4 corridor. With a few billboards, the idea took only a year to catch on.

Tom formed a franchise corporation so Bob could sell the business plan to individuals. The name "Homestead Creamery" was registered as a trademark. The co-op agreed to supply the milk products needed for the stores and the logistics to deliver the milk products to the drive-through stores.

Then, Frank and Bea hired a corporate team to manage the business. They identified markets throughout the South, then the Northeast, then the Mid-West. The team hired the marketers and the franchisers. Then came a legal department, and Tom was out of a job. He was asked if he wanted to run the legal department. Tom declined. He would go back to criminal law and continue to oversee the operations in Belize.

Frank and Bea didn't have time to run Plantation #7, so Jenny was designated the manager to oversee the operation as she continued Law School at University of Florida.

***

Jenny stayed at the Plantation when she was home from school, and now, during Spring Break in Daytona. Spring Break was drinking beer on the beach and concerts at night-Wilson Pickett, Peter, Paul and Mary at the Islanders' ball park. Spring was also the season for crawling in a car at night parked on the beach and watching the shrimp boats from the shore with their lights twinkling in a black, moonless sky.

Jenny was the new woman. She was free. She spoke her mind, embarrassing Frank and Bea with her trash mouth and ideas about emancipation. She would date colored if she was so inclined. Shocking.

Marla tried to keep ties with Jenny, and had coaxed her home for weekends and vacation, but Marla could exercise less control once Jenny had a Ten Million CD gaining 8% interest per annum in Daytona Beach Federal Bank. The CD was the largest single account in the bank and even when Jenny slinked into the bank in one of her braless outfits with everything hanging out, she was greeted by the bank manager and helped with her transaction like a rich little old lady.

Marla had told her to be cautious with her money. Though it seemed like a lot, it could evaporate if she was not careful. She would be back living at the Homestead with Bob and Albert if she lost her money.

Ugh, thought Jenny. She knew Bob and Albert were already broke.

Marla engaged Jenny with the arts and with exercise. She had her walking to the ocean early in the morning and swimming with the surfers and catching waves with a boogie board. At times she was au natural. Marla didn't mind the nudity on the desolate strand of beach, but if she was going to be running around nude, Marla thought Jenny should at least be a classy lady and not project herself as a slut.

Marla spent a lot of time with Jenny. They would go to Orlando to shop. Orlando had an Ivey's and Maas Brothers. A real downtown. Marla taught her colors and fabric. Visual and tactile experiences.

They were like a mother and daughter. They dressed impeccably. They went to Winter Park and activities at Rollins College. They drank wine in the sidewalk cafes on Park Avenue. Jenny collected Florida painters, the artists N.C. Wyeth, Frederick Frieske, Herman Herzog, Ernest Lawson and David Burliuk.

Marla and Jenny endowed the Ormond Art Center and they loaned their artwork to the museum.

***

Meanwhile, Marla was being flattered by Mr. James M. Reynolds, who sent fresh flowers every day. Marla arranged them in the library on an oak table. He visited. Flying in on his jet and then flying them to dinner in Atlanta or Savannah or wherever she desired.

Mr. Reynolds drank only when he was nervous. He was nervous around Marla, she was that exquisite. He was small and a little fat and a little bald but he gave advice to the President of the United States, and he was sometimes accused of being a bully.

Marla calmed the savage breast.

Marla's bedroom was decorated like the interior of a tent in the desert. Mr. Reynolds was nervous when he first entered the room. There were no electric lights. The room was lit with flickering hurricane lamps. The floor was the bed. It was covered with thick oriental carpets and pillows. There was an open bath in the corner of the room with curtains made of bamboo fabric. There was a shower and toilet and bidet behind the curtain.

There were no windows but there was cool air flowing and ceiling fans rolling the air softly. It was very quiet. After you entered the room and sat on the pillows on the floor and drank a glass of wine, all the tension in your body was released. When you awoke, your face was smooth with no wrinkles. You wanted to sleep. Deliciously.

***

They were married in St. Patrick's in New York City. Marla wore white. She had never married before.

Tom was there. He was happy for Marla. She had asked him about a pre-nuptial agreement. Both Marla and Mr. Reynolds presented each other with agreements. But for the perks of his office as President of JRD Corporation, the apartments and the home in Rochester, and the plane and the cars and his dog, Reynolds had only a few million dollars. Marla wasn't worried. Marla had money, what she didn't have was power, and she would gain status and power from the marriage. That is what she wanted now.

Frank and Bea and Albert and Jenny were in the wedding party. Frank gave Marla away. Albert was an usher, Jenny was bridesmaid and Bea cried. They loved her very much.

Bob didn't come to the wedding, but he sent Marla a letter, a poem really, in which he professed his love for her and that he would not be able to live without her.

When Marla read the letter she called and talked to Bob. He answered the phone line "Barnes Lime Rock". All he wanted to talk about was the lime rock and cement industry. At that point, Marla knew he was all right. He wasn't going to kill himself. She promised she would invest in his company when he asked.

"How much do you need?"

"Probably a million would do it."

"Do you have any of your money left?"

"Not much."

"What about Albert? Does he have any money left?"

"No. We spent that first."

"Do you have any contracts?"

"We have plenty of work and plenty of receivables but we are starved for cash."

"I will send you the million and I will talk to my husband about your situation. How much do you have in receivables?"

"Twenty five million, about."

"Who owes you the money?"

"The State of Florida."

"Sounds like the State would be a good risk. My husband can help you. They have a bank and they can loan you the value of the receivables or they will buy the debt at a discount and they will make the collection from your customers."

"That would really help us if you could talk to him."

"I will," said Marla. "You know I will always love you."

"Thank you Marla. I love you too."

Chapter 40
Cellmates

The Pinellas County Jail administration had a section of cells for the inmates they felt were the most dangerous. The jail placed two inmates Tom represented, who were considered dangerous, in the same cell in that wing. They were Logan and Grant. The special holding area was called "the wing". All of the inmates in the wing were housed two to a cell. The jail architect had intended that these cells should be for only one prisoner. However, due to extreme overcrowding, the cells contained two inmates, and sometimes there were three men in a cell.

The wing was two stories tall, with a walkway for the guard who delivered meals, and responded to emergencies involving the prisoners who were housed in cells that were constructed on each of the two floors.

The conditions were poor at best. There was only one cot to the cell and the other men slept on the floor on mats. The men had tin cups and burned newspaper to heat water in the cups and make coffee. Fire was against the rules. The guards knew the men were breaking the rules, but the inmates controlled the wing and the guards did not stop the men from cooking. The entire floor was full of smoke because the men were cooking and smoking tobacco products. It was hard to breathe.

There was also an alcohol still. The men were often intoxicated and the guards could see the effects of the moonshine in the prisoners. The guards only confiscated contraband if the inmates were open and flaunted the possession of the booze or marijuana or drugs or coffee.

Cigarettes were a substitute currency. Hand-rolled smokes were accepted for barter, but machine rolled brands like Camel and Pall Malls and Lucky Strikes were the most prized. Sex was a commodity in the rest of the jail, but in the wing, the men were not let out in groups larger than three or four, and there were two guards watching when the men showered. For sexual release, the men were left to their own devices.

The wing was torture for most men who were waiting for their fate to be decided. The men who had been sentenced and would be shipped out to the prison system could hardly wait to leave. Even the State system allowed men more dignity than that which the jail administration allowed the criminals in the wing.

Michael Grant, who had been imprisoned for seven years in Attica Prison in New York, thought the wing was worse than anything he had seen. The men were denied all amenities because the guards were in fear. The guards used brute force to manipulate the inmates instead of coaxing them to comply with the guards' orders with better treatment. Rewards such as books and magazines, access to commissary, and venting the wing so fresh air entered the cells, would have cost nothing, but could have been used to give the guards something they could trade, so the guards did not have to use brute force to obtain compliance. The use of force degraded the guards.

The guards had long ago relinquished power over the men.

Grant and Logan developed a joint degree of mutual trust and Logan told Grant as soon as he first heard the murmurings of a plan of an escape. Grant began to gather information from his friends and acquaintances in other cells. The men passed notes through the bars and the notes spoke of the escape.

The plan outlined in the notes was to kidnap the guard on the floor and force the other guard who operated the master control of the cell doors to open all of the doors, which would allow the men on the two floors of the wing out of their cells.

Grant and Logan saw nothing that they could gain by participating in the attempted escape. They could perhaps get out of their cell but they could not get out of the jail to the outside and ultimately to freedom. Further, Logan and Grant had no reason to escape. Grant had been sentenced to a year in jail, and he had already served two months. With gain time he would be released in eight more months. If he tried to escape, and if a guard or an inmate were killed, he would be charged with accessory to murder and he would be sentenced to life in prison. Grant knew, because that is what happened to the participants in the Attica riot who were not shot and killed by the guards. They ended up in jail for life. Grant was sentenced to an extra two years in New York just because his cell door was found to be open when the troops re-took the prison. He had not participated in the riot but still he was punished.

Logan was waiting on an appeal by the State Attorney. He was confident he would prevail and he didn't want to try to escape. Logan and Grant knew that the only way to distance themselves from the participants of the escape was to tell the authorities about the plan. If they were unsuccessful advising the authorities or if it was discovered that they snitched they could be killed. They did not trust the guards with the information, and they thought the guards probably would not believe them but would think it was a con.

They decided to tell Tom and hope he could convince the jail personnel that there was a real threat of an attempted escape or a riot.

The plan was that inmates in cell 205 would grab a guard through the bars and pull him to the cell and threaten him with a shiv to his jugular vein in his neck. All three inmates in cell 205 had agreed to participate.

Grant and Logan's proof of the conspiracy was contained in a hand written note that had been intercepted by Logan and the note described the plan.

Communications between a prisoner with an attorney were most likely to be confidential if the prisoner and his attorney were in court. The attorney and the inmate could try to talk in the jail and in the worst case they could pass notes back and forth. Logan was due in court the next day for a rehearing on setting a bond on appeal. Logan's mother had convinced wealthy family friends to post a property bond using their house for collateral. The house was worth $250,000. Logan and Grant agreed that Logan would tell Tom about the escape plan while they waited for the hearing to begin.

Logan was disappointed when Roger Adams appeared in place of Tom. Logan was afraid to tell Roger about the escape, but he was able to get Roger to convince Tom to come and see him the next day. Logan told Roger it was important, a matter of life or death. Further, Grant insisted Roger was to tell Tom to bring his transistor radio.

***

"Sorry I was unable to make the bond hearing yesterday," said Tom to Logan. "I was in New York City at a wedding."

"Roger did a good job at the hearing," said Logan. "I think if you can get the bond lower by another $100,000 I can make bond."

"We'll try again," said Tom. "Do you want me to turn on the radio?"

Logan nodded. "Put it on a country station." The music would mask their conversation.

Tom complied. Logan whispered and wrote out a description of the escape plan and that he and Grant were concerned. They wanted to tell the authorities, but they didn't think the administrator would believe them. If they were believed and the guards arrested the men in cell 205, the other conspirators would take revenge on everyone else in the wing until they found out who snitched. Logan wanted Tom to negotiate the removal of Logan and Grant to solitary confinement and away from the wing.

Tom understood. He reread the handwritten note. "This is pretty clear. What if I spoke to the Sheriff? He's in charge of the jail and he would work with me to solve the problem."

Logan agreed and gave Tom the note. Tom turned off the radio and gave Logan an update on the appeal. Tom agreed he would return the same day he spoke with the Sheriff.

***

The Sheriff met with Tom and the Chief Administer of the jail. Neither believed Tom's clients.

They thought Logan and Grant were trying to parlay this information into better accommodations. The Sheriff told Tom security in the wing was under control and he had no intention of taking any action against the inmates in cell 205, or moving Tom's clients out of the wing.

Tom reminded the Sheriff that if anything happened, his clients had warned the Sheriff.

"Fair enough," said the Sheriff.

As soon as Tom finished with the Sheriff he went to the jail and told Logan what happened.

"Do what you can to get my bail reduced," said Logan. "These men are going to do something soon and I don't want to be here when they do."

***

At 1:00am a guard was grabbed by the three men in cell 205. One of the prisoners placed the shiv to the guard's jugular and another guard grabbed the guard's legs causing the guard to slump downward and his neck was impaled by the shiv severing the jugular. The blood pumped out of the man's neck, spewing on the floor. The scene was so slimy the inmates let loose of the guard and he gurgled and suffocated on his own blood as he tried to breathe. There was a clock on the wall. The timer showed that only two minutes passed before the man quit moving and lay still on the concrete floor. None of the inmates on the second floor of the wing said anything as they saw the murder occur with their own eyes. They were in shock. The men on the first floor who were locked in their cells could see nothing but they knew what was happening was not going according to plan and they began to howl.

Then the doors to the cells were unlocked automatically and the men came out of the cells.

The jails extraction team entered the wing with shotguns loaded with bird shot and the guards fired repeatedly into the mass of men until they could retrieve the body of the dead guard. The men retreated into their cells and the guards methodically closed each of the cell doors and locked them with a key so each door was locked independently. Most of the prisoners were wounded and bleeding. The three men in cell 205 were hit with pellets many times and bled to death before the door was opened for first aid responders.

Logan and Grant were each hit by bird shot but they were not seriously wounded. Some of the inmates were transported to the holding facility in St. Petersburg at the courthouse, and some were placed at the Police Department. Logan and Grant were kept together and locked in the hospital ward in a two man cell. They did not speak to anyone. They just waited for the next shoe to drop.

The jail went into lockdown. The Sheriff issued no statement. The St. Petersburg Times newspaper was unable to print the story to make the deadline for the morning paper, except to state that there was a riot at the jail. They printed what they could, expressing many caveats regarding the accuracy of the story. The reporters got some facts right and some wrong. They got right the fact that there was a riot and that four people were dead.

***

Tom was in his pajamas when the police sergeant came to his door and told him to dress quickly and come with him. There was no other explanation. Tom complied. He was driven to the County jail. All of the lights were on in the facility. They were conducting a sweep of the jail doing a head count of all the prisoners.

Tom was taken to the medical ward and he was put in an examination room. Logan was in the room. John Hale, who had recently been elected State Attorney, was in the room with a guard.

"Logan wanted to speak with you. He wanted an attorney present when he was interviewed. The same with Mr. Grant. He wants to speak with you."

"What is the charge?" asked Tom.

"There is none," said Hale. "I intend to grant them immunity from prosecution for any crime that arose from the riot and the four deaths and other injuries here at the jail tonight. We are trying to identify who the conspirators were in this incident. The men in cell 205 are all dead. We know the dead men were involved but there were others who were complicit. We need their names."

"If my clients talk they will be dead," said Tom.

"We will protect them," said Hale. "It's absolutely imperative that we get all of the men who were involved. If we don't get them all, no guard will be safe ever again in this jail."

"Do you have a subpoena for my clients?" asked Tom. "They have to be compelled to testify and we need an immunity agreement for you to sign as State Attorney."

"You explain they must testify truthfully and I will provide the subpoena and the agreement."

"They will testify. They have little or no choice."

Tom spoke to Grant and Logan separately. Both understood they would be given immunity and were under subpoena. There was a chance Tom could help them with a deal or reduced sentencing if they co-operated. They understood and agreed to testify.

Epilogue
Book I

Marla and Tom approached middle age. Marla, Tom's first secretary, has just married James M. Reynolds and has a chance to make her mark on American society. She is independently wealthy. A sharp business person, she is wise and well liked. She is well read but has only a high school education. The question is whether she will succeed in New York City.

Tom continues to flounder. He has sparks of genius but seems exhausted and weak at times.

To succeed, Bob, Albert, and Jenny just need to stay out of the back pages of the newspaper – the obituaries or the police blotter.

Frank and Bea have struck gold again, this time with the consumer, selling milk nationwide at drive-through stores. As a franchise operation, they are partners in businesses located in all 48 contiguous states, with hard working Americans who want to own their own business and participate in the American Dream by owning a franchise of Homestead Creamery.

Chronology of Important Dates

1920   Frank Barnes and Tom Night are born

1922   Beatrice "Bea" O'Brien is born

1929 – 1939 Great Depression

1936   Jimmy Barnes is born

1937 – 1943 Frank Barnes and Tom Night meet at Stetson University in Deland, Florida. Frank becomes a forester. Tom attends law school at Stetson.

1940   40,000 Acres of timber is foreclosed on between Deland and Daytona. The Senator, Francis Aloysius Barnes, buys the cut over timber land. Frank learns to re-plant it.

1939 – 1945 WW II

1941   Bob Johnson born to Albert and Mary Johnson

1943   Little Al born to Albert and Mary Johnson

1945   Tom graduates from Stetson University, College of Law

1946   Mary and Al Sr. and Bob and Little Al move to Holly Hill, Fl., next to Bea and Frank

1947   Jenny is born to Mary and Albert Johnson

1948   Mary, Al Sr., Little Al and Jenny move to Daytona Beach. Bob stays with Bea and Frank in Holly Hill.

1949   Frank and Bea adopt Bob, Little Al and Jenny. Their last names are changed to Barnes.

1967   Tom and Roger Adams become law partners

1970   Tom convicted of Contempt of Court

Maps

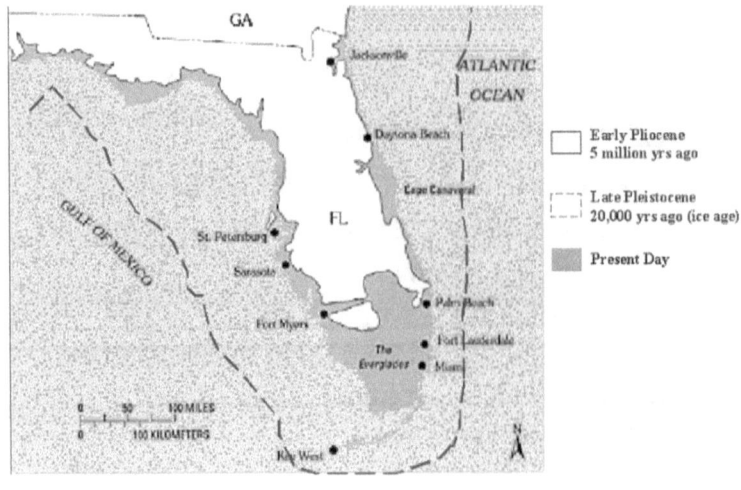

Map 2a
Boundary of Florida as a result of ice age, 20,000 years ago

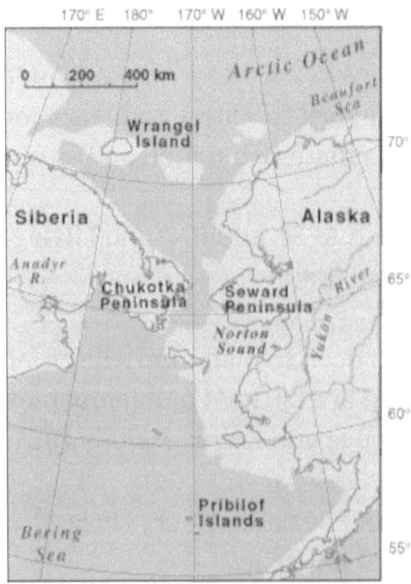

Map 2b
Beringia, possible locations for land bridge

Map 3

Florida Indian Tribes prior to European presence (1492)

Map 4

French Map showing fort on River of May (1562)

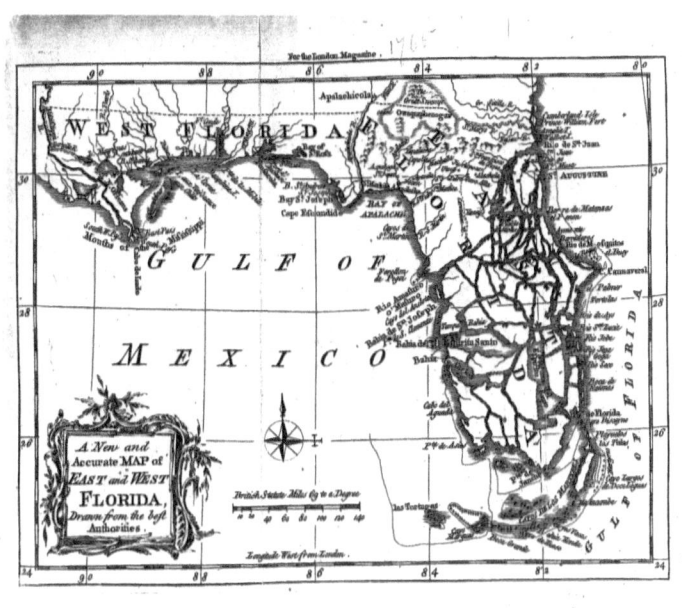

Map 5

English Map of Florida during Revolutionary War (1765)

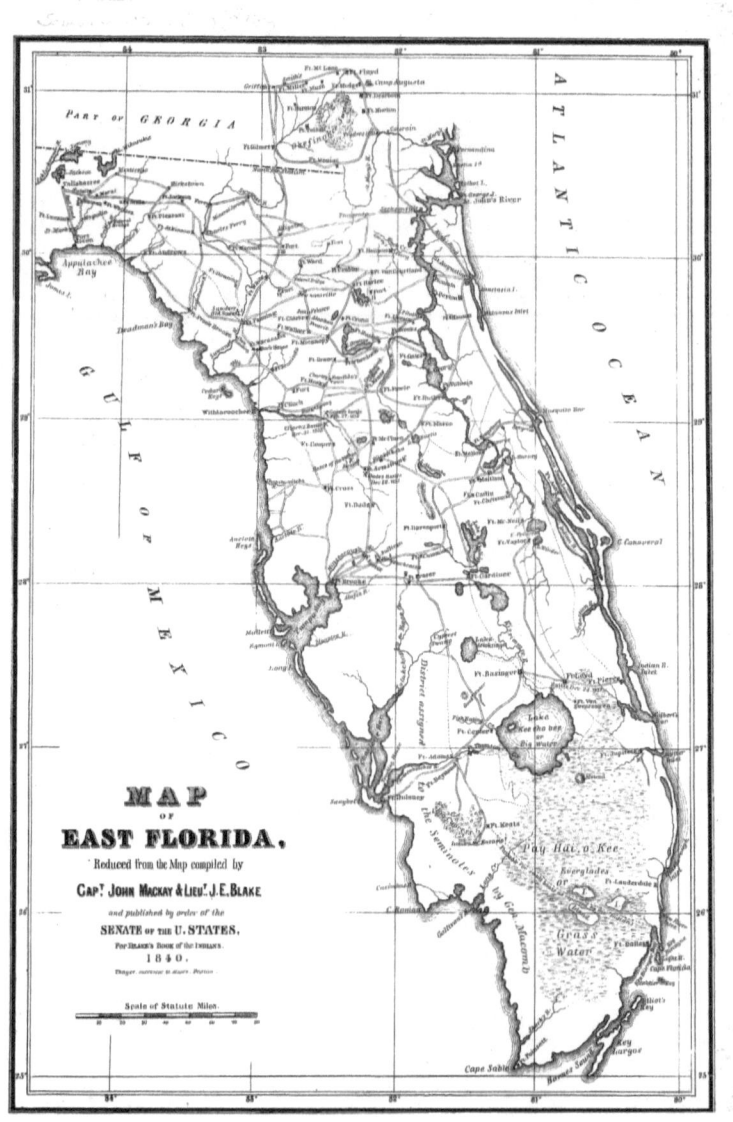

Map 6

East Florida, showing major cities, Indian trails,
rivers, and major lakes (1840)

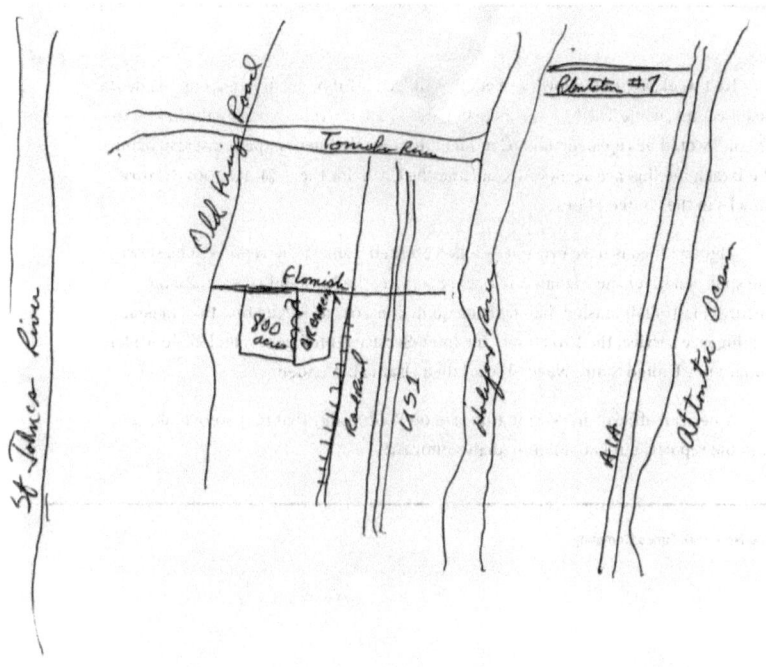

Map 7
Hand drawn map showing location of
Homestead and Plantation on opposite sides
of the Halifax River (1900)

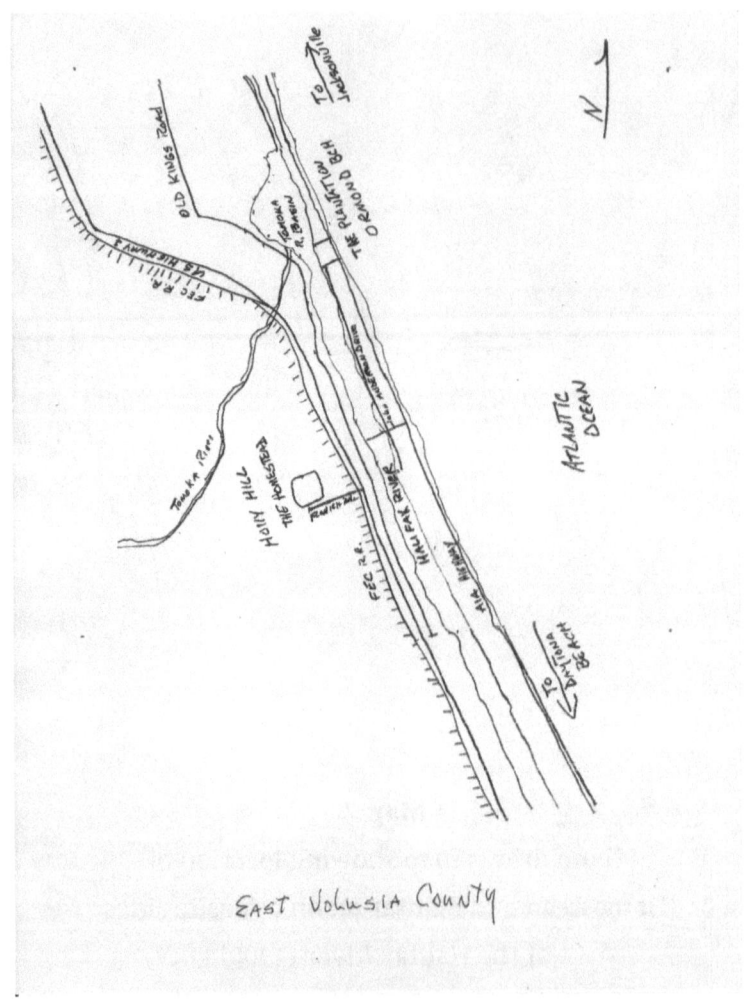

Map 8

Hand drawn map showing Intracoastal Waterway,

railroad, and major highways (1942)

Map 9

Modern Map of Florida

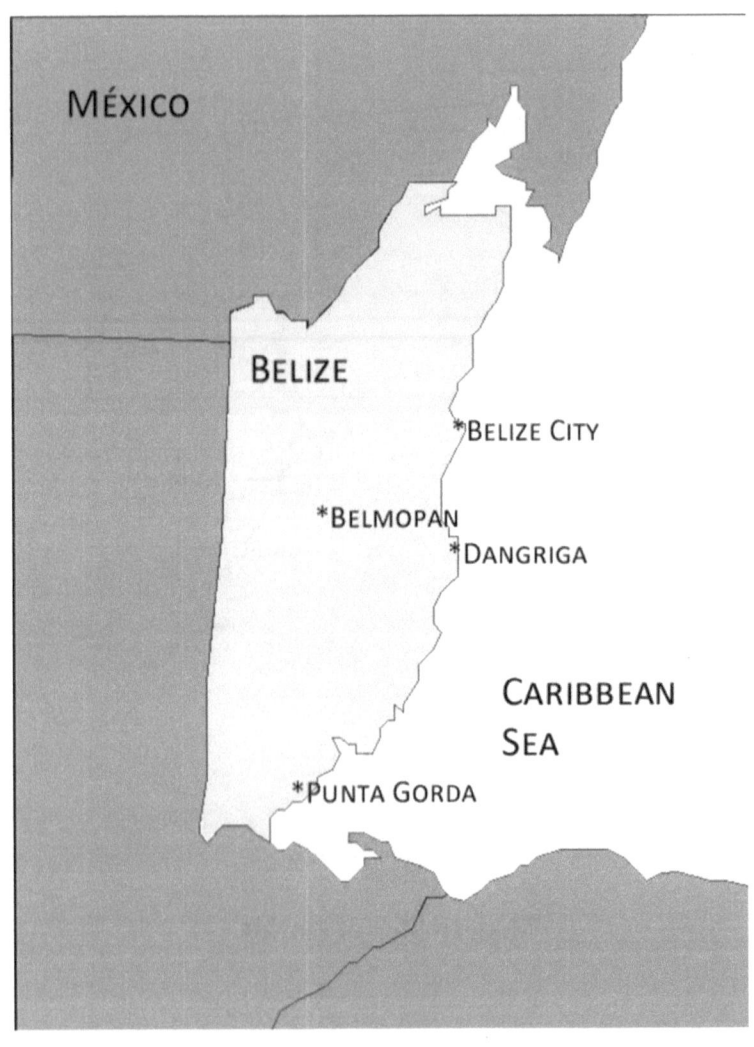

Map 10

Map of Belize

Preview of Book 2: Punta Rosa

"I need to be sure Mr. Anthony will not know I was the one who ratted on him."

Jorge Mendez was calling from a pay phone located on the side of a gas station on US 1 in Key Largo, Florida. Jorge was a crewman on one of two small ships that Anthony Arnold was motoring from the USA to Belize on the Yucatan in Central America. Jorge, a Mexican, was short, with a dark skinned complexion and with black shinny hair. He was handsome with European features but at the moment, he was very nervous and frowning. He did not want to be seen speaking on the phone.

Anthony Arnold's two boats had tied up at a dock in a canal in Key Largo, Florida and the crew was loading the boat with fuel, ice, beer and food that Anthony purchased for the voyage from a marine supply house. It was a long trip and they intended to avoid land until they were in Mexican waters. The ships would encounter the Florida Straight with its volatile currents and storms that kicked up high seas. This time of year hurricanes and low pressure systems would also be a danger.

Neither boat was designed for rough seas. The M.V. Cap de l'Ile was an old coastal freighter on its last legs. The other vessel was newly constructed for diving charters. It had a barge-like hull and an opening cut in the floor of the hull for a moon pool that allowed a diver to enter the water from inside the boat. Both boats were designed to operate near shore and in shallow water. In the ocean, if the seas were rough, the boats bounced like bobbers on a fishing line. The men were counting on calm weather.

Besides Anthony and Jorge there were two Honduran men who had agreed to help crew the small ships. Their pay was their pas-

sage, food and drink, together with a few pesos they would receive at the end of the voyage. They were content because they
could re-enter Mexico without going through customs. The Hondurans said they were trying to get back home to their families in
Central America. They appeared to be uneducated and had little
knowledge of the modern world. Anthony thought they were
probably criminals. They answered only to Spanish. Jorge was
from Cancún, México and Spanish was his native language but he
could also speak English fluently. He had spent many years illeg-
ally in the United States.

Anthony was born in the USA. He learned to read Spanish from
a lexicon and by reading Spanish pulp fiction novels. He tried to
learn to speak the language when he was in jail but never learned
to speak Spanish. State prison in Florida was segregated - blacks,
whites, and Latinos. So, "Mr. Anthony", as he was known by the
crew, could not speak Spanish fluently and had to rely on Jorge to
speak to the Hondurans. Anthony Arnold had been in and out of
prison all his life. He was a brilliant mechanic - boats, planes, cars.
He could fix anything with an engine. He was in his 40's, strong,
blond, tanned, with a smile on his face, but which was scarred
from acne when he was a teen.

Jorge was still on the phone. "Look I need to be assured that
Mr. Anthony will not know I turned him in."

"He won't know. We couldn't stay in business if the people we
arrested knew how we found them" said the Bounty Hunter. The
Bounty Hunter's business was arresting fugitives from courts in
the United States.

"If something happens to me, how will I know you will pay my
wife the fee for the information I want to sell?" asked Jorge. "I
don't even know your real name."

"You have to trust us on that. We are offering you a lot of
money, ten percent of the bail bond premium for the information,
that's $17,500.00 US dollars. You got our phone number from
someone, so you know our reputation. We will make payment for
the information as we have agreed. We could only remain in busi-

ness in the future if we make payment for the information we receive."

Seventeen Thousand Five Hundred US Dollars was a huge sum of money in 1970. The amount was 10% of the bail bond the insurance company had paid the court in Bushton, Florida. The insurance company paid the clerk to assure the court Anthony would appear for trial on a charge of theft of an airplane. Anthony was a no show and the company had to pay.

"So tell me, where are you now?"

"We are in the Florida Keys at Key Largo," said Jorge.

"How long will you be there?"

"Not long. From here we head toward Isla Mujeres, México. But we don't intend to make port until we reach Punta Rosa."

"How do you know that?"

"Anthony has charts. I got a look at them."

"What is your route of travel?"

"We skirt the Florida Keys and then head west past the Dry Tortugas and then we go south from the Dry Tortugas heading for the east coast of the Yucatán," said Jorge.

"You do not stop in Isla Mujeres?"(See map of Yucatán, page 11).

"Correct. We go south to Punta Rosa, México. We land in Punta Rosa and take on fuel there. The gas is cheap in México and that is the last Mexican port before Ambergris Cay in Belize. The fuel is very expensive in Belize."

"We have a man in Punta Rosa," said the Bounty Hunter. "He will contact us when you land. Do you know that there is a storm in the Caribbean Sea heading north?"

"We were told about the hurricane when we landed here in Key Largo. Mr. Anthony believes we will miss the storm. He is betting it goes north and then east toward the west coast of Florida. If that happens the storm will be behind us and all the shipping will be out of the area and we will be able to slip into México quietly."

"I hope you are successful." The phone was breaking up. "If Anthony changes his mind and decides to wait out the storm in Key Largo call us back. It would be easier to capture him in the States. Otherwise we will wait for our man's call from Punta Rosa. He has a marine radio and we can stay in touch. We can fly fast. If you see a black Lear jet overhead, that's our plane. Good luck to you."

"Thank you," said Jorge.

When Jorge got back to the ship, Anthony was working on the flying bridge of the dive boat. Jorge went to help and fell into the routine of stowing gear and lashing crates and cargo that would be exposed to the elements if their vessels were hit by the storm.

***

They had good luck for the first part of the trip and made it through the Florida Straight to the Dry Tortugas in calm seas. There was no fresh water on these keys or islands. The largest island was occupied by Fort Jefferson, built in the early 1800s. The occupants of Fort Jefferson had to rely on rain water and transport ships for potable water. The water was stored on the island in cisterns. Fort Jefferson had been built to protect Florida from a raid from an enemy who made an approach by sea from the south. After the Civil War the fort became a prison. Its most famous inmate was Dr. Samuel A. Mudd who treated the injury to John Wilkes Booth's ankle after Booth assassinated President A. Lincoln.

The fort was a tourist trap now. It did not have a ship's store or fuel. It was for day trips only and did not sell necessities, only souvenirs.

Arnold's ships passed the fort at night. It was low on the horizon and but for the lights on the ramparts, the fort would be invisible to a passing ship.

The weather held until they made the Straight of Cozumel (Mayan Riviera) just south of Isla Mujeres and they were heading south to Punta Rosa. The sky turned grey and the wind was from the east peppered with stinging raindrops. The Isle of Cozumel with its high coast line protected the two vessels but once they passed the south end of the island the ships began to struggle with the wind. The boats had to head south west to keep south. But they were making progress and the men on the boats were confident they would make Punta Rosa before the storm would swamp their ships. Anthony had bet wrong that the storm would head north. All the signs were that it first headed north and that it was now heading west in the direction of Punta Rosa.

Punta Rosa was located at the end of a strip of land that was about two miles wide and 30 miles long that extended south from the town of Vigia Chico. Vigia Chico was in the coastal wildlife preserve that surrounded the town. Punta Rosa was at the end of a dirt road. The dirt road was cut through the mangrove jungle and began at Cancún and passed the Mayan ruins at Tulum.

South of Punta Rosa there was nothing but water to the front and left of you and a vast mangrove swamp to the right until you arrived at Ambergris Caye in Belize.

Jorge was smiling when he saw the low buildings of Punta Rosa all tucked into the shoreline on a 20 foot rise of shoreline. The promontory was probably the base of a Mayan lime rock tower or temple. Many towers had been built by the Mayans along the coast of the Yucatán. One could suppose that if the Mayans constructed a tower on the high spot at Punta Rosa and built a fire on top of the tower, the natives would have a lighthouse of sorts to use for navigation. To the west of the fishing village there was a small but deep bay that would offer a safe harbor in a storm.

Anthony, who was operating the dive boat, contacted Jorge by two way radio. Jorge was behind but in sight of the dive boat piloting the M.V. Cap de I'lle. Anthony instructed him to go south past the port and tie up behind and to the west of the village in the bay at the Ship's Store. The men docked and topped off the fuel tanks and took on drinking water, beer and soft drinks. They did not remain tied up at the docks extending into the bay but instead each vessel moved into the bay and set out a single large anchor hooked into the lime rock at the bottom of the bay. Tying to the bottom out in the bay would prevent the boats from colliding with the pilings around the docks if the storm hit. Once the boats were secured, a small craft came to them and carried them to the Ship's Store. The building was the largest on shore and was a combination warehouse, fuel depot, bar and restaurant.

When the low pressure storm threatened, all the 20 or so residents of the fishing village named Punta Rosa wanted to huddle in the warehouse, named the "Ship's Store", because the building was new and strong, constructed to withstand a hurricane. It had been built on top of 30 foot long pine pilings. The pilings were sunk in holes that were dug ten feet deep into the highest point of the promontory. Then lime rock and sand were wedged around the poles and the sand was pounded tight against the pilings.

The pilings were set every four feet along the perimeter of the building and then the outside of the poles were covered with 8' by 4' sheets of ¾ inch marine plywood. There was a second wall of plywood inside the building so that the pilings were enclosed inside the plywood skins. The building was 48 feet long by 24 feet wide by 10 feet high at the eave of the roof. The roof was made of corrugated tin panels nailed on to manufactured rafters. The rafters were attached to the walls of the building with metal hurricane straps. There were screen windows cut in the walls but each window had a shutter that closed over the opening. The shutters were to be attached with screws to the wall over the screened windows if a heavy storm approached.

This was the first time the building had been tested by the full force of a hurricane.

The building had a floor made of 2" by 8" boards. The floor was constructed five feet off the ground. The idea was that if a storm pushed a surge of water over the promontory, the storm surge would flow under the floor of the building from the Caribbean Sea into the bay behind the building.

There was a kitchen inside the Ship's Store with a grill and oven and refrigeration unit. The oven and grill ran on propane gas and the refrigeration ran off a gas powered electric generator that also powered the lights and the fuel pumps for the diesel and gasoline tanks. The only system that was outside of the building were the toilets that were nothing more than outhouses built over the water of the bay on a dock about 100 yards from the Ship's Store.

The building was much more secure than the houses built by the residents of Punta Rosa. Their homes were simple shacks. They were idyllic until a storm hit and then they offered the owner little protection.

The owner and operator of the business was Felix Mercado, a Mexican national from Cancún. He and his wife and three children lived in an Airstream travel trailer that was parked to the west side of the store. The trailer was tied to the electricity and propane systems in the store. The trailer was not strapped to the building but it had been parked close to the leeward side of the building. The wind from the sea would be the most destructive if it came out of the West and the Ship's Store blocked the wind from the storm hitting the Airstream trailer directly.

Felix knew Jorge and his family. They grew up together in Cancún, Mexico and they recognized each other immediately. They struck up a conversation in Spanish as soon as they saw each other. Jorge was concerned about his wife and family. Felix offered Jorge the use of his ship to shore radio to call Cancún. Jorge's brother, Pablo Mendez, was the Cancún Police Chief and the police department was able to patch Jorge through to his brother while Pablo was in his police car.

Jorge learned from his brother that his family was safe. They had worried about him, knowing he was at sea with a storm in the Gulf. He told his brother, Pablo, he should be back within a week but he was safe now and would ride out the storm in Punta Rosa. Pablo told Jorge he would watch out for his wife and children until Jorge got home.

Jorge and his brother, Pablo, looked like twins but they had taken different journeys to middle age. Pablo was a respected and an important member of the Mexican Judiciary. Jorge was a criminal.

After he made the call, Jorge introduced Felix to Anthony. Felix offered to let Jorge, Anthony and the Hondurans stay inside the building with the other residents of the small community during the storm. Anthony was very appreciative and told Felix that he would purchase all of the remaining supplies needed for the trip south at the store because of the favor. Felix reminded Jorge and the rest of the crew that they should take advantage of the outhouses before they blew away.

Felix went to his radio to make another call to the States. He talked to the Bounty Hunter to tell him Anthony was there in the store and would be there until the storm passed.

Felix would be paid by the Bounty Hunter for the information. The Bounty Hunter was an American and flew a black Lear jet but no one knew his name or address, not even the people who worked closely with him. Everyone just called him the "Bounty Hunter".

After the call, Felix made two rules for his neighbors and the others who would ride out the storm in his store. If anyone took a beer or food they were to write down the purchase in a tablet on the counter and second they were not to light the propane because the storm might cause a leak in the gas line and it could cause a fire.

Felix then went to the Airstream to be with his family.

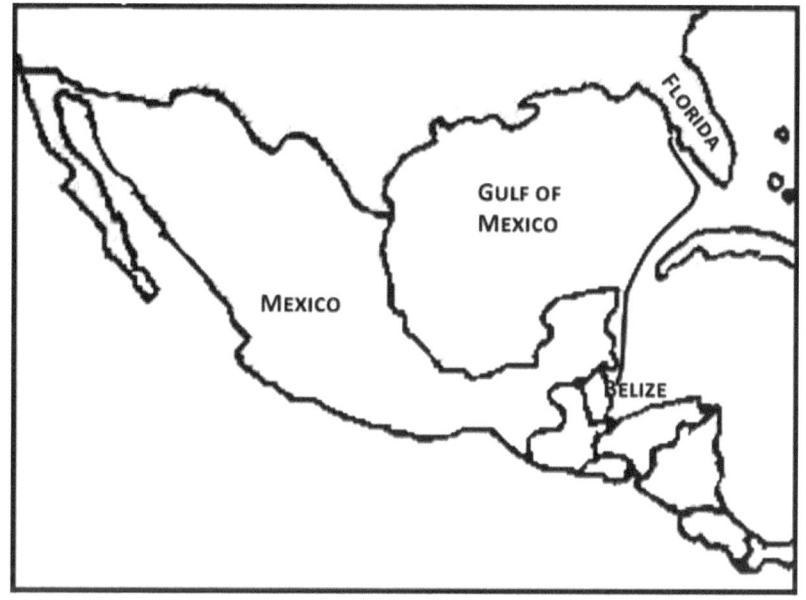

Route from Tampa to Punta Rosa

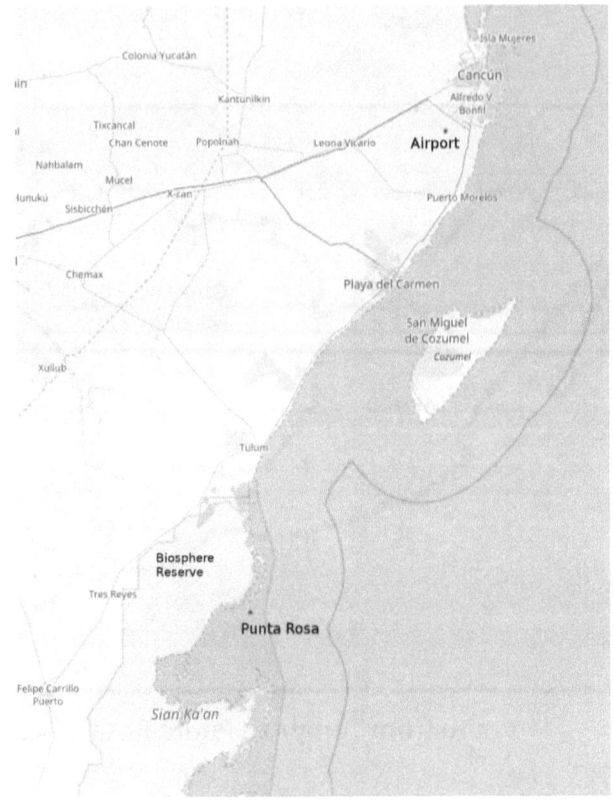

Yucatan Peninsula

Quintana Roo Province, Mexico